MW01235646

TRANSCENDENCE
THEORY

Z. L. GRAY

TABLE OF CONTENTS

First Paperback Edition May 2024

Paperback ISBN: 979-8-9904208-0-9
Ebook: ISBN: 979-8-9904208-1-6

Edited by Willow Heath
Cover Art: Kieran

Published by Stitched Dead Trees

AUTHOR'S NOTE

This book was inspired by the character Melanie Stryder in The Host by Stephenie Meyer. However, it quickly evolved into an allegory for the stroke I suffered at the age of 21. After my stroke, I felt like I was trapped inside my own body. This story perfectly encapsulates the emotional turmoil of losing myself, as well as the healing journey of regaining my independence.

Transcendence Theory is a slice-of-life-esque story in the Biopunk subgenre of Science Fiction. Some of the topics in this story are heavy and may contain graphic depictions of violence that could be triggering to some readers. Below is a list of trigger warnings. Please keep your mental health safe above all else.

★ Ableism
★ Coercion
★ Death/Mention of Death
★ Drugs/Mention of Drugs
★ Eugenics
★ Gore *sangue*
★ Gun Violence
★ Hospital/Hospitalization
★ Hostages
★ Kidnapping
★ Manipulation
★ Mention of Torture
★ Murder
★ Needles/Syringes
★ Suicidal Thoughts, indirectly
★ Poisoning
★ Profanity
★ Violence

THANK YOU

To Kieran, the sole reason I strive to be the best that I can be. You're the best daughter and greatest cheerleader one could hope for. Also, for making my really nice cover.

To Jessi, my best friend and one of the most amazing people on the planet. Without your continued support this book wouldn't have become a reality.

To Justine, the second-best cheerleader around. Your constant encouragement and continued support helped me finish this book.

To everyone that reads this book.

CHAPTER ONE

AWARENESS IS ALL I have. Awareness of the dark that surrounds me. Awareness that my consciousness is disconnected from my body, suspended in limbo. It's almost as if I'm shrouded by a dense fog preventing me from being able to do the simplest of movements. Twitching my fingers or wiggling my toes should come easily, but I can't feel them at all.

Is this just a very vivid nightmare in which I have no control over my own body? Is it possible for someone to be this coherent in a dream?

"The transitioning stage is nearing completion." A muffled male voice slices through the heaviness. His words are rushed, as if he's in a hurry.

Transition stage? I repeat.

Am I being operated on? *Of course not, I wouldn't be awake for that.*

If this were an operation, anesthesia would prevent me waking up before I'm supposed to. Besides, if I were going under the knife, I would remember it, right?

Am I having a nightmare involving plastic surgery? *Possibly.*

A strong, distinct feminine voice infiltrates the cloudy dome that I barely recognize as my mind. "How much time before the patient wakes up?"

Wake me up! I'm awake! I can hear you! I scream hopelessly into the void.

With full consciousness, how am I not awake right now?

I want to panic. I *should* be panicking, but in its place there's only emptiness. Not only is it impossible to reach my physical body, but I also can't reach my emotions. Hearing these people talk through this barrier seems to be the extent of my sensory range.

"Let's see. Approximately one hour," the man says, speaking as rapidly as before, but much closer to me.

An hour? I can hear you now! I'm awake now! I scream into the void again, desperately trying to will my mouth to form any words.

Their footsteps disappear as their voices fade into oblivion—or, more likely, down a hallway. I'm alone now with rather obnoxious beeping as my only company. The beeps call to mind associations of surgery or an intensive care unit. Even if it is coming from hospital machines, it doesn't cause me to panic.

I feel empty. Could this be a side effect of whatever is creating the inability to feel my body?

Am I calm? Perhaps I was administered some sort of medicine to help me remain calm once I come to.

I can't fathom why I'm in this position. If this isn't a dream, then I must be in a coma, right? Was it a car crash? Or was it the result of an outrageous stunt going horribly wrong? Maybe it's something far more mundane, but it's possible I incurred a head injury that's preventing me from remembering anything. Although, if it's any of the former options, I'm surprisingly at ease to be in a potentially life-threatening situation.

The beeps intensify, creating a claustrophobic feeling inside the empty space. The continuous beeps echo louder inside my head, so the heaviness must be dissipating now.

As grateful as I am for the machines probably keeping me alive, my perceived comfort is beginning to turn into what I can only guess is annoyance as I sit here inside the vacant space of my mind in-definitely. While I don't feel annoyed, the discernable blissful aura dwindles into nothingness.

The only thing I can focus on is the incessant beeps. Possibly to the point that they might be screwing with my perception of time since it feels like far more than an hour has passed. Perhaps my ap-parent sensory deprivation is the reason for my inability to tell time.

The return of two sets of footsteps is a stark reminder of my cur-rent absent state. I thought that by the time someone returned this weightless feeling would be dissolved.

I desperately want to stop feeling like a thing *floating aimlessly in space.*

"Hello, 607," the woman says, sounding much harsher now.

607? Did she just refer to someone as a number? Has someone else been in the room with me the entire time? He must be the one they were referring to earlier about transitioning.

She interrupts my thoughts, "I assume you're adjusting well."

"I think... I am," he says. His voice sounds groggy.

He sounds closer to me than the two people who were spouting their nonsense earlier. Is he lying close to me?

Do I know this person they're calling 607? His voice is strangely familiar and unmistakable.

"I just seem to be incredibly tired."

Close and familiar... Wait! That's my voice! I yell.

Faster than I can comprehend, questions fill my mind.

How does this man have my voice? Why can't I open my mouth to hear my own voice? Why can't I flutter my eyelashes or even feel the tiny hairs against my cheeks? Why can't I do anything but listen?

Unable to voice the thoughts, they'll remain unanswered, swirling frantically around in my head.

"It's a commonality among the transitioned patients. It will pass soon enough. Just rest for as long as you need. The button is here. Press that and someone will be here to check on you," the man says, forcing the words out in nearly one breath.

A commonality among the transitioned? I echo.

The word "transitioned" is beginning to taunt me. It's almost like a threat, spoken with certainty, but it reverberates malice and fear.

Does transitioned mean replacement? Am I being replaced? Is that how this man has my voice? No way. It's... it's not possible.

"We'll just have to wait," the woman states coldly. With that, they quickly exit the room, heel on heel.

Wait for what? I wonder. Probably an assessment of some kind.

Returning to the forefront of my darkness is the beeping. Now it's accompanied by *my* deep breathing lulling me back into the dense fog I thought I had escaped.

Am I falling asleep? Can I go to sleep? Of course I can. This is all one giant, vivid nightmare. Everything will return to normal once I wake up again. This time without someone else using my voice.

I'll wake up from this overly realistic dream soon enough, I assure myself before drifting into an unconscious state.

Time disappears. I'm aware again—just aware and nothing more. Seemingly nothing about my predicament has changed. The same noises from the same medical equipment resound in my tiny space. My body is still inaccessible and I'm still unable to feel my fingers or toes.

I have no memory of being alive. I only have a vague feeling that

I should be. However, I'm beginning to question if I'm even real. If I am real, shouldn't I know how I ended up in limbo? Can something with this much consciousness be fake? Perhaps I am nothing more than a figment of this person's imagination. I certainly resemble a parasite more than a person right now.

I wish I was dead. Death would be better than whatever this is, but then again, anything would be better than existing and not truly being alive.

A softer, and far more welcoming, woman interrupts me this time, "How are you adjusting to your new body, uh... 607?"

New body? What do you mean "new body?" I ask, pointlessly. She's referring to my body that this jackass has apparently taken from me.

It's my body, give it back! I demand, childishly. Fitting since the idea of a childlike tantrum of flying fists and kicking legs attacking the ground furiously comes to mind. There isn't an accompanying image, however.

This must be a sick joke, right? There's no way these people can actually steal my body and give it to this person. They would have to kidnap me, incapacitate me, and somehow put his consciousness into my body. None of this sounds possible, and yet I'm imprisoned inside my own head.

It seems more likely that I have died, and this is the hell I've been subjected to. But that doesn't seem right. This all feels too real. I feel too real. I don't feel dead, either; just nonexistent, floating around in this endless darkness.

My mind returns to the word "patients" that was unintentionally skipped over earlier. They've done this before? Of course they have— six hundred and six times before, to be exact. Although, what *this* is, I'm not entirely sure.

Are they really stealing bodies? It appears so, but why? Why are they stealing bodies? Why does this person have my voice and why can't I reach my own body?

If I had my physical sensations, I'm sure I'd be sick to my stomach.

"I'm not sure..." My voice trails off.

"What aren't you certain about?" she asks, gently.

Someone clears their throat and judging by the proximity, it's mine. An eye-rolling gesture would be appropriate. The thought of someone else controlling any part of my body is difficult to process.

Even insignificant things like clearing *my* throat or rolling *my* eyes.

"Um, I keep hearing things that aren't my thoughts."

He can hear my thoughts and everything I'm thinking? I can't hear his thoughts. I hate you. The last part is directed at him to make me feel better. It doesn't.

"Really? That's weird, but I'm sure it's just leftover remnants from the first owner." Concern fills her voice.

I want to spit at these people. *I'm still the owner of this body. I mean, my body. It's all mine; my voice and every other part of my body, intimate or not, belongs to me. I may not be in control of the body, but while I'm still conscious, this is* my *body.*

"We'll monitor your mental status over the next few days. By then the only thoughts in your head should be yours."

Does she think he's schizophrenic? Probably not, but I'm sure he feels like he is since he can hear all my interminable thoughts.

"Uh, one more thing." My voice hesitates. "It's just dark when I open my eyes. Was he blind?"

"Shit. This body seemed perfect before transitioning you. It didn't seem defective." A much younger-sounding man interjects. "You'll have to wait until we find another body so you can transition again, alright?"

Defective? I'm not some broken item to exchange, you asshole! I've been blind since birth!

A slew of memories infiltrates my mind—memories of me using various vibrations and textures on the ground. From sinking my feet into the warm sand on a windy day to sopping wet grass after a heavy downpour to feeling the rumble of cars against my soles. For a moment, thinking of the physical sensations reminds me that I'm real again.

I would give anything to smell the delightful scents of the world again. Like spring flowers in full bloom or freshly baked desserts that taste as good as they smell.

Perhaps it's a good thing they think my body is defective. I might get my body back from this jerk and not exist in this crappy meta-physical presence anymore.

"If I transition into a new body, what will happen to this one?" he asks, listening to my thoughts again.

These are my internal thoughts. Not yours. Go listen to someone else's unspoken words, I think, but I'd be lying if I said I wasn't a little curious to know the answer to his question.

"It will either be used for testing or destroyed like all the other useless bodies." His callous tone matches his inconsiderate answer.

Testing? Destroyed? Useless? It's clear now that I'm not viewed as a person. To these people I'm a damaged item; just an object for this sick experiment they're conducting. I and the six hundred other victims who've had the misfortune of encountering these wretched people.

"What about the original owners?" my voice asks.

Is he worried about me? Of course not. He wouldn't have stolen my body if he was worried about me. More than likely, he just doesn't want someone's death placed on his conscience.

You're not allowed to feel remorse for my impending death after you stole my body.

"Nobody survives, so don't worry about that," he says with an air of arrogance.

I survived, asshole. Even if I'm not living in the technical sense of the word, you didn't get rid of me that easily. I'm still here, and I will continue to be until the moment my body is destroyed. I think to him, uselessly.

"What if they did live through it?" Another question by my voice earns an abrupt chuckle from the cocky, young asshole. Imagining a fist to his face is the most pleasant thought I've had since waking up.

"Ignore Avery. He's a teensy bit vulgar and crass. If they happen to survive, we cremate the bodies to ensure everyone's safety," the calm woman explains.

Ensure the safety of who? The people who require that safety and protection are the ones being stripped of it. With the blatant disregard for human life, it's unlikely that she's referring to anyone who isn't directly involved with the kidnapping.

The calm tone she has while talking about killing someone isn't exactly comforting. Her demeanor is preferable over the guy who seems to enjoy killing innocent people, though.

Questions continue popping into my mind. *Shouldn't I be excited about the promise of a more permanent solution? Shouldn't I be happy that I won't be in this desolate existence if they cremate me?*

Death would be better than living this false existence. But somewhere outside of the emptiness, there is a fear of nonexistence. The thought of permanent death before I even learn my name is beyond disheartening. I suppose it doesn't matter what happens to me or my body, since I can't even remember who I am.

"The cremation is so we don't get exposed," the asshole says.

What exactly do they not want exposed? What are they doing? How are they doing it?

Kidnapping people, stealing their lives by somehow putting a new consciousness into their bodies. If I wasn't actively listening to this insane jargon, I wouldn't believe it was true.

What reason does anyone have to justify this cruelty? I wonder if the person who stole my body is a willing participant. It's nearly impossible to comprehend someone agreeing to undergo this vile process, but he must have, right? If he didn't, I don't think they'd be treating him like a patient recovering from surgery.

Why, though?

I'm sure if my head was mine again, I'd have a massive migraine. I wonder if he has a headache right now from my constant thoughts.

Why do I even care? He's a thief.

"Here's a walking cane so you can move around easier. Hopefully you won't be inconvenienced much longer," the young woman speaks, courteously.

Inconvenienced? Him? I'm the one that's been robbed of nearly every sense and of my life. But, sure, the man wielding my voice is being inconvenienced by a lack of eyesight. Poor him.

"We'll notify you once we've got a new body for you," she says.

The close set of footsteps reveals to me that she's likely leading him to the entrance of the building. Consumed by my thoughts, I didn't pay attention to anything that might be important. Not that it really matters since there isn't anything I can do in my current position.

Nothing is more important than preparing to die, anyway.

"Thanks for all your help." The car door closes. "Take me to the address written on this paper, please."

A cab? *Where are we going? I mean, where is this thief taking my body?*

My thoughts prevent me from listening to the verbal exchange between the guy with my voice and the cab driver.

How am I going to get used to being a false presence in my own mind? Is it possible to be okay with merely existing in a space devoid of every sense except hearing? I don't think so, but it doesn't seem as though I have much choice. I'll never again be able to feel the cool concrete against my feet, the wind brushing against my skin—

nothing. Death really would be better than this.

I catch their goodbyes followed by the car door slamming shut.

"Fuck!" My voice exclaims, loudly. Probably from smashing his foot into something as he makes his way to the front door.

That's what you get for taking someone's body—my body.

Another door slams and keys jingle erratically, clinking against themselves inside of a wooden object. It seems the blindness isn't slowing him down much.

"This isn't what I wanted." My voice sounds defeated.

Yeah, no one wants a defective, stolen body. Sarcasm doesn't suit me. It feels foreign as it quickly sputters through my mind.

"I didn't know you'd be alive when I transitioned," he says, and I wonder, *Is he talking to me, or himself?* "I didn't know anyone would be aware after all this was done."

You must have known. How could you not know you were stealing someone's body? How could you be transitioned into a body without being informed of the specifics?

They wouldn't want to divulge specific information if they feared doing so would make people shy away from transitioning. Unless someone is sadistic like that jerk from earlier, I highly doubt anyone would willingly kill someone to have a new body.

"No one told me that I'd be taking someone's actual body for this. It was worded in a way that sounded like it would come from a deceased person or like it would be a fabricated body. Maybe that's just what I assumed," he says.

Although it's my voice and I can hear the sincerity in it, I can't help but think it's just a mask.

How can you hear me? Why did you transition? What is the point of this transition bullshit anyway? What did you think would happen if you didn't know they were taking and killing people for it?

"Just one question at a time, please. First, can we start by calling each other by our names?" The question catches me off guard. "It makes me uncomfortable to hear you refer to me as 'your voice.'"

Hi, 607, not-so-nice to meet you. I don't even know my name, so don't bother getting sentiment from anything we exchange.

He erupts into a surprising bout of laughter.

"My name's Gaddreol," he says, his laughter fading with each word, "your name is Tristan."

CHAPTER TWO

THREE DAYS HAVE passed since initially waking up and I still feel like a mere figment of Gaddreol's imagination. I often find myself wondering if I'm nothing more than a simple creation of his mind. There isn't much I remember about myself—bordering on nothing at all, in fact. Remembering what certain sensations feel like against my skin seems to be the only thing cementing the idea that I'm actually real.

Remembering next to nothing about myself is difficult to deal with. Both frustration and anger come to mind, but there isn't the slightest hint of either. Being stuck inside my own mind should entitle me to swim around, accessing knowledge at my leisure. My name is Tristan; at least, that's what one of the doctors told Gaddreol during the time I was absorbed in my thoughts. Aside from my name, the only thing I know about myself is that I've been blind from birth.

However, relearning that hasn't helped me cope with the darkness at all. Prior to the transition, I don't think the darkness felt as forlorn as it is now. This emptiness is both isolating and exhausting. If I had control over my body, I'm certain this feeling would translate into physical sensations, such as my throat feeling closed or my lungs struggling for air.

I don't expect anything they said about me to be truthful. Can I believe my name is Tristan when their incompetence seems glaringly obvious? They had been observing me for a long time and the only thing to show for it is a name. My body being physically well-kept was all they surmised to be enough for their experiments. How could they be oblivious to the fact that someone they kidnapped is blind?

For such a unique—and not to mention illegal—operation with an allegedly advanced system, there's a substantial lack of effort put into it, and the people running it seem lackluster at best. Not that I want them to perfect their asinine procedures, but the mental and emotional states of the victims should be held to the same standard as their physical state. Hopefully, their incompetence will ultimately lead to their demise.

Since leaving the hospital, the doctors appear far too often. If he has any neighbors, I'm sure they are increasingly curious as to who continues coming at all hours of the day. It'd be weird if other residents weren't suspicious of their new neighbor receiving so many visitors in a short time. Once or twice a day is more than enough to routinely check on someone.

During a visit with Taz, the most pleasant doctor, she mentioned that Gaddreol is being monitored far more than previous patients due to *my* faulty body. My blindness is a major concern for them despite people living with it without much difficulty. Even with the extensive stalking, they were unaware of my condition, so it clearly didn't affect me negatively. The idea of strangers following me around, watching my every movement brings the urge to shudder accompanied by the thought of goosebumps covering my body.

Taz is the only doctor I don't intentionally try to ignore. I know I should hate her for being a part of this aberrant organization, but there is nothing in this dark abyss that hints at that. I suppose I have an inclination towards her. Could it be the first step to achieving an emotional sensation? Maybe. At least there isn't a sensation of hope to be crushed.

My surrounding darkness would probably feel less isolating if I had someone I could communicate with regularly. Just the idea of being able to speak with someone seems comforting despite having no semblance of the feeling. We're not able to converse often with the frequent interruptions, unfortunately.

Gaddreol speaks to me when he's alone, presumably to ease the loneliness he must feel. His experience with sudden blindness seems isolating, but it's nothing compared to the encompassing emptiness I'm languishing in. Perhaps the reason is just because my constant summarizing of events is difficult to ignore. Hearing myself endlessly recount moments in the day is something that would likely annoy me if I had access to my emotions. So I imagine it must be utterly exasperating for him to listen to me maundering all day. Regardless of the reason, I'm appreciative of the company.

"You may not believe it, but I appreciate your company," he says.

The door closes gently, followed by the jarring sound of jingling keys as they hit the wooden bowl. "Sorry, I'll be more careful."

You made it home safely?

"I hope I made it home safely." There's a playful smirk in his tone. "Otherwise, I just broke into someone's house."

For a moment, the urge to laugh flows freely through my bubble, but dissipates rapidly. *While you're in public, recapping is the only thing I can do unless I want to listen to you constantly counting your steps.*

"You noticed that, huh?"

You don't need to feel embarrassed. It's admirable that you're adapting so well to being blind. I don't understand how counting is effective, but it's working for you. At least now you have something that helps you move smoothly so those doctors can't keep saying that it inconveniences you. Is that why you started counting?

"It's not why. But it's definitely a good reason to perfect it." I hear a dresser drawer opening.

Did you learn anything today? I ask, ignoring how awkward it is that another person has full control over my body, clothed or naked. I can't feel the discomfort, but I know it exists somewhere in my tiny void. If only I could shake the speculation away.

"Well, the organization that conducts these experiments is called Forced and Rapid Evolution, but everyone just calls it FREE," he says.

That's... not an apt acronym for this revolting program.

"No, it's not."

The shower valves squeak as he turns the water on. The water pressure is high enough that it resembles heavy rainfall instead of a light rain shower. Immediately, embarrassment tries to invade my bubble and my face wants to flush at the thought of someone else washing my body. It's not the first shower he's taken, but it's the first one with us actively conversing.

"Sorry, I didn't think about that," he says. "I should've let you keep thinking about things."

It's fine. What else did you find out?

"I didn't learn anything else about FREE. Delicate information can't be given so openly in the trial stages, apparently."

The people who have consented to transition are aware that their consciousness will be placed into a new body, but they are kept at arm's length for everything else. The secrecy they have towards the active participants for fear of potential retaliation is contradictory to the indiscretion they have when heedlessly kidnapping people.

The only apparent indicator of a good body is being physically well-kept. Surely, they would observe the person they're snatching to ensure whoever they take is living a relatively solitary life. Many of the people taken are likely outcasts of society.

Does that mean I don't have any friends who are curious about my missing existence? Did my family not care enough to notice my absence? Does that mean no one cares about me? Accompanying the sadness that wants to wash over me is the thought of tears flowing down my face.

"I'm sure you have people who care about you," Gaddreol says, "Maybe you should stop speculating for a bit."

Speculation is rapidly becoming a good acquaintance of mine. I think, easily falling back into theorizing things about the horrible organization.

With the technology they have to remove consciousness from one body to put it into a new body, shouldn't they have the technology to create a synthetic body? Creating a fabricated body would give them a blank canvas to implement the superior traits they want instead of hoping the victim has the genetic lottery they're looking for. It would also prevent accidental exposure of their organization, which is something they're apparently worried about.

Here I go again, theoretically helping them enhance their system. At least if they did make synthetic bodies, their horrific experiments would be downgraded to questionable at best.

"Synthetic," he mutters as the water shuts off. "Sorry for laughing at you earlier."

You laughed at me?

"You didn't notice?" he asks, confused. "I laughed at the idea of you swimming around in your mind like you're in space."

He lets out another chuckle, probably visualizing me swimming inside my mind accessing the libraries of my own memories and knowledge again. A two-way connection would be optimal in this terrible situation; I'd be able to experience a visual stimulus for the first time if it were double-ended. A passing thought of envy crosses my bubble.

"I've actually been wondering since you don't have memories, how do you know what your reactions to situations should be? Like, how do you know you want to feel envy right now if you can't feel anything?"

Even without memories, I have perceptions of how I would react. My subconscious reactions help me gauge my speculations. I hear everything objectively, but my mind seems to automatically know which emotion or reaction I would convey.

"That's strange," he says, pensively.

It's possible that my lack of sight enabled the perfect conditions to prevent my brain from discerning details from my past. Whereas emotional reactions stem from the lasting impression a scenario has on someone rather than the scenario itself, so memory isn't needed.

"That makes sense when you put it that way. When I think about a memory, it starts with an image," he says. "I want you to know that I really do feel awful for taking your body."

Honestly?

"Of course. Why do you think I've been trying to convince them to not transition me again?"

I just thought you didn't want my death on your conscience.

"I don't want you to die. I don't want anyone to die. I thought they were dead already. You know, like those people that donate their bodies to science?" Each word he speaks drips with regret. "I can't imagine being in the same position as you."

I can't say that I can either.

"I think I would lose my mind. No offense," he says.

None taken. If it wasn't the only thing anchoring me to this non-existence, I would have lost it, too. Can I ask what they're doing with your body?

"I don't know what they're doing with my body. I stayed in pretty good shape, so maybe they're using it to transition someone else into. That sounds disgusting. I'm really sorry about all of this," he says, almost choking on the heaviness in his words.

I assume the realization of his actions hit him hard. *You really jumped into this entire situation without any knowledge of how it all works. Why did you just throw yourself into this chaos?*

He lets out an exaggerated sigh and plops loudly onto what I assume is his bed. Maybe he's feeling as defeated as I should be. I don't know why defeat feels accurate, but it's a fitting description for someone who's stuck in his own mind. It's not like I have an opportunity to claw my way out of this darkness into a lit opening.

"I did this for my little sister, Vera." He exhales softly, seemingly to steady his voice. "She has been paralyzed since she was a small child. She has full consciousness, but she can't communicate since she can't move or speak. When I spoke to Avery about it—"

That asshole who was overly excited about killing people? I ask, interrupting.

Another large sigh escapes his lips before he continues. "Yeah, that's him. He wasn't like that before. I don't know what changed or when—"

Did you know him well? I ask, unintentionally interrupting again.

"I want to say yes, but right now it feels like I don't know him at all..." His voice trails off. I want to ask more, but his somber tone is like a weight against my bubble, so I don't want to pry further.

"Thanks. Anyway, I told him about my sister's condition, and he told me about this experiment he was working on. It was still in the trial phase and needed more participants. He promised if I signed up for the trials and joined the experiments, he'd make sure my sister was given a new chance at life. I was so excited. None of the small details mattered. After I filled out some paperwork, I was contacted about a body. *Your* body."

The sadness in his voice is nearly tangible. The most appropriate response would be a hug, but with only words at my disposal, I think, *It's reasonable to want to give your little sister a chance at a better life.*

"Did I really give her a chance at a better life? I joined this to change her life, but I ended up taking yours instead." I can hear his voice straining, trying to hold back tears with each word. "It's finally sinking in that she's going to be placed into a healthy body that belonged to someone fully alive and well—"

You couldn't have known that at the time though. That asshole made sure to omit that information from you.

"I know you hate him, but can you please stop calling him that."

I'm sorry. I didn't mean to upset you more.

"No, I'm sorry. I'm just really worried about my sister. Not only will someone's life be taken away to give her a chance at one, but what if they're strong-willed like you?"

Strong-willed like me? I repeat.

Am I strong-willed because I survived a horrendous experiment that kills off the original person? I wouldn't consider myself strong-willed. Stubborn, maybe. What reason would a person without any friends have to live? Does that mean there's someone or something that's giving me a sliver of hope to cling to whatever this version of life is?

"You are strong-willed. You survived the transition process for a reason," he says, trying in vain to mask his sadness to cheer me up.

Are you worried that the owner of your sister's body may retain their consciousness?

The words are nondescript, but as the questions form, a forlorn heaviness follows them that nearly smothers my void. Thinking of someone else possibly experiencing this disheartening existence is sickening.

"Even if they're not conscious after, someone's life will be taken to give my sister the chance at a life she'll never have otherwise. I am glad she'll get to live her life to the fullest extent, but why does someone else have to lose their life for that?" The sorrow in his voice is almost strong enough to penetrate the heaviness around my bubble. I hear muffled fabric rustling like he's curling up in a blanket. It'd be ideal to bundle up inside a blanket and forget about all the horrors.

His words provide me with a sense of solace that I didn't know I could find. His involvement comes from good intentions. Even now, he has zero ill will towards me or anyone else. The guilt of what he's agreed to is probably eating away at him. I assumed the prominent emotion I would have towards that revelation would be happiness, but Gaddreol doesn't deserve such an abhorrent response. He only wanted to do what he could to better his younger sister's life, and who could fault him for that?

As much as I want to offer something valuable or comforting, there's nothing I can say that would do that. If it were possible, I would offer empathy to him. If things were different, I think he and I could've been friends—good friends at that.

CHAPTER THREE

AN INTENSE BRIGHTNESS surges into my small space, replacing the darkness and displacing the suffocating, desolate remnants with an uplifting embrace. Instinctively, I want to shield my eyes, even though I have enough cognizance to know that I'm not seeing this phenomenon with physical sight. There's a slight semblance of warmth within this light; a true figment of the imagination, but a soothing one at least.

Aggressive pounding against the front door interrupts the light. The engulfing intensity rapidly decreases with each bang until I'm plunged back into the bleak darkness that's become so familiar. The abrupt shift makes my already small space feel even more claustrophobic than it did before.

Confusion tries to force its way into my space. *Did I really have a visual experience?*

The banging against the door persists, becoming progressively more violent and urgent. I hear Gaddreol start shuffling around, probably trying to gain his composure from the abrupt wake up call.

"Just a minute!" he calls out, groggy and slightly annoyed.

"Open up!" The voice of the self-important, overzealous man yells from outside. Avery makes anger want to boil through my bubble.

Go away.

"I don't have all day! I can't be waiting on you forever!"

The chain clanks as it drops, and the deadbolt is unlocked. I sense Avery shoves his way through the opening, tipped off partially by his emphatically rude demeanor. That and the soft grunt that escapes Gaddreol.

He certainly knows how to make an entrance, doesn't he? I ask.

"Why don't you come in? Make yourself comfortable," Gaddreol says, irritation playing at the edge of his words. He softly closes the door. "I'm a little glad that you showed up. We have to talk."

"Aren't you just so happy to see me again?" Avery asks. His vanity and conceit are unrivaled. The thought of my eyes rolling because of his arrogance is too strong to ignore.

"No. In fact, I'm pretty content with not being able to see you right now." Gaddreol's frustration steadily increases.

"Whatever." I can practically hear the frown in Avery's voice. The words that follow roll off his tongue with utter disgust. "I'm here to tell you we're ready to take you out of this deformed body."

Deformed? I repeat. Disgust towards this man wants to settle.

Pedantry aside, this man is loathsome. How Avery and Gaddreol were ever close is an absolute mystery. I can't fathom there's even the faintest bit of compatibility between an easygoing person and an unlikeable asshole filled to the brim with contempt.

"I told you," Gaddreol says; his voice is disconnected, quiet, but harsh. "I want to stay in this body."

You told him before? I ask. *I don't remember you talking to Avery about keeping my body.* Unsurprising since he's the only doctor I actively attempt to drown out with my perpetual rambling. His gross excitement for these experiments is enough to make anyone recoil in disgust.

"Don't you miss being able to see my face?" His usual arrogant tone is gone, in its place is a taunting, playful, possibly seductive sound.

The urge to shudder floods my mind. *How close were they?*

"I wasn't kidding when I said I'm glad I can't see you. Besides, my memory serves me well enough," he says, hints of anger seeping into his words.

Gaddreol's anger over the question is confusing. Before this, their interactions seemed fairly tame without even the slightest bit of discomfort, so it's strange to hear it now. I wonder if it's something that was brought up last night or if it's something Avery said during this interaction.

"Tell me something," Avery says, annoyed. He's much closer to me now, his voice penetrating my minuscule space. "What is it about *this* body that you like so much?"

He doesn't wish me dead like you, asshole. I think, immediately following it with, *I'm sorry, it slipped.*

Gaddreol sighs. "I just don't think his blindness is a problem."

Genuine laughter comes from Avery, likely dissipating some of the tension between them. "Walk over to the kitchen without tripping and tell me it doesn't hinder you."

"It's a learning curve," he says. "I'll figure it out."

"It's been a week," Avery says, his too-close voice shrinking my already confined space.

A week isn't enough time for anyone to get acquainted with this new existence. Especially not this horrible false existence I'm stuck in. For someone thrown into a new body and life, with the addition of blindness and an ever-present second set of thoughts, I'd say, Gaddreol is faring surprisingly well.

I don't understand how blindness is considered a hindrance to their unorthodox experiments anyway.

"I just need time to—"

His words are cut off by an abrupt bang that I assume is Avery's fist slamming against a coffee table. "Dammit, Gaddreol! You don't get to keep *his* defective body." His anger is nearly palpable, but at least he's not invading my space anymore.

His body? He actually acknowledged my body.

Every person who speaks with Gaddreol has referred to me as 'the body.' I never expected anyone to consider me as anything other than a vessel. Least of all this man with all his unpleasantries. Astonishment wants to consume me, but I'm likely reading far too much into this discrepancy. In all actuality, he was just mirroring Gaddreol's language.

Following the loud outburst, Avery trudges off until his sounds are muted. Less than a minute passes before his brisk footsteps return. "Do you know what this is?"

The sudden burst of laughter from Gaddreol catches me off guard considering how much tension there seems to be. Probably from imagining the petulant man holding up an unknown object. I hear a rumbling bellow from Avery as Gaddreol attempts to stifle his giggles.

"I'm sorry, I don't know why that's so funny. What is it?"

"Ha ha. So funny. It's a camera." Avery's curt explanation is more than enough to quell the abrupt laughter. "Why do you think you had so many visits the first few days?"

Camera, I repeat.

It's just a word. A word with so many potential implications that I don't know where to begin. With Avery's reaction to the camera, I suspect it's abnormal for them to place a camera inside subjects' homes alongside the house calls. It's pretty easy to place a camera anywhere when your subject is sightless in a foreign environment.

One of the initial conversations with one of the women pops into my mind, *"We'll monitor your mental status over the next few days."*

At the time, I hadn't thought about the insinuation. If they were concerned about residual thoughts from the former inhabitant, why didn't they just perform a test to rule out multiple consciousnesses? Unnecessary, when you can set up a 'hidden' camera in plain sight due to the fortunate circumstances where everything is hidden.

"I was being monitored for things besides standard procedural things?" he asks. It's probably rhetorical, but it's wracked with worry.

"Yes." Avery's curt response is pensive.

What could this deranged man be thinking to cause a simple word to hold so much meaning behind it?

They're listening to our one-sided conversations. Everything that Gaddreol has said to me over the past week is immortalized on that camera. His vulnerable confessions and his inner thoughts about the entire process. His reminiscing about his life with his sister before the transitions, and the fears and regrets he has for his little sister's transition process. Not to mention the guilt he feels about his own involvement with this unlawful activity.

"You speak to Tristan."

They've listened to every conversation he and I shared; one side of it, at least. They heard him speaking to me as if I wasn't just a fragmented piece in his head. As if my existence is as corporeal as both his and Avery's.

"The problem wasn't his blindness."

The words left unspoken hang in the air, swirling in my tiny hole. *"He survived,"* I mock, almost hearing his tantalizing voice instead.

My minuscule existence is the actual issue that makes my body unworthy of this unethical experiment. Somehow, my survival throws a wrench in the metaphorical machine.

"Avery, I don't understand," Gaddreol says, devoid of all emotion. "Why does someone have to die so that I can have a new body?"

Silence falls between them. Anticipation is the only emotion that suits this verbal exchange as I find myself waiting impatiently to hear what Avery will spew next. *Why do I care what this insensitive bastard even has to say?*

He scoffs, before bluntly saying, "What we're doing isn't exactly public knowledge."

"Why can't you use the deceased bodies that people donate for medical research?" he asks. There's a mix of distressed emotions I don't recognize in his voice. It's like an emotional rollercoaster of anger and sadness and I can't figure out the trajectory.

"You want to transition into a fifty-eight-year-old body with heart failure?" Avery retorts. "Besides, those bodies are claimed. We take what we can get."

His pragmatic tone is soul-crushing, which is unfortunate as it's the only state I currently exist in. It's a truth better left unsaid. They take whatever—whoever—they want. They have taken six hundred and seven people already.

Six hundred and eight, excuse me. Probably more if I'm honest with myself.

Nausea or dizziness is an accurate reaction to the realization of how many people have been taken away from their previous lives for someone else to inhabit it. If I had the body that was so graciously ripped away from me, I'm certain I would puke. How can these people just callously throw lives away without the slightest bit of remorse?

"Why do I have to give up his body just because you guys are aware of his conscious state?"

A simple question that hadn't even occurred to me. *Why does my metaphysical presence cause them to be so adamant that I need to die? Why are they so eager for my permanent end? This is the most defenseless I can be and yet they want to destroy me as if I'm some incomprehensible monster.*

I might have pissed in someone's cheerios.

He takes in a sharp breath and lets out a small whimper before continuing, "I don't want to keep his body, but I don't want you guys to just kill him if I transition. Why does Tristan have to die?"

"His body is defective," Avery says again as if it clarifies everything.

I. Am. Not. Defective.

I wish I could scream at Avery. He and all the other despicable people who want to dispose of me simply because of my physical impairment. People go blind all the time for various reasons; do they deserve to be killed due to their vision loss?

Yes. The answer is yes, according to these absolute lunatics. Why do I deserve to be killed because my eyes aren't functional?

Avery's quiet now, bringing the deafening silence back, causing me to wait impatiently to hear his guttural voice again. Nothing he can say at this moment can make anything better, but at least he can't make it worse either. Hopefully.

"He's not defective. And is that really a reason to kill someone?"

"It's too risky," Avery says, deflecting the question.

Too risky?

"Avery, please." *Why are you pleading with this emotionless man?* "Please just figure out how to get more time. I don't want him to die."

Avery releases an exaggerated sigh. "I'll see what I can do, but I make no promises."

"Thank you. Has a body been found for Vera?"

The emotional rollercoaster returns. Relief, hesitation, and fear racing through the metaphorical rails. Hopefully, there will be a slow descent instead of a crashing halt at the end of this ride.

"It has." The cocksure tone that seems to be synonymous with Avery returns. "She's already been transitioned. I'd take you to see her, but you know."

"Know what?" Gaddreol asks, sounding furious now. It doesn't need to be said, but it feels important for him to hear.

"You can't see her even if I take you to her," he says.

The somber atmosphere around the words nearly suffocates the energy in my void. I get the impression the words are like a lightning bolt to Gaddreol's heart. I find myself wishing for true solitude to get away from this uncomfortable situation.

I'm blind. You're blind.

I don't know why I state the obvious, but for the first time, my blindness is more than an inconvenience. His little sister is the most important person to him; the entire reason he subjected himself to this and he can't see her with his own eyes. He can't see her facial expressions or her walking and moving about—nothing. I want to apologize for hindering him in such a significant way.

I'm sorry.

"Where is Vera now?" Gaddreol's anger evaporates as he says her name again.

"She's at a community home right now," Avery says. "Unlike how they're treating you, she's being well taken care of. They're helping her refine her motor skills and teaching her all sorts of things."

"That's amazing. Thank you."

"Yeah, no problem.

* * *

Much to my surprise, Avery agreed to drive Gaddreol to Vera. I didn't think he was capable of performing any action that required a little consideration. The monotonous roaring of the wind rushing into the windows offers me a convenient, mind-numbing distraction from my unrelenting thoughts and the idle chatter between the two men.

They arrive at the place Vera is at too quickly. She must not live too far from Gaddreol.

The engine cuts off and a bunch of nonspecific shuffling sounds follow. Car doors slam, one after the other, and then Avery plods away. Gaddreol doesn't move an inch.

Are you nervous? I'm sure she'll be ecstatic that you're here, so don't stress too much.

I doubt it's from my weak encouragement, but the light rapping on the front door gets louder as he closes the distance. Who knew Avery could knock without punching the door?

"Avery! Come—" A gurgled sound forces its way out of her. She was probably pulled into a surprise hug by Gaddreol. My suspicion is confirmed when she manages to squeak, "I can't breathe!"

From the cluster of muddled thuds against the solid door and the sharp inhale, being abruptly pulled into a hug and then quickly released unsteadied her.

"Sorry, I didn't mean to hug you so hard! Are you okay?"

"I, I'm fine," she stammers, presumably straightening herself. Her demeanor whiplashes when she squeals, "Gaddreol, it's really you?!"

"Woah, easy," Avery says, calmly as a muted grunt comes from Gaddreol. She most likely returned the friendly gesture with equal ferocity. Hopefully, my body is strong enough that it's not easily toppled.

"It's so nice to hear you speak." Gaddreol's words are strained.

I can't imagine what must be going through his mind to hear his little sister's voice after all these years. How many years has it been since her paralysis? I don't know. I don't know how old Vera was when she became paralyzed, nor do I know her age now. Come to think of it, I haven't learned anyone's age, not even my own. It's all insignificant in the grand scheme, but it feels like something I should know about myself.

"I know! And watch this!" she exclaims.

I hear Avery attempting to suppress his laughter. Of course, this pompous jerk is reveling in the uncomfortable exchange between siblings. Any resemblance he might've had to an actual human with real feelings all but disintegrated with this cruel act. Nothing would have been lost by informing her that her older brother is sightless.

It would have taken two seconds of forewarning to prevent this awkward interaction. I direct my words at him, uselessly.

"I'm sorry, Vera." He chokes out more strained words. I know he's fighting back tears now. "The body I transitioned into is blind."

"Oh, gosh. I'm so sorry. I didn't even notice your walking stick." Her sweet voice sounds small and fragile, her sadness mirrors his. "Oh, come in, come in. We don't have to stay on the porch."

All three of them entering the house together sounds like a quiet stampede. So many things happen at once. Gaddreol fumbling with his walking cane, bumping into a couple of things, disrupting his whispered counting, Vera offering drinks and clambering about the kitchen to get everything for said drinks, despite both men politely declining, and Avery making unspecified sounds, possibly removing a coat and shoes. Normally, listening to an assortment of noises is relatively unnoticeable, but right now all the sounds rushing in are incredibly overwhelming.

"How do you like your new body?" Gaddreol asks after settling.

The question is simple, but it creates a small hole in my bubble, allowing curiosity to pour in. *Is she alone? Can she hear the original person's consciousness? Ask her.* I Impulsively think to Gaddreol.

Ask her for what? It would just cause unnecessary worry for her. *I'm sorry, I don't know what came over me.*

Somewhere inside my bubble of isolation, I find myself hopeful that I'm not alone. While I don't want anyone to experience this ethereality and its accompanying confusion, if someone shared my experience it would be reassuring, encouraging even.

Quickly trailing the feeling of hope is disgust. *Why am I hopeful for someone potentially sharing my predicament? Why would I want someone, especially his little sister, to be subjected to this horrible reality?*

Ice clinks against the glasses. "I… love it!" she exclaims. Each word is an excited yelp. Gaddreol laughs softly at her excitement. "I can carry this tray of glasses now! Not only that! I can dance, and sing, and just anything I can think of!"

"I'm so happy that you have your life back," he says.

Now, I just need to get my life back.

Why am I having all these insensitive thoughts? The objectivity I usually have has subsided for an unfavorable, crass subjectivity.

"Yeah! And I am going to start school after I finish doing physical therapy. They said I tested at a middle school level, but I'll be going to high school. One of the doctors said she'll help me if I ever get stuck. I don't remember her name, but she's super cool."

"That's great! I'm so proud of you!" Gaddreol exclaims.

"Thanks! I'm so excited. It's kinda crazy, too. They made my new body real close to my old one!"

Did they tell her that this body was made for her? A knot in my false stomach wants to form.

"The blonde in my hair is a little bit more golden than honey now and my eyes are a bright blue like yours used to be instead of hazel. I'm about the same height, I think. But I'm not atrophied anymore! I'm even gonna go to the gym like you always did."

"That's great! Do you have someone to go with you?" he asks, trying to hide the worry in his voice.

"Not yet, but I'm gonna find someone to go with. Do you like your new body?" The excitement in her voice dissipates with the question, realizing his situation is far less ideal than her own.

"Yes, I like the body I have now. I can't tell you what it looks like, but I can tell you I've gotten pretty good at counting." He laughs. "It's been pretty interesting learning how to do things without being able to see."

"Well, I can tell you they made your body look *way* different than you do. Did you wanna be anonymous? It looks like they gave you a default body and forgot to color it in." She giggles. "You almost look like a ghost now. Your tan skin and blue eyes are both basically white. Your sandy blond hair is pitch black. Kinda creepy... Sorry."

"I didn't really care what I looked like, to be honest," Gaddreol says, plainly.

"Are you blind because of the transition? Did something go wrong?" she asks, anxiously.

She thinks they made these bodies for them. Her ignorance is truly bliss, but her question is disconcerting. *What are you going to tell her?*

"Avery and the other doctors want me to transition into another body, but I don't want to." Gaddreol redirects the conversation with ease. "I don't think it's necessary."

"I told you; I will try to convince them to give you more time." Avery's interjection reminds me that he's included in this gathering.

"Gaddreol, I don't like you having to deal with this handicap," she says, genuinely concerned. "Your real body is in perfect health, so just go back to that one, okay?"

I can sense Gaddreol's internal panic as the conversation shifts to the organization's flawed system. On the surface, Vera being lied to is a good thing, but her questions are slightly problematic when it comes to her lack of understanding of the nuances.

Avery seems to sense the inner turmoil swelling inside Gaddreol, so he attempts to soften the blow. "The experiments that we run on the bodies of transitioned patients may prevent that. I don't know how long he'll have to wait for something like that."

The consideration he has for the siblings' sensitive situation is as unexpected as his uncharacteristic kindness. But at least it saves Gaddreol from awkwardly trying to beat around the bush without revealing impertinent information to preserve Vera's innocence. Is Avery the one who originally told Vera that they tailored her body specifically to her? I didn't think someone as self-serving as him would even think of creating a subtle ruse for her.

"Oh, okay," she says, resignedly. "Well, I think you should get a new body when you can."

"Really, it's fine. This body is fine for me. I like the challenge," he says playfully, trying to lighten the mood.

Why does everyone find my blindness to be so constraining?

The realization of Vera's perspective crushes the space I reside in. She has every reason to be upset with her brother's vision loss. He can't see her moving the muscles she couldn't move for so long, the curvature of her mouth as she speaks, screams, or sings, or the subtle changes in her facial features as her emotions change. She can finally do so many things that she couldn't for so long and he can't watch her do any of it.

It makes sense to me now why Avery is sympathetic enough to preserve her innocence. Also, Gaddreol's genuine empathy and guilt makes sense regarding my entrapment. My ethereal state mirrors Vera's extensive circumstance that she grew up with. Just as I am now, she was always just conscious. Hyperaware of the muscles she couldn't move, the voice she couldn't use, and the environment she couldn't interact with.

She's a baby bird, ready to spread her wings.

My revelation makes me feel more sadistic than Avery right now. Essentially, my impulsive question to Gaddreol would cause her to relive the tormented life she lived for so long. The entire point of this was to free her from that life and I was more than willing to shove her right back into it. My intrusive thoughts are repugnant, and even though Vera can't hear them, I find myself wishing I could profusely apologize to her. Instead, I apologize to Gaddreol.

I'm sorry. I wasn't able to perceive the parallels between Vera's condition and my present ethereality before now.

My spiral of thoughts causes me to miss part of the conversation. I catch the end of Vera's sentence, "—getting better, I think."

Wait, what's getting better? I ask, but Gaddreol quickly clears up my confusion. "I'm glad that you've been singing your heart out! Can I hear you sing one day?"

"What?!" No way!" she exclaims, playfully, probably feeling a little embarrassed by the thought of someone, even her brother, hearing her sing. "You gotta wait until I get some lessons, first."

"Ah, I bet you already have a majestic voice," he says.

Her voice is mellow, mellifluous even, so her singing could be phenomenal once she gets a grasp on different tones and pitches.

A notification sound interrupts the conversation. Avery's voice sounds frustrated when he says, "I'm sorry to cut this reunion short, but I have to get back to the hospital."

The three exchange goodbyes as they make their way towards the car. Vera tells Avery to get Gaddreol a blind-accessible phone, which he promises to do. The fondness he seems to have towards Vera is still confusing to me.

CHAPTER FOUR

A FEW DAYS have passed since Gaddreol and Vera reunited, but the interaction between them still lingers. So much so that ignoring the numerous daily encounters is relatively easy. I've had a calm and unrelenting river of rhetorical statements and unanswered questions flow through my mind.

My existence is unknown to Vera.

I find myself wondering how she would react to discovering the truth of my current state mirroring hers. I expect nothing short of a raw, visceral reaction from the lively young girl. Discovering the truth would likely entangle her with sullen memories of her former body.

Would she feel rage and resentment towards her older brother? It's a possibility, but she doesn't seem capable of feeling that way toward him. No one knows how one would react when faced with such a harrowing revelation. Could she ignore all of these sickening details for her new lease on life?

My rampant introspection is difficult to ignore, I'm sure it's not helping in the slightest. My buoyant thoughts are likely intensifying his. I'm not sure how invasive his thoughts are about the encounter with his sister because the inescapable doctors have doubled down on their intrusive tendencies.

The other doctors involved don't appreciate Avery changing his mind. Their insistence toward Gaddreol has increased immensely; trying all but physical force to convince him to switch bodies. Very rarely do they acknowledge my existence. Gaddreol still makes it a point to not talk to me in their presence. Presumably, to not give them any more incentive to push him out of my body.

Even with the multitude of possibilities invading my invisible void, I have yet to come up with a scenario that favors me while also incentivizing them to let me live. It seems if it doesn't benefit them or their organization, they are unreasonable and uncooperative.

To these disturbing doctors, I'm merely a guinea pig to use until they've exhausted my worth. According to their arbitrary standards, I've exceeded my value and now I've been deemed unsuitable for their revolting experiments. In their minds, any potential utility I might have had is entirely fictitious due to my survival. My existence is a small gust of wind in an unabating hurricane.

They can easily find more people with their desired qualities. One guinea pig doesn't matter when you have access to countless more. *Six hundred and eight guinea pigs and counting.*

Shamefully, a disagreeable scenario has crossed my mind more than once. The only apparent qualifier for becoming a transitioned patient is the awareness of the trials. I've got that going for me. Sign non-binding contracts and be subjected to unspecified tests? Easier than whatever I'm being subjected to now. Arguably, it's the only idea I've come up with that wouldn't instantly be rejected.

However, if it were that simple, why wouldn't a single person offer that as a compromise? They can't rip my minuscule consciousness away from my body and put it into an unsuspecting one? Most likely, it's just because they despise my existence that much. I was never meant to survive. My demise was planned from the beginning and nothing will change their minds. Their infallible experiment is proven to be flawed and my survival is a persistent reminder of that.

Logically, it makes sense for them to cover their tracks. If someone like me survived the transition, there isn't much stopping them from going to the authorities about it. While it's unlikely to amount to anything, the potential suspicion wouldn't be worth the risk.

None of that changes the fact that this nonexistence is a far worse condemnation than death would be. *No one seems to share my sentiment, though.*

"I do," Gaddreol exhales the words quietly. "I don't want to give up yet."

Yet. I push away the thought and listen to the doctors mumble nearby, before asking, *Did you escape to the bathroom?*

"Mhm. Only for a second. I needed a minute. Josephine's overly pushy," he whispers.

Presumably, he's near the door because the doctors' conversation clears up slightly, although it's still muffled.

"We just need to give up," the rapid-talking man says, sounding frustrated. "He's not going to give up so we shouldn't worry about him anymore. We've got other things we need to focus on anyway."

"This is the most important thing we're focusing on. Submission is not an option," the authoritative woman states. "He can't keep *this* unusable body."

Gaddreol clears his throat, an unnecessary action from a blind man stumbling out of the bathroom. "Is anyone going to tell me why Tristan's body is unusable?"

This is the first time he's said my name to anyone besides Avery. He's frustrated with them now; probably tired of everyone referring to me like I'm an inanimate object. Vera's situation floods my mind again. I can imagine the absolute rage he would feel if she was regarded in the same way.

Do you feel protective of me because of your little sister? I ask. I'm met with a sound possibly made in agreement.

"We are looking for results. Results you can't provide us with in *this* body." Josephine closes the distance, and her voice resonates uncomfortably inside my space.

"I'd appreciate it if you keep your hands to yourself outside of a medical context," he says, making no effort to hide his anger, but his voice is still clear and concise.

She put her hands on you? There isn't an accompanying sound occurring with the accusation, so I assume she poked him when referring to my body.

"I'd appreciate it if you would just relent." Hostility grows in her tone.

"You can leave now," he says.

The demand earns a scornful huff, but surprisingly, they follow the command. The door opens seconds later, and they both shuffle out of the apartment without another word. Gaddreol collapses onto what I think is a couch.

I thought they would be here forever.

"Me too. You'd really consider transitioning?" he asks, jumping straight back into the unpleasant thoughts. Exhaustion is thick in his voice now. "I don't think it's necessarily a bad idea."

You don't? It's the most plausible idea, but still an unwelcome one.

"Well, if there's a body that's just being used for experiments then maybe they'd let you use that one," he says.

Wishful thinking. Even if there's an unused body, the idea would undoubtedly be met with insurmountable rejection. Nearly everyone trudging through your front door has attempted to talk you into transitioning with the sole intention of cremating me. I don't think I am in anyone's favor to be considered as a candidate.

"Avery—" Gaddreol says, but my thoughts interrupt.

My only saving grace when it comes to him is the history you two share.

Our weak attempt at a conversation fades until it's saturated in silence. He's too tired to keep up the façade and I don't have much more to dwell on when it comes to contemplating such an egregious idea.

I don't know how much time passes before he starts snoring softly. I expect to slip into a false state of unconsciousness, but it doesn't come. Due to our bizarre connection and his lack of vision, he's had abnormal sleep patterns, but this is the first time I haven't been dragged into his sleep state, too. Instantly, a feeling of panic wants to become a permanent resident of my ever-shrinking space.

Why is panic attempting to settle inside my black hole? Sleeping is little more than an insignificant concept for a metaphysical being stuck inside his head. Could this be the first indication of us being separated? But why? How? Disconnection. Am I going to find out what true isolation feels like in my tiny void? Or am I beginning to fade into pure oblivion?

Confusion and fear want to replace the unoccupied space. Before I can continue questioning the surreality of my situation the blinding light returns, illuminating the nothingness surrounding me. It's still a vague and mystifying sensation. The intense brightness is difficult to see in my mind.

How am I able to see this at all?

Without warning the blazing light dims. Images flash through my mind in an incomprehensible, dizzying blur of motion in what I can only imagine is comparable to the unfocused, blurry images taken with a camera.

It's an unintelligible, ancient language comprised of many colors, shapes, and objects that my mind is desperately trying to decipher. An impossible feat made worse with everything spinning around. It's all so overwhelming and confusing. If it were possible I think I would puke.

The images slow to a crawl, removing the fuzziness. Everything is unrecognizable, but Gaddreol's memories automatically lend words to me, filling in the gaps with a distinct familiarity. Which allows me to intuitively take in the vast stimulus before me.

I'm experiencing Gaddreol's dream.

A small child with bright blonde curls, fair skin, and hazel eyes is sitting in a wheelchair. A rich purple dress overwhelms her tiny frame. The young girl is frail but high-spirited. Her chair is bulky, dwarfing her, causing her to look even more fragile. Attached to the right arm is a controller for her tiny fingers. Her eyes, large with adoration, are fixed on the large metal box framing a movie of cartoon cats. The room is relatively unstimulating by comparison, with shades of beige and brown on the furniture, walls, and carpet. It still has a unique beauty, though.

My gaze drops to my arm that's extending towards Vera. My out-stretched hand, with a single piece of popcorn between my fingers, goes straight up to Vera's mouth and carefully feeds it to her. She smiles a weak, toothy smile and then returns her attention to the animated cats frolicking about once more.

Suddenly, we're no longer sitting in front of the television. Now we are outside, the sun is shining brightly between sparsely strewn fluffy white clouds. The wind is blowing enough for the leaves of the trees to sway and the blades of the lush emerald grass to bend in its direction. Her wheelchair is secured on a metal platform suspended by shiny silver chains. I am pushing her from behind, watching as her blonde hair bounces slightly. I can't see her little grin, but she is radiating happiness.

The clouds transform from sparse soft, fluffy ones into heavy, dark ones that engulf the sky. Gray washes over the picturesque environment; everything looks dull and bleak now. The sky lights up briefly with bright streaks of lightning, followed quickly by crackles and booms from thunder.

The vibrancy in Vera rapidly fades, as well. She, too, is tinged with gray now. Her fair skin is pale, and her bright blonde hair dims to a washed-out ashen color. The remainder of her strength seems gone as she is slumped in her chair, unable to move. I slowly come around the swing to see her mouth slightly ajar and a blank stare in her eyes.

"VERA!" Gaddreol screams, instantaneously thrusting me out of the colorful dream and plunging me back into the black pit again.

An intense disorientation wants to consume me. I'm stupefied. I don't know how to process this intense visual hallucination. I don't know what I should be feeling. Happy? Sad? Confused? Fearful? I want to feel everything, and simultaneously nothing at all.

At least I have one of those things going for me.

Although the dream itself isn't very long, the entirety of it is heart-breakingly beautiful. Vera's drastic shift from an exuberant young girl to a frail husk is excruciating to watch, but both scenes are inconceivable and enigmatic in their beauty. Every minor detail fits seamlessly together to form a larger image that is indescribably sublime.

It feels as though the edges of my confined space are fraying; the black pool is being infiltrated by the small remnants of his dream trying to force its way beyond the frayed edges. Gaddreol's dream exists in my small space as a million shattered pieces. To the best of my ability, I put them together like a puzzle. Thin, fractured pieces that I now recognize as colors, in the form of strings are dancing just outside of what would be considered my peripheral vision if I had functioning eyes.

If I could shed tears, I think a raging waterfall would be an apt description. Vision is a true blessing.

I don't deserve to die because I don't have it, though.

Now that I've been given the chance to be on the outside looking in, I have an empathetic comprehension of Gaddreol's situation. I truly appreciate the deep-seated protection he feels for Vera and his leap of faith into this concealed project.

More relevant to my situation, I understand his determination to help me break out of my prison. I don't fault him for any decision he's made. Everything he's done up until now has been with the best intentions.

There's a loud thud, followed by fabric swishing against a wall, he's probably sliding to the floor. I imagine him curled into the fetal position, holding himself tightly. All I can do is listen intently to his excruciating sobs as he finally lets himself feel all of the emotions he's pushed away time and time again. I want to offer something comforting, but there's nothing that comes to mind that would be helpful.

"I tried so hard," he says, choking through his sobs. I don't think he's talking to me.

You did everything you could.

"I tried so hard to do the right thing. I saved Vera just to hurt someone in her place. I'm so sorry." He wails, crying so hard that his breathing is ragged and forced.

It's okay, Gaddreol. Breathe.

He struggles to his feet using what sounds like the cabinet to pull himself up, and then water begins flowing from the faucet alongside his unyielding cries. Either rinsing his face or getting some water to calm down, perhaps.

I was too consumed with admiring the extraordinary visuals to consider what the painstaking dream means to him or how reliving such an agonizing event would affect him.

I'm sorry for my constant incoherent babbling. Are you okay?

"I wish I could lie and say yes," Gaddreol admits. His breathing is short and rapid. "Truth is, not in the slightest. I've tried to hold it all together since day one. I was doing good, but after having that dream…"

His voice trails off as he crumples into a heap on the floor again. He's hyperventilating. My constant never-ending thoughts are at a complete loss for something to say that might provide solace. An 'I'm sorry' only feels like an apathetic response. Given the unique circumstances, the typical 'I'm here for you' doesn't feel appropriate either.

Calm down. Breathe slowly. Close enough.

His breathing calms enough for a brief chuckle to break through the tears. The cries are still steady and persistent, but at least he's not going to black out. I don't think I'm equipped to handle that.

Laughter plays on the edge of his voice as he says, "I have to say that's a pretty good inkling to have. Your 'incoherent babbling' isn't a detriment, just so you know.

Why do you say that? My rambling was wildly inappropriate for your emotional well-being.

"You just experienced my dream. Even though it was one of the most depressing things ever, you actually experienced something visual. I'd be seriously worried about you if you weren't babbling incoherently about it. Besides, your constant rambling may be the only thing keeping both of us sane at this point." He laughs half-heartedly, and I want to join in.

We're going to have to agree to disagree on that last statement. But I'm glad you're able to laugh about it. Hopefully I provided a small bit of comfort.

CHAPTER FIVE

OVER THE PHONE, the unfamiliar doctor, Sai I believe, stressed that it's of the utmost importance to arrive at the hospital in a timely manner for testing. I'm not even sure Gaddreol had enough time to brush his hair before stumbling towards the cab parked outside. He hums a quiet sound of agreement, although I'm not sure if it's supposed to be a yes or no to the hairbrush.

Now that Gaddreol is here, there isn't any urgency as the doctor suggested. It seems to be little more than a routine clinical visit for various tests and screenings. For fifteen minutes, he's been sitting in the lobby, while I'm treated to the repetitive clicking of a mouse and tippy-tapping on a keyboard. Not to mention the phone ringing every other minute on the receptionist's desk, followed by the well-rehearsed greeting for the "Samson Hospital."

This must be the hospital that FREE is discreetly using as a front for their disgusting operations.

Accompanying each sound pulsing through the dark is a swirl of dancing colors. They're faint and barely noticeable now, almost like there's not enough room in this cramped hole to fit both vision and hearing simultaneously. As devastating as the dream was, I wouldn't mind seeing it again if it meant the vibrant colors could return.

"Mr. Adair," a gravelly voice belonging to an older woman calls out, breaking up the monotony. A heavy smoker, perhaps. Gaddreol collects himself.

Gaddreol Adair. His name is unusual. Not that I have memories of names to call upon, but his seems exceptionally strange. *If I can remember, I'll ask him about his name.*

He dutifully follows the nurse as carefully as he can by tapping his cane and quietly counting his steps. I'm not sure if she's keeping pace with him or vice versa, but their steps are surprisingly in sync. When her footsteps come to a halt, he mirrors the action.

"The doc told me to skip triage and bring you straight to the eighth floor." As if on cue, a quick ding emits. Their quiet footsteps walking on the wooden flooring echo against the stark metal floor of the elevator.

The elevator's sequential beeps accentuate the uncomfortable silence between them as they ascend. The nurse escorting him seems unapproachable, only saying things of relevance and nothing more. At least she doesn't think he's incompetent and in need of constant assistance. I must say, even I'm impressed by his ability to navigate using sounds. It shames me to admit that I thought it would have been a much steeper mountain to climb.

"Here we are, room 809," she says, rapping the door. "Here's your patient, Doc!"

The pitter-pattering on his keyboard stops. "Thank you, Mildred. Gaddreol, come in, please. Sit down." His tone is unemotional and flat, and his approachability may even be less than Mildred's. "I apologize for asking you to come in early. An unexpected meeting came up that required my attendance."

"That's okay."

"We can skip the formalities and get straight to it. First, I have everything ready to get your bloodwork done. Afterwards, we will get a full-body MRI done. Then a colleague of mine will perform a mental evaluation to ensure you are still suitable to continue our program." The doctor's voice is soft, but authoritative.

If he's deemed unsuitable for their absurd program, what will they do with him? Would he lose his life if it came to that? It wouldn't benefit them to dispose of the patients that are mentally unstable. Stabilizing their conditions to monitor and studying their behaviors would be optimal for furthering their experiments while satiating their morbid curiosities, with the possible upside of actually helping the patient. They haven't seemed to learn that the tiny details are as significant as the grand scheme of things.

Setting aside my theoretical fine-tuning of the minute details of their sickening organization, I know this situation is different than the ones before it and the outcome hardly relies on Gaddreol at all. The fixation is on me and my survival and how that affects their momentum.

"Can I ask you something, Dr. Sai?" he asks, cordially.

"Sai is fine, and of course," Sai's tone mimics Gaddreol's. "What is troubling you?"

An ever-present looming darkness, a lonely nonexistence, and imminent, probable death. Despite my unwarranted response, it's a good question.

With everything that's happened since the transition, I honestly don't know what Gaddreol's response to this question will be. I'm not sure if any response to this question would be adequate for a doctor who lacks good bedside manners.

"What other sorts of things happen here?" he asks, skipping over Sai's question entirely to ask one that would fall under the category of 'inappropriate.' "Obviously, there are other people like me. But switching people's bodies can't be the only thing that happens at this hospital."

I admire Gaddreol for asking questions to any doctor that will humor him. Most of them are highly unreceptive to anything he has to say now. This one probably won't be any different since he's silent, steadily tapping away at the keys.

Just keep making it worse. He's going to assume you're fishing for information for some incriminating evidence or something. He probably won't answer a question like that.

"Well, we are also researching various physical impairments, such as your blindness. The transitions are the most reliable method to cure impairments, so we are working tirelessly to improve them."

He actually answered you.

"If you guys are already experimenting with these impairments, why can't I stay in this body as a participant in that study group?"

Somehow, I know he's implying that I should be allowed in the study group.

"Typically, we perform experiments on the bodies we get from the transitions, both with impairments and without. The tests are rigorous, and most would not wish to be subjected to them. So, I do not think this is an applicable solution to your situation." His words are direct and studious.

What kind of horrific tests would prevent people from wanting to participate for a chance to change their lives for the better?

"Would I be able to join anyway?"

I don't think he's going to appreciate you weaseling your way into things you haven't been invited to.

"The director would need to approve that decision," Sai states. The tapping finally ceases. "I apologize for keeping you waiting with these intrusions. Something else unexpected came up that I needed to address. I am ready to begin now. This may hurt."

I don't know if it hurts or if he can really feel it at all, since he isn't making any noises of discomfort. He is just letting the doctor perform his duties without interruption.

"I want to ask you something." Sai's voice is neutral. "Why are you so insistent on remaining in a sightless body?"

Does he know? He must know, right? It seems everyone at this confounded place knows, don't they? If he doesn't know, anything you say will tip him off.

"I just don't get why I have to change bodies when this one is still capable of being used for these trials." The last word has a slight hint of aggravation in it.

"Your role in this process is to help us assess the discrepancies between your body and this new one. We document your personal recollections so that we can ascertain the effects of the transition. We worry that this body being blind may cloud your judgement, which would prevent us from obtaining the results we seek." The doctor sounds very pragmatic now.

Sai is the first doctor to put into actual words how my blindness would be unsuitable for their transition. But after what Avery said, this feels more like an attempt to deflect Gaddreol with objective reasoning rather than outright admit their hatred of me.

While he hasn't said anything particularly damning, it's what's left unsaid that stands out. These vile people despise me for simply surviving their imperfect transitioning process. Outside of their absolute hatred of me, there is no reason I can't be a participant in these ruthless tests for my blindness. I wish I knew what caused them to have so much contempt for people in my position. My guess is that I was right in my thinking that allowing me to live is a constant reminder of their failings.

"So if the director somehow agrees to me participating in the blind studies, what would that mean?" Gaddreol asks, ignoring the blatant opposition.

"Are you sure you want to experience that excessive amount of discomfort when you could just transition into the body that was found for you?"

How can he ask that so nonchalantly? How can he speak of this person, who is alive and well, as if they are nothing more than a new place to reside? No matter how superficially nice any of them seem, beneath the surface, they are all despicable people.

"With all due respect, Sai, there's not really anything that's more uncomfortable than knowing that transitioning into another body means I've killed two people," Gaddreol says, trying to disguise the sadness in his voice. "I'll go through pretty much anything to not take another person's life away."

"Understandable," Sai says, plainly. "The MRI is ready for you now."

Both men stand up without another word. Sai leads the way and Gaddreol walks closely behind him lightly tapping the cane against the tile.

"Lie down. Easy now. This is going to be extremely long, loud, and tiresome, but you must stay as still as you possibly can, okay?" Nothing comes from Gaddreol; I assume he nods an affirmation.

Loud and tiresome is an understatement. Unfaltering sounds of clicking, beeping, scratching, and whirring reverberate throughout the machine. The colors from the dream swirl around my mind, trying to latch onto the sounds. A pale yellow-beige color like the walls clings to the clicking. The lush green of the grass adheres to the beeping. The deep brown of the tree bark attaches to the scratching. Lastly, the whirring is assigned to a soft gray color like the looming clouds.

Clicking. Yellow. Scratching. Brown. Beeping. Green. Whirring. Gray.

The sounds invade the all-consuming darkness, imprisoning my full attention with the rapidly switching colors. The yellow and green pulsate with a consistent pattern. The brown rapidly oscillates and the gray spins in a constant circle.

Clicking. Yellow. Scratching. Brown. Beeping. Green. Whirring. Gray.

Even when the sounds are distant, they still reverberate inside of my cramped space. I think I've died and exist in this hellscape. The inescapable fiery pit of hell is an accurate depiction. *This is hell.*

Clicking. Yellow. Scratching. Brown. Beeping. Green. Whirring. Gray.

I can't tear my focus away from the unabated loop of sounds and colors. *This. Is. Hell. Make it stop. Please. Just make it stop.* I beg, pointlessly.

Clicking. Yellow. Scratching. Brown. Beeping. Green. Whirring. Gray.

I have no idea how much time passes before the noises circling my bubble finally cease and the colors disintegrate like wisps of smoke. There isn't any reprieve as the subsequent silence is equally deafening.

I never want to experience an MRI again.

"That was awful. I feel so dizzy," he says.

The horrendous carousel of swirling colors is likely the culprit for the dizzying feeling. *I'm sorry.*

"We'll get you a wheelchair." I hear footsteps rapidly exiting the room and then return with equal haste with a set of squealing tires in tow. "Once you're finished with your mental evaluation you are free to return home."

Vera's wheelchair pops into my mind. Although her chair in the dream was immaculate and wouldn't match these abrasive sounds it's the only visual representation I have. I try to imagine it with rust, but it's impossible.

As the doctor helps Gaddreol into the chair it creaks and groans with every movement. Its onslaught of squeaky protests continues as they wheel him back to the room. More creaky groans erupt when they help him out of the chair.

They replace people when they are slightly disadvantaged, but they can't replace a wheelchair that seems to barely be holding itself together?

The wait isn't long before a polite, unfamiliar voice says, "Good morning, Mr. Adair, Dr. Sai. I'm Dr. Sands. I will be performing your evaluation today. Are you ready to begin?"

Dr. Sands didn't introduce himself by his first name, but he seems friendlier than many of the ones on a first name basis, Sai included.

Sai is mystifying. There's something about him that's intriguing, but I can't figure out what.

"Yes, just a little dizzy from all the uncomfortable sounds in the MRI." Unconcealed discomfort is thick in his voice.

Good luck.

"Okay. The first question. Are you satisfied with the results of your transition?" Dr. Sands' voice is indifferent but polite.

No.

"Kinda."

"Care to elaborate further?"

No.

"I didn't know that transitioning meant murdering someone. So that sucks, but if it was a different bodily circumstance, it wouldn't be a big deal."

"A different bodily circumstance?" Dr. Sands questions.

Gaddreol repeats to this doctor what he said to me. "I assumed the bodies were, you know, already deceased and preserved. Or, well, created artificially. Something that isn't this."

Something that isn't kidnapping people. Something that isn't taking my life away and forcing me into this abysmal existence. Something that isn't killing innocent people because of a deranged ideology.

"I see, thank you for that insight. Do you feel you've returned to a relatively normal life?" he asks, ignoring the creeping distress in Gaddreol's voice.

If listening to the nonstop rambling of a disembodied voice counts as relatively normal, then yes.

"All things considered, I think I'm adjusting to things fairly well."

I concur.

The ensuing questions pertain to his emotions and moods, and his thoughts regarding physical and social activities. Emotions are chaotic, moods are intense, and there are too many thoughts on everything. Not too many physical activities unless catching yourself from tripping over something counts. The potential positive is that his social status can't be exhausted with so many people coming and going like his life is a revolving door. However, even with the massive number of social interactions, he could still feel alone while surrounded by people.

Hopefully, his answers are a bit more succinct and positive than my internal analysis. I don't know though, because I find myself struggling to follow the droning conversation. My thoughts wander to flashes of the dream—the remnants I can remember anyway.

Fundamentally knowing that hair is made up of thousands of thin strands is far different than seeing them combined to create a full head of hair for the first time. It's mundane but absolutely mind-blowing. Her eyes were shown briefly, but it was enough to see the pale green and brown gradient speckled with gold atop the intricate ridges of the iris. Even something as boring and uninteresting as grass has multiple components to create a soft, lush appearance. It looks exactly like I remember it feeling.

Oh, how I wish I could run my hands through my hair or across the grass again.

"Thank you, Mr. Adair. I think we're done now that I have what I need. I appreciate you taking the time to do this assessment."

I don't think he was given a choice, Doctor.

"Of course. Thank you, Dr. Sands. Thank you, Dr. Sai," Gaddreol mutters, bleakly, but still cordially.

"Sai is fine," he repeats, sounding amiable now. Perhaps he needs to become accustomed to someone before letting his guard down. "I will be assisting you to the lobby to ensure you make it to your ride safely."

The ride down mirrors the ride up. The intervals of short beeps are the only sound until the doors slide open to the main floor. They step into the lobby, but Sai stops suddenly, and Gaddreol probably bumps into him from the grunt he makes.

"Avery, what are you doing?" Sai asks.

"Hey, Sai. I'm apparently watching you make Gaddreol trip. You, okay?" Avery asks, keeping his voice low, a feat I didn't think he was capable of. Before now, I assumed his voice could only be adjusted from loud to louder. He's closer when he asks, "How'd the tests go?"

"I'm fine," Gaddreol says, straightening himself.

"The tests were fine," Sai says, matching the half-whisper. "Why are you here?"

"I'm taking Gaddreol out to eat." His voice is as smug as ever.

As another urge to punch him passes through me, an image of a hand crosses my mind. It loosely resembles a fist, but hardly one capable of doing anything significant.

I can't remember them making plans, but perhaps it was when I was too consumed by my thoughts to notice.

"Avery, you should not be his personal cab. We've already spoken about this." It's hard to place, but Sai sounds disappointed.

Sai's disappointment in Avery is baffling. Aside from him bringing personal affairs into a professional setting, I can't fathom why it would bother the aloof man. Perhaps he's a stickler for the rules, but I have a hunch it's a little more personal than a strict set of rules he abides by.

"Since you asked so nicely, yes, we can go out to eat," Gaddreol sarcastically joins in.

"See, Sai," Avery says. His snarky demeanor earns a sound of disapproval, but nothing else comes from the other doctor. "There's nothing to worry about."

"Be careful, Avery," Sai says, sternly.

Why does he need to be careful? Can he get in trouble for being a personal chauffeur? That seems as unlikely as it is surprising that Avery is choosing to personally escort him around. But the concern Sai harbors for the obnoxious man is strange to me.

There's something about Sai, bubbling just beneath the surface of his distant demeanor, that's fascinating. However, there's no time to analyze the oddities of this strange man before Gaddreol is ushered out the door by Avery.

✳ ✳ ✳

The two men are at a nearby restaurant waiting for their burgers, fries, and drinks. According to Avery, the hospital staff come here for lunch often because it has the best burgers around. He, himself, has been here a few times a week since he started working at the hospital.

Based on the clashing of cutlery and soft murmurs from every direction it is fairly populated. Too many people are unintentionally fighting to be the clearest, and the loudest, voice. To prevent the indistinct, constant chatter from becoming overwhelming, I focus on the conversation between Avery and Gaddreol.

"Why did you start working at the hospital?" Gaddreol asks.

I don't think that's the right question. *You should ask 'why did you join FREE,' instead.* Though that's a little too direct for a public outing.

"I started working at the hospital right out of med school," he responds without the zealousness I expect to hear. "My internship started here, and I completed that along with my residency."

"So, you've always worked at the hospital," he muses, and then adds, "Is that why you joined the organization, too?"

Avery shushes Gaddreol as a waitress brings their food to the table. "Here you are. Two classic hamburgers and fries. Do you need refills for your drinks?" she asks.

They agree in unison, waiting quietly for her to return and refill their respective cups.

"Thanks," Avery calls after, then lowers his voice into a cold, steely tone I don't recognize. "It was just the natural progression of my employment once my residency ended, so I joined. Plus, I'm very good at what I do."

Just as he starts opening up and softening around the edges, he returns to his cold-hearted nature. *The same cold-hearted person that is waiting on the day Gaddreol relents, allowing him to murder me.*

What exactly does Avery do? What does Sai even do? Why do I care about what Sai does? It seems Sai is versatile; Avery must be, as well, as much as I don't want to admit that.

"I don't even know what you do."

"Everything." Another curt response.

It's a cop out answer. To say everything, he is admitting nothing. By admitting nothing, he has plausible deniability. Hearing the most prideful man I've encountered so far have such guarded answers is something I struggle to understand. Although, it's most likely to keep the conversation vague since so much of what his answer implied is, in fact, illegal.

"Everything" includes stalking, kidnapping, transitions, countless experiments, and ill-advised taxi driving. Does he really do it all? Although I don't know what his role actually is, the entitlement he has suggests that he wouldn't allow himself to be subjected to the menial aspects of his job. Physical labor doesn't suit him.

"Look, I'm not going to press you since you clearly don't want to talk about your involvement in all this," Gaddreol says. His voice is soft but stern. "But I want you to get me a meeting with the director."

The abrupt laughter from Avery startles Gaddreol, causing him to smack the table, scattering the clanging silverware onto the tile. The restaurant falls silent momentarily, before roaring to life again with the muffled chatter.

Avery leans down to grab the fallen objects, mumbling, "I've got it, don't make a fool of yourself again."

"Anyway, can you get me a meeting or not?" he asks, ignoring the comment.

Recollecting himself, he sits back down. With a mouth full, the rude man asks, barely audible, "You seriously think you can get a meeting with the director?"

Avery and I may never find common ground again, but we both agree on this. Why would an important, powerful person consider meeting with someone so low on the hierarchy? The amount of tenacity Gaddreol has to confront the director is borderline insane.

"Why can't you believe that?" Gaddreol asks as Avery tries to calm his laughter but fails miserably.

"There's no way in hell. What makes you think he'd want to talk to you?" Avery's laughter slowly dissipates with each word.

Gaddreol is quiet, probably chewing his food before opening his mouth, unlike the man across from him. Then he says, "Sai said the only way I can join the experiments for physical impairments is to 'take it up with the director,' so I'm asking you if you can make it happen."

"Doubt it. I'm barely in his good graces at the moment because I'm standing by your decision to not transition from this—" he's interrupted, which may be a good thing since his voice is growing astronomically louder as he keeps talking.

"Tristan's."

"Right, Tristan's." Accepting the correction, Avery's voice returns to a soft whisper. Then he adds, "That doesn't feel strange to you? To speak of his body, while choosing to stay in it?"

"Yeah, it does, but I don't care about how uncomfortable I am if my comfort is tantamount to a death sentence." The intentionally vague words sound harsher than I think he intended.

The mention of my impending death caused their conversation to end abruptly. Only sounds of chewing and clumsy fumbling from Gaddreol to grab his drink or scrape food from his plate. I don't blame them, since the mention of my demise tends to leave an uneasy feeling that's difficult to navigate. Even I'm left equally thoughtful and thoughtless regarding this morbid topic.

On one side of the proverbial coin, I want to encourage him to forget about me and move on to a happier life with his younger sister. If I was unimportant enough to be whisked away without anyone thinking or caring, it should be okay to be unimportant now. All of that is currently irrelevant as I know thoughts don't have any influence on his resolve.

On the other side of the proverbial coin, I want to thank him for his valiant efforts to ensure my safety and for trying to make me feel like an actual person despite my ethereal state of being. Most of all, I want to tell him that even though this is possibly the worst existence imaginable, I wouldn't want to go through this craziness with anyone else.

The waitress returns, interrupting their presumably tense silence. "Are you guys ready for the bill, or did you want to order something else?"

"I would actually like another burger with fries." Avery's stomach groans in agreement. "And some chocolate pie. You want anything else?"

"I'd like a piece of chocolate pie, too. With whipped cream, if possible, please. Thank you."

"Of course. I'll be back with your food soon," the waitress says, leaving them once more to sit in uncomfortable silence.

Gaddreol is the one to speak up first. "So, you don't think the director will even consider meeting with me?"

Absolutely, not. I answer without meaning to.

Avery sighs, "I want to tell you he'll consider it, but he won't. He doesn't like to be bothered with trivial things. Besides, now that I'm advocating for you, he hardly acknowledges me. I don't even know who he's masquerading as, literally."

Avery doesn't know who the director is? How is the face of the hospital unknown to one of the doctors? With the technology he has readily available to him, he could be anyone. It's predictable coming from a man involved in explicit criminal activity wanting to remain hidden in plain sight, but the doctors working for him should at least know who he is.

"Why does it even have to be approved by him if it's so trivial?" Gaddreol asks, irritation growing in his voice.

"It's trivial because it's against policy. It has to go through him." I want to say Avery sounds sympathetic, but I'm still not sure he's capable of feeling that.

The policy is ridiculous. These horrific experiments are available for physical impairments, but if a transitioned patient wants to join them, they can't because their contract specified transitions only. What was the reason behind signing a contract? I can't imagine any of this is even remotely legal to be challenged in a court. Is it merely a façade to make patients believe it's a real organization? But what is the point of that, if they're willing to resort to murder to conceal their disgusting secrets? None of it makes sense.

One day, I'd like to meet the director just to ask him questions. More than he would answer. He probably wouldn't give me a single answer, but I would ask the questions anyway.

Why did he create this horrible organization? What is the point of this entire operation? How does transitioning people even work? Why murder the survivors of the transitioning process instead of the more reasonable option of allowing them to transition too?

The last question is little more than a redundant theoretical. The answer is simple: fear. Fear that allowing them to live will expose the horrors occurring behind closed doors.

However, it brings up more questions I hadn't considered before. *How does this operation run entirely unnoticed? How do the doctors remain secretive about everything? How do patients like Gaddreol in less drastic circumstances not run straight to the authorities?*

For a lot of patients, the truth likely remains undiscovered, and they continue assuming something like Gaddreol did. It's possible that some are even fed the same lies that Vera was told. As for the doctors' disposition and willingness, it must be blackmail. Though, that seems too minor to maintain their obedience to this twisted operation. I'm fairly certain there are others like Avery who are far too excited about certain aspects of the *job*, but I doubt all of them are like that.

I hear a metal object scraping a glass plate. Gaddreol must be eating the pie he ordered. I find myself wanting to know what pie looks like. I know it's a triangular prism, but I don't know what any of the components making up the triangle look like from the crust, the filling, or the toppings.

I guess that doesn't even matter when I don't remember what it tastes like, either. Have I eaten pie before? *Probably.* The first thing I'm going to eat if I get my body back will be a piece of pie. *Maybe.*

"This is delicious!" Gaddreol exclaims, shoveling another piece onto the utensil.

"Told you. It's the best." His smugness makes its return again.

The waitress hands the bill and a to-go box to Avery. Gratitude is expressed on both sides and then she walks away. Gaddreol stands first but waits to follow Avery's lead out of the restaurant.

"Thanks for going out with me today. It reminds me of how it used to be." There is a genuine smile in Avery's tone.

"I didn't really have a choice," Gaddreol retorts, laughing softly. "I wouldn't mind doing it again. Now, take me home, please."

The car ride is another mind-numbing experience. My usual black void is colored with streaks of gray matching the sporadic gusts of wind.

CHAPTER SIX

I HAVE COMPLETELY lost track of the days. I don't know how long it's been since I initially woke up in this state. The daily interactions are on a rinse-and-repeat cycle, barely anything new finds its way into the repetitive routine. All the doctors, excluding Sai, still argue with Gaddreol and Avery about the decision to remain in my body when so many perfectly healthy bodies are available to use.

So many perfectly healthy—stolen—bodies.

Taz never argues about it; she offers her gentle encouragement for Gaddreol to live his best life. His best life is apparently at the detriment of mine, unfortunately. She rarely shows up now, though. It's probably best that she stays at the hospital, anyway. I'm sure her gentle manner is very helpful in keeping transitioned patients calm and comfortable once they've woken up.

Sai's solution isn't very popular with the other doctors, either. Too many variables that could go wrong with the experiments that wouldn't be worth the risk. An excellent excuse. There's hardly any risk to Gaddreol if he undergoes the available tests; it's not like his eyesight can get any worse.

It's likely to be nothing more than the doctors being angry that he refuses to follow the procedures according to their discretion. That and his outright rejection of their apparent discriminatory ideology to perfect the human race that they seem to use as an excuse to kill anyone with physical impairments. They would rather murder someone like me than improve their life.

To the dismay of the other doctors, Avery is still fully supporting his decision to continue inhabiting my body. I think Gaddreol being passionate about something besides his younger sister is helping Avery sympathize with his plight. He is still the same arrogant, overcompensating asshole, but him going against his own organization to help is bringing the smallest sliver of hope to Gaddreol. While I don't really understand their relationship, I'm glad he has something to hold onto.

Sai is another person I don't understand. Something about him is strangely tranquil. Superficially, he seems cold and calculating; beneath that, friendly and humble. He still advocates for Gaddreol to be a participant in the blind studies despite the backlash that comes with that. This uncivilized organization is seemingly beneath his dignified disposition, yet somehow, he fits in perfectly.

It's difficult to fathom that not only one, but two doctors from this disturbing place are choosing to stand by Gaddreol. He is a microscopic fraction of the people involved and yet two people are trying to give him what he wants. Within reason, of course. Though, what constitutes reasonable to this organization is anything but.

Gaddreol? Can you hear me? I ask, but I'm met with silence. I don't hear any doctors, so it's unusual to not get a response as I prattle on.

Are you alright? No answer.

Despite his lack of response, my mind continues to wander. It skims over Avery, Sai, Vera, and even my impending death until it finally settles on the inexplicable nightmare we shared. I don't think Gaddreol has mentioned it to anyone. Which is probably for the best since neither Sai nor Avery are likely to care about me experiencing sight for the first time. There hasn't been another one, sadly. There may never be another one.

Thanks to the short-lived connection with his subconscious, some words are now associated with a fragmented image. For the most part, the visual aspect has faded. Many of the colors have muddied, running together and the shapes have blurred into nearly indistinct blobs. Sometimes, a bit of the visual residue finds its way to the forefront of my space, reminding me that it was real—as real as whatever this is, at least.

Even though the pictures are dwindling, I'm forever grateful for the incredible experience. Witnessing the exquisite scenes almost makes being stuck in this horrid solitary confinement worth it.

Needless to say, I never thought I'd be happy for being trapped inside of my own mind.

The emotional range inside my ever-shrinking bubble shifts from gratitude to the emotion I can only recognize as regret. It's an ill-fitting emotion, but it's the only one that wants to take over. There's an uncomfortable prickly sensation hovering over the emptiness.

Why? I don't have any reason to feel remorseful, do I? Yes... I do.

Remorse because my unconcealed, impulsive thoughts could've ruined the siblings' reunion. Remorse for surviving the transition or for simply existing. As if by continuing to live in this ceaseless space I'm being incredibly selfish.

"There's no reason to feel that way," Gaddreol says. His drowsy voice offers reassurance, causing the prickly sensation to fade.

I'd breathe a sigh of relief if I could. *I was getting worried about you.*

"I'm sorry for being absent tonight," he says, languidly. "I've been dozing off."

I can imagine how utterly exhausting everything is.

His heavy breathing is the only sound, so he's effortlessly drifted off again. His light sleeping causes me to feel alone. His ability to briefly fall in and out of an unconscious state while I'm stuck without any hint of drowsiness to drag me into a sleep-like state alongside him is a glaring reminder that I'm just an ethereal being stuck inside someone's head.

Being reminded of my metaphysical state is really difficult to deal with. No one wants to be constantly reminded that they're incorporeal, unable to feel emotional or physical sensations. The only thing to somewhat remind me of my true existence is being able to listen to all the sourceless sounds that my mind desperately tries to make sense of. In this relentless isolation, the only solace I have is that I still have remarkable mental capabilities with the exception of my memory loss.

Apart from not remembering things about myself, forgetting how textures or physical sensations feel may be the worst part about losing myself in this endless darkness. I know how I would feel and how my body should react to things, but the tactile sensations I used to experience the world with are gone. Not knowing how tangible objects should feel is like missing a large part of myself.

I'm missing a lot more than that, obviously.

The best thing to come out of this is Vera being able to live her life in a healthy body. Grief tries to settle inside my already cramped space. The young blonde-haired, blue-eyed girl whose body was taken away for Vera to have this opportunity flows into my mind. From the dainty, sweet voice, the girl likely hasn't even graduated high school yet. A teenage girl being snatched away from her loving family makes me wish it were possible for me to cry. Instead, the encompassing sadness makes me feel as if I'm sinking deeper into my empty hole.

Thankfully, she didn't live through the transition. The thought slips into my mind before I can stop it. *Thankfully, she didn't live.* Those are words that actually came from my own mind.

"Death is better than this." That's what I said the first day I woke up. Now I'm unintentionally resigning this young woman to the same fate I initially resigned myself to.

The relief I should feel due to her not sharing my unbearable existence is short-lived as I realize that I don't know for certain that she doesn't live this same existence. What if she did survive the transition, except she doesn't have the same connection with Vera that I have with Gaddreol?

Tears would be flowing uncontrollably from my eyes right now if I could cry. Assuming she didn't survive is dismissing the very real possibility that she might be in an even more isolated nonexistence than I am. The thought of her probable demise makes me want to cry, but the possibility of her living an even lonelier desolation is far more devastating. With the former, she would be at peace instead of trapped inside this torturous hell.

Aside from the unyielding sorrow I know I should feel, there is another emotion trying to weasel its way into my claustrophobic hole. Alongside the despair I want to feel for the young girl, I also want to be envious of her. Envious because she likely experienced death instead of this inescapable abyss. Although I can't confirm she's resting peacefully, there's no evidence to contradict it, either.

A truly disgusting thought to have. I'm sorry. I pointlessly direct the thought to the unnamed girl.

Competing with envy is resentment towards Gaddreol. For not affording me the same peace. For keeping me locked away in this prison once known as a mind—my mind. And because he has full control over my body while all I have is my disembodied voice.

Why didn't you just let go of me? You're the only reason I'm still here and I hate it.

I know I'm as drained as Gaddreol is, I just can't feel it. All these emotions trying to take the figurative spotlight is taxing. My mind is on edge tonight, which I suspect is because I have been listening to his soft snores. There's absolutely no reason to spare his feelings from my abrasive thoughts, allowing them to flow freely. His heart is in the right place, but his personal decisions feel self-serving.

Perhaps it really is me who is the selfish one. I think, intently. I try to think of how I would feel in his place instead of my own.

Could I transition into a new body knowing that someone will die as soon as I do?

No, that's heartless and cruel.

Would their death be on my hands if I could?

It'd definitely feel that way since my action would be the one that sets it into motion.

Would I be able to give them up for death if I believed there was a chance to give them their life back?

I don't know.

The hypothetical role reversal is crushing. My life or death is the unintended result of this transition and the heavy burden he's forced to carry. It is a balancing act he has to carefully teeter with every encounter. Despite the responsibility paired with all the opposition he faces every day he continues to remain positive. I imagine that juggling all of these things plagues him internally, but he takes it in stride without complaining. The mental fortitude he has to navigate this delicate situation is astounding.

In a sinking ship, everyone is drowning, but he's holding his head above the water, hanging on to things floating by until a lifeboat comes along.

"A lifeboat?" His groggy voice interrupts my stream of rambles.

Ignoring his question, I ask, *How come you hardly talk about what you're feeling?*

"I don't like bothering people with trivial things."

Your feelings aren't trivial. You listen to me nonstop, but barely give yourself time to talk. Everyone needs an outlet.

"Especially you."

* * *

"It's a lovely day for a picnic!" Vera exclaims.

Even without having a visual depiction, Vera's energy seems like a shaken soda bottle, always on the verge of a bubbling explosion.

"We can make sandwiches and pack 'em up with some chips and cookies! No, you sit down! I'll get all the stuff on the table," she says, as she buzzes around the kitchen, noisily grabbing all the ingredients for them.

She's sweet, but, I think, *maybe a bit too worried about your sight predicament.*

However, Gaddreol complies with her request, probably feeling a bit anxious about navigating another unknown layout. Her concern may not be unfounded since he only recently became familiar with the layout of his own apartment.

At some point, Avery placed different textured rugs in the entry-ways and in front of the stove and bathtub for him. It is thoughtful gestures like the rugs that make me think he's not as callous as he seems on the surface. After all, he's to thank for the uninterrupted day. Just an elder brother and younger sister doing whatever they want without the persistent doctors disturbing either one of them.

Nearly every movement Vera makes as she gathers the items is accompanied by loud clangs and bangs. After she gets all the items, she haphazardly releases everything into a noisy clattering heap onto the table. She has the personality of a doe, but the clumsiness of a fawn.

After straightening up all the items, she says, "Here's a butter knife, be careful. The bread is next to your left hand."

"Thanks for getting this together," he says. I can hear the smile in his words.

"It's only fair! You took care of me for so long, now I get to return the favor. Here's some mayo." Containers and bottles are opened followed by muffled sounds from a butter knife scraping the inside of the plastic container. "The lunch meat is directly in front of you, cheese to the right of that, pickles to the left of the bread. And here's the mustard."

The mundane small talk between siblings is a refreshing change from the constant arguments with the doctors. I didn't realize a little humdrum conversing would be enjoyable, but it's a delightful respite for sure.

"What are you smiling for?" she asks, gleefully.

"No reason. Just happy that we get to spend time together like this." The loving tone in his voice expresses how much he cherishes his little sister. "We're making sandwiches together. It's something that shouldn't be possible, but it is. And you even got all the stuff for us."

"And we're gonna walk to the park in the neighborhood. It's super pretty, I know you'll…" Vera's excitement disintegrates, realizing that Gaddreol won't experience the lovely scenery as she can.

He calmly reassures, "Don't worry, you can tell me about all the pretty things, and it will be just like I'm seeing it, too."

With the limited visual details I saw in the dream, I wonder if I will be able to picture any of the things she might describe. Probably, if it's relative to the contents from the dream. If not, it will remain an unfinished puzzle. Gaddreol retained his memories, so he will be able to clearly see the mental images of what she might describe. A pang of jealousy wants to form, but it's the wrong emotion. Gratitude is the emotion that should be expressed. I should be grateful to know what anything looks like.

"Here's a tote bag to bring the food in. I don't have one of those cute baskets, sadly," Vera says as she snatches up the ingredients to put them in their rightful place. As careless as before, she sounds like she's destroying the room instead of putting things in order.

"Maybe one day we can find one at the store."

"I'd like that. Come on, Bat. I'm ready to go." Faintly, I hear her finishing up and getting ready for their leave.

"Bat?"

Yes, because you're 'blind as a bat' now.

At the same moment, she says, "Yeah, you know, blind as a bat?"

They laugh as they make their way outside. The younger sibling is half skipping, half walking to maintain pace with the older sibling as he gently scrapes his walking stick ahead of him. Her energetic bounce sounds like she wants to run all the way to the park, but she's trying to be polite and remain at her brother's side.

At least she didn't call you a mole.

It's a baseless thought that pops into my head for no reason, but it causes a whirlwind to form in my mind. A bat is a suitable description for him and unfortunately, a mole is fitting to my present state of being. After all, I am burrowed deep within this solitary hole. The analogy unintentionally reminds me of how alone I am. Perhaps it's because moles choose to be in their hole, unlike me, restricted to this invisible box.

"Oh, shoot!" The young girl's yelp brings my attention back to the outer world. "I forgot the blanket!"

"It's okay, we can just sit on the grass."

Sitting on the grass would be wonderful. *I wish I could sit and feel the individual blades of grass against my skin.*

Vera begins to protest, but the soft grunts from Gaddreol as he sits on the ground squash any rebuttal she can offer. She follows him to the ground, plopping down to her knees by the muted thud. The bag rustles and they waste little time eating their meal. The momentary silence between them seems to be relaxing instead of ominous as it so often is.

"So, you wanna know what things look like?" Her voice sounds timid as the question forms.

I hear a hard gulp from Gaddreol, probably trying to quickly swallow the food he's chewing to answer. "Of course!"

"Okay! There's a gigantic pond in the middle of the park. In the center of the pond, there's a giant fountain with large jets shooting water up to the sky. It's blocked by a fence, but people are sitting next to it watching the ducks. Oh, and feeding them, too. We should have brought food for the ducks!"

"We can do that next time." He laughs.

I can't see the imagery of anything she's saying, but I can hear the ducks honking and flapping their wings against the surface of the water. The raging jets from the water fountain sound more akin to a waterfall. Although the water overshadows them, groups of people are scattered around the park chatting and laughing, just enjoying their time together.

Focusing on the sounds, I miss part of her explaining the scenes going on in different parts of the park. Returning to the sound of her voice, she's describing a couple of dogs playing fetch with their owner.

"One of the dogs is a golden German Shepherd, like the dog you used to have when I was real little. I miss Harley; she always knew exactly when I needed company. Maybe you should get a service dog."

A service dog isn't a bad idea. I don't know why I hadn't even considered it as an option.

Would this horrible organization forbid him from getting a dog? Are they allowed to do something like that? That'd be an onerous process, but if he is able to stay in my body for a lengthy amount of time, it may be worth it.

How would that work, though?

From a slightly irrelevant connection, it reminds me that I don't understand the logistics of this disturbing operation. Now that I'm contemplating the legality of it, I wonder if now that he's in my body, is he still legally Gaddreol Adair? Or is he Tristan Whatever-My-Last-Name-Is? Even with the incompetence everyone within the horrid organization seems to have, I'm sure the legality of it is carefully planned and structured. Have I simply been eradicated from all legal systems? That makes sense considering their urging for my death.

The high-energy voice drags me away from my mental tangent. "The other dog is large and honey colored. I dunno what he is, but his fluffy face is gigantic!" She giggles. "They're playing tug of war now. The German Shepherd is putting up a great fight."

"It's probably a mastiff. The other dog, I mean." He laughs with her. "Hey, so this is a little awkward, but since you're describing what things look like, I was wondering, what do I look like now?"

Pitch black hair, creepy, ghostly eyes, and white skin. Was this really the only time my appearance was mentioned? I know what these elements look like individually, but I can't combine them to create the mental image needed to visualize myself. Maybe that's for the best with that description.

Vera lets out an exaggerated gasp. She sounds perplexed when she asks, "You still don't know what you look like?"

"It just never came up. Something was always more important to talk about. My appearance was never the focus, except when you told me I have black hair and white eyes and skin," he says with a mix of excitement and anxiousness.

"Well, let's see. Your hair is straight and fluffy—kinda just going in all directions—like that dog. Your eyes, well like I said before they are creepy ghost eyes, but they're upturned, maybe almond-shaped. Ooh, almonds sound good right now."

A pained noise comes from Gaddreol. "Ow, easy! I may be blind, but eyeballs still hurt if you poke them."

"Sorry! I'm tryna get a closer look so you can get a good picture of how you look, too."

"Maybe I should try using my fingers to see," he jokes, and they both erupt into joyous laughter.

"Oh, hush! I'll be careful. Anyway! Above that you've got real thin eyebrows. Your skin is like a porcelain doll. You look like you could break any minute. Oh, and your face is either heart-shaped or a little triangle. Your nose is thin and straight, kinda dainty, but it fits your face well. Honestly, you look a little feminine, especially compared to what you actually look like." She states all of this matter-of-factly, before adding, "Sorry, that sounded really mean, but I didn't mean for it to! But you look a little feminine because you're on the shorter side. Maybe five-six and real lean."

Feminine porcelain doll. Straight, fluffy, black hair. Triangular, heart-shaped face. Upturned almond, ghost eyes. Dainty, thin, and straight nose. The unintelligible alien language returns as I try, and fail miserably, to decipher the words she is saying.

All of these words are baseless, aimlessly swirling around in a sea of nothingness. The only image that forms with relative ease is the pale color of my skin since it was a part of the dream that my mind observed. Everything else feels like trying to force something into a space where it clearly doesn't fit.

"Thank you, Vera," Gaddreol says, sincerely. "It's so strange to think about how different I look and how different my life is now."

From Vera's description of me and the details she mentioned about Gaddreol with the little bit I viewed in the dream; he really does look immensely different than I do. While I only saw his arm, it was long and muscular, so his stature is likely far larger than mine. I can't imagine how jarring it must be to transition into a body much smaller than your own, even without factoring in blindness. Still, it's better than the complete loss of a body.

"Crazy, right?" she asks, sounding contemplative. "None of the stories you read to me as a kid ever mentioned anything like this. Who knew I could be living in a brand-new body someday?"

"I never knew anything like this was possible, either." His voice is unrecognizable to me. I think he is attempting to hide his guilt and sadness by attempting to match her enthusiasm. "But here we are, having a picnic you prepared for us."

"I'm so happy to spend time with you again. You just don't even know." An indistinguishable mix of sadness and happiness takes over the softness in her voice, aging it slightly. Somehow, I know there are gentle tears rolling down her cheeks. "I'm so happy that I can speak and move and just do things again. Thanks, Gaddreol."

Gaddreol speaks softly. "Come on, let's get you back home, and then call Avery to pick me up."

"Sounds good," she says, gathering things.

CHAPTER SEVEN

SO MUCH HAS happened, making it difficult to keep track of every little thing from inside my prison. Free-flowing information comes and goes effortlessly. The lack of privacy from the doctors allows little time to contemplate the intricacies and complexities of the whole ordeal. Today is no exception to that.

This time, Taz shows up unannounced, first thing in the morning. Her arrival leaves Gaddreol without any time to prepare himself, for which she apologizes. She tells him to take all the time he needs to dress and groom himself while she cooks the bacon, eggs, and pancakes. At least she brought breakfast for the two of them. He accepts, taking a little longer than usual to get himself together.

"I don't know what to do," Gaddreol mumbles softly.

Play along, I guess. Why did I think that? It's a useless thought.

The "game" started way before Gaddreol was aware it was being played at all. Turns were made on his behalf before he could join for himself. Now, it is unrelenting on both sides—a stalemate. Is there even a move to make at this point? I don't think anything can be said to change anyone's mind. Having Avery and Sai as allies doesn't seem to make a difference, either.

"I am not in the mood to listen to Taz's attempts to convince me to discard you."

Exhaustion is wearing him down; I don't know how much more of their constant insistence he can endure before it tears him down completely.

I offer weak reassurance. *Hopefully, she won't bother you too much.*

Even as I think it, we both know it isn't true. She's probably here to be as much of a nuisance as she can manage without being obnoxious. She isn't ruthless, or tactless, but is equally persistent as the rest of them. Gaddreol closes the door behind him and makes his way to the kitchen.

"Smells amazing." He exaggerates a long sniff at the air. "Thank you for making breakfast. I don't think anything compares to having a home-cooked meal first thing in the morning."

"My pleasure. Help yourself, please," she says. From the minimal movement surrounding her voice, I deduce Taz is already sitting at the table. "Do you mind if I ask about your name? It's a really unique name. I meant to ask sooner, but there was always so much to do without a moment to talk like this."

I completely forgot I was going to ask about your name! I listen attentively to his answer.

"The name belonged to my great-grandfather. My mother used to tell me stories of all the heroic and kind-hearted things he would do; she would say she always knew I would grow up to be just as wonderful a man as he was."

Immediately I find myself wondering what his mother is like. She must have been an incredible, good-natured woman to have raised a man with strong values like Gaddreol.

What is my family like? I wonder, absently, without any way to scrutinize the thought as he continues, "What about you, Taz?"

"Taz is short for "Tasmanian Devil." Despite my calm demeanor now, as a child, I was rambunctious and a bit messy." She laughs briefly, before saying, "I didn't come here to discuss your unique name, though. I wanted to ask how you're adjusting to everything."

"Fine," he responds, before shoveling food into his mouth.

A very blunt answer. He wasn't kidding when he said he wasn't in the mood for this. I can't blame him, though. This has been ongoing for what feels like an eternity at this point.

Another sad thought forces its way into my mind to remind me of my desolate position. *For me, it may as well be an eternity.*

"And Tristan?" Taz asks.

The piece of silverware in Gaddreol's hand clanks against the plate, clattering loudly inside my small space.

"And Tristan?" Taz acknowledged me. This is the first time that my existence has been acknowledged without encouragement from Gaddreol. My ethereality feels lighter than ever before as if floating through a breeze of serenity.

How is Tristan adjusting? I mean, how am I adjusting? Not very well, if I do say so myself.

Being acknowledged by another member from this monstrous

organization is incomprehensible, but Taz's acknowledgement of my existence makes more sense than Sai's or Avery's. The negative traits that both of those men portray are completely absent in Taz. She is apprehensive, possibly timid, which makes her the most ill-fitting doctor for this nightmarish operation. How did someone so calm and so sweet end up here instead of in pediatrics or care for the elderly?

"Sorry, sorry." He apologizes for his clumsiness. The disbelief in his voice mirrors what I imagine mine would. "Tristan is doing as good as anyone in his situation, I guess. So, if I may, can I ask why you're actually acknowledging Tristan?"

There is a hint of distrust lingering in his words, which is sensible given the amount of hassle everyone—including Taz herself—has given him. I know it should make me ecstatic to be addressed in any capacity, but his caution is reasonable given that neither Avery nor Sai has directed words at me of their own volition. Neither of them even feigned the slightest interest in my well-being.

"I know you're guarded right now. However, I want to apologize to you, and Tristan."

And Tristan. I echo.

Taz's voice quivers slightly, but she continues. "After speaking with Sai yesterday, I understand the significance of your situation."

Why would this conversation be paramount over prior ones they must have had regarding my state? What did he say that provided more clarity? Was the conversation to understand the significance of my promised death? Or that Gaddreol is trying to do anything and everything in his limited power to prevent that from happening? She already knows all these things, so what makes this conversation different?

What exactly did this conversation about me pertain to? I think, at the same time, Gaddreol asks, "about what, exactly?"

"Well," she says, sounding almost too nervous to talk about it. "He told me that Tristan has total cognizance of his surroundings; that you speak with him when we aren't around."

"I thought all of you guys were aware of that because of those recordings." His tone is accusatory as annoyance settles into his voice.

"I never knew what was on those recordings. I never listened to them. I didn't approve of them setting up the camera. Samuel set it up, per Josephine's request." Taz speaks frantically, before taking a deep breath to calm herself. "I'm ashamed to admit that when you first told me that you were hearing his voice, I just dismissed it. It was wrong, I know, but most of the voices from previous owners dissipate within a few days of transitioning."

The previous people who survived the transitions gradually faded into oblivion. More answerless questions and potential implications invade my bubble, flitting around me.

Do they survive, but stay silent out of fear for the promise of their imminent death? Are they conscious without the new owner of their body being aware of their presence? Are they dormant and waiting for their bodies to be returned to them? Do they officially die?

"If you believed that, why'd you encourage me to switch bodies, too?" Gaddreol asks, trying to suppress his growing anger.

"I didn't want you to deal with unnecessary hurdles that come with being blind when you don't need to. Even with Sai trying to get you included, I don't think the team running the department will let you join the blind studies." She sounds genuinely remorseful for her role in encouraging another transition.

As she finishes speaking, I say to Gaddreol, *I don't think she had any ill intentions towards you.* However, I can't help but wonder, *why did it take a conversation with a mysterious man to understand that transitioning Gaddreol is the end of me? She should already know that when patients transition, they cremate the body.*

Of course, she knows. She's the one who confirmed the cremation would occur. Why, then, is she being so capricious about it now? The amount of uncertainty surrounding her words tells me she is willfully omitting something. Although it doesn't feel ominous in nature, her intentional secrecy is a little unnerving.

Why does it make any difference to her, or to any of them, that I survived more than a few days past transitioning when they allowed it to go on in the first place? I was never going to make it out of here alive, despite Gaddreol's best efforts.

Listening to my concerns, the accusatory tone he has dims to one of disapproval when he asks, "Why does it matter now that Tristan survived?"

The unspoken words ravage my brain. *You both willingly carry out transitions knowing that the original person will die, so what makes me special? Avery cares because Gaddreol cares, but why do you?*

"I know it doesn't make sense right now, but I think it would be best to talk to Sai or Avery about the rest."

Why should he talk to either of them, when you are the one who brought it all up?

"Why can't you tell me now?"

"I don't like what we do any more than you do," she says, dismissing his question.

You don't have to live this miserable existence. You can go home to your family and friends. So why do you continue to do this if you really don't like it? The intrusive thoughts flood into my mind before I am able to stop them.

My thoughts sound much harsher than intended, but if I allow myself to analyze the question, I know that she likely doesn't have a choice. I don't know what it could be, but something is being held over her to force her participation in these vile experiments. No one as delightful as she would willingly engage in something so heinous.

Avery, the right—and simultaneously, wrong—man lets himself in. Almost as if she summoned him herself.

"You should really keep this door locked. A blind man like you doesn't have a way to defend himself properly."

"Please, sit down and join us." Gaddreol's invitation is anything but amicable, his usual positive attitude stripped of all friendliness. "You're just the person I was hoping would show up."

"What's going on here?" Avery asks, sounding uneasy as he walks closer toward the pair sitting around the table. With each step he takes, I can almost feel the growing tension in the room seep into my void.

"I'm sorry, Avery." Taz's apology is riddled with nervousness. "I just wanted to apologize to Gaddreol. And Tristan."

And Tristan. I repeat, again.

The acceptance from Taz is difficult to wrap my mind around, but I appreciate it all the same. Avery starts to speak, but Gaddreol cuts him off abruptly.

"Sai spoke to her about Tristan's situation, but apparently I need to talk to you or Sai about why his survival matters at all." There's full-blown anger in his voice now. It sounds uncomfortable—foreign even. I don't know if it's because he hardly displays any negative emotions or if I'm not used to hearing my own voice sound irate.

"Wait, what? Of course, Tristan's survival matters," Avery says, as if he wasn't excited about my demise not too long ago.

"Why, though? Why does it matter now? To Sai? To Taz? To you?" he asks, through gritted teeth.

"Hold on, Gaddreol. Where's all this coming from?" Avery says, sounding genuinely taken aback.

"None of this makes any sense, Avery. Why do I have to push back against everyone to keep Tristan alive? Why do I have to keep up this exhausting charade when there are so many better options. Why are these options not available because of some arbitrary rule? Why do you, Sai, and now Taz, care when no one else does?" A loud sound screeches that I recognize as the chair scraping against the tiled floor. "Why did you sign me up for this gross organization!? Why did you let me take someone's life away!? Why did you let my sister kill someone!?"

All the words he's wanted to say pour out of his mouth as the anger breaks down into a mix of sorrow, agony, and pure rage. It seems the pain and frustration he's held onto since the transition is finally being felt in its entirety, as each word is accompanied by a sporadic, muddled thump.

Are you punching him? A quick pang of jealousy wants to enter as I think of how much I've wanted to do that since first hearing his arrogant voice. The thought quickly dissipates as I consider the pure despondency he must be feeling to physically assault Avery.

The muddled thumps lighten up, but there is silence from the man on the receiving end. Gaddreol demands, "Answer me! Why were you going to let me kill Tristan!?"

The mention of my name makes me feel more real and less like a spirit trapped in an infinitesimal hole. The fact that I'm in this state because Gaddreol was supposed to kill me causes a sense of dread to want to overwhelm me.

Has my life always felt this insignificant?

"I didn't know," Avery's voice is barely above a whisper.

"Like Hell, you didn't know! Tell me the fucking truth." Gaddreol's voice is nearly pure rage now.

Inadvertently, strobing lights invade my bubble as my mind tries to decipher the color that should match his emotion, but red wasn't in the dream sequence. Once the flashes of strobing lights cease, I settle back into the dismal black. I redirect my attention to the back and forth between the two men.

"I didn't know," Avery repeats, raising his octave slightly.

"Tell. Me. The. Fucking. Truth. Avery," Gaddreol demands, again, forcing each word out.

"I didn't fucking know! If I had known, my little brother would still be alive, and I wouldn't be in his fucking body right now! I wouldn't have fucking killed him!" Avery yells completely dejected now.

There's an abrupt crash consisting of dishes clanging against each other and more harsh scraping sounds, followed by a loud, vague thud. From Taz's gasp and rapid movement from the chair to the ground, I assume Avery retaliated by shoving Gaddreol into the table.

"Are you alright, Gaddreol?" she asks, calmly.

"Fine," Gaddreol says, collecting himself. "What did you say?"

"I'm sorry, I didn't mean to react like that," Avery says. His rage disintegrates, dejection and despair rapidly taking its place. "When I first told you about all this shit, I didn't know."

"Avery..." Concern mixes into the anger he feels so strongly. "What happened?"

"Everything happened so fast. I just finished my residency when my younger brother was finally done with nursing school. He was so excited to get a job working with me." Avery's voice trembles as he speaks. "The director approached me with this new project he was working on. Said it would change the world as we know it and give everyone a new chance at life. Burn victims wouldn't have extensive operations or long recoveries. Survivors of tragic accidents wouldn't need to undergo major reconstructive surgery or the intense healing that follows. I was skeptical, of course. Even told him he was batshit crazy."

He is indeed batshit crazy.

I can't begin to comprehend the intricacies and nuances of this gross organization. How was the director able to learn about such an outrageous experiment in the first place? How did he happen upon the knowledge and know how to remove someone's soul from their physical being and put it into someone else's? It seems like it would be nothing more than a precarious experiment and yet he somehow perfected all of the complexities to create the relatively desired—or undesired—outcome.

Avery takes a few deep breaths to calm the shaking in his voice. The despair in his voice remains, but he tries in vain to keep it blank. "He laughed, saying 'We're all a little crazy here.' Told me if I wanted to see what it's like for myself, I just needed to give him a description of what I wanted to look like. I didn't give it a second thought until you told me about Vera and her condition."

"So, this is all my fault?" Gaddreol whispers softly to himself.

No, it isn't. You didn't know. Don't beat yourself up over this.

"I told him I wanted a body that kind of looked like I do now—did then, just a little younger looking so I'd be ahead of the game, you know. Stupid, cocky shit." A long pause, no doubt pondering how negligent that decision was in retrospect. His breathing is labored, a panic attack coming on, perhaps. "He said he's got the perfect body in mind for me already."

His breathing quickens and he takes intentional deeper breaths to steady himself. "During that conversation, I told him I had two candidates that would be interested in trialing if it worked for me. He told me to bring you both in, right away. I didn't hesitate. You didn't hesitate. You signed the papers the same day I transitioned into my own baby brother's body."

His voice is overflowing with agony. His breathing is coming in rapid intervals, but he keeps talking despite that. "I demanded the director take you out of the trials, to rip up any papers you signed, and forget about everything. You weren't going to be a part of it if I had anything to say about it. Except… I didn't have anything to say about it. I, as my little brother, would be framed for the kidnap and murder of myself. I know it was selfish, but I couldn't do that to my family. They already lost one son…"

He trails off, trying to stifle his cries. Through the ragged breaths, he continues, "My family thinks I'm missing when it's my brother that everyone should be mourning instead. I lost my brother. I lost you. Somewhere along the way, I lost myself, too."

His hitching breath coupled with pained cries evolves into the most heart-wrenching sobs I never thought possible from the man whose outer shell is made up of snark and egotism. Listening to his excruciatingly loud wails of pure anguish makes me want to comfort him despite the numerous times he has gone out of his way to make me uncomfortable. Who could listen to those devastating shrieks and not feel anything but empathy for him? I may be an ethereal soul, but I am not heartless. Gaddreol is close to him, likely holding him tightly.

Pointlessly, I think, *I'm sorry, Avery.*

"I'm sorry, Avery. I'm here." His whispered voice is stricken with sorrow.

I can hear soft cries from Taz, too. I find myself wondering if she's crying because of how distressed Avery is right now or because of her own possibly twisted situation.

They attempt to console the inconsolable Avery with shushing sounds bolstered by mantras of "it's okay," "it's going to be alright," and "it's not your fault."

"The perfect body..." Avery's raspy voice croaks as his piercing wails grow louder, which I didn't think possible. But he manages to choke out the words, "was my brother's."

I know that I feel sorrow for Avery, or at least, I would. I'm stuck in this unforgiving limbo, but I think it might be preferable to the indescribable hell Avery is experiencing right now. To unknowingly kill your brother on a whim, to be forever trapped with his face as a constant reminder of the devastation your decision caused. And then to be forced through blackmail to continue the same process onto more unsuspecting victims. I doubt I could bear the burden of the exhausting reality Avery is facing. He is far more remarkable, exceptional, even, than I gave him credit for.

Between the harrowed cries and shallow breaths, he continues despite the hoarseness of his voice. "I'm sorry, Gaddreol. I'm sorry for breaking up with you over the phone when you needed me the most. I couldn't face you. Not like this."

Avery and Gaddreol were in a romantic relationship? Hardly the most important thought, but unfortunately the first one my mind settled on. They must have truly cared for each other for them to maintain a relationship, albeit a strained one, after breaking up.

"No, Avery. You needed me and I wasn't there. I'm so sorry." His whisper is muffled, probably from his face nuzzling into Avery. With his kindhearted nature, Gaddreol is probably beating himself for not realizing that it was something beneath the surface level.

You couldn't have known.

"You couldn't have known, I didn't want you to," Avery says.

Told you. The least helpful thing I could think of, so I quickly follow up with, *I'm sorry, that was insensitive.*

"The day after, I couldn't take it anymore. I lost it and smashed all the mirrors in the bathroom. Sai found me, bloodied and in a sobbing heap just like I am now—minus the blood. He held me like you are now and let me cry until I was too exhausted to continue crying. Afterwards, he helped me with everything from stitching up my hands to helping me fully transition, to become my brother. Hell, he even helped me with cleaning up the blood in the bathroom."

Sai doesn't seem capable of displaying that type of affection. He certainly doesn't give off the impression of being the consoling type.

But if he has been forced into a similar situation, it makes sense that he would have enough consideration to offer commiseration to his colleague. An unlikely friendship, maybe, but exactly the one Avery—and possibly Sai—needed.

"I didn't know what to do. I was angry, confused, and repulsed. Horrified by what my decision caused... by my new reflection." The raw emotion in his voice is undisguised by his weak, raspy voice.

Is that why a blind person was chosen for transitioning your ex-boyfriend? The directed question is futile, but it causes a pang of sadness to want to encroach on my small space. To be chosen because of my blindness, not in spite of it, somehow feels worse after all the things Gaddreol has been put through.

I must have sparked intrigue in Gaddreol since he regurgitates my question. "Is that why I was transitioned into Tristan's body? So, I couldn't see you as you are now?"

A startling, pained laugh emerges from the dejected man. "No, that was just a very fortunate coincidence on my part. I honestly didn't know he was blind."

His words linger, momentarily. How does a significant detail go unnoticed, while still conveniently being the perfect safeguard for Avery's situation? *Sai.* The name infiltrates my mind. I don't know why, or how, but Sai seems to be the missing link in this convoluted mess.

Gaddreol iterates my concerns again, "How does Sai fit into this?"

A heavy sigh comes from Avery, and Taz softly says, "It's okay, you don't have to talk anymore, Avery."

"Sai chose Tristan for you." If I had access to my heart, I think it would stop entirely.

Despite more information being shared, it only throws questions into my tiny, claustrophobic hole. *My body was chosen for Gaddreol to use, by Sai specifically. How? Why? That means he must know me personally, right? Is that why he feels vaguely familiar to me? If we knew each other previously, we must have been enemies. Why else would he put through this horrendous operation with an abhorrent outcome?*

I can only infer he must truly despise me to offer me this cruel existence; one which initially was intended to be my promised death that turned into my inescapable, personal hell.

My space sinks into near nothingness. Nausea tries to force its way into the nonexistent opening. I'm struck with the realization that the two people offering their help with this catastrophe are the same two people who caused my miserable position to begin with.

Should've never trusted an apathetic doctor or an unstable one.

I immediately push the belligerent thoughts away and return to the present situation. Assuming Sai was aware of my blindness and the stipulations surrounding the experiments and trials, why would he willingly place Gaddreol into my body when he knows it wouldn't be sufficient?

My sporadic thoughts wander, pondering the possible reasoning. *Does he hate me? Does he have a strong desire for my eradication? Was he hoping Gaddreol could detransition and resume life normally due to transitioning into an unusable body leaving me to die? Was my body used to give Avery the reprieve he didn't realize he needed?*

My persistent rambling blocked out part of the verbal exchange. I catch the end of Avery saying, "—knew Tristan."

"None of this makes any sense." Gaddreol's confusion matches the questions fluttering in circles around my void.

"There was nothing I could do to get you out of the contract with the director. Sai helped me clear my head and think of our options," he says, meekly. His breathing has slowed. If he still has tears falling, they are silent ones without the heartbreaking sobs.

Whose options? Not mine. Gaddreol's and Avery's, or Avery's and Sai's, or the organization's as a whole?

"Options..." It's not a question or a statement, really. Gaddreol sounds disconcerted, probably contemplating all of the possibilities, maybe some that weren't even mentioned during this conversation.

Silence fills the small space between the two men, and I realize Taz is moving quietly around the kitchen cleaning up the mess of their unfinished meals. I hear small clinks as she collects broken plates and scattered silverware, followed by a deep, mellow metal thud from placing the dishes in the sink. She grabs a bag, lightly crinkling it, followed by soft sounds of cardboard brushing against itself as she puts away what I assume are the used packages of eggs and bacon and the open box of pancake mix.

Is Taz okay?

From her silence and the tears she shed earlier, I don't think any of this heartbreaking situation was shared with her before this moment. Aside from it being a devastating revelation, I wonder if it is causing her to dwell on her own personal torture. Maybe one day she will open up about the horrific event that forced her into this nefarious organization. I'm sure it must plague her mind as much as Avery's.

There's a knock on the door that captures my attention again. Abrupt, unexpected disappointment wants to come over me when I hear Taz say, "Dr. Sands."

Disappointed by what, though? Am I expecting someone else to be at the door? If so, who? I am uncertain, but Dr. Sands' arrival leaves me with a peculiar sinking sensation. The realization hits me.

I expected Sai to be here. I wanted him here to answer all the unrelenting questions that are nagging at me.

"I thought Sai was supposed to come," Avery says, swinging the door open. I was too consumed by my reaction to the absence of the elusive doctor to notice Avery move away.

"Dr. Sai asked me to fill in for him here while he finishes up some paperwork before the deadline tonight." Dr. Sands' voice is as cordial as it was the first day he met Gaddreol.

"That bastard," Avery says, his sadness has nearly disintegrated despite his croaky voice. "Come on in."

✶ ✶ ✶

Dr. Sands, for the most part, is keeping to himself during his stay. A few questions have been raised, but I'm sure the doctor recognizes that Gaddreol is not in a healthy state of mind to answer any mind-numbing inquiries.

Since Avery and Taz left, Gaddreol has basically remained silent, undoubtedly replaying the events that just unfolded with Avery. I can't begin to imagine the thoughts ruminating in his head. A two-way connection would be more than ideal at the moment.

I don't even know how I would feel in his situation. To learn so many appalling truths one after the other, all crammed together and hurled at him at once. It must be nearly impossible to comprehend the sheer magnitude of Avery's pained words.

Understandable. It's an incomprehensible mess. Most likely, the words are suspended in his mind, indefinitely, as he aimlessly wades through them. That is, until he can discern them, allowing them to properly sink in. At least, once Gaddreol is able to compartmentalize the vast information he's been given, escaping the confusion may be a little easier.

I, however, am not sure I'll be given the same luxury. Especially, since after that devastating conversation, I am left with far more mysteries to uncover, many of which surround that elusive man.

When Sai wasn't the one at the door, the emotion that circled my space was recognized as disappointment. He didn't show up and, bizarrely, it leaves me wanting to feel discouraged. Now I just want to feel angry, sad, or betrayed. All those emotions seem too subtle for how it should be affecting me.

Mostly, I just want Sai to talk to me, or well, to Gaddreol. I want to know why I was thrown into this; why he chose me to be replaced by someone else. All this time, I assumed that I was stalked, hunted down, and captured. But my reality is much worse. I was handed over without seemingly any remorse. The devastation I'd feel would be insurmountable if it was possible.

I wish more than anything that I could remember my life before this. It wouldn't be a waiting game for answers then. I would know who Sai is, who he was to me, and why he decided to hand deliver me to my sacrificial ending. No one deserves this twisted fate, and yet here I am, still faced with this unending torment. So, I can only think that I must have done something to warrant this atrocity.

I hear water running for a shower. *A nice warm shower right now might be the perfect thing to help you relax.*

"It's not to relax in," Gaddreol quietly responds. "I wanted to take you up on that offer now. If that's okay, I mean."

Offer? I ask, and then quickly remember. *Oh right, go ahead.*

"Thanks, I really need someone to talk to, and Dr. Sands really isn't the person I want to talk to." There is intense desolation in his voice, while simultaneously sounding emotional and emotionless. "I'm not okay if I'm honest."

I don't know what to say, or think, so I just wait patiently.

"When Avery broke up with me, I was just lost and confused. I couldn't grasp it, but I ignored the pain so I could focus on giving Vera the life she deserved. Now everything just feels upside down."

Upside down, I muse. *You're right about that.*

"I never gave myself the chance to actually be upset over the break-up because I was so excited about Vera living a new life. But after all that was said today, I realized under the surface of holding it all together for my little sister, I was mad at Avery. Mad that he would just abandon me during one of the scariest moments of my life. Mad that the love of my life turned his back on me when I needed him the most. Now, I know the truth and I just feel regret and shame for feeling those things. He needed me just as much, if not more than I needed him and I didn't even try to understand."

Hindsight is invaluable, sure, but you can't beat yourself up for knowing now that you didn't know previously. Even if you had known everything that you know now, no one would blame you for focusing on you and Vera. You were dealing with an incredibly new and very stressful experiment. On top of everything, the person you expected to guide you through the uncertainty abandoned you for seemingly no reason at all. I can't imagine the fears and emotions that you were feeling at the time.

"After I transitioned, when I heard Avery speak, I suspected it was him, but it didn't sound quite right. I wondered if the transition warped my sense of hearing or something. Now... Now... every time I think about his voice it just makes my heart hurt and a knot form in my stomach. It makes me sick to think he was tricked into taking the life of his younger brother."

I understand. What happened to Avery is truly despicable. What he went through is nothing short of a repulsive, treacherous thing. But his painful situation does not detract from your own. You've also been through your own personal hell.

I have a strong inkling that most of the members participating in FREE are not doing so of their own volition. I wonder how many people have become victims of this revolting organization.

"It makes me feel horrible because I don't want to be involved in this anymore. What happened to you and Avery is horrific enough. I don't want to even think about what has happened to anyone else, including the person my little sister has taken over..." His voice trails off and the water beating down against the shower floor fills the momentary silence, before he says, "But I don't want to take away my sister's new life, either."

As someone who is experiencing firsthand what it's like to live like your sister lived previously, I don't want her to remain in an unusable husk either. None of this makes you a bad person, just someone who cares deeply for their sibling.

The deplorable circumstances that have happened to so many people overshadow my words.

Anyone faced with a burdensome situation like yours would feel conflicted, but I think it is in our nature to look after those closest to us first and foremost. As unforgivably selfish as it feels to choose your sister's life over another, I think many could relate. If the girl whose life your sister unknowingly took over is truly dead, then there is no reason to end her transition. I know that causes an additional layer of guilt for you since you're dealing with a personal dilemma about our unfortunate circumstance. You can remain in my body, stuck with me in a perpetual nonexistence, or transition into another body, effectively taking away someone else's life.

The hypocrisy I have concerning Vera invades my sense of self.

How can I advocate for her to live her new life in someone else's body when I want my body back? I want to be able to wiggle my fingers, stretch my toes, and everything in between. But if I'm okay with Vera taking over someone's body to be able to have the same opportunity, should I even be entitled to feeling those sensations again?

There are so many layers to this complicated system all made worse by the large amount of deception involved.

"You are entitled to your life and being able to feel those things again. You deserve your body as much as anyone else."

There is a gentle knock on the door and Dr. Sands calls from the other side, "Everything alright, Gaddreol?"

"Fine, just finishing up."

It must be frustrating to deal with doctors monitoring everything. To the point that even stepping away to take a shower for more than fifteen minutes is long enough to be checked on. Gaddreol's sigh confirms my speculation.

He shuts the water off and then grabs his towel from the rack. After quickly drying off and changing into fresh clothes, he shuffles quietly out of the bathroom.

So much time and energy were spent on perfecting the extraction and implantation of souls without taking time to develop an ethical way to obtain the result. All of this could have been resolved if they would just use synthetic technology instead of living people. There would be no illegal implications, no pain, no suffering, no blackmail, and, most importantly, no unnecessary deaths. Whoever is at the helm of this operation is truly one sick individual.

I find myself wondering where Dr. Sands fits into this unethical organization. He is probably being blackmailed like Avery is to keep him complicit. Can a psychologist be tricked into participation even through coercion? Unlikely, but it's possible. If he isn't being forced, what could he possibly gain from being a part of this? And why is he being reduced to menial tasks? Monitoring a blind man is hardly a task for a psychologist.

Dr. Sands and Sai must know each other on some personal level if he is willing to take on this tedious task. I wonder if there is a way to question the doctor. Probably not. It's unlikely that Dr. Sands will reveal any information about his colleague. It's not like Gaddreol has anything to offer that would be enticing or beneficial anyway.

"You seem pensive, Gaddreol," Dr. Sands' says, interrupting the silence. "Would you like to talk about what's on your mind?"

"Nope." An unexpected curt response with a childlike pop sound attached to it, earning a dissatisfied grunt comes from the doctor. Gaddreol ignores it and asks, "Why are you a part of FREE?"

The direct question throws me off, but Dr. Sands shows no signs of bewilderment as he says, "Observation and analysis, of course."

An all-encompassing answer, but a nondescript one. Observing and analyzing the participants must mean he's running his own experiments. Does he find the experiments exciting, appalling, or a morbid mixture of both? No answer will change the fact that his own experiments align with the horrific nature of this organization; it seems almost as disturbing as the experiments themselves.

"You may very well be one of the most intriguing subjects, Mr. Adair." Dr. Sands' flat tone is bordering on ominous now.

"Why's that?"

"You're one of the most selfless people I've come across." The friendly façade disintegrates, replaced by a venomous tone toying at the edges of his words.

"I don't have the patience for this right now." Gaddreol is unconcerned, but the threatening tone from the doctor should disturb him a little.

The returned silence from Dr. Sands is hardly a comfort. Is he trying to get a reaction from this broken man? If he accepted Sai's request to take his place for the sole purpose of getting closer to Gaddreol, today was the wrong day. After the intense conversation earlier, I imagine the mental exhaustion he feels is too great to care about the emotional response Dr. Sands is attempting to stir.

"I am going to bed now."

"Good night, Mr. Adair," he says. The malice is gone now, back to the same monotonous tone as before.

Had I imagined a sinister tone? *Am I going crazy?*

CHAPTER EIGHT

AN AMALGAMATION OF colors and shapes forms. The images are not as clear as before, but thanks to Gaddreol's memories the words are readily available once more. This time it's hardly even a scene; just a man, standing in the middle of a barren field.

The man is standing with a bright white smile plastered on his face, oblivious to the desolate landscape. Dark brown corkscrew coils frame his face, contrasting beautifully with his striking amber eyes that hold the same smile in them as they look directly at me. The rich chestnut color of his skin pales the wasteland around him, causing an alluring glow to radiate around him.

He raises his arm in a polite wave. Despite the small gesture, it reveals powerful muscles beneath the plain red shirt. Effortlessly, I move towards him, taking in everything I can of him. His skin looks toned and flawless like a statue. The tattered jeans he's wearing only slightly conceal some of the muscle definition in his legs. The bottom of the jeans hangs loosely over the worn tennis shoes that are almost too dirty to be recognized as white.

'Avery!' An unfamiliar voice calls out. It's not my voice, but I know it's coming from me. Gaddreol's voice is a gentle, comforting sound.

"Gaddreol!" His name is called by a voice that doesn't belong to the cheerful man. It's a high-pitched, sing-song sound.

"Gaddreol!" The word is dragged out with emphasis on every syllable. The man before me fades into the abyss, fragments slowly breaking off until only one eye and the curve of his beautiful smile remain.

Darkness covers the last part of the image and it's almost like it never happened. I try forcing my mind to reconstruct the image into a whole piece, but I can only see fragmented sections. His dark brown corkscrew coils, striking amber eyes, and the bold red shirt bounce around the emptiness not wanting to remain stationary.

It's difficult to thoroughly see the restless images, but at least I now know what the color belonging to the phrase "seeing red" looks like. Although, the bright color doesn't seem to do it justice.

That's Avery? I ask, absently. The rhetorical question doesn't need an answer, but he makes a sound of affirmation anyway. *He's gorgeous.*

"Are you awake in there?" Vera's voice chimes loudly against the door. "You better be dressed, I'm coming in!"

She opens the door with a dramatic loudness that echoes in the room, presumably, due to a lack of decorations around the room for sound reduction. A loud but softened plop is followed up by a groan from Gaddreol.

He laughs, heartily, saying, "Good morning to you, too!"

"Good afternoon, sleepyhead," she playfully mocks. "I just got done with testing at the hospital and I asked Avery if he could bring me to check on you, so here I am!"

"Well, you checked, so am I still in one piece?" Gaddreol laughs again.

His sister brings out a playful side in him that I think would be nonexistent otherwise. The charade he continues to make her happy is admirable.

"Mostly," she says, giggling. "Can I ask you about Sai?"

"I think Avery's a little more suited to answer questions about him than I am," Gaddreol says, sleepily. He yawns loudly, which I assume is accompanied by a full-body stretch.

"You don't know Sai?" Vera asks, her fragile voice is filled with nervousness and concern now.

"Not really, no. Why, what's up?" He sounds confused but tries to suppress it to not worry Vera. He situates himself on the edge of the bed, the sheets hissing with his movements.

"Oh..." she says. "It's just that, there is a collage of pictures of you like this on his desk. I thought maybe you were dating him..."

"What? No." Gaddreol laughs, nervously, unsure of what to say to alleviate her discomfort. How can the situation be explained to her without breaking the illusion that her body was specially made for her? "Are you sure it isn't just someone that looks similar?"

Sai has pictures of me on his desk. Not just one, but multiple. I must be happy in them if she assumes it's a romantic relationship. It just adds more confusion surrounding the situation with Sai. If we shared an intimate relationship, why would he put me in a perilous position for this abhorrent experiment? Absolutely nothing involving this man makes any sense.

"No way. Your eyes are totally unmistakable!" she says, before immediately backtracking, "I mean, maybe it is someone else and I possibly filled in the gaps. I'm sorry for bothering you with these crazy thoughts."

"No, it's fine. You're fine. You didn't do anything wrong. I don't have the answers, but nothing you can say will ever bother me," he says, fumbling about the bed. "Sorry, I was trying to find you to give you a hug, but I have no idea where you are."

"Thanks," Vera exclaims, leaping from her spot into Gaddreol, earning another grunt from the startled man.

This is a very delicate situation for Vera. Her inexperience of the world is not obscured by her innate intelligence. At some point, she is going to piece together the unrefined, mangled puzzle that makes up this deranged organization. Starting with Sai's negligence. It seems I have a protective feeling towards the young girl, wanting to preserve all of the innocence she still holds deep within herself.

"What's this I hear about Sai stealing you away?" Avery sounds as conceited as he did when I first encountered him.

"You and Avery?!" Her excitement sounds too potent to contain.

"I don't know, Avery—me and you?" He asks.

"If you'll take me back, that is." Avery's defenses drop in that one sentence, and he sounds almost as vulnerable as he did yesterday. "I'm sorry for all the shit that I put you through. I don't want to do anything else without you, again."

A restrained squeal escapes the excited young girl between the two vulnerable men. Despite the exhilaration she feels, there seems to be a lot of tension between the three people. It doesn't feel hostile in nature, just a lingering uncertainty. Presumably, Avery is hoping his apology is accepted and Gaddreol is still adjusting from being asleep to being utterly confused, while Vera anxiously waits for her older brother to respond.

"Of course I'll take you back," Gaddreol says.

The few words seem to dissolve the tension as fast as it arose. Acknowledging and mending the sadness, frustration, and anger from yesterday; almost entirely rectifying the pain and confusion on either side of this horrific situation.

"Thank you," Avery whispers, invading my bubble, and making me want to recoil. "You don't know how happy that makes me."

Their lips connect in a tender kiss, and the caressing sound makes me wish I could withdraw further into my hole. The sound is far too intense, and too intimate, inside my cramped space. That paired with the muted moans from Gaddreol makes me feel like I am the one kissing Avery and that thought is almost enough for a shudder to run through my nonexistent body.

"You two are super cute!" Vera's barely contained enthusiasm is like a young puppy ready to play relentless games of fetch.

"I'm sorry, that was inappropriate," Gaddreol says, but I'm sure he's addressing me without being so blatant since neither person before him is bothered by the action.

"It's just like the stories you used to read to me, Gaddreol!" She half-yells the words. "Is he the boy you used to tell me about?"

"You used to talk about me?" Avery smugly interjects.

"Yes, he is the one I used to tell you about. We both just went through some difficult things and separated while we sorted things out," Gaddreol calmly explains.

"But nothing can stand in the way of true love! He even loves you when you look a little ghostly!" She giggles, causing Avery to burst into a boisterous belly laugh. I suppose it's a good thing I don't have any emotional responses since she is unintentionally ruthless.

After he catches his breath, he says, "Casper can't scare me away that easily."

A distant knock at the front door interrupts their friendly banter. Muted shuffles from Gaddreol and Avery, alongside an abrupt thud sound that I know is from Vera leaping to her feet.

Avery calls toward the door as they approach it. "Who is it?"

"Sai." The muffled, word comes from the man on the outside.

The door opens, likely with Sai surveying the three individuals who decided opening the door is a group activity, before saying, "Gaddreol, I need you to come with me."

Avery inserts himself before Gaddreol can respond. "Where've you been, you cheeky bastard?"

This is the second time I agree with Avery's sentiment. I'd like to know where Sai has been, as well, so he can hopefully answer the innumerable questions floating tirelessly through my tiny space.

"Irrelevant," Sai says, ignoring the interrogation attempt, then adds, "I apologize for interrupting your personal time with Vera, but this is important; Gaddreol, will you please come with me?"

"That's okay! I've got dance class soon!" she squeals, oblivious to the seriousness of Sai's tone.

Desperately trying to visualize her dancing gracefully brings forth a shattered image of the lively girl into my mind. I can sort of see her standing, but the inactivity of both people in either dream prevents me from being able to fill in the gaps with the visuals required to see her dance.

"That's great! I hope you have tons of fun! And don't forget to tell me all about it!" Gaddreol says, excitedly, before addressing Sai with a calmer tone. "Can you give me like five minutes to get ready?"

"Of course," he states, monotonously. "I'll wait here."

"You can wait inside if you want."

They close the door after it sounds like everyone nearly stumbles impatiently into one another.

"I'll take Vera to her practice and then catch up with you later." Avery plants another tender kiss on Gaddreol's mouth. I don't think that particular sensation is something I'll be able to adjust to.

"Thank you, Avery." Gaddreol kisses him again briefly, and then says, "I appreciate everything you've done for me and Vera."

I want to feel anxious, overwhelmed, or even distressed, but just as always, there's nothing besides the emptiness. Suddenly, I feel moderately exposed listening to Avery and Vera take their leave. I'm ill-prepared for Sai and Gaddreol to be alone together.

"If you prefer, we can speak here, now," Sai says.

Gaddreol agrees and both men take a seat preparing to have a seemingly uncomfortable conversation.

Finally, I'm presented with the opportunity to ask this detached man all the questions that have plagued me for so long. And yet everything I've wanted to say to this man has all but abandoned my consciousness. An indestructible wall erected itself around my void, preventing anything from passing through it. It seems no amount of willpower will give me the questions I desperately want to relay to this man.

"Tristan," Sai addresses me directly. If it were possible, I think my heart would skip a beat. "I apologize."

For what? My initial reaction is a lot crasser than I expected it to be when finally addressed by the man I ostensibly know. I want to be forgiving—accepting, even—but the betrayal and disdain he has shown me cause the forefront of my perceived emotional response to be indignation.

The chance to talk one-on-one with this stoic man is something I have longed for. Now that it's here, every thought and question that has tormented my mind has simply disintegrated into nothing.

"He wants you to continue," Gaddreol says, reluctantly.

"Of course," Sai says, his voice remains flat and emotionless. "I apologize for subjecting you to this unforgiving reality."

"Why d'you put him in these experiments?" Gaddreol asks one of the questions I have waited impatiently to hear an answer to. "Vera said you have pictures of him on your desk, so you must've been close?"

"I apologize for my negligence regarding Vera's observations," he states plainly. "I presume Tristan's memories are unavailable at present?"

"Correct," he says, mirroring the monotony Sai maintains.

"Then what I say next is going to sound outlandish," he states, candidly. "This situation was arranged with Tristan's full cooperation prior to transitioning you into his body."

My cooperation? The words sound like an audacious attempt at deception. *Why would I cooperate with this awful organization and the horrific things they stand for? More importantly, why would I let myself be subjected to my own imminent demise?*

Gaddreol's facial expression must match my skepticism, causing Sai to clarify. "I would never have allowed Tristan to participate in this experiment or be put through this atrocious reality if I had not thought I could ensure his safety."

My safety? If I could laugh, I would. *The existence you imposed on me is hardly deemed safe.*

Since the beginning, almost every person Gaddreol has met from this transition process is in support of my impending death. Only three doctors, including Sai, aware of my situation have been slightly reasonable regarding my current condition.

"How's any of this considered safe for him? Ever since all of this started, I have been encouraged nonstop to replace his body, which will end his life," he says, his emotions are starting to break through his voice.

"I personally performed the transition to ensure Tristan's survival. He was never going to die." Sai's confidence wavers slightly, slipping through the cracks, to reveal that he can feel something other than apathy. "I will also perform the detransition."

"So will Tristan be able to get his body back?" Gaddreol asks, and then quickly adds, "Will I?"

"Tristan will be able to get his body back. At present, I don't have the information regarding your body. If you would like, I can find out if your body is available for you to transition into. Although, it's a very slim possibility."

"If it's not too much trouble, I would really like to see if my body is available." Gaddreol's flat tone fades with fatigue slowly replacing it.

"Of course," Sai states. Then, asks, "Tristan, do you have anything you wish to ask of me or say to me?"

Being addressed directly is still a bizarre phenomenon that I will need to adjust to. The direct question doesn't elicit any of my own questions. The other night there were so many potential questions flowing freely through my mind for when the chance finally arose and now, they elude me. Frustration is the only thing that comes to mind. Did I subconsciously block my own inquiries to protect myself from the possible horrors his answers may uncover?

Why do you hate me? The most intense, personal question fills my small space, its presence almost allowing a heaviness to form. Unfortunately, it's the one that's broken through the impenetrable wall I created.

"He wants to know why you hate him." The words are strained, as if it's painful to say them.

"Hate him?" Sai repeats, sounding disgusted and saddened. "I do not hate you, Tristan. I promise."

Are you certain? I ask, but it feels like the wrong question with the emotional response he had to my initial question. Even so, I can't help but think the promise is more for his own benefit than mine, to convince himself instead of me.

Thoughts of screaming and crying out from frustration pass through me, but of course, that's not possible. Nothing is possible, except listening to the words coming from the indifferent man. His words sound authentic, and they don't come off as deceitful, but that doesn't prevent me from not wanting to believe him.

"He asked, 'Are you certain?'"

Hearing Gaddreol reiterate my question makes me realize how insufferable I sound right now. The antagonism I have towards him is incomprehensible when he has given me no reason to believe he is anything but genuine.

I'm sorry, Sai.

Gaddreol dutifully adds, "He apologizes for being rude."

"Your aversion towards me is reasonable. I have not presented any reason to be deemed trustworthy in light of your predicament. I apologize for putting you through this hardship, Tristan. If I had another choice, I never would have put you through the transition." Sai sounds simultaneously reasonable and slightly unhinged.

How did you not have a choice? I think, as Gaddreol asks the same aloud.

"Tristan and I agreed to this arrangement because I need his help. Without him being included in the experiments, he wouldn't be able to provide the aid I require." His tone sounds sensitive, which is a lot different from the stoic tone he had before.

Despite Sai allowing himself to be vulnerable, nothing that he's saying provides any clarity to my frustrating conundrum. There's no feasible way that I could be of any help to anyone in my current position. Even if I wasn't trapped in this ethereal nonexistent state, what could I, as a blind man, do to be helpful in any way? Without prior knowledge to help me navigate this horrific organization—with or without my other senses—it is doubtful that I would be of any use at all.

What aid could I possibly provide in a state like this? I think, and Gaddreol reiterates my concerns. "How can he help you like this?"

A heavy sigh comes from the other man before he says, "I should not divulge this information to you, but it is important for you to know. Tristan is an assassin."

A sound comes from Gaddreol that is a cross between gurgling and choking, resulting in a violent coughing fit. Once the coughs subside, his voice is hoarse as he asks, "A what?"

Assassin. I am an assassin? No, definitely not. That is the most absurd thing I've ever heard. That doesn't make sense, at all.

There is no chance that is true in any shape or form. A blind man simply cannot be an assassin. Sai does not come off as the type to make jokes, but this sounds too ridiculous to be anything else.

"I understand the confusion that arises with that statement. If you have any questions, please ask. I will answer all of them," Sai clarifies. Gaddreol must be physically expressing the same disbelief I am experiencing.

"A blind man? An assassin? That's not possible." Gaddreol's voice is the embodiment of bewilderment.

"It is possible. As it turns out, assassinations can come naturally to a blind man, resulting in an effortless undertaking."

I can't tell if Sai is being intentionally guileless or if it's his natural demeanor.

"How do you know that?" Gaddreol asks.

"I know everything about Tristan," Sai responds.

How do you know everything about me? I wonder.

Nothing comes to mind. Nothing about myself, this mysterious man, or our supposed relationship to each other. *How do we know each other? Who are you to me?*

"He wants to know how you two know each other," Gaddreol says, sounding slightly more grounded now.

"Oh." Sai sounds caught off guard by the statement. "Tristan and I have been partners for twelve years."

Twelve years? How old is he? How old am I? How old were we when we met?

Allegedly, I've been with this man for twelve years, and yet I don't remember him at all. I don't know why that is startling to me when I recall so little of my own self. Still, I want to grieve a relationship I can't remember.

"How old were you when you two met?" Gaddreol reiterates my thoughts again.

"We met when we were fifteen," he answers, plainly.

Then for the first time, Sai shares unprompted information. "His blindness never held him back. Dare I say it made him resilient? Despite the perceived disability, he trained relentlessly to be the fastest and strongest—and deadliest—he could be. Tristan is the sole reason I became a doctor. I wanted to offer my assistance to him if he ever required it. I never imagined it would be me that required his assistance in my line of work."

I feel inclined to believe the unorthodox words he speaks. Although, it'd be easier to believe if it wasn't about me specifically. I don't think killing in any capacity is something I'm even remotely capable of. Let alone something I would personally train myself for. The thought is not as repulsive to me as it probably should be, but it's not appealing either.

How can I be an assassin?

"How did you end up working with this organization?" Gaddreol asks, probably trying to focus on anything else.

"Any doctor working at the hospital involuntarily signs up for FREE." The matter-of-fact tone returns, removing the personable attitude he displayed briefly. "The director discriminates little when it comes to who he incorporates."

To be expected from a sadistic man; presumably, anyone that enters the hospital is marked to become a member of his horrible organization. Sai must have been involved longer than Avery since he chose my body to act as a placeholder for Gaddreol due to my alleged skillset. None of this makes any sense.

A migraine would be pulsing against my skull if I could feel it. *I'm sorry if that's what you're feeling right now.*

"You never told Avery the truth about Tristan, did you?"

Sai quickly mutters, "No. I did not think it was necessary."

"Hopefully, this doesn't come off as rude, but I think that would have been pretty important to tell him." I expect annoyance, but there isn't even the slightest hint of irritation.

"I understand your concerns. I ask that you try to see things from my perspective about why I didn't tell him." Sai's tone remains flat.

Trust—or the lack thereof—is the likely culprit as to why he didn't tell Avery about my survival. There is a chance that there wasn't enough trust between the two doctors to share the sensitive details with him. Who could blame him? If what he's saying is true, it would be difficult to trust anyone.

Inversely, it's possible that he trusts Avery too much to risk his safety by sharing delicate information with him. The shattered man has been through so much, it makes sense not to add anything to his metaphorical plate.

"Tristan said it's either because you trust Avery too much or you don't trust him at all." Gaddreol iterates my reasoning.

"I do trust Avery." He sounds approving of my analysis. "I have learned that my assumptions were a bit too hasty and misguided. At the time, my thought process was that it would be safer for everyone if Tristan's identity, or rather his career choice, remained a secret. My decision was made because it can be potentially harmful to share nonessential information. The only reason I am informing you now is because I was not sure you would trust me otherwise. If you still don't, it is understandable, but my options are limited."

"I don't think my trust is really necessary, but I appreciate you considering it, anyway." I can hear the slight smile in his voice.

Sai seeking Gaddreol's approval is an interesting concept. He must consider Avery a friend to some degree to want to earn the trust of his boyfriend—an unnecessary formality, indeed. He could have performed the transition without ever speaking to Gaddreol.

Instead, by sharing this unbelievable information, he's displaying vulnerability in an attempt to gain friendship.

"Perhaps not. However, you have been nothing but courteous to Tristan. The least I can do is treat you with the same respect." A notification sound interrupts the conversation. A brief silence, and then Sai speaks again. "I apologize for my discourtesy, but during our talk, I sent a message to my colleague regarding the status of your personal body. It is unavailable for transitioning currently, but another body is prepared for you if you would like to proceed."

I can hear Gaddreol shift uncomfortably. "I suppose I don't really have a choice, do I?"

Are you sure you're okay with this?

Gaddreol responds to me directly, "No, but it'll be okay. Should we go ahead and get on with it?"

"If you are ready, I will take you back to the facility to perform the transition."

If you're ready, I repeat. *Am I ready?*

I should be. This is what I've been wanting since initially waking up in my imprisonment. The solution to my personal hell is finally available to me. It's really happening, and yet, the excitement I expected to feel is entirely absent and in its place is a consuming apprehension that would be suffocating if I could feel it.

"Alright, but will you let Avery know?" Gaddreol's voice trembles.

"Yes, of course."

Everything will be okay. I try to offer what little reassurance I can. I doubt it's very effective when I don't feel assured.

"I hope so."

Me, too.

∗ ∗ ∗

Once everything was decided, Gaddreol took a few minutes to get himself ready. During that time, Sai left a voicemail for Avery, who's probably giving his undivided attention to Vera. Hopefully, Vera's dance practice is going well. Undoubtedly, she is enjoying herself a lot more than her older brother who is most likely mentally prepares himself to transition again.

Despite the ride to the hospital being filled with the whirring noise from the wind, there is a distinct tapping sound that I recognize as a nervous tic. Gaddreol isn't prone to fidgeting, so that, paired with his shallow breathing indicates his anxiety is bordering on a panic attack. Which is understandable given the current circumstances. I can't imagine my reaction would be much different.

I want to offer reassurance, but there is nothing I can say at this moment. This is something I do not understand and offering another feeble attempt at reassurance feels like a disservice to us both. I can't imagine the thoughts that must be running through his mind. He has already been through this once without any support and while that isn't necessarily the same situation as right now, Avery is still not here to support him.

If you want to wait for Avery, I think Sai will understand.

He doesn't respond, but his silence tells me that it's okay—that he's okay to proceed without Avery at his side. The hospital is quiet with small bundles of indistinct chatter as they navigate through the building. Instead of slow meticulous taps, he's rapidly tapping the walking cane against the tile.

"The room is on your left," Sai states. "The hospital bed is in the middle of the room."

"Good afternoon, Gaddreol. Good afternoon, Tristan." Taz says. Clear in her quiet voice is the exhilaration she's feeling. "Everything is ready for you two to be separated. I'm so excited, I can't wait to meet you, Tristan."

I'm glad to hear her voice since her calming demeanor is a lot more relaxing than Sai's. Hopefully, her attendance will help Gaddreol feel a little more at ease.

I can't wait to meet you, either, Taz, I think, hoping that he's calm enough to relay that to her.

"He's excited to meet you, too. I'm about as ready as I'm going to be," Gaddreol says as he lies on the squeaky fabric.

"It will be the same as before. Taz will administer the anesthesia to Tristan's body first. And then to the new body once you are unconscious so there will be enough time for you to adjust to the new body. Administer the anesthesia, please, Taz. Gaddreol, please count down from ten."

"Ten, nine, eight… Seven. Six. Fi…" Gaddreol's voice fades away.

"Initiating the extraction in three… two… one…" A low hum starts up, accompanied by a continuous buzzing sound.

Is anesthesia necessary because the transition is painful? How painful could an extraction of an ethereal entity be, though? Is it attached to every part of our body on a microscopic level? Or does it aimlessly float around like I imagine my consciousness does at all times in my own mind? Perhaps the anesthesia is simply because the subconscious would instinctively reject the new body if it were given the opportunity.

Without warning, a sudden mix of aggressive gurgling sounds and guttural groans interrupt my thoughts. Accompanying those horrifying sounds is an array of noises from the squeaky fabric and sporadic, firm thumping sounds. A strong sense of alarm surrounds these unspecified sounds that my mind desperately tries to make sense of.

What's happening?

"Sai! What's happening!?" The panic in Taz's tone reverberates through my space, matching my own perceived panic.

"He's convulsing! Grab a capsule! I need to extract him now!" The frantic tone in Sai's voice sends a nearly tangible sensation of pure terror through me.

"Here!" Taz's attempt to remain calm is futile. Her voice cracks and I can hear the stifled cries pushing their way through. "Hang in there, Gaddreol! We're getting you out!"

The buzzing and humming sounds start up again. I try to think of the capsule they are placing his ethereal being into. He won't retain his consciousness inside the vial, but if he transitions back into his body will he be able to resume a normal life? Is this capsule specifically designed to allow a soul to survive outside of the body? Will he be okay?

Convulsing, I think. The gravity of the situation settles in. *This new body is rejecting his consciousness.*

How is that possible? This procedure is supposed to be fairly safe, especially with Sai overseeing the entire thing. But now the man I've grown accustomed to sharing my space with is seizing and the only solution to save his existence is placing his soul into a tiny capsule. Despite his consciousness being removed entirely from my body, the connection I share with him doesn't feel severed.

I do the only thing I can do in my microscopic space—I cry out, pointlessly, *Gaddreol! Don't die! Please! Your sister needs you! Avery needs you! I need you!*

For the first time since the initial transition, I feel a sensation weave itself indiscriminately across every inch of my body. It is a ghastly mix of both dread and fear.

I'm afraid—no, I am terrified.

I attempt to force my body to scream, but nothing happens. I focus all my energy on the throat I can't feel and the vocal cords I don't remember how to use, urging anything to happen. Finally, a sound escapes from my throat, but it's little more than an inaudible moan. The diminutive action takes the remaining strength I have and regardless of my attempts to stay tethered to consciousness, I slip away.

I don't know how much time passes until I come to. My sense of time is still warped. *I feel... heavy? I feel heavy. I feel something!*

Not the most pleasant sensation, but it is far more comforting than the absolute dread I experienced before falling unconscious. It's nearly inconceivable to go from a borderline nonexistent state to finally being able to experience any sort of sensation, but I will be happy if I never experience that type of fear again.

An abrupt thud that I recognize to be a punch reminds me of the dire situation and my relief is short-lived. *Gaddreol!* His name is the only one I can summon to the forefront of my consciousness.

I strain through the fogginess, trying to listen to my surroundings. The voices sound like whispered echoes through the hazy mist.

"What the hell did you do?" Avery asks, sounding torn between breaking down into tears or screaming until he loses his voice.

"Sai didn't do anything, Avery," Taz says. "He saved Gaddreol from dying with the body."

"Now, he's inside of a tiny vial!" Avery's voice trembles.

His essence is diminished to a tiny vial and a strong twinge of guilt tears through the shrouding fog. If I hadn't selfishly taken my body back none of this would have happened. Gaddreol should be here instead of me. He should be here to greet Avery as he comes to. He should be awaiting the return of his sister from her dance lessons to cheerfully congratulate her. Instead, I am here in my own body, and he is trapped in a state of nonexistence possibly worse than my lived experience.

I'm sorry, Gaddreol.

Logically, I know that none of this is my fault. However, I can't help but feel responsible for his current state of being. A foolish thought to latch onto, like I could have done anything meaningful to prevent the outcome. If two people who have conducted countless experiments think this is the right course of action, who am I to disagree?

"Sai, your lip is bleeding," Taz says.

"I'm fine," Sai's weary voice sounds weak. "The body rejected his transition. If it weren't for this vial there would be nothing left of him. Once we get another body, we can remove him from the vial."

"What if..." Avery's voice trails off, leaving his words unfinished.

What if? I repeat.

As if reading his mind, Taz responds, "He will be strong enough. This is just a one off."

The fear Avery is displaying feels slightly unfounded because of the absolute strength Gaddreol has displayed since the beginning. The sheer willpower he's had throughout this entire process shows a commendable amount of resilience. However, it is understandable for Avery to be afraid of losing the love of his life again after seeing the current state of his condition. He has lost so much already and now the man who promised him a second chance is diminished to a capsulated existence. I can't begin to comprehend the feelings that must be coursing through him right now.

"What's that?" A familiar voice breaks through the fog.

"Go away, Sands. This doesn't concern you, at all." Avery's voice hardens. He sounds on edge now, wary of the new addition.

"That is a beautiful specimen, Avery. Mind if I get a closer look?" Dr. Sands sounds intentionally cloying.

"Yes, I mind. This doesn't concern you," Avery repeats himself.

"May I show Josephine, then?" he asks the question as a threat.

I recall Josephine being the antagonistic woman who had the audacity to put her hands on Gaddreol, but the significance of the threat regarding her involvement is perplexing. Almost as baffling as the menacing tone coming from the doctor; it is nearly the same tone he attempted to use as an intimidation tactic the other night.

"I know that is your lover, Avery. I am not brainless."

"Dr. Sands, please," Sai pleads. "This is an unnecessary display of bravado."

Before this moment, I thought there was an unspoken respect for one another among the doctors. This tense interaction proves my inherent ability for perception is vastly underwhelming when my senses are limited. Something else I failed to discern is that there's a doctor here who has a more rage-inducing personality than Avery. My observational skills seem tremendously lackluster making the assassin claim even more preposterous than my initial revelation. That or I'm an exceptionally inadequate assassin.

"I just want to see the soul. I've not been acquainted with this aspect of the experiments yet. What better occasion to witness it firsthand than a soul conveniently trapped in a small vial? I am quite fascinated with the dirty work you three perform."

It's clear that he looks down on them, but I'm uncertain whether it's just their line of work he views as insignificant or their individual characters, too.

Did Dr. Sands sabotage the body? A baseless question that may be too ridiculous to even be considered a real thought. What would he gain by disturbing an ongoing experiment? How could he even tamper with the body to trigger that type of reaction?

"Don't touch him," Avery demands. "Here he is."

The image of Avery raising his arm in the same fashion as the dream crosses my mind. Replacing the friendly waving gesture is a loose fist holding up an unidentified object. Instinctually, I know it's the vial, but since I don't have a visual representation of it, it's a cylindrical object that remains out of focus.

"Absolutely stunning. An almost indistinguishable blend of colors. Who knew a soul would be a mystifying gradient silhouette of silvers, blues, and purples? Far smaller than I imagined; two or three inches of a formless shape—a spasmodic blob, restlessly moving about inside the vial. Captivating. Would it be possible to experiment on this?" The excitement in his voice is repugnant.

"No." Three distinct voices remark in unison.

None of the doctors agree with the experimentation, especially with the implication that Gaddreol's soul would be an unwilling test subject.

"It doesn't have to be your lover. It can be any soul really."

The restraint the three people adjacent to him have to not beat this man into oblivion is astounding. The heaviness still holds me uncomfortably still or else I likely would have tried to do it myself. It would be nothing but satisfying to wipe that smug expression off his face.

Instead, I attempt to activate my voice again. This time, it's far easier, but the only sound I can manage is a very raw, continuous scream. The sound fills the room until everything plummets into silence.

CHAPTER NINE

ON A SUBCONSCIOUS level, I knew if I made it to my body again, processing all the sensations would be an arduous task, bordering on impossible. Knowing this, however, did very little to prepare me for anything. The physical sensations come first.

This room is freezing. The beeping is ear-splitting. The mattress is stiff. The blanket is crushing. The clothes are constricting. My limbs are feeble. My stomach is ravenous. The throbbing inside my head is excruciating. Everything is simply too much.

A single tear rolls down my cheek, ripping open the floodgates, allowing a continuous stream to pour from my eyes. The physical sensations are a lot to deal with, but the emotions ravaging through me are far worse. My mental state is in shambles as I attempt to process my inner turmoil.

The intense emotional exhaustion that reawakening from my ethereal existence has caused is incongruous with the happiness I feel because of the uncontrollable tears flowing down my face. The strange satisfaction I have from the liquid pooling on either side of my neck, soaking into the ends of my hair is a stark contrast to the grim despair I feel due to my role in taking Gaddreol's life.

Gaddreol...

The tears that were starting to slow are reinvigorated as my mind moves to the small vial containing the entirety of his being. A brief thought of him attempting to break out of it pops into my mind. If it all wasn't so devastating, it might have been funny.

Quickly replacing that is a thought of Gaddreol being in my mind with me again. Being alone inside my head is a melancholic isolation that I was underprepared for. While I don't miss being an obscured presence in someone's mind, I find that I miss the unique symbiotic relationship—the amity and closeness we shared.

More than that, though, I miss him.

"Tristan," Taz speaks softly. "Are you alright?"

Am I alright? *No.*

What am I supposed to say? Can I say anything at all? The last time I attempted to use my voice I fell unconscious. Nonetheless, I try again. Uncertain of what I will say—what I even want to say. I force myself to respond.

My mouth opens, but the only thing that comes out is, "Nnn."

The low vibration in my throat grabs my attention, fixating on the scratchy feeling in my throat, most likely irritated from my deafening scream. The low hum moves against my lips, causing me to notice the cotton mouth I have. An unintentional, brief grimace forms. A cold glass of water would be the most amazing thing right now.

"I'm so sorry, Tristan," she says. Her voice trembles slightly. "The anesthesia should wear off completely soon."

I hope so.

My focus wanders to the lesser sensations I didn't notice before. My nostrils are flaring as air fills my lungs. The rhythmic rise and fall of my chest engrosses me. With the small amount of strength I can muster, I deliberately disrupt it, by inhaling as much air as I can, holding it, and then releasing it into one long exaggerated breath.

It's by far the most pleasant physical sensation I have felt since reacquiring my body. With it, the steady stream of tears begins to slow again. I repeat the process until I am calm enough for my breathing to return to its rhythmic pace and the tears finally stop altogether.

One after the other, I attempt to move various parts of my body. Open my eyes. Close my eyes. Roll my eyes. Open my mouth. Close my mouth. Move my tongue against my teeth. Open my fingers. Close my fingers. Curl my toes. Stretch my toes. Every movement is a small one, but all of them require more effort than I remember. Hopefully, when the anesthesia wears off completely these things will be effortless again.

Someone tiptoes into the room, possibly trying not to disturb my rest. Whoever it is, walks over to me, possibly examining my current physical state for any apparent changes. The simple action leaves me feeling inescapably vulnerable and exposed.

"Hello, Tristan." Sai's voice inexplicably causes tears to fall from my eyes again.

Did I really ask for this existence?

This is the most difficult adjustment I think anyone could ever go through. So many irrational things are eliciting extreme emotional responses within me. Since accessing my physical body, every minor incident that occurs is amplified, allowing these intense, involuntary reactions. I doubt anyone would agree to this arrangement if they were aware of the emotional turbulence that inevitably follows.

Incapacitated and feeble.

Those are the only two things that come to mind about myself. Neither characteristic is appropriate for an alleged assassin. If my deteriorated emotional state is any indication, I may be the worst assassin in history. Submitting to these intense reactions is the exact opposite of what is expected of a ruthless killer. To be an assassin I should be vigorous and impenetrable.

Suddenly, Sai's hand caresses my tear-streaked cheek. There is a comforting warmth from his hand as he glides it gently across my cheek. The subtle gesture short circuits my brain. I can feel my eyes widen and my lips part slightly; my breath catches in my chest, and the tears abruptly dry up for a split second. As quickly as everything stops, the emotions rush over me once more, allowing another flood of tears. The tears threaten to reach his hand, so he pulls it away. To my surprise, a cloth is used to wipe away the liquid from my face.

"Oh, Tristan..." he says, softly.

Hearing my name said with so much intimacy causes a memory hidden deep inside my mind to push against the invisible barriers surrounding my mind. It's unexplainable to feel something that is phantomlike have a tactile sensation. It's almost as if I can tangibly feel the memory trying to push through so it can be accessed.

"The most intriguing part about this abhorrent experiment is how different you are in your own body versus someone sharing your physicality for a month. Even as relatively motionless as you are at the moment, the distinct differences between you and Gaddreol are apparent." Sai is soft-spoken, but his matter-of-fact tone returns.

I'm unsure if he is attempting to comfort me or just making an astute observation. Either way, I am grateful that the man I have shared my life with for more than a decade can distinguish me from someone who shared my features for a short time. Finding solace in such a strange thought is bizarre, but it's a much-needed change from the extreme emotions I have been experiencing.

"This is the first time I am seeing Tristan for Tristan, and I can't believe how different their expressions are." Taz sounds awestruck.

I can imagine the differences between the two of us are rather large. He is a genuinely wonderful man who puts everyone before himself. Everything he does is done with consideration of those he deeply cares for. I suppose in some regard, I do that too if I willingly subjected myself to this wretched abomination. However, my status as an alleged killer may detract from any redeemable qualities that may be hiding beneath the amnesia.

"Tristan," Sai says. "Do you remember who you are?"

"Nn…"

The answer is a simple 'no', but I don't have enough coordination to form the word. I can communicate with inaudible groans. I can even open my mouth slightly. However, getting the two actions to cooperate so I can form a word seems to be an unattainable task.

Somehow, I am a formidable executioner. A laughable thought.

"Shouldn't his memories start coming back to him now that his consciousness is fully attached to his body again?" Taz asks.

"Yes. Maybe I can gather some items to stimulate his explicit memories." Sai states firmly.

My curiosity is thoroughly piqued and rampant now. What items will Sai use to activate my memories? Do I have a prized possession that, before all of this, I wouldn't have gone without? Perhaps I have a preferred weapon I use over any others that he will bring for me to hold. A weapon may be far too brazen to be considered an option. Will he bring me a favored book written in Braille? Do I even know how to read Braille? Surely, I do, or else the thought wouldn't have even crossed my mind.

"Oh, that's a great idea!" Taz says excitedly. "Do you have some items in mind?"

"A few." Sai sounds contemplative. "I'm going home to retrieve the items. Is that okay, Tristan?"

"Unn." An indistinct sound that hopefully he understands is my weakened attempt to say, "yes."

"Don't worry, I'll keep an eye on things here," Taz reassures him.

Without another word, Sai's soft footsteps grow distant. My mind wanders to Gaddreol, his final moments flooding my mind, causing an abundance of tears to flow down my face again. The endearing mechanism he adopted to sightlessly navigate the world was the last thing he said before being encapsulated. He counted down his final moments. He was alone and scared, but I hope being with me in his last waking moments provided him solace.

Avery must have Gaddreol's capsule put away somewhere safe.

The safest place would probably be on his person considering the lack of privacy. Even though Avery probably has Gaddreol with him, he is most likely feeling debilitated right now. Although I have full access to my emotions, I'm not sure how I would react or feel about his delicate situation surrounded by all of the heartache.

"Tristan," Taz whispers. "How are you feeling? Oh, wait, I mean are you feeling okay?"

No. I think, but I try to lie. "Ye…"

I am so close to full control over my body again. Being able to produce an intentional sound, broken or not, should fill me with joy, but the strenuous effort is far too draining.

"Good job!" Taz exclaims excitedly.

I should feel infantilized by the statement, but her intention is seemingly meant to be an encouraging sentiment, one which I'm grateful for. She really is the personification of calmness.

I compel myself to utter my thanks. "Th… thaa… thnk—."

"You're welcome!" She cuts off my pitiful efforts at expressing myself and continues her encouragement. "You're doing great!"

Even though the anesthesia is almost dissipated now, and I have only been awake for a little while, I want to rest more. There's an unfounded optimism in hoping that after resting the connection between my nervous and muscular systems will be revitalized. With comparative ease, I slip into a state of unconsciousness.

⁎ ⁎ ⁎

Awakening with a sharp jolt, I automatically sit upright. The simple action fills me with euphoria, curling my mouth into an unfeigned smile. I'll never take for granted being able to move my body without interference again. Once my memories return to me, my gratitude will never be displaced, either. For reasons unknown, I consented to this experiment, but in hindsight, I'm not sure if I would have agreed to this disorienting experience. Almost everything is leaving me with an intense discomposure.

"Good morning, Tristan." Sai sounds relieved.

"Good. Morning. Sai," I say, speaking with a deliberate slowness to ensure the signals between my brain and mouth function properly. They are, so I say, "It feels so good to have my autonomy again."

The full range of my newfound functionality was unimaginable just a short time ago. An assassin requires a fluidity that is entirely absent from my prevailing range of motions. While the clumsiness is incompatible with the claims of being an assassin, I'm so happy to have the ability again.

"I've missed that beautiful smile of yours. How are you feeling?" His voice sounds as if he is erring on the side of caution, afraid to say the wrong thing in this precarious situation.

"Very little, thankfully," I answer, "which is greatly appreciated, considering the tumultuous whirlwind of utter chaos that burdened me on my initial awakening."

"Are you hungry?" he asks.

Before I'm able to respond, my stomach grumbles. Sai chuckles briefly, a wonderful sound I haven't heard since transitioning. His soft laughter is alluring and soothing, like gentle waves rolling over the shore. The first manifestation of a memory pops into my mind.

Hand-in-hand, Sai and I are walking along the shoreline. With each step a molded footprint is left behind as wet sand coats the bottoms of my feet, filling in the small gaps in my toes. The tranquil water flows over my feet, just above my ankles, washing away the clinging sand. The calming sounds of the waves instill a sense of serenity.

"Tristan?" Sai grabs my attention. "Are you alright?"

"Huh? What?" I ask, reorienting myself. "Yes, I'm fine. We were on the beach together, holding hands, sauntering through the sand and the rolling waves."

"That's so sweet!" Taz's excitement is reminiscent of Vera's.

A brief pang of guilt passes over me, but it's quickly pushed away as my cheeks flush from the burst of embarrassment. Despite her presence inciting this confusing reaction, feeling the heat rising in my face is an amazing sensation to experience. It's mind-blowing to have a physical sensation match my emotional response after being in an ethereal state for so long. I'll have to thank Gaddreol for giving me the ability to envision my cheeks turning red.

Hopefully, I'll get the chance to.

"I'm sorry, did you say something after asking if I was hungry?" I ask, regaining my composure.

"Yes. The hospital food is a disservice, so I brought you either a fruit smoothie or a yogurt with some fruits on the side," Sai repeats himself.

"Both of those things would be amazing right now. I'll go with the fruit smoothie." While I reacquaint myself with my limbs a smoothie may be the best option with the least humiliating outcomes.

He hands me a plastic bottle. I inspect the object with my free hand, finding it has a secured lid with a straw in the center. Eagerly, I bring it up to my lips and take an enthusiastic gulp of the liquid. I have no idea if this is the best smoothie ever made or if I am beyond elated to be tasting anything, but the combination of fruits mixed with what I assume is milk and yogurt creates a delicious symphony of flavors.

"This is divine," I say in between drinking the heavenly liquid.

To my disappointment, the noisy slurping of mostly air indicates the end of my delicious meal. I'm almost desperate enough to take off the lid and scoop out the remnants by hand. Compromising, I unscrew the top and tilt the cup upside down against my mouth in hopes of getting every drop of the delicious liquid, while hopefully not looking as ridiculous as I feel. This draws out another beautiful laugh from Sai.

"I am elated that you remember walking along the beach with me." He sounds like he's reminiscing about the event as well. "Have you had any other recollections?"

"He remembers something?" Avery's solemn voice was the last one I expected to hear. Surrounding his presence is looming sorrow so tangibly heavy it's almost suffocating.

"Yes," Sai responds. "I have some items that I am going to give him soon that will hopefully stimulate his memories."

"That's great." His uncharacteristically empty tone is absolutely heartbreaking to listen to. "When you're finished, I would like to talk to Tristan."

"If this is important, I will wait," Sai says. He grabs the now empty cup from me, his hand gently brushing against mine. Light tingles follow the movement and then vanish.

"It is and it isn't. It can wait. By the way, hi, Tristan." He does not attempt to sound anything more than the melancholy he is feeling. I want to reach out to him, but I don't think he would appreciate the gesture, so I remain in place.

"Hello, Avery," I reply, wanting to say more.

He's not in the mood to hear about the horrible outcome, and saying anything about it wouldn't be good for him, so the thoughts roam freely inside my mind. *I'm sorry we didn't meet under better circumstances. I'm sorry for what happened to Gaddreol, for being here instead of him. I'm sorry his existence is a tiny vial. I wish I could change everything that has happened.*

"Avery, go ahead. Then, go home to rest," Taz interjects.

The worry in her voice makes me wonder what Avery must look like for her to suggest that. Disheveled, or even sullen looking, at the very least. I imagine he hasn't been able to sleep much or keep food down very well. It wouldn't surprise me if this broken man didn't even have the energy to bathe himself. My heart aches for him, and for Gaddreol.

"Alright." He exhales, possibly to maintain his brittle composure. "It's about Vera. Tristan, if you can, I need you to pretend to be Gaddreol. She can't know he's like this. Please."

Without thinking, I respond, "Of course I will."

Panic swells inside me. As genuine as he is, I am pretty sure no matter how good my potential acting skills might be, she'll know that I'm not him. The bond that they share is not something I will be able to confidently emulate. Besides, if Taz, who had never met me, can tell the difference between Gaddreol and me, I'm not sure how I can pretend to be him well enough to deceive his baby sister.

"Thanks so much." I can hear the relief in his voice slipping past the desolation.

"Take care of yourself," Taz says, concerned. "We'll find a new body for Gaddreol soon."

Avery offers a simple okay as he takes his leave. He is far more admirable than I originally gave him credit for. In a short time, he's lost both his brother and the love of his life, but he's still putting Vera and her situation above himself. Despite facing extreme adversity, he's taking the time to speak with me to ensure she's not exposed to the ensuing chaos. Selflessness isn't a word I ever thought I would associate with Avery, but it's befitting.

"Will he be okay?" I find myself asking without meaning to. *Who would be okay after everything he has been through recently?*

"I think so," Sai says, sounding slightly unconvinced by his own words. "Do you want to hold the first item I brought?"

I breathe deeply, trying to push away the consuming sadness to focus on the two people before me, trying to help me remember who I am. "I'm ready."

"Are you sure?" he asks, probably worrying about how the short interaction affected me.

"Yes." I stretch my hand out.

He places a small item, barely an inch or two in length, in my hand. It's a circular shape, smooth to the touch, and hollow inside; a ring. The thick band has an engraving on it. I run my finger along the engraving. A tear rolls down my cheek as I realize it's my name written in braille.

⠠⠞⠗⠊⠎⠞⠁⠝

The ring fits perfectly on my ring finger. The connected memory flows effortlessly into my mind.

My arms are both outstretched against a satin-clothed table, Sai's hands clasped around my own. I can feel the happiness radiating from both of us.

'Will you marry me, Tristan?' His voice is faint and hazy.

Unlike the vivid "Yes!" from myself as the unadulterated euphoria engulfs every inch of my body. Sharp prickling sensations trail along my body as goosebumps cover my skin.

The sensation occurs physically, pulling me out of the memory. A melodic bout of laughter comes from Sai probably recalling similar physical sensations. He asked me to marry him. I don't have a boy-friend; I have a fiancé.

There's no uncertainty anymore of who this mysterious man is. He is the man who loves me unconditionally, despite his inherently reserved nature. The man who always stands with me, supporting every decision I have made over the last decade. He is the man who requested my help in one of the most unorthodox ways imaginable. He is someone I willingly put myself into this unthinkable situation for because I love him with every fiber of my being. I am not sure I have ever felt so sure of anything in my life.

"I love you, Sai." The words flow naturally.

His mouth meets mine, every controlled movement brimming with affection and passion. I wrap my arms around his neck and pull him closer to me. He wraps his arms around my waist, pulling me to the edge of the hospital bed, the fabric noisily squeaking in protest. Closing the distance between us, his body presses firmly against mine.

The exuberant energy encircling us grows as our kiss deepens. His lips part and I match his movement, allowing him to explore my mouth. My hands find their way to his silky hair and run my hands through it. A soft moan escapes my throat as his hands graze my thighs.

Leaning away, he ends the intense kiss with a quick, tender peck. Breathily he says, "I love you, too, Tristan."

"That must've been an intense memory you shared," Taz says, reminding me of her presence.

The color red flashes through my mind as the same creeping heat of embarrassment flushes my cheeks again. I catch my breath and attempt to regain my self-control. At this moment, I just want to hide under the thin blanket and pretend I don't exist.

"I'm sorry, I didn't mean to embarrass you!" She unsuccessfully tries to conceal her laughter.

"I didn't mean to get carried away," Sai says, sheepishly. "It's the engagement ring I gave Tristan when I proposed to him."

"The two of you are so adorable." I honestly didn't know her voice could go so high from excitement. I hear a light thump sound and realize Taz playfully hit Sai when she squeals, "I didn't know you were engaged!"

"I apologize. I never mentioned it before because it was not of any relevance," Sai admits.

His thought process is perplexing since he was trying to conceal my identity from everyone, sort of. There was enough secrecy to the point that he didn't give any information to anyone unless he felt it was essential, but he didn't hide the fact that he knew me on a personal level since he was displaying pictures of me for anyone to see. His priorities are slightly skewed, but it's most likely due to his intrinsic introversion than anything else.

"At this rate, you won't need any other items. How many did you bring, anyway?" Taz asks curiously.

"Four."

"I can't wait to what else you have," she says with anticipation.

Fearsome assassin. Another laughable thought pops up, realizing I lack confidence in my ability to carry myself to the bathroom. An essential bodily function is causing me to feel utterly helpless, but I'm supposed to be a formidable force. *Right.*

"This is a little embarrassing, but do you mind helping me to the bathroom?" I ask, accepting my vulnerability.

"There is nothing to be embarrassed about," he says, grabbing both of my hands with a gentle grip.

Using his strength, I pull myself to my feet while my legs shakily protest every slight movement. Thankfully, I have just enough self-preservation to request help, because if I had attempted this on my own, I think my face would have become well acquainted with the cold tiled floor. Having full control over my limbs does not seem to reduce the incoordination I still have. Sai wraps his arm around my waist and supports my weight as he guides me to the bathroom. I trip over my clumsy feet, stumbling repeatedly into Sai. He remains unwavering despite my constant staggering.

"Careful. The toilet is right in front of you," he says, releasing his grip on my waist.

I have enough strength to support myself for my much-needed relief. Once I finish, Sai resumes his position at my side with his arm wrapped around my waist, supporting my weight as I lean into him again.

"Thank you," I say.

My voice has a diffidence that sounds unnatural to me. He lifts me back onto the bed, effortlessly. The simple action causes the inevitable heat to flush my face again as thoughts of the strength he possesses to pick me up with such graceful ease fill my mind. Red flashes into my mind again. I am beginning to regret feeling content with this sensation since it's currently betraying my thoughts.

"I didn't know you could be so doting, Sai," Taz teases playfully.

"Of course," he says.

A lively bout of laughter comes from both doctors. I'm uncertain if it's because of her comment or from the bright red that's coloring my cheeks. Probably both.

Sai asks, "Would you like to hold the next item I have?"

"Yes." *Please.* Anything that can distract me from the thoughts causing the increased blood flow to my face. I hold out my hand, waiting anxiously.

He bypasses my hand and puts it directly on my lap. It's larger and heavier than I expected. Examining it with my hands, I realize it's a folded fabric. Clumsily I unfold the item to inspect it closer. It's a blanket. An intricately knitted blanket, so soft and warm; I instantly wrap it around myself, and Sai takes it upon himself to straighten the blanket, wrapping it thoroughly around my body.

Allowing myself to fully take in and feel the pattern against my skin, I try to force a memory to form. This must be special to me, right? Nothing comes to mind, so I run my hand along the material and just take in the elaborate design used to create it. I pull the blanket closer and nuzzle my face into the edge. The softness is comforting and peaceful. *Home.* This blanket reminds me of home.

This realization leads the way for a memory to flow through.

I'm lying down in my bed, tightly wrapped in a cocoon with a thick comforter pulled up to my chin. A hand gently smooths the hair away from my face.

"Are you alright, Tristan?" Sai asks faintly.

"Miserable, so no," I mutter.

"I was going to wait to give you this until Christmas, but I think it is appropriate now." He pulls on the blanket wrapped around me and I let him remove it completely.

He drapes a thinner blanket on top of me. It instantly provides a warmth that the thicker blanket lacked. It's far more comfortable as it wraps tighter around my form.

"Is this what you've been working on for so long?" I ask.

"Yes."

A wet sensation coats my cheeks.

The tears materialize in the present, pulling me from the memory. Bewilderment sweeps over me. *Shouldn't I be experiencing happiness since the man I love made me something so precious?*

I wipe my eyes to stop the tears from continuing, and then ask, "Why am I crying? I remember you giving me this blanket that you made for me. And I was miserable, but before I could find out why the physical tears pulled me out of the memory."

"I was a bit reluctant to bring this one, but it is one of your most cherished items." Sai's words are heavy, the weight of them seems crushing and burdensome. Instantly, I feel guilty for asking. "I was making this blanket for you for Christmas. But… You lost your family in a drunk driving incident. It seemed like the right decision, so I gave it to you right then."

I barely process the audible gasp that comes from Taz.

Drunk. Driving. Incident. I think, each word piercing my heart. The agony I feel contorts my face and Sai wraps his arms around me in a tight embrace.

He whispers, "I'm sorry."

Words rapidly race through my brain incoherently. *Funeral. Car. Mom. Court. Ambulance. Totaled. Tears. Mountain. Dad. Man. Judge. Sisters. Police. Insincerity. Brother. Target.*

"The man was found not guilty?" I ask, coldly, desperate to make sense of the words racing in and out of my mind.

"Yes." His answer is devoid of all emotion.

"I'm so sorry, Tristan," Taz says.

Unsure of what to say, I just sit in silence, using Sai's embrace to ground me. I've experienced so much pain and heartbreak in such a short time. First being a front row spectator to Gaddreol's, and then an adjacent witness to Avery's. Now I'm reliving my own pain. My only saving grace is that by some miracle my mental fortitude is strong enough to not crumble under the enormity. That might be the only attribute I possess to indicate truth to the claim of an assassin.

"What's the next item you have?" I ask, sounding distant and shaky. I barely recognize my own voice. I take a deep breath to calm myself.

"Are you sure you're ready to proceed?" he asks. I nod, hoping he is looking directly at me. I mumble a sound of affirmation just in case he isn't.

"I want you to be careful with this one." I hold my hand palm up and in it, he places an item that has a woven grip.

Grasping my hand firmly around the slim object, it has a short, wrapped grip with a small bit of metal exposed at the end. A hilt, most likely. Is it really a weapon?

Tentatively, I trail my finger along the item. At the top of the grip is thin metal that diverges into three dull blades that gradually taper off into blunt points. I cautiously glide my hand along the length of the three sections. The blade in the middle is roughly a foot in length, while the two on the sides are about half the length.

Sai really brought a weapon to the hospital. That doesn't seem like an appropriate item to help memories come to fruition. *Sai.* The word pops into my head.

An abrupt chuckle rips out of me before I can think about it. "You really brought me a weapon that matches your name?"

"Yes. Is it evoking any memories for you?" he asks, maintaining his usual uneventful tone.

"Unfortunately, no. Nothing, but it's delightful to have a weapon with your name," I say, my brows creasing slightly from feeling a little ashamed that this item didn't bring forth anything significant.

"That's alright. Admittedly, I only brought it with me because it is amusing. You specifically chose this weapon because it matches my name." A small stint of laughter escapes from him, before his voice is stoic again. "The last item is not something I brought. But I think it will prove significant to you."

"Alright, so what is it?" I ask, feeling a little anxious.

"Is it alright, if I lift your shirt?" I nod.

Tentatively, he raises my shirt. My breath hitches. Gently, he grabs my hand and guides it to a raised ridge on my skin. He lets go of my hand, allowing me to explore the raised line. A scar running from the top of my right hip diagonal towards the left side of my chest. The length of it is roughly a foot in length. The inch width is uniform all the way through except for the middle around my belly button. The scar splits into a cluster of diverging paths that rejoin to a singular point at either side.

"Are you alright?! What happened?! Tristan!" Sai's voice sounds almost drowned, distorted.

My legs are as heavy as lead, as I stumble through the doorway. Barely managing to make it inside before collapsing against Sai. Incoherent mumbling ensues. He picks me up and puts me gently on the sofa. My hand raises to my stomach, the thick liquid coating it instantly. Sai returns to my side before I notice him leave.

"This is going to hurt. Forgive me."

I flinch, ripping my attention away from the memory. My hands absently holding my stomach. Gaddreol must have felt this long scar. There's no way he wouldn't have noticed something this large. Why didn't he ever mention it? I suppose it wouldn't have mattered if I couldn't have provided any significant answers about it.

"You saved my life." It's the only words I can manage. There is no context as to why I stumbled inside on the brink of death, but I believe Sai did everything he could to save me. "What happened?"

"You were attacked by someone. They stole everything you had on your person." His monotonous tone is struggling to remain flat.

Was it a random encounter or a calculated one?

"That's quite the gnarly scar you gained," Taz says, her voice a mix of horror and fascination.

"Yes, I saved your life. No moment holds more significance in my career as a surgeon. Well, as a doctor with an interest in surgery."

"You did that when you weren't a surgeon yet?" Taz asks. "That's amazing!"

"Thank you," I say to Sai.

The words I'm too overwhelmed to speak spin around inside my head. *If it weren't for you, I don't know how far I'd have come. Even without all of my memories, I know you're imperative to my success, an essential part of my life, in every aspect.*

"Of course," he states. "I would do anything for you."

"I feel so bad for thinking this, Sai, but I didn't think you'd even have a partner," Taz admits. "I assumed you were aromantic since you're so aloof."

"A fair assessment."

"It was a lot of fun getting to experience all of this with you guys. I need to get home and rest, too. I'll stop by Avery's first," Taz says yawning.

"Goodnight, Taz."

"Night, Sai, night, Tristan. See you later."

After she closes the door, Sai's footsteps are light, but noticeable as he crosses the room. I hear him rummaging through a cloth bag until he finds whatever it is he's looking for.

"There's another item, but I didn't want to share it with Taz here."

My breathing quickens and my stomach flutters as the flustered feeling returns. The image of my pale cheeks being painted red from the creeping heat pops into my head again.

His sweet melodic laugh returns, and then he says, "I apologize. I did not think about how my words could be misconstrued as an innuendo."

Embarrassment overflows and I want to hide, again. At least no one else is here to witness my mortification. I open my mouth to say something, anything, but nothing comes out, so I close it and pull the blanket closer to me in a pitiful attempt to cover my shame.

Why did my mind immediately jump to a crude assumption?

Sai gives me a quick kiss on the cheek, and I can feel the smile on his lips when he pulls away. The simple action calms my nerves.

"This is another weapon that I want you to be careful with. It is a knife, sharper than the previous one." He guides my hand to the hilt.

Cautiously, I skim my hand along the intricately detailed hilt. It has a lined design that is comfortable against the palm of my hand. It feels designed specifically for my hand, perfectly fitting against my palm as I tighten my grip. The knife is lightweight and easy to wield. Lightly tracing the blade, I recognize it's a dagger.

Unthinking, I ask, "This is a weapon I regularly carry with me?"

"Yes, for protection."

"Am I actually an assassin?" I ask, barely above a whisper. "Do I really kill people?"

Gently, he touches my hand which is still clutching the dagger. A subtle request for me to release it so he can put it safely back where he retrieved it from. His delicate touch sends chills up my arm.

"Yes." He states, but his tone softens as he asks, "Does it bother you now?"

"It seems rather ill-suited if I'm honest. I don't remember any of the potentially heinous acts I have committed." Hearing myself say it aloud is unsettling.

"If it is any consolation, you have never targeted anyone that did not explicitly deserve it," Sai says, sitting on the edge of the squeaky bed in front of me. He grabs my hands, holding them between his. "The horrific incident involving your family initiated your desire to redirect your attention to assassinations. That vile man lacked any remorse for his actions."

"Thanks. That does make me feel significantly better."

It's the truth. It's a huge relief to know my targets are people who have proven themselves to be nothing more than despicable pieces of trash. The idea of me being an assassin felt undeniably nefarious. Now it seems to resemble immorality more than intrinsic evil.

"Off-topic, but may I ask a question?" I ask, unable to conceal the worry I feel.

"Anything," Sai responds, sounding worried.

I exhale deeply, trying to maintain the little bit of composure I have left. Even though I initiated the inquiry, I'm not sure if I'm prepared to hear the answer. Although I've done fairly well to keep my attention away from Gaddreol's newfound surreality, it lingers in the back of my mind.

With another quick exhale, I force the question out, "Is that vial a maintainable, temporary existence for Gaddreol? Is he going to be okay?"

Two questions, actually, I think, immediately regretting asking at all. An unsettling tension grows between us quickly as silence falls upon my questions.

Sai's remorseful voice cuts through the brief tensity, "Honestly, Tristan, I am not sure. Rejection like this has not occurred since I began performing the transitions. Despite the countless transitions and extractions I have performed, this is still a perilous experiment with many potential outcomes that I am incapable of predicting."

His words confirm my justified reluctance. It is an answer I didn't want to hear, but one I expected to hear. Unless another stolen body comes into their possession, Gaddreol will remain an encapsulated essence. Even if another body becomes available, I'm not sure if he would appreciate it over his current residence. If it isn't his rightful body, I don't think he wants to take anyone else's life away at the expense of his own. After everything he has been through and done for everyone, this is the undignified compensation he gets.

Please forgive me. If I had known... The sudden knotting in my stomach interrupts my thoughts and, finally, after all this time, I might actually *expel* the contents of my very *real* twisted stomach.

"Are you okay?" His troubled voice must mean my affliction is evident on my face.

I don't have time to respond before I lean over the side of the bed and retch. The smoothie comes back as easily as it went down. The loud heaves, acidic taste, and putrid bile smell are more than I could've prepared myself for. The overwhelming sensations cause me to retch more, only acid burning its way up my throat.

Sai moves away unnoticed, until he returns, standing next to the bed, asking, "Would you like some water?"

I nod, hesitantly, and he places a fresh cup of water in my hand. For fear of spewing another round of vile stomach acid, I don't dare make another sound. I take cautious sips to not upset my stomach further. A damp rag is placed in my hand to clean my face with and then he cleans up the disgusting mess I adorned the bed and floor with.

My voice is hoarse when I say, "I apologize, Sai."

"Please, do not apologize. It is understandable. My current line of work is nothing more than revolting," he says, matter-of-factly.

"That might be the biggest understatement of all time." I reach for the blanket but freeze. "Did I ruin the blanket you brought?"

"The blanket is unscathed," he says.

Wasting no time, I bundle myself up, as I think, *Scary assassin.*

"Why did we do it this way?" I ask. "Was there really no other way?"

"There was not another way, no." Sai sounds pensive. "Tristan, I need to apologize to you and Gaddreol. I wasn't entirely honest with him when he questioned me in my office. You are a part of the blind studies."

My heart skips a beat. My breathing stops altogether, and I can feel the panic rising in my chest until I remind myself to breathe. Gaddreol could have been a part of the blind studies; so why isn't he here now doing that instead of—?

"I don't remember, but I don't think you're one to lie, so why did you tell him he wasn't able to be a part of the experiments?" I say, cutting my own ramblings off before rousing the extreme physical reaction again.

"After what has happened, this is going to sound monstrous." He sighs. "I know that this situation left a mutual appreciation between you and Gaddreol. However, he was never meant to remain in your body. From the beginning, you were always meant to be a part of the blind studies. I needed you to be a part of them. That way you can be a participant in the experiments while maintaining the skills you've honed."

Everything he says I already knew on some level, but hearing it said out loud puts it into perspective for me.

"So, I will be a part of these studies. Are they as daunting as you made them out to be?" I ask, feeling moderately intimidated at the thought of being a part of it.

"Unfortunately, many of the tests will be excruciatingly painful." He certainly knows how to instill confidence in me. A grimace forms on my face. "I'm sorry, I just don't want you to go into it thinking anything less."

"I appreciate it. All of this is unbelievably overwhelming. I hope I can remember more things soon." Exhaustion washes over me.

"I know, I am so sorry for asking so much of you." Sai wraps his arms around my self-made cocoon. "I should have never put all of this on you. Unfortunately, it is an untimely observation."

"Sai," I say, bluntly. "Kindly, stop talking. Sure, everything you've said about me sounds preposterous, but I know there is truth to it. I understand why you requested my assistance. And I know that you orchestrated everything to get me up close and personal, which is a rather necessary formality. I am glad you trust me enough to involve me in this harrowing process. I just wish it wasn't at the expense of Gaddreol. Since the beginning of the transition, he's been faced with nonstop hardships that he never deserved—and now this."

"I understand." He sounds remorseful, but only adds, "I love you, Tristan."

"I love you, too, Sai."

He lies on the too-small bed with me and pulls me against his body. Every inch of my body fits perfectly against his. Tranquility washes over me as I inhale the familiar scent of sandalwood and vanilla.

"I promise," Sai whispers, "I'll do everything within my abilities to give Gaddreol his life back."

"I believe you."

Heaviness sweeps over me and my breathing settles into a deep, deliberate pace as I listen to his rhythmic heartbeats. Sai gently kisses the top of my head. My eyes close and the soft beats against my ear lull me to sleep.

CHAPTER TEN

"ARE YOU READY?" Sai asks me.

I'm nervous but calm enough to not let it show.

"Never been better."

He takes my hand in his and says, 'Be careful, I'll be at this same spot when you return.'

I squeeze his hand, release it, and walk along the path. This is the moment I've practiced countless times. I'm ready. With my walking cane in front of me, I head directly for the man I know is walking along the path. His grating voice carries on the wind and his pace is nothing more than a stroll.

Catching up to him takes no time at all. I tighten my grip on the small syringe in my hand. Forcibly, I trip over him, partially landing atop him. I quickly plunge the needle into his neck and then retract it back into my sleeve. Scrambling to my feet, I apologize profusely for my clumsiness.

"What the fuck!?" he yells before, presumably, getting a good look at my walking cane and intense white eyes. "Man, my bad. Are you good?"

"I'm fine, thank you. Take care."

An unexpected tear rolls down my cheek. My first dream since regaining full control is one without any visual stimulus. I don't know why it is upsetting to have a sightless dream again since it's what I've had my entire life, but I push back more tears attempting to follow. I have no idea if it's because I won't have any more glimpses of the beautiful world to discover or because it's a stark reminder that Gaddreol isn't here with me. Or anywhere outside of that tiny vial.

David Lewis. The name lends itself to me. My first assassination. The man who got away with remorselessly killing my entire family. In spite of the blatant disregard he showed during the trial, he was given nothing more than a valediction of "take care."

I remember just feeling relief when Sai shared his obituary with me. A few days after our encounter, his heart stopped. The cause of death was ruled natural causes. No matter how confident I was in my ability to pull it off, I was still anxious it would be traced back to me. It was a risk I was willing to take.

"Morning, Tristan." Taz's voice is a whisper as if she's uncertain if I'm awake or not.

"Good morning, Taz," I mumble, earning a loud yelp from Taz, who is closer to the hospital bed than I thought.

"Sorry, I thought you were still sleeping. There is a small table on your right with a cup of water, another smoothie, a yogurt cup, some fruit, and two pieces of toast for you." My mouth starts watering before she can finish listing the mini buffet. "Once you're finished eating, the shower is ready for you to use."

"Thank you so much for all of this," I say, sitting up completely to indulge in the delicious food.

"Sai did all of this. He got all this food together for you, but was called away to deal with another patient, so I'm here to keep you company," she says, sounding nervous and excited.

I start with the bread. Toasted to perfection, topped with salted butter. Sai knows me better than I know myself; this bread hits all the right notes. Stopping myself from gorging on all the bread at once, I turn my attention to the fruit and take my time eating that. A wonderful mix of berries: strawberries, blueberries, blackberries, and raspberries.

I take a small sip of the smoothie, it's even better than the one from yesterday. One sip quickly becomes half the bottle before I set it back down. The velvety texture of the yogurt is comforting, but the tangy taste is more jarring than I was prepared for. Nonetheless, it's eaten nearly as fast as everything else.

Taking a break from stuffing my face with all the delicious food prepared for me, I ask, "How is Avery doing?"

Another question with an answer I'm not certain I'm prepared to hear. Perhaps an unfounded thought, but I feel if I don't ask, I am doing a disservice to Avery and Gaddreol. Gaddreol has been here for me since the beginning and I want to be here for him, or well, the people he cares the most about.

The heavy sigh Taz releases tells me all I need to know, but I listen intently to her response, anyway. "Avery isn't doing well. He is taking the day to himself, but he will be back tomorrow."

The words left unsaid are more disheartening than what she said. Avery can't take any time for himself to process anything that has happened. The man who was already blackmailed into submission will continue to face coercion if he considers allowing himself a few days away. The enormity of this organization is undeniable, just as the director intended.

I nod in acknowledgment, hoping she's looking at me to notice it. My words escape me, so I return to the small amount of food on the table.

Scarfing down the rest of the food is challenging. Everything is delicious, possibly a little too good. The discomfort residing in my stomach agrees with that assessment. A distinct, raw sensation rises into my throat and panic washes over me until an exceptionally loud burp rips out of my mouth.

"Wow! I didn't think you had that in you!" Taz sounds amazed, with a hint of disgust mixed in.

"Neither did I. I'm sorry about that," I say, getting a boisterous rise out of her. After she calms down, I ask, "Are you okay, Taz?"

"Me? Totally. Just worried about everyone." She sounds distant, but still trying to sound upbeat. "I'm fine, though."

There's no point pushing. She's dealing with the situation the best she can. Maybe one day she'll open up to me if she feels it necessary.

Feeling around the tray, I straighten up my mess. Stacking the plates together, and any scattered trash or silverware on top.

"Oh, don't worry about cleaning up, I'll get it," she says, walking towards me.

"Thank you. Did Sai happen to bring a change of clothes for me?"

"Yes. Everything's ready for you in there. So, just wash up and get yourself looking—er, feeling—good again." She sounds apologetic.

At a loss for how to navigate the awkwardness she seems to feel I just softly chuckle. I'm unsure if that's a reasonable response, but I focus on the daunting task at hand, ignoring the discomfort. With deliberate slowness, I practically slide off the bed to my feet. Still feeling uncertain about supporting my own weight I take cautious steps.

Despite clumsily stumbling my way through it, I make it to the bathroom relatively unscathed, maybe just a bit frozen from the icy tiles beneath my feet. Directly next to the door frame is the vanity. Continuing with my graceless movements, I fumble my way around the countertop until finding a toothbrush and its essential pairing.

Feeling the bristles scrape across my teeth is a jarring sensation I didn't miss at all. The refreshing feeling following the discomfort is almost enough to make the action worth it. Grabbing the brush next, I rake it through my hair which I'm sure is an unrestrained version of Vera's description. Surprisingly, it's not the rat's nest I expected.

Now, it's time for a much-needed shower. More fumbling ensues as I figure out how to turn on the water. The setup is easy enough and the water warms up quickly. I'm excited to feel the water rain onto my skin. It is probably one of the most soothing things I can recall. Stepping inside, I nearly slip, barely catching myself against the wall. Not the best start to something that is supposed to be relaxing.

After I stabilize myself, I focus on the water as the soft droplets repeatedly hit my skin. like gentle rain. If it weren't so slippery, the idea of dancing in the rain might have been at the forefront of my thoughts. The water gliding gracefully over my skin brings the sense of serenity I was hoping for. I could stand here for an indeterminate amount of time and just remain in this blissful downpour.

With things requiring my attention, though, remaining under this showerhead is an implausibility. Instead, I allow myself some time to just feel the sensations flow through my hair and roll over my body. The water predictably runs into the drain and for a moment, it's as if it takes all of my worries, pain, and troubles along with it. If only things were that simple.

I begin washing my hair—a task I should be able to finish quickly. However, I wasn't anticipating the surreal emotional reaction the simple task elicits. The unintentional scalp massage brings tears to my eyes again. I missed being able to perform the simple action of running my fingers through my hair. Putting my hair beneath the showerhead once more is too overwhelming to process.

The phrase "too much of a good thing" comes to mind. To reduce the sudden overpowering emotions, I quickly wash my body without giving myself time to think about it. Carefully, I step onto the icy tile, a stark contrast from being engulfed by the warmth of the steam. My skin tightens as tiny, raised bumps immediately cover my body, but dissipate at nearly the same speed.

My towel is folded over a bar and instantly I regret grabbing it. The material is soft and plush, but coupled with my overstimulation, the towel feels akin to an abrasive sandpaper scraping my skin raw.

As quickly as possible, I pat myself dry and get dressed. Not very effective since my clothes grip my damp skin with each motion. After squeezing the excess moisture out of my hair, I collect myself and leave the bathroom.

"Tristan, are you okay?" From the concern in Sai's voice, I didn't do a very good job of minimizing the overstimulation.

"Yes, I'm okay," I respond, trying to not give away my apparent discomposure. "Thanks for breakfast and setting the bathroom up for me."

"You're welcome."

I hear footsteps that I know belong to Sai. He moves towards me and places his hands gently on my shoulders. Most likely looking me over since I seem to currently wear my emotions like a fashion statement. After a few seconds, he pulls me into a loving embrace that seems to disintegrate all the intolerable sensations at once.

"Thank you," I say. He deepens the embrace, nestling his head against my cold, wet hair.

"Please, do not lie to me, Tristan. It serves no purpose, and I can see through it," he says. There's a playful tone in the last words he speaks.

"I'm sorry. I won't lie to you, again."

Saying the sentence sounds strange. Deception is likely a part of assassinations, but lying to my partner of twelve years is ludicrous. Honestly, I'm not sure why I attempted the futile action. I assume it's because the overstimulation I feel is relatively inconsequential compared to the bigger things going on right now.

"Thank you," he says. "Did you enjoy your breakfast?"

"A bit too much. It was all very delicious." The sweet, melodic laugh returns, and it brings with it a sense of solace.

"I know it's a bit sudden but are you ready to start the trials?" he asks, the concern undisguised in his voice.

Moments ago, the very mundane task of showering proved to be an unsettling one even with knowing exactly what I was getting myself into before stepping into the bathroom. Now, without the foreknowledge or understanding of how any of these experiments work, I am still diving headfirst into it. A laughable notion.

Am I ready? *No.* Do I need to do it, anyway? "Yes."

"The room is ready if you are. I need to return to my office, but if you would like, Taz has offered to stay with you." He plants a tender kiss on my forehead.

"This may be the most prepared I can be," I reply, truthfully. If we wait any longer my feet may miraculously get even colder.

✳ ✳ ✳

Taz is pushing the wheelchair that I reluctantly agreed to. It's out of my comfort zone to travel through the hospital in a chair instead of on foot, but she wants me safe. Unfortunately, her idea of safety leaves me feeling uncomfortably vulnerable. Navigating the world with bare feet provides a sense of security for me that most don't understand.

"Are you nervous?" Taz asks, sounding nervous herself.

"A bit, yes."

The feeling isn't exclusive to the experiments. Nor is it solely from the wheelchair I am uncomfortable with. While it is a bit of both of those things, there is another element to the unpleasant feeling. An insecurity left from a hole deep within me; I am missing a part of myself, and it's left me with an exposed meekness.

I wonder if sighted people experience the same disorientation from riding in a wheelchair. If not, perhaps this is comparable to the games people play blindfolded where they spin until they can no longer stand upright. Or more likely it's because of the relentless overwhelming sensations I've been experiencing since waking up. She is patient and calm, but I think Taz may secretly be hiding a love for speed. I almost want to ask her to stop so I can take a break, but I think adapting to the change in motion would be even more difficult to deal with than this is.

"We're almost there, but we have to take the elevator up." Her sympathetic tone tells me that I'm inadequate when it comes to keeping my distress hidden.

"It's fine," I say, as she pushes the chair over the threshold.

I may have spoken too soon; fine is not the most accurate word. As soon as the elevator starts descending, my stomach follows suit. I hold my breath as if doing so will remove the intense crushing feeling that encumbers me. Alongside the sinking feeling in the pit of my stomach is a bizarre psychological sensation where my body feels like it's sinking deep into the chair. The anticipated ding sounds off and she pushes me onto the floor.

Thank God, I think, forcibly exhaling the breath I was holding.

"Tristan..." She says, sounding uncertain. "Are... are you afraid of elevators?"

No, I don't think so.

All at once, the realization hits me. I'm unable to find my voice to provide her with an answer. Taking another deep breath, I focus on steadying myself. Her observational skills are making mine look like a disgrace. Everything I rediscover about myself discredits the idea of being an assassin.

"We made it!" She exclaims, but she stops abruptly, jerking the wheelchair. Her voice is unrecognizable when she says, "Josephine, what are you doing here?"

"I am just here as an observer, Tessa," the rude woman retorts. "Is that a problem?"

"You know I don't like that name. Please refrain from using it." Taz's frustration is clear in her voice. She continues pushing the chair into the room. "And yes, it is. You're not involved in these studies."

"Neither are you, but here we are," Josephine snidely replies.

"I am just lending a hand. Your observations aren't needed." The growing tension between the women is so thick it's suffocating.

"Is everything okay?" asks the rapid-talking man who was with Josephine the day she was pestering Gaddreol. He feebly attempted to convince her to leave Gaddreol alone. Although judging from how quickly he gave up, his resolve might be weaker than my eyesight.

"Samuel, yes, everything is great. We were waiting for you to get started." Josephine's voice turns sickly sweet.

"Oh, alright. Well, Tristan. Is it Tristan? Doesn't matter. You're here for experiments with your blindness, yes? Bring him over here, Taz. This is going to be mildly uncomfortable. There might even be some pain. Are you ready?" He says everything in nearly one breath.

Mildly uncomfortable, sure.

Without allowing me much time to process the words, he plunges a needle into my left eye. The blatant euphemism leaves me severely unprepared for the molten lava released directly into my eye. From the deepest depths of hell, a coalescence of screams, shrieks, and growls rip through my body into the condensed space of my throat, and out of the small opening of my mouth.

I'm going to die! Panic shreds through every line of defense I've created.

Every muscle in my body contracts in response to the pain my mind simply cannot comprehend. I can hear cracking sounds in my mouth from the weight of my clenched jaw. Instinctively, my hands reach for my eyes to claw them from their sockets. I'll do anything to stop this excruciating pain.

Mustering all of the strength I can bring forth, I grip the arms of the wheelchair. Digging my nails so hard into the fabric I rip through the first leather layer, then into the second foam layer, until my nails are just scraping against the metal frame.

Make it stop, please. Just make it stop! Send me back to my non-existence! I beg, hoping anyone, everyone, can miraculously hear my frantic thoughts.

I pass out momentarily from the pain, long enough that the same molten lava ignites every nerve in my right eye propelling me back into consciousness. My voice is nearly gone from the first stream of screams, but more ragged screams rip through me. This time it's a mix of gravelly, guttural growls and feeble shrieks that force their way out of me.

The raw, searing pain in my fingers pales in comparison, but the occasional twinges pull my attention away from the lava ravaging the inside of my eyes. The muscles throughout my body are constricting so much that it feels like I'm practicing rigor mortis.

Please, please, kill me! Let this torture end.

"Is it supposed to hurt that much!?" Taz yells, but I can't focus on her voice well enough to hear it clearer than a distorted whisper.

I hope not.

In between the strained, forced noises shredding my insides are rapid gasps. Breathing hurts nearly as much as the raw screams, but it's still hardly noticeable compared to the excruciating liquid that's swirling around inside my eyes.

I can't catch my breath. I can't think.

All I can manage to do is feel. Feel the molten lava obliterating my eyes. Feel my nails shredding against the metal frame—the only thing stopping me from digging my eyes from their cavities. Feel my destroyed, raw throat dutifully carry unidentifiable sounds out of my body. Feel the ragged breaths like mini explosions going off in my chest.

The euphemism Sai said to Gaddreol finds its way into my mind. *"These are rigorous tests that most would not wish to be subjected to."* Then the straightforward words he spoke to me follow. *"Many of these tests will be excruciatingly painful."* I wish I had recalled them before the onslaught of scorching liquid fire pooled into my eyes. Despite Sai being direct with me it's still a massive understatement.

I'll keep my blindness, I think, pure exhaustion taking over me.

All the strength in my body evaporates, causing my head to fall forward, my chin nestling uncomfortably into my chest. A constant, low hum of electricity covers every inch of my body. My screams dwindle to incoherent mumbling and my body falls lax. My breaths are still ragged and rough, but they're not on the verge of a panic attack. I do the only thing I can do; I listen. The voices around me are distorted and distant.

"Thank you, Samuel, for that brilliant display," Josephine says. "It was a pleasure, as always."

"What is wrong with you?" Taz asks. "What did you do?"

Faintly, I can hear footsteps, hopefully belonging to Taz, closing the distance to the chair that is doing its best to hold me together in one piece. She asks me if I'm okay, but I lack the strength to perform even the most basic action. I want to beg her to take me away from this room, to anywhere but here, but all my energy was forcibly eradicated from my body, so I'm stuck here at everyone's discretion.

"What happened?" Sai's panicked voice sounds just as distant and distorted as the others, but I know he is at my side. I can hardly feel his touch through the electrifying sensation prickling all over my body.

"Samuel was doing what you asked him to do, isn't that right?" The sinister edge in Josephine's voice should make me uneasy, but I simply don't have it in me to feel anything.

"Samuel?" Sai's voice is both pleading and irate.

"I did exactly as you asked of me. I included him in the studies. I injected his eyes with these syringes like you wanted. Maybe a little more than you insisted, but I did what I was told." A soft thud causes a grunt from the rambling man, but it gets him to stop talking.

"How much did you put in there?" Sai's words are strained as he tries to stifle his anger. It sounds like he bumps into things, knocking them over presumably to frantically grab one of the syringes. "Show me."

After moments of silence, even through the distortion, I hear a hard, violent thud that I presume is a punch. Sai starts hauling the chair off somewhere in a hurry and I hear the start of a muddled argument between the two women until the distance is too great.

He stops the chair, picks me up, and puts me onto an empty bed. Carefully, puppeteering my limp body into place. The last thing I hear is Sai saying, "Everything is going to be okay."

I don't know how much time passes before I'm awake again. My eyes flutter open, but I remain still, trying to process what I'm feeling or what I'm supposed to feel.

I don't think, when I agreed to this, that I truly understood how utterly exhausting this transition process is. I certainly would not have subjected myself to any sort of molten hot liquid in my eye if I had known the extent of the pain I would endure. At least the agonizing pain is gone now. The prickly electrical sensation is gone now, too. Everything is gone; in its place is just a numbness that covers my entire body.

With less effort than I expected, I sit up. The blanket Sai made for me hugs my body, causing a smile to touch my lips. I extend my arm to the side of the bed to find the table is stocked with more food. My stomach grumbles so I eagerly grab whatever is closest to my hand.

I'm acutely aware of the bandages wrapped tightly around my fingers. After several awkward attempts, I finally fumble my way to success. My reward is a sandwich. At this point, I feel so ravenous it doesn't even matter what kind.

"Woah! My god!" Taz's half scream and distraught voice snaps my attention to her.

With half-chewed food I forgot about still in my mouth, I try to ask, "What's wrong?"

My words sound more like Scooby Doo trying to talk and less like a coherent question. Quickly, covering my mouth, I swallow the food. Before I can ask something else, I hear fast-approaching footsteps echoing in, presumably, the hallway.

"Sai, was that supposed to happen?" Taz asks, worried.

"No, it wasn't," he states. "Tristan, can you see anything?"

"Um, no," I say, feeling guilty.

I went through with this trial, experiencing something that's far more excruciating than anyone, me included, can comprehend. To make matters worse, the effects were unavailing, hardly anything more than an ineffective torturous experiment that I never want to participate in again.

"Are you alright?" Taz asks.

"Much better, now. Thanks. What's wrong?" I ask, coherently, this time.

"The irises of your eyes are orange. Vibrant, glowing, orange," Sai says, sounding truly confused.

My mind scans over the visual fragments that I experienced to find the color orange. The closest thing would be Avery's amber eyes without the radiation, of course. Behind his eyes, I try to imagine a light source to produce a glow effect, but nothing substantial makes the orange glow.

Unexpected silence cloaks the room with an air of mystique and uncertainty. Neither of the doctors can comprehend why my eyes are now radioactive orbs. From their startled reactions, it's highly unlikely something like this has happened before.

"Sai, this is an adjacent topic, but did you punch Samuel?"

The question brings with it an undeniable shift in the room from confusion to anger. Immediately I regret asking the question. Not only because of the energy shift, but I realize how impeccable my timing for saying the worst things is when an unrecognizable voice calls into the room.

"Taz, you're needed for an awakening."

Sai waits until Taz follows the unknown person down the hall. Then he answers, "Unashamedly, yes. I am sorry. I would never have left you with him if I had known he was capable of conducting the trials with full abandon of his professionalism."

"It's okay," is all I can manage to say.

Hardly the correct response, but what else do you say to the man who is internally beating himself up for all the horrific events that have occurred? The guilt he has must be astronomical.

He grabs something large and pulls it to the side of the bed. He sits down and I realize it's a chair. He crosses his arms beside my leg, and lays his head on my lap, his hair grazing lightly against my skin. Ignoring the bandages, I rub his head, hoping it provides him with the comfort my words lack.

CHAPTER ELEVEN

"HOLY HELL, TRISTAN! Are you okay?" A voice disturbs the calm. An indeterminate time passes before I realize the voice is Avery's.

I'm on my side, dozing in and out of lucidity. Sai is passed out, lightly snoring with his head pressed against my chest. He wakes abruptly, finally sensing the other man in the room.

"Sorry, I didn't mean to wake you, but Jesus Christ."

Sai yawns and I can feel him stretching against the edge of the bed. "Oh, no. You are fine."

My eyes open, causing Avery to gasp loudly. "What happened to you? To your hands? T-to your eyes?"

My attention is drawn to both body parts that he mentions, a sharp pulsing pain radiates in my fingertips while an intense all-encompassing burning fills my eyes. I wince involuntarily. The pain steadily increases in intensity, causing my face to contort.

Sai rises to his feet and returns, placing a hand gently on my head. "Lean your head back and keep your eyes open."

I follow his directions, feeling a couple of eye drops filling each eye. The liquid is cool and soothing, instantly subduing the pain in my eyes. "Thank you."

I open my mouth to ask for more medication for the pulsing in my fingers, but he speaks before I can. "I am adding medicine to the IV for your hands."

I can't help but feel my lips curl upwards. *He's always prepared.*

Sai fills Avery in on the chaotic situation. "Samuel proceeded with the experiment while I was performing a transition. I had no idea Josephine was going to be there to manipulate Samuel, nor that he would blatantly attempt to maim or kill Tristan under her influence."

"The little shit is her puppet. If I get my hands on him," he says, through gritted teeth, trying to stay calm as he listens.

The guilt is still thick in Sai's voice, but he continues. "Instead of

Transcendence Theory

the half milliliter, he put five milliliters in both eyes. His fingers are bandaged because when he redirected the instinctive reaction to claw his eyes out, he hollowed out the chair."

I wince, remembering the horrific clawing. Sai takes notice and puts his hand on top of my arm. I reach for his hand and gently hold my bandaged hand above it.

"If it provides some clarity, the metal frame he was gripping and clawing is stripped of the paint and has some indentations now. The same cannot be said about the extensive damage to his fingers. They are obviously worse than a little lost paint and indentations. Tristan's condition is stable; everything has been flushed out of his system, and all wounds are tended to. The unexplainable eye color I am at a loss for."

"Normally, I'd make a joke about it, but, man, that just sucks. I'm sorry. Just half a milliliter is bad enough. You okay?" Avery genuinely sounds concerned. Trying to feign enthusiasm, he adds, "Your eyes look cool, at least."

There seems to be no shortage of chaos surrounding my life at the moment. In a sea of unrelenting mayhem, I am so appreciative of Sai and everything he does for me. Right now, that appreciation extends to the usually obnoxious man as well. He is doing his best to hold himself together and attempt to be an integral part of my reintegration despite being so distraught at his circumstances.

As if to cement my rambling, Avery says, "That's not why I'm here, but I'm sorry you're dealing with all this shit. Including, no, especially, all that I did to you. I shouldn't have treated you with contempt. I shouldn't have been jealous of you—your survival, I mean, but I was."

"Thank you," I say, sinking back as much as I can into the rigid mattress. "With everything you've been put through, I don't blame you for anything you've felt towards me."

"Thanks. I'm actually here to ask if you would spend time with Vera tomorrow," he says, reluctantly. "But with everything you have been through today, I'll think of something to tell her so you have time to recover."

Vera wants to spend time with Gaddreol.

Something I had not even considered since Avery initially asked me to pretend to be him for her sake. Do I even have it in me to pretend to be him? I've spent about a month with him, but I don't think I have enough charisma and charm to convince her that I'm her older brother.

"I do not think Vera seeing Tristan—Gaddreol—in this state is a good idea. It will just cause unnecessary worry." Sai's matter-of-fact tone returns. "They are still looking for a new body to transition him into."

"What happened to his body, Sai?" Avery asks. Just asking the question seems to bring the usually self-assured man to tears. I assumed he'd know what Gaddreol's body is being used for, but it makes sense he would distance himself in any way he can from the horrors involved if given the chance.

"His body was given to the research team. I will check with them if they are finished with it."

"I hate this fucking place." A defeated sigh escapes the broken man. "I doubt they're going to leave his body in a usable condition."

Usable condition, I repeat, unwilling to say the possibilities aloud, my mind wanders. I ponder the ridiculous ideas that might make that statement an undeniable reality.

Without any ramifications for potential screw ups, there isn't any reason to be cautious. So they could be trialing previously untested medications, which could be causing adverse effects. Perhaps they are pushing the limits of dosages—not unlike Samuel's apparent gross negligence. A little more barbaric in thought, but they could be experimenting on limb removal and reattachment. Another morbid idea comes to mind of them repeatedly killing and reviving the body, testing the effects after so many resurrections.

"I know, Avery. We will figure things out." Sai sounds sympathetic "If you stay here with Tristan, I'll go ahead and talk with the research department."

"Yeah, definitely. I can do that." Avery tries to hide his hope, trying to not become too excited at the possibility that Gaddreol may have his body back. "Thanks, man."

The absurd thought of me being a contract killer pops into my head. So scary that I require a babysitter. I guess anyone who has been deliberately attacked would need a babysitter, even with sight. Or at least protection.

My memories can't come soon enough, though. I'd like to know how I'm supposed to be this fearless, potentially revered assassin. Right now, I'm anything but. Not that remembering the kills I have performed will bring me a sense of relief, but I am tired of feeling afraid, confused, and overwhelmed.

"Of course," he says, stepping out of the room.

Avery sits down on the chair that Sai pulled next to the bed. "You alright?"

"Yeah, I'm fine," I say, dismissively. It's not entirely a lie, since I survived the most agonizingly painful experience of my life, so I'd say I'm doing pretty well.

"What about emotionally?"

His question disarms me, stripping away the defenses I created after the string of overwhelming breakdowns. I just shake my head, not trusting my voice.

"Yeah, me, too."

The conversation shifting to his emotional state helps me find my voice. "Gaddreol will make it through this. After surviving nearly a month with my ceaseless thoughts, he can survive anything."

A sense of accomplishment surges through me as I manage to weasel a laugh out of Avery. Something I wasn't even sure he was capable of. It's a pleasant sound to hear after all the hellish noises I made a bit ago.

"Ah, you don't seem that annoying to listen to."

"When disembodied sounds are the only thing you can use to decipher the world around you, recounting it constantly is probably pretty frustrating to listen to all the time. But he took it in stride, always listening to what I thought," I say, a soft smile curls at the corners of my mouth.

"Not that he had much choice." Avery laughs again, a sound I am grateful to hear. "He's always been like that, though. Always there for everyone in every way he can. No matter what, he always showed up for everyone."

The somber tone infiltrates his voice again. No doubt reliving the moment he abandoned Gaddreol during one of the most frightening experiences he's had. My outstretched hand reaches to the spot I heard him move his hand to last. Upon finding it, I gently place my tightly wrapped hand on top of his. I'm unsure how comforting that can really be, but he doesn't move.

"He doesn't blame you."

"I know. He always sees the good in everyone. Even me after I treated him—and you—like absolute shit. I treated the love of my life with absolute disdain because of my own self-loathing." His voice shares an insight into the mental torment inside his mind.

"Your anger may have been displaced, but beating yourself up about it right now doesn't help him. Nor does it particularly benefit you."

He rolls his hand over, wrapping it loosely around mine, hopefully, giving him the slightest bit of comfort since my face is the last one Gaddreol wore. I don't move, allowing him to outline the bandages.

He shifts a little closer to me. "I feel so bad for wishing he wasn't transferred out of your body. You deserve a life, too. But if he didn't transition out of your body... Maybe this wouldn't have happened."

"You're not alone in that thought process. I almost wish he never transitioned from my body. Gaddreol doesn't deserve the existence he's been forced into, and I'd do anything to get him back." My voice cracks as I force back the tears that sting the creases of my eyes. If it weren't for the soothing drops, the tears would be reigniting the unrelenting fire.

"My uncontrolled anger destroyed me inside and out and I did despicable things I can't take back because of it. The shit I did to Gaddreol, and to you, can't be taken back. I can't take back the jealousy I had towards you. Or that I demeaned your life because you lived while my brother didn't." The pain is riddled in every word he speaks. "You deserve to live just as much as Gaddreol does and my brother and anyone else that lost their life to this sick fucking place."

Avery puts things into perspective for me that I hadn't thought about. *Why should Gaddreol's life be deemed more important than mine to me? Why didn't I consider how utterly devastated Sai would feel if Gaddreol was in my place instead? Never once did I think about the trepidation Sai was likely wracked with during the entirety of the transition process. Or the lingering dread that must have persisted until my survival was confirmed. It was something I foolishly overlooked. Avery's desolation is no more important than what Sai would feel if he were faced with the same position, but wishing Gaddreol to take my place is contradictory to that.*

My introspection is likely evident on my face if Avery's actions are any indication. He grabs my hand with both of his and pulls it to him. He presses his forehead firmly against my wrapped fingers, and his thick brows cause a ticklish sensation against the exposed skin of my hand.

"I don't deserve him, but God, I miss him," he says.

"I miss him, too," I admit, aloud.

He tilts his head down as he releases one of his hands from mine. After readjusting himself, his hand rests on my cheek for a moment.

He quickly removes it before bringing it back, pressing something small against my cheek.

Gaddreol.

"Thank you, Avery," I whisper.

With my free hand, I put it over the hand against my cheek. It's just a small vial, sure. But it's Gaddreol—his entire essence—right here with me, again. Although it's impossible to see the enigmatic beauty that's inside the capsule, Avery allowing me this closeness is comparable, if not preferable. Silent tears fall without resistance, stinging my eyes. Ignoring the discomfort, I fixate on the tiny object pressed lightly against my cheek.

"Am I interrupting something?"

Avery stiffens at the sound of Sai's voice, but he doesn't make any sudden movements. My movements are far more frantic and rushed as embarrassment creeps over me, dropping my hand from my cheek and pulling my other swiftly out of his loose grasp. A mistake my fingers are paying for as throbbing pain rips through my fingers. Carefully, he brings his free hand up to my face and slowly pulls away the small vial.

"I was showing him Gaddreol," Avery says, shifting away from me.

"His body is relatively intact," Sai states matter-of-factly.

"Relatively, meaning what?" Avery asks, jumping to his feet.

"His body is a double amputee now," Sai says, monotonously. "The director needs to approve getting his body back to transition into."

My head drops. *I wasn't serious about the limb removal. I didn't think it would actually happen.*

A heavy sigh escapes Avery, most likely an attempt to quell the rage trying to bubble inside him. "I knew it'd be some shit like that. It was stupid to be hopeful that it wouldn't be."

The director truly is a puppet master. Pulling all of the strings to strategically set up the stage to his perfection. With what Avery said about him before, I highly doubt he would agree to Gaddreol getting his body back—amputee or not.

Maybe Gaddreol's tenacity wore off on me, I think, as I find my voice, and ask, "What if I speak to the director?"

* * *

Neither Sai nor Avery agreed with my idea to confront the director myself. I understand their reservations and honestly, I am not even sure what came over me to be that assertive. The more time I have to ponder my own suggestion, the more misguided it seems to have been. The director is a man of self-importance who would view me as nothing more than an insignificant pest.

It's highly unlikely he would accept an invitation for an audience with me. To pull off something like that I'll need to provide something of value to him, which is practically impossible until I'm able to remember who I am. That thought implies there's something inside me that leads me to think that I do in fact have something of note to offer. A man of his caliber who's mastered the art of deception and extortion has no need for someone as insignificant as me.

Hopefully, when my memories return to me, I will have something valuable that will pique his interest. Until then, my surroundings will remain at the forefront of my focus. Starting with the burning pain radiating through my splintered fingers. Sai is rebandaging them for me and each faint touch is as abrasive as the surface of a brick scraping across my fingertips. I resist the urge to recoil by gritting my teeth to keep as still as possible.

"I am almost done."

Sai seems to distance himself from things that bring him some discomfort. Likely to suppress any potential negative response he might have. Undoubtedly, a defense mechanism, but whether he developed it because of his childhood or more recently due to the prevailing circumstances, I can't be sure. Does it offer protection against his perceived frailties?

"Why are you looking so pensive?" he asks, inquisitively.

"You," I say, answering honestly.

"Me? What about me?" Curiosity breaks through his rigidity.

The shift in his demeanor warms my heart and brings a smile to my face. However, my rumination is not nearly as heartwarming. It's more of a demoralizing dissection of his personality than a favorable interpretation.

I shake my head with a soft objection. "It's unimportant. Just a circuitous way of trying to remember who you are, and indirectly who I am."

His melodious laugh returns before he says, "Understandable."

The absence of conversation allows the unfortunate displeasure of focusing on the radiating pain in my fingertips, again. A nervous feeling twists my stomach, which makes me want to fidget with my fingers.

Ignoring the strong urge, I focus on the nervousness, finding the courage to say, "About yesterday. I want to apologize for…"

My voice fades. *What do I want to apologize for? The moment Avery and I shared with Gaddreol? The embarrassing reaction I had to his presence?*

He drops my hands from his and wraps his arms around me.

"Tristan, you don't have any reason to apologize," he says softly pressing his forehead against mine. "When I first walked in, I was confused, but I know that you share an intimacy with Gaddreol that I may never understand. After what I put you through, I'd honestly expect nothing less."

My face relaxes and my shoulders slump against his body. I wrap my arms loosely around his waist. I was apologizing for the moment with Avery, but Sai's right. The moment with Avery could only occur because of the closeness I have with Gaddreol.

Without him with me, there is an exposed hole, like an integral part of myself is missing. Gaddreol's existence is unintentionally disparaged by my callous inarticulacy, but he has become a piece of the puzzle that is my being.

The separation made it possible for the darkness to not feel as forlorn and unwelcoming as it was inside my inescapable prison. Now, it provides a sense of serenity that was previously impossible to grasp. Unfortunately, though, alongside my dark tranquility is a grim melancholy that overshadows me; a loneliness I didn't expect to feel once gaining full access to my body again.

"Thank you for being understanding," I say, tightening my arms around him.

"I asked this of you," he states. "The least I can do is attempt to understand what you are going through right now."

"I'm sorry for being so emotionally distraught," I say, but I'm not even sure what I'm apologizing for.

Closing the space between us, I press our bodies firmly together. He gently brushes his lips against mine. I deepen the kiss, eagerly pressing my lips harder, melding with his. His hands are fervently caressing the small of my back. A shiver runs up my spine, leaving goosebumps in its wake. His touch is passionate and electrifying.

He pulls away, breathing heavily. "Your emotional state is nearly unassailable. The resolve you have is admirable."

I assume that's his way of trying to comfort me, since we both know that isn't true. This may be the most vulnerable I've ever been. I'd laugh if I weren't so overwhelmed by my very assailable emotional state.

"Right now, my emotional state is fragile," I say, and he tightens his embrace.

"A little faltering is to be expected with the numerous things you have experienced over the past month. The strength you display is extraordinary. Allow yourself a little bit more time to reacclimate," he says pressing his lips against my forehead.

"I never got a chance to tell you," I begin to explain, trying to bring forth the beautiful colors I've grown to love. "Through a couple of Gaddreol's dreams, I witnessed the absolute beauty of the world. The unbelievable synergy between lights and shapes to create an awe-inspiring picture is a mystifying phenomenon I never imagined I could experience."

"Tristan!" he exclaims. "That's fantastic! I didn't think that was possible! What did you get to see?"

There's a soft knock at the door, followed by Taz's anxious voice. "I really hate to break up your cute moment, but I have to tell you the director is demanding a meeting with Tristan."

Immediately, there's a palpable shift in the air, from a feathery lightness to the condensed heaviness, making it harder to breathe. Maybe that's more from the lingering intensity of our kiss, though.

The phrase "be careful what you wish for" comes to mind. When I suggested approaching the director I felt a tentative confidence. However, with the situation flipped, I feel a foreboding trepidation. Now that he has requested my presence, I don't have leverage to help me navigate this meeting. I suppose that was never something I had to begin with, but if I had been able to request his audience, that could have been misconstrued.

"I am sorry. I do not mean to interrupt your fantastic news," he says.

I shake my head and wave a hand. I remove my arms from him and place them carefully in my lap as he sits back, dropping his arms from my waist.

Sai turns his attention to Taz and asks, "Do you know what this meeting pertains to?"

From what I've learned about the director, his question almost feels rhetorical in nature. The director seems like a man who only divulges enough vague information to get things done and nothing more.

That doesn't stop me from thinking of the potential questions. *How was it discovered that souls could be extracted? How did you discover souls could be placed into new bodies once extracted? Why don't you use synthetic bodies instead of living people?*

"I don't. I'm sorry." Her voice is timid. "I do know he is allowing you to wait until tomorrow morning."

"This room is being monitored because of me," I remark. "While you were helping with a transition, I suggested a meeting with the director."

The room being monitored was a massive misjudgement. Why an obvious thing escaped me, and everyone else, is beyond me. It can probably be chalked up to logic and rationale being eclipsed by the intense emotions, though.

If his familiar fragrance serves me right, Sai hasn't experienced transitioning firsthand. Outside of Avery, I don't think anyone else is closely intertwined with the experiments. He may have been the only one with any inkling of the devastation that follows. Not to mention the traumatic failed transition that overshadows all of it.

"You are right. I apologize for my lack of awareness." Sai's voice is almost indescribable, but I assume he's feeling shame or regret. He pulls away from me, standing upright. "Unfortunately, I cannot see where a camera would be placed."

"Sai, look," Taz says, moving toward the area she's talking about. "It's inside the console."

Sai's body tenses as he whispers unintelligible expletives, then says, "Shut it off, please."

"Tristan," He sits back down in the bedside chair, placing his hand gently on my leg. "Why did you suggest a meeting?"

Honestly, I haven't figured that one out myself. I can't stop my facial expression from displaying my uncertainty. My brows crease and my lips pull into a thin-lipped frown. "I doubt there is anything I can say that would appeal to the director, but I owe it to Gaddreol to at least try."

He exhales loudly, before saying, "Unfortunately, now that he has requested your attendance, you will have to meet with him."

I can hear the defeat in his voice and feel the subtle tremors rippling throughout his body. The man who lacks typical emotional responses is terrified of the orchestrator behind this dysfunctional symphony. When it comes to the grandeur of the deranged man behind the scenes my apprehension is not misplaced.

"Will you be okay, Tristan?" Taz asks, sounding as frightened as Sai. At this point, it feels like the only thing I've managed to accomplish is causing emotional turmoil within everyone around me.

Will I be? "According to what I've been told about my life, this should be an easy task." Although my words hold the truth, they're still hidden deep within me.

I feel a shift in Sai's stance, his fear evaporating in an instant. "Taz, will you stay here with Tristan? I need to retrieve more things."

Presumably, she gives Sai a nod, since he abruptly rises to his feet, giving me a quick kiss on the cheek.

"I'll be back soon."

CHAPTER TWELVE

"ARE YOU OKAY?" Taz sounds uncharacteristically uncomfortable. "Your eyes and hands, I mean."

My attention is drawn to the stinging pain nagging my eyes and the dull pulsing vibrating through my fingertips. Absently, I hold my hands up to my face as if to examine them. "They're recovering, but still borderline unbearable. The bandages are less restrictive now, but moving my fingers causes radiating pain. The burning in my eyes is still excruciating without the eye drops."

"I'm so glad you're doing okay." I feel her sink into the bedside chair. "After what happened with Gaddreol... I was so worried."

The immense pain was all I could focus on. By the time it was over I didn't have enough mental capacity to grasp the severe danger my life was in. If it weren't for Sai's quick wit and natural ability to remain calm under stress, I don't know what the outcome would have been. How would I have reacted if I had known how close I was to death? The death that I had accepted not too long ago.

"Sai is exceptional. Can you tell me what he looks like?" I ask impulsively before I can fully process asking at all.

"Tell you what he looks like? Sure, but you've been blind since you were born, right?" she asks, sounding utterly perplexed.

"Yes, but with Gaddreol I was able to experience dreams that were accompanied by sight. I know what Vera and Avery look like, although the images have all but disappeared. When I try to recall images or colors, I can see shattered fragments of it or unfocused strands of colors." My uncontained excitement forces a smile to take over my features.

"What?! That's amazing!" She yells, excitedly.

"While the only definitive pictures I can kind of access are what was shared with me in the dreams, I have a slightly clearer idea of what things are now. I should have a decent perception of what he looks like," explaining a little further.

However, I think it's mostly directed at myself. An undisguised attempt to remind myself not to feel discouraged if I can't visualize a mental image. I take a deep breath to calm the nerves I can feel growing restless.

"Okay, so you said you saw Avery, right? He and Sai are similar in stature. They're both tall and muscular, but I think Sai is a smidge taller. His skin tone is closer to Vera's. A light tan, but not as golden as hers. His hair is short, straight, and dark brown with lighter brown highlights. He has an oval face, bright blue eyes and thick, rounded eyebrows, and a prominent nose." She excitedly spouts all the words. Her hands are animated, waving around my vicinity, so much so I can feel slight gusts of air against my face. "Did you get all that?"

Taz's description allows my mind to splice pieces of Avery's and Vera's appearances to form my own frankensteined picture of Sai. Despite the woven image being the most monstrous version ever concocted of Sai, knowing what he looks like brings me immense joy.

"He is beautiful," I say with a peaceful smile resting on my face.

"He is, isn't he?" The smile in her voice is tangible.

"Do you have a partner?" I ask, feeling crass for inquiring about her personal life. "I apologize, that was probably rude."

"Me? No way. It's not rude to ask questions, how else would we get to know each other." She giggles with little snorts here and there. I can't help but laugh with her.

Her genuine laugh is boisterous and infectious, causing me to join in. My rolling laugh reinvigorates hers until a nonsensical bout of laughter continues to roll between the two of us. Every time one of us calms down, the infection bounces back in a continuous fit of hysterics. The octaves of my laughter increase until it's so intense that I'm laughing without sound coming at all. Taz does the same and she starts playfully smacking my chest.

Soon, we're just a heap of two people struggling to breathe. The muscles in my stomach contract from the sudden fit of laughter and tears well into my eyes again. I'm sure she is experiencing similar sensations.

When she catches her breath, she says, "I tried dating while I was in college. It was a disaster."

"Really?" I'm doubled over from joyous pain, but I spew more rude words before I can stop myself, "I figured you wouldn't have difficulty with dating."

"Wipe that worried look off your face!" She playfully smacks my arm. "You're too proper, like Sai. Loosen up a little!"

"I'm sorry. It is presumptuous to speculate about people, but for the last month it's all I've been able to do." Heat creeps into my cheeks.

"Don't worry so much." She giggles softly. "I'm an open book, so you can ask me anything!"

I open my mouth to say something, but nothing comes out. The embarrassment of being put on the spot mutes me.

Thankfully, she takes control of the conversation. "Well, about my lack of difficulty with dating, you're right. Dating was easy for me, but I didn't enjoy it. The cuteness between you and Sai is not something I want for myself."

"You don't want romance?"

"Nah." The air from the wave of her hand gently sweeps across my cheek. "Friendships are great. Romance, ah, not so much."

"That isn't lonely for you?" I ask, feeling incredibly rude, but also intrigued, which is apparently winning against my respectful nature.

"Not in the least. I'm happy with my friends and furballs. While I wouldn't mind having a few more of those, intimate relationships just don't do it for me." She laughs again, before adding, "Besides, who can be lonely when they have two cats impatiently waiting for them every day?"

"Cats? What are they like?"

She claps her hands together with a little gasp. "Butler is a fancy tuxedo cat. He's a black cat with a large white patch on his chest, but he has a cute little black bow-tie mark on his chest. His name is refined, but he's not. Truffle is a tortoiseshell calico. She's mostly dark brown with beige and light brown splotches coating her body. She's kinda lazy, always lounging."

I'd like to appreciate what she is describing about her cats, but there's nothing that stands out as memorable that I can visualize. I don't have a depiction of cats, just the vague clusters of colors she mentions. The texture of cat fur isn't something I can recollect either, so my only working knowledge of them is that they're fluffy animals with exuberant tails.

"Sounds like the two make quite the pair."

"Yeah, they're a handful, but the highlight of my night is going home to them." She lets out a sigh and sags into the bedside chair that creaks with the movement. "The only thing that's been good about working here is being friends with Sai and Avery."

"I'm glad you are friends with Sai and Avery. I think they needed you in their life." A large smile spreads across my face. "Everyone could use someone like you.

"Thanks! That's too kind of you," she says, dismissing my words with another wave.

"Can I ask you the dreaded question?" The higher octave of my voice startles me. "I'm sorry, that may be too forward."

She lets out a chuckle before saying, "I promise you don't have to be so reserved around me, even though it's a little endearing. Go for it."

The boldness I managed to squeak out is nearly gone despite her encouragement. My hands twitch, wanting to rub together from the rapidly growing anxiety. Exhaling deeply, I calm myself enough to ask, "How did you get involved with this deplorable organization?"

"Well, if it makes you feel better, it isn't anything like Avery." She speaks his name with a tinge of hollow sadness. "When I was told about the experiment, I shared it with my mom right away. She was excited about it. She fell off a ladder and messed up her back. Two back surgeries later and her back was still in too much pain to do anything. So, the director signed her up and I signed my life away to FREE. Ironic, really."

"Does she know?"

"About the kidnapping? God, no. I didn't know about that part until after I saw her." Her voice sounds hollow again. "She was transitioned into a woman I thought was a patient. A thirty-four-year-old brunette. All of that is really gross as-is, but I feel bad for being weirded out by the fact my mom is just a few years older than me now."

"I can imagine how major an adjustment that was for you along with the massive revelation."

"You have no idea," she says, voice returning to normal. "My mom has been loving life again. Going out with friends and she's even dating again."

A disabled woman likely in her late forties, early fifties is now in her mid-thirties again. It reminds me of when I questioned the legality of my own situation. Is she legally the same person she was before transitioning? Or did she take the identity of the kidnapped woman? Was a new, fabricated identification provided for her? The latter two questions don't make sense if she's not aware of her situation, though.

"What are the legalities of that?"

"Honestly, I don't know the ins and outs, but I do know her new body is written off as cosmetic surgery."

Cosmetic surgery is something that never crossed my mind. It's a perfect cover up for the extreme 'changes' of the individual. That begs the question, though; what happens when a loved one of the unwilling participants spots them in public? A question that may never get an answer.

Taz is involved with the organization through coercion. While her situation isn't as harrowing as Avery's, to see your mom wearing the face of the patient you were treating is horrifying in its own right. Not to mention the adjustment it must have been to see her mom as a much younger woman than she likely ever remembers.

The fact that she is attached to this vile place through threats and blackmail might mean Sai is in a similar position. Now that I think about it, I'm not sure how or why he is involved at all, just that he requested my help for it. Is Sai in the same body he's always had or is he discreetly hidden due to my innate blindness and memory loss?

Speaking of Sai, his entrance is a sudden assault on my senses. The unmistakable greasy aroma from fast food fills the room, and my nose, as the door cracks open. Paper bags loudly crumple between him and the door he is pushing open. Taz gets up to help, calming the crumpling sounds instantly. He drops everything into a condensed spot on the bedside table, creating a loud bang that snaps against my eardrums. My hands defensively cover my ears.

"I'm sorry! If it wasn't for the last-minute decision to get food, the files would be neatly organized." He kisses the top of my head, bringing the overpowering salty grease smell closer to me. I resist the urge to plug my nose as he hands me a box of fries.

"Thank you for the food."

I force a weak grin, hiding the queasy feeling swirling inside my stomach. I'm not sure if the sick feeling is from the abrupt sensory overload or the atrocious smell. Despite my protesting stomach, I shove the offending fries into my mouth. The sublime saltiness of the shoestring potatoes soothes the ill feelings.

"Here you go, Taz."

"Aw, thanks! I'm going to eat on the way out. Gotta get back to my house." She rises to her feet. "I'll stop by Avery's again to check on him."

"Thank you," Sai says, plainly. My mind fills in the blank space of his appreciation. '...for looking after Tristan and Avery.'

"My pleasure. Also, good luck tomorrow. I'm going to treat Vera to a girls' day. Fill me in on everything, okay?"

Presumably, Sai gives a quiet affirmation as she closes the door behind her without another word.

Vera. I haven't forgotten about Avery's request for me to visit her acting as her older brother. It feels wrong to be grateful for the horrific trial preventing me from being able to fulfill that request. Going through that pain again would be far easier than pretending to be the man who is her favorite person in the world—her best friend. The upcoming meeting with one of the most sadistic men in the world is less daunting than impersonating Gaddreol.

Even after being with him for a month and feeling as though he is a part of me, I do not think I can competently act like him to deliver a convincing performance. I fear that no matter how well I do, it will still feel deceptive.

A partially unwrapped burger is placed in my hand. I can't help the smile that forms on my face as I say, "Thanks, gorgeous."

"What?" Sai asks, bemused.

"Taz described how you look to me. It's not the most accurate, but from what I could assemble, you are beautiful." Satisfaction isn't the feeling I anticipated, but I'm pleased to create a semi-cohesive picture by piecing the fragments together. "Hopefully, this doesn't come off as rude, but is your body the one I've always known you to have?"

"Thank you. And no, it is not rude. The answer is yes." The tone is inquisitive as if he knows it is leading to another question. I can feel his eyes watching me. He waits patiently for my question.

"How did you get involved with this horrible place?" I drop my head. The answer isn't something I'm ready to hear, but I need to.

His hand rests on my leg, a comforting gesture I didn't realize I needed. *He always knows what I need, even before I do.*

"At first it was procedural. The procedure was taught to me far before understanding the true horrors of it. I had suspicions, but I remained blissfully ignorant regarding the true nature of the horrid experiments. Maintaining moral ambiguity was easier than facing the truth: that I was aiding in killing innocent people. The gravity of my situation became so crushing that the truth was impossible to ignore; I was—I am complicit in murdering innocent people."

Automatically, my brows furrow and my lips compress into a thin line. My loss for words is evident as I search for something, anything, to say. He wasn't forced into the experiment, nor was his life ruined like Avery's was. Instructions were given along with the equipment to produce results. Sai accomplished the task without question or argument.

He takes a steadying breath, before adding, "The assistance I offered Avery caused me to become a liability. I was no longer the obedient doctor following orders. Instead, I was the doctor with an emotional tie that needed to be kept in line. My personal life was investigated; you became a target. I needed to protect you and help Gaddreol. After a moment of panicked clarity, I chose you for his transition."

To ground myself, I take deliberate bites of the burger. Initially, he wasn't coerced, but he formed a companionship with someone that the director maliciously destroyed. Inciting the director to feel it necessary to obtain leverage over Sai to maintain control that originally wasn't needed. That way, when Sai inevitably turned on the director, it wouldn't be possible without it being pernicious to himself, too. Tears threaten to fall, but I blink them away.

"Everything was impromptu?" I ask, but the answer is already apparent. "Getting me in the blind studies was a way to circumvent the inescapable because I'm the solution."

"Yes," He answers anyway. There's a tremble in his voice as he says, "This was the only way I could protect you. Regrettably, my negligence has nullified my precautions. Because of my oversight regarding the camera, the director is aware of your chosen career path. However, there's a possibility that he only knows of the first one you performed."

"Do you know how that will affect the meeting tomorrow?" The question I ask doesn't match the worry I have. The better question is, if he knows I'm an assassin, is he going to end my life during the meeting?

"Unfortunately, I don't. The sudden request prompted the need for these much sooner than I anticipated." He grabs the stack of folders and places them on the bed. "If you are still comfortable with moving forward, these are files that I put together for you over the years."

While finishing my food, I allow myself to contemplate what all of this means. The director's awareness of me being an assassin may cause him to deem me too much of a threat to keep alive, this might be the angle I need in order to present something valuable to him. Evidently, it's something I am capable of, so hopefully, I can prove my potential to him.

A shudder runs up my spine as I consider the possibility that his chosen target may not align with my preferred targets. After his callous actions toward Avery to maintain his obedience, I doubt he cares at all who he targets. He has no reason to be considerate when he's choosing victims since all he seems to care for is their physical health.

After wiping my hands free of the residual crumbs, I finger the tabs of the folders. Each name is written in Braille along the tabs.

⠃⠗⠑⠞⠞ ⠺⠁⠗⠝⠑⠗ *Brett Warner*

⠁⠝⠙⠗⠑⠺ ⠎⠉⠕⠞⠞ *Andrew Scott*

⠛⠗⠁⠙⠽ ⠎⠍⠊⠞⠓ *Grady Smith*

⠞⠽⠇⠑⠗ ⠉⠁⠗⠎⠕⠝ *Tyler Carson*

⠛⠁⠃⠗⠊⠑⠇ ⠏⠁⠗⠅⠑⠗ *Gabriel Parker*

⠉⠁⠗⠇ ⠓⠁⠙⠙⠕⠝ *Carl Haddon*

⠙⠁⠧⠊⠙ ⠇⠑⠺⠊⠎ *David Lewis*

Seven folders, seven people, seven targets. My assassinations. Outlined, detailed, and organized. Different people with different lives, all connected by one common denominator: me. They met their inevitable end because I marked them to become acquainted with their fates. Poisoned. Murdered. Assassinated. By me.

"I did this." My voice is a mere whisper.

The top file is of Brett Warner, so I grab it first and move my fingers along the dots. Outlined in the folder are the horrific crimes he committed along with the acquittals and the light sentencing that followed.

File after file, they're all the same; with their crimes detailed and then the outcomes of the prosecutions for each crime. At the end of each file is a section detailing the relatively unchanging portions of their schedules.

The only thing missing from the details regarding their heinous crimes is the blatant lack of remorse each of these men displayed on trial. Even with the knowledge that I am the responsible variable in their deaths, it doesn't prevent my face from scrunching in disgust when reviewing the information beneath my fingers. My eyebrows lower, my eyes close tightly, and the wrinkling in my nose pulls my top lip with it.

Ignoring the fact that the information at my fingertips details the crimes that these horrible men committed, running my fingers along the cells is comforting. Feeling each of the raised bumps against my skin would be relaxing if it weren't for the cells seamlessly making up the horrors of their crimes.

With each cell I read, the tactile memories penetrate the invisible barrier and flow through my mind. The familiarity of the files and the documents sink in. Sai created these files for me in braille. Organized them into easy-to-read documents, aiding in my assassinations. I studied each of these folders front to back before initiating the task.

Alongside studying the information in the folders is the physical aspect. Sai set up a training dummy for me to practice my strikes. After each person was selected, the dummy was adjusted to match each target's height, maximizing my efficiency.

My stature is short, and my muscularity is lean, allowing me to appear unassuming. Although my physicality appears fragile, my strength is maintained through practicing calisthenics, Tai Chi, and Judo. With each assassination, I diligently held myself to a rigorous training routine, ensuring my physical prowess was on par with my frame of mind.

"I couldn't have done any of this without your support." I find his leg, putting my hand on his knee.

"You remember?" The uncontained excitement brings his voice an octave or two higher than it's been since I came to.

"I remember studying these files, training for each target, but not performing the acts. Except for the dream I had about David Lewis the night you brought those items for me. I imagine each act pretty much plays out the same."

"You had a dream about the assassination?" he asks. The high tone of his voice gradually degrades back to its usual octave.

It reminds me I never got the chance to tell him about it. "Yes, we started on a bench at a park, and then I followed him around, tripping over him intentionally, but in an accidental manner. The act was quick, and he died a couple days later."

"Although, I'm sure that isn't a preferential memory, I'm glad you are remembering things. You are correct, by the way. Each act was similar in execution," he states, then excitedly adds, "Since you have finished reading through these files, I brought colognes with me."

"Can we get rid of the greasy smell in the room first?" I ask.

An unabashed smile takes over my features as Sai immediately begins cleaning up the offending trash. He throws it into a bin and then places the bin outside of the room. An unscented aerosol sprinkles my skin.

"I'm ready." I hold out my hand and he sprays it on my wrist.

The scent is a blend of blackcurrant and peach with undertones of floral and earthy notes. It's the cologne I wear casually sometimes, but mostly it's reserved for dates or going out to events. Whether we're going hiking, to dinner, or to the movies, and anything in between. This is the one that suits me and compliments the scent he wears regularly.

"I already know the other cologne you brought."

My smile reinvigorates as he sprays his sandalwood and vanilla cologne in the air in front of my face. The same one he wore the night we shared the uncomfortable hospital bed. It's the scent he wears daily; the scent that has become synonymous with him. It's the scent I've grown to love more than anything in the world.

The two scents blending pulls an intense memory forward. I lean back, close my eyes, and allow myself to be enveloped by it.

"Wow! You look amazing!" A deep, baritone voice exclaims.

Sai's father, my soon-to-be-future father-in-law, straightens the lapels of the linen suit. My face beams and I shift excitedly beneath his loose grasp, rocking back and forth anxiously on my toes.

"Are you ready, Son?"

"Yes!" I yell, failing the battle at containing my composure.

He mists the elegant fruity spray against my neck, arms, and wrists and then wraps his arm around mine to guide me through the building. The plush carpet feels like walking on a luxurious cloud. It takes everything in me to not scream or jump up and down. I focus on my steps and the man leading the way.

"Here we go," he says.

The door swings open and the music begins playing. The breeze brushes against my skin and ruffles my hair as it wafts the familiar sandalwood and vanilla towards me.

With our arms linked, my soon-to-be-father-in-law walks with me through the threshold towards the man waiting for me at the end of the aisle. With each step, the dewy grass flattens underfoot as my feet sink into the soft dirt. The delicate blades of grass lightly sweep across my skin.

At the end of the aisle, my father-in-law quickly pecks my cheek before handing me off to his son. Sai lightly grabs my hands, pulling me into my spot. I squeeze his hands excitedly, and he gives me a gentle squeeze in return. I can feel the smile radiating from the wonderful man across from me.

"I do," I say, aloud, removing myself from the precious memory. I was wrong. He's not my fiancé. He's my husband.

"I do, too."

CHAPTER THIRTEEN

AS IT TURNS out, I'm not afraid of elevators. I just do not enjoy the disorientation that comes when I can't plant my feet firmly on the ground. The ride up to the director's office is silent. Sai's arm loosely hangs around my waist. The elevator dings and I take a deep breath before stepping out onto the floor. The floor is still freezing, but at least the uncomfortable sensation isn't overwhelming anymore.

At my side, Sai stiffens. The muscles in his arm are now prominent against the thin fabric on my back. Intuitively, I keep my head held high and remain silent as we cover the length of the hallway. Sai touches my side once we make it to the office. He shifts his weight to be partially in front of me.

"Sit down, Sai. The director is going to speak to Tristan alone." Josephine's shrill voice echoes down the empty hallway.

The threat Dr. Sands made regarding Josephine makes sense now. She is the director's assistant—possibly the only person in the hospital who has consistent communication with the evasive man.

Sai's stance is defensive now. I can feel the heat emitting from his rigid back on my face. "He's not going in alone."

"You don't have a choice."

The stiffness in Sai's muscles fall limply as he faces the bleak reality that we have no alternative options. I want to reach out, but my body remains unmoving. My instinct is more reliable than my desire. He steps to the side, allowing Josephine to guide me.

"Walk." The vitriolic woman barks orders at me. "Wait. Go."

Josephine leads me through two sets of doors. Following her commands feels strangely ominous. Instead of being escorted into a meeting, I feel like I should be wearing chains around my wrists and ankles as I walk to my death. Digging her nails into my forearm, she forcefully pushes me into a comfortable leather chair.

"Sit," she demands.

"Thank you, Josephine." His voice is vaguely familiar. A mellow tone that shifts into a more authoritative one when he says, "It's magnificent to have a private moment with the man who's become rather famous as of late. Oh, my. Your eyes are rather bold, aren't they? Please, allow me to offer my sincerest apologies for Samuel's inadequacy."

Rapidly, I dissect my brain to discern who the voice belongs to. Despite his best efforts, his honeyed voice can't mask the sinister undertones. "Dr. Sands... you're the director? Why pretend to be a psychologist?"

Dr. Sands is the director. The other night with Gaddreol makes a lot more sense now.

"Pretending? I must say, I'm appalled you think so little of me. Let's keep that little tidbit between us. But please, Director is fine." Something tells me he is making a dramatic show of exaggerated movements. He sounds like a predator toying with his prey, trying to lure me into feigned security with his sickly-sweet voice. "Just as I expected, you have a keen intellect. An assassin needs to be sharp-witted. I assume this is especially true for one with an impairment such as yours."

Briefly, I consider how to approach the open-ended comment. Do I match his standoffish attitude or just be forward? Deciding against being disingenuous, I give a flat response. "Thanks."

"Outspoken, aren't you? Not what I expected from someone who wants an audience with me. Let's begin with that." The cloying tone of his voice clashing with the malice is grating. I resist the urge to shudder.

"Well, there are a lot of questions I want to ask." I straighten my spine against the chair.

"Questions for me? Audacious. I like it."

Unsure of how to begin, I blurt out the first question that comes forth, "What is the point of this organization?"

"Have you heard of the Transcendence Theory?" he counters.

"No." My eyebrows crease slightly.

"To understand the importance of our work at FREE, you must first understand the Transcendence Theory." He sounds offended at my ignorance. "We strive to transcend morbidity and mortality."

Obviously, morbidity is being used as an umbrella term to put any medical issues that don't fit his ideal health standards. Usually, my blindness wouldn't fit into that category, but according to his beliefs, it does. If the goal he is pursuing is health, then why was Gaddreol's healthy body mutilated? It seems these cruel operations are masquerading as experiments simply to appease their macabre curiosity. Perhaps it's just another calculated measure to keep Avery constrained.

"You're using a theory of transcendence as an excuse to maim and murder people?" I question unapologetically.

"Sacrifices must be made in order to achieve greatness. All that enter this building are a part of a greater purpose."

"Why not just use synthetic bodies to get the desired results?" I ask, but think to myself, *That way you don't have to take anyone's life away.*

I find myself absently gnawing on the inner lining of my cheek, so I snap my teeth together.

"Synthetics are unreliable for several reasons, but the important reason is that production for synthetics is far too slow." There is an amused tone in his words. Deliberately omitting something, daring me to question it.

I take the bait, even though I'm not ready to know the answer. "Too slow for what?"

"Customers. They're waiting for their perfect bodies. Whether that be through our retrievals or through genetics, eventually their patience will run out."

People are paying for this loathsome "service". Customers are either waiting for a stolen body or someone's offspring to become available. Retrievals. Kidnappings. Genetics. Reproductions. Actual children are involved. The words flood into my mind, reminding me of the disturbing reality I didn't allow myself to think about before.

Is it his intention to cause discombobulation by sharing this with me? Or was it merely a Freudian slip? If it's the former, it may be working. My stomach is knotting, and a lump is forming in my throat. I take a deep breath to steady myself.

Forcing my face to remain unmoving and my voice to stay flat, I ask, "You're breeding people like livestock?"

"Hardly reprehensible when every patient agrees to their bodies being used for reproduction."

The papers are signed before undergoing transitioning. Anyone who read them probably assumed it was simply a formality for an unlikely scenario. Not knowing it was an intentional facet of this organization. Or maybe, they were aware and intentionally agreed.

Whether it's under false pretenses or general acceptance, I'll never know.

My revulsion is completely unveiled now. "Where are the children you're forcing these people to have?"

"They are being taken care of, I assure you."

I feel completely assured now, thanks.

"Why kill people who happen to survive the transition?" I ask, pushing down more stomach acid.

"Anyone who survives is a liability. As I'm sure you've noticed, your survival created a large disturbance here."

Technically, he's not wrong. Anyone who may survive won't have the same forced loyalty as the doctors working for him. However, agreeing with him for any reason is sickening. I shake my head to distract from a shudder writhing beneath the surface.

"Why are you allowing me to live, then?"

A dull ache presses tightly against the center of my forehead, so I forcibly relax my furrowed eyebrows.

"I wasn't going to let you live, and while I still might kill you, you are rather fascinating. Your optimism and confidence intrigue me. How often does one encounter a blind assassin? How many people have you killed?" He laughs.

"I don't remember," I say, hoping I won't be betrayed by my facial features and mannerisms.

"Pity. I'm sure you have captivating tales to tell. You remind me of myself, you know," he says, but I'm sure it's only to provoke me.

We are absolutely nothing alike. My stomach knots again, but this time I'm unable to suppress my gag response. I want to retch and expel all of the contents knotting inside my stomach, but I take a deep breath, regaining what little composure I have.

"How'd you even learn how to extract souls and reimplant them inside of other people?"

"At the turn of the century, a physician conducted experiments to determine that the human soul weighed twenty-one grams." He sounds as if he's been waiting for someone to ask. His excitement is repulsive. "Working with a scientist and an engineer, we discovered that he was, in fact, correct. After that, we designed and developed a machine to capture the souls. There was a lot of trial and error, but with some delicate fine-tuning, the machine was perfect."

The mastermind of this entire operation is a trio of like-minded sick individuals. *Fantastic.*

"Where are they now?"

"Brazen, as well. But that doesn't concern you." His voice returns to the malicious tone that suits his voice a little too well.

My irritation twitches at the corners of my lips and creases the center of my forehead. Forcibly, I smooth my features to become stonelike. "Fine. But why am I privy to this information? It was only recently that my blindness condemned me to death?"

An uproarious laugh erupts from the otherwise composed man, causing me to flinch. "Your blindness didn't condemn you to death; it simply served as vindication. You were condemned to death by Sai when he so graciously underhanded me."

"So where does that leave me, now?" I state flatly, desperately trying to hide feeling exposed.

Another shiver accompanies the goosebumps coating my skin. Unable to suppress it, my entire body trembles. I ball my hands into fists. The excruciating pain from tightly curling my fingers into my palms provides the perfect distraction to quell my unwanted bodily reactions.

"I am giving you one chance to prove yourself. If you succeed, you will work directly for me and Gaddreol can have his *mangled* body back." His voice is exceptionally enthusiastic.

Quietly, he closes the distance. Then his fingers trail along my balled fists, up my arm until he's behind me with his hands rubbing my shoulders. He leans in with his hot breath against my ear when he asks, "Do we have a deal?"

Shrugging him off and suppressing another full-body shudder, I ask, "If I decline? Or fail?"

"It would be in your best interest, and Sai's, to accept my offer. And if you fail? Let's just say, I wouldn't test that out if I were you."

"What do you propose?" I ask, stiffening my spine that wants to curl up in a ball against the chair.

"Sadly, it's nothing as adventurous as murder. But a formidable assassin such as yourself can accomplish the paltry task I have in mind. I just want you to obtain a new body for me." He walks away from me again, presumably around his desk.

Kidnapping someone for him and performing the murder with my own hands are essentially identical tasks. In the end, whoever the unfortunate person is, they are losing their life. If I refuse or fail, both Gaddreol and Sai will suffer from the consequences neither of them deserve. Gaddreol will be transitioned into a new body that will leave him guilt-ridden and my refusal will force Sai to receive an unjustifiable punishment.

I hold my head up high. "Deal."

"Very well. Avery will assist in your endeavors. He will receive all the information you require." I stand and make my way to the door. When I open the first set, he calls out, "It will be a pleasure to work with you."

Avery being allowed to assist me in this undertaking isn't all that surprising. He will work tirelessly until the task is accomplished due to his emotional investment. With the limited information we have, Gaddreol has the most to lose if this fails and by extension, Avery does, too. If the kidnapping is pulled off, Gaddreol will go back to his rightful, albeit, amputated, body.

Exiting the second set of doors, I hear a screeching sound from Sai abruptly standing. "Are you okay? Are you hurt?"

Without breaking my stride, I pass him and continue walking down the hall. Focusing only on keeping my head held high and my back straight as my legs diligently carry me to the elevator. Rushing towards me, he catches up to me and matches my pace.

"I'm fine," I say, keeping my voice firm. "Let's go."

Once we enter my hospital room, I immediately grab the blanket from the bed and cloak myself in it. Barely managing a whisper, I say, "Take me home, please."

* * *

No matter how tightly the blanket is wrapped around me, it can't replace the vulnerability coating every inch of me. Even though I'm home now, surrounded by things that are vaguely familiar, I can't shake the uncomfortable feelings.

The softness of the cotton sofa is barely noticeable past the perturbed feeling crawling all over my skin like tiny invisible bugs. The warm blueberry green tea isn't soothing enough to quell the butterflies violently fluttering around in my stomach. The pulsating pain radiating in each of my fingers eclipses the other sensations, calling attention to them every other second.

My glaring incompetence is on full display. I severely misjudged my readiness and miscalculated the director's cunning abilities. His sadistic nature affected me in ways I couldn't comprehend until it left me in complete disarray. His unwinnable ultimatum stripped me of everything, leaving me utterly defenseless.

I curl into a ball against the sofa, feeling as small as I do weak. *Maybe I can sink into true nothingness.* The unintentional thought popping into my mind makes me gag. I never want to experience that state of oblivion again.

"Are you okay?" Sai asks. His melodic soothes my discomfort. I rest my head in his lap, his hand absently runs through my hair.

"Far from it," I admit. The conversation swirls around inside my head wanting to come out of my mouth, but it anchors itself in the pit of my stomach unwilling to surface. Mustering the tiny amount of willpower I possess, I ask, "What was our original plan?"

He pauses for a moment. "After separating you and Gaddreol, you were going to assassinate the director."

A simple statement with a complex execution. "That may not be the plan anymore."

"Why do you say that?" His hand stops, presumably because he's pondering my words.

I open my mouth, but no sound comes out. *Why do I say that?* The engineer, the scientist, the children, and the customers. *Just say that.* "FREE is a lot more convoluted than you may know."

He brushes his hand through my hair again but remains quiet. I rub my arms, forgetting about the radiating pain in my fingertips. The surging pain counterbalances the self-soothing action, but it gives me enough push to finally say something of note.

"The director isn't the only one pulling the strings; a scientist and an engineer were involved to some degree in the development. There are a lot of impatient customers for this vile organization either waiting on a body to be stolen or a child being concealed somewhere."

"I see," he says in a pensive tone. "What else did he say? If you are ready to talk about it, that is."

The question lifts the weight within me. "The director has given me an ultimatum to kidnap someone. If I fail, you and Gaddreol will be given undeserved punishments, and I'll be a living test subject. If I succeed, he wants me to work directly for him."

An unexpected guttural roar rips through Sai. Wide eyed and slack-jawed, my head snaps in his direction. It's the first raw sound of pure frustration I've heard from him since transitioning. It's a brief reaction, but for someone who struggles with expressing his emotions, it's monumental. It makes me feel better about all of the uncontrollable reactions I'm having to the whole ordeal.

"That meeting reverts everything I was trying to prevent. The security I managed to provide for you is eradicated. Your choices have returned to complicity or death—or worse." There's a shift beside me. Carefully, I reach out to find his head hung in defeat inside his palms. "I'm so sorry. I never wanted any of this for you."

"Me, too," I say wrapping my arm around his waist and leaning my head against his shoulder.

"Are you going to follow through with the task?" A polite way of asking, *Are you going to send an innocent man to his death?*

"Yes. I don't have a choice, unfortunately." My voice is feeble.

In accepting this, I am probably leading an innocent man to his death. While this person may be someone who isn't morally good, the probability of that seems low. If I don't do it, I'm inadvertently putting two people I care for into unfathomable situations. Neither choice is ideal, but the lesser of two evils is apparent.

I let out a breath I didn't realize I was holding to say, "Maybe in working with him, I'll be able to learn important information."

"Only if he is true to his word," he says. The words suffocate the air in my lungs, crushing my chest. I struggle through it until I can take a few stabilized breaths. "I'm sorry, I shouldn't have said that."

"What do you think he has in mind?" I ask, nibbling on my lip.

Men like the director are conniving and deceitful, so it doesn't surprise me. Still, I don't know how to navigate something I can't predict. Most likely something was phrased in a way to create a loophole that I missed. Scanning over the interactions in my mind, I still can't think of anything.

"Honestly, I'm not sure." His uncertain tone matches the words. "Without a doubt, he has concocted something to give himself an advantage."

My turbulent emotions veiled my perception, but Sai's right. The director likely doesn't perceive the ultimatum as beneficial to himself. He succeeded in trapping me in a corner, but the choices he gave me were more passive than he seems to prefer. Based on the options he has given me I have liberties that don't align with his malicious methods. Unlike the sheer devastation he caused Avery to create the perfect underling.

How could I have misjudged the interaction so poorly?

"I messed up."

"You didn't mess anything up." Sai's posture straightens as his arm rests loosely around my waist. "The director is unscrupulous; everything he does is by unethical means. To say he is exceptional at it would be an understatement."

More things that were discussed in the meeting flood my mind to tell Sai. *Dr. Sands. Transcendence Theory. Avery.*

"I have a few more things that I almost forgot about. The first is, do you know anything about Transcendence Theory?"

"Yes, it was explained to me. We are transcending our worthless existences through transitioning." He almost spits the words out.

"Second thing is the director is Dr. Sands. He told me to keep it a secret, but I don't really understand why it's that important, since Avery and I are going to steal him a new body." The words fly out of my mouth before I can stop them. "Oh, that was the third thing, Avery was assigned to help me carry out the task."

"Avery? Why?"

I shrug, saying, "It wasn't clarified, but I assume it's because of his unwavering obedience."

"That makes sense," he says. His voice is sullen, but it returns to its usual monotonous tone when he asks, "Anyway, would you like me to run you a bath?"

"Yes, please." With his absence, I readjust into a ball again in a futile attempt to comfort myself.

Push away the discomfort and read between the lines.

We discussed more horrific realities of the organization, but it's not personal enough to be used against me. Automatically, Avery's disqualified since his submission is already forced. Not that we are close enough anyway. Gaddreol is promised his body back, but the condition of it wasn't. While it still could be in worse shape before getting back to him, that is too indirect to serve as an underlying imposition.

Sai is the obvious choice. He's my partner, but he also covertly deceived the director. The only notable ambiguity was in my initial choice of accepting or declining his assignment. Sai went against the director and came out of it relatively unscathed. My initiation probably gave him the perfect incentive to move forward with any plans he had to punish Sai for his disloyalty. My impending success or failure is likely nothing more than an irrelevant diversion.

How do I contend with something that's unidentifiable? Remain as calm and collected as possible. Continue moving forward and take whatever is thrown my way in stride. Most importantly, try not to let my senses and emotions overwhelm me again as they are now. Maintain my equilibrium and my self-control.

Starting now.

With that, I uncurl my body and stretch my stiff limbs. I fumble my way to the bathroom just as the water is shut off. A smile curls my lips as the sweet smell of lavender fills my nose. The sweet smell of relaxation.

"I was coming to get you." He guides me gently to the bathtub.

"That's okay. It's about time I stop wallowing in my misery," I mumble as Sai eases me into the water. Once he lets go, I sink into the abundant bubbles.

I'll start tomorrow.

CHAPTER FOURTEEN

THE DAY I'VE been worrying about is finally here. Vera is waiting anxiously for her older brother to listen to all of the fun things she's been doing. Which is concerning. Not only do I not remember my passions or talents, but I also have no idea about his either, or the things they enjoyed together. Except that he would read books to her all the time. Pretending to be Gaddreol is a daunting task that will be difficult to pull off. Hopefully, she gives me easy, traversable things to respond to.

"You ready to go yet?" Avery calls from the living room, waiting not-so-patiently to take me to Vera. It seems he may be as anxious about the entire thing as I am.

No, I'm not. I inhale deeply. *But I need to be.*

"Yeah!" I yell back, buttoning my pants and adjusting my shirt. As ready as I'm going to be, at least. "Coming!"

The smooth wooden flooring feels good beneath my feet. As I make my way down the hallway, I run my hand along the plain walls, unobstructed by any decorations or frames. The transition from the smooth panels to the plush carpet reminds me of the rugs Avery set up for Gaddreol.

"What's got you beaming?" he asks. The amusement in his voice captures my attention. When he sounds pleasant, he comes across as likable.

"I was reminded of the tactile sensations you placed around the apartment for Gaddreol." The words come out before I realize how insensitive they may come across. The smile disappears from my eyes first, and then my mouth until only a twitch at the corners of my lips remains. "Gaddreol really appreciated when you did that."

"I'm glad." The sad tone returns, but he quickly clears his throat to remove it. "Let's get to Vera. She, uh, wants you to go dancing with her."

Oh, no. I think, but say, "I guess we're going to find out if that's possible."

At least if I fumble while dancing that will be believable. It's not like Gaddreol is secretly a professional dancer who could conquer blindness just to show off an unlikely skillset, right? Of course not. This may actually prove to be a better choice than it appears on the surface.

"Are you going without shoes?" Avery asks, confused, as I exit the house barefoot.

"I don't wear shoes. Tactile sensations are how I process the world around me," I say.

"Have you ever stepped in dog shit?" He erupts into laughter.

"Twice." Answering his question makes me realize that Gaddreol probably wouldn't go anywhere without shoes, so I sigh, resignedly. "I'll get shoes and the cane."

"Don't sound so defeated," he says, soft laughter trailing him as he descends the stairs.

After putting the shoes on, I struggle with the laces, trying to tie them until accepting the bandages makes it too difficult. I leave them untied, loosely hanging around my feet, nearly falling off with every step. Before exiting again, I grab the walking cane out of the closet next to the front door.

Feeling uncertain without the tactile feedback against my feet and the too-loose shoes, I keep my feet planted on the ground and drag them across the veranda. Once I make it to the top of the stairs, I brace myself with the railing and carefully take each step. Every time my feet lift into the air, I stretch my toes to secure the shoes from falling off.

Avery's laughter grows from a breathy snicker to a boisterous full belly laugh as he watches me struggle. While attempting to stifle his laughter, he offers, "I can tie your shoes if you want."

Trying to ignore the humiliation washing over me, I sit on the last step and accept the help. "Yes, please."

"Maybe you should invest in slips-ons," Avery says, after tying one shoe.

"It's not like this is a regular occurrence for me," I say.

"True. I'm sorry for laughing so hard." He stands up, helps me to my feet, and then walks me to his car.

"It's fine," I say. "I can imagine it was a pretty funny thing to see. Plus, as weird as it is to say, I'm glad you can laugh at me like that."

He gets into the driver's side, and then asks, "Why's that?"

"Because by laughing at me, you must see me as someone who isn't completely helpless."

I'm not even sure why that stands out to me or why that would hold any significance at all. If anything, as an assassin, people viewing me as completely helpless is a fantastic thing. Unassuming and unthreatening, viewed as nothing more than meek and feeble, able to easily slip in and out without drawing the wrong attention.

Right now, though, I feel acknowledged, a feeling I am not sure I've felt from anyone other than Sai in a long time. As good as it feels, being acknowledged by Avery is not something that would have crossed my mind as a possibility.

A grin settles on my face once I realize the bizarre hilarity of my current predicament. This may be the weakest I've been in a long time and now I must appear even more so. Since the shoes make my steps feel uncertain and off balance, the cane is a necessity. It should be easy to pull off the feeble look without much deception.

"Helpless? Not even close." Another brief laugh escapes him. "From what I've heard about you, you're more capable than most people."

More capable than most? Hardly.

Nothing I've done has been on my own. Everything I do requires assistance in some form or another. Especially from Sai, who has been an integral part of everything I've accomplished.

I laugh before responding, "I couldn't even tie my own shoes."

"That doesn't count." His boisterous laughter returns.

"Since it's a task I was incapable of doing, I have to respectfully disagree," I say, chuckling even more.

"Nope." One word said with an exaggerated pop. It reminds me of Gaddreol doing the same to Dr. Sands the other night. This time I know it's meant as friendly banter and the childish counter to my argument brings me tears from laughing so hard.

I feel bad for misjudging Avery. Although, in the beginning, he didn't give me a reason to question my judgements. He is far more genuine under his now-cracked exterior than he appeared initially.

"I needed that," he says, laughter still trickling in his voice. "We're almost there."

"I did, too." I close my eyes and allow myself to relax.

* * *

"I'm so glad you could make it!" Vera exclaims running towards us. "Are your fingers okay?"

Instinctively, I raise them up in front of my face as if to inspect them. My eyes almost fly open, but I focus my attention on keeping them closed so she doesn't see the neon orange. I'm unsure of how she'll react to them, and I really don't want to ruin her day if I can help it. It should be as wonderful as possible.

"Ah, this? Yeah, it's fine," I say, feeling completely out of my element trying to mimic Gaddreol's speech patterns. I should be used to it since he was with me for a month, but it still feels out of place coming out of my mouth. "Avery yelled to me from outside the window. So, I poked my head out and hit the window coming back in. It came crashing down on my fingertips. No big deal."

Vera grabs my hands into hers and gingerly kisses each of my fingers, reminding me that her experiences are still very limited to the interactions she had with her older brother. Tears well behind my eyelids, fighting for their exit. I want to blink the tears away, but in trying not to reveal my irradiated eyes, I squeeze them shut, forcing the tears out instead.

"I'm sorry!" she squeaks. "I didn't mean to hurt you."

"No, no. You didn't. It was just really sweet," I say, with a large toothy grin.

"You always did it for me, so it's nice to return the favor." I can hear the smile return to her voice. "Come on then."

"Have fun." Avery leaves and my heart sinks into my stomach.

Hand-in-hand, she gently guides me toward the building. I can hear faint music already playing. Accompanying the instruments are faint colors that find their way into my mind. The closer we get to the doors, the louder the music gets and with it, the dancing strands of colors get brighter.

Red, green, blue, purple, and yellow. Twisting and swirling to the beat and rhythm of the music. I can't pinpoint which color belongs to which instrument as they all blend together.

Once we make it inside, the music is too loud and the colors are too bright, which puts my nerves on edge. The increased anxiety is unintentionally disorienting, causing my pace to slow, and allowing a downward spiral of unfortunate events to transpire.

Vera loses her grip, so she turns to face me, presumably to see what's going on. She accidentally shifts her body into mine, crushing my fingers between us. The surge of pain causes me to forget about keeping my eyes closed as I try to stifle the shrieks trying to escape my body. Vera screams, which is exceptionally noticeable when the scattered movement in the room abruptly stops.

"Gaddreol!" she yells. "What happened to your eyes?"

This is a disaster, I think. Trying to ease the pain, I unclench my jaw.

"You guys okay?" Avery's out of breath after sprinting to us.

"I'm sorry. I'm sorry," she repeats, sounding remorseful.

The panic and remorse in her voice rip my attention away from the pain long enough for me to respond. "I'm fine. It's okay. Just a little sore."

"Show me your hands," he says, and I oblige. "You're bleeding."

"I'm so sorry. I didn't mean to hurt you more." The guilt in her voice hurts almost as much as the renewed pain in my fingers.

The amount of damage to my fingers makes me glad I can't see them. I've never seen blood or gore, so I don't know how I would react. Sai's efforts to heal my fingers have become futile with the number of times I've damaged them in some way. I can't imagine they are looking very good with everything I've put them through.

"You're fine, Vera. You didn't do anything wrong," Avery says in an unexpectedly calming voice. It changes abruptly as he calls to the stunned crowd, "I need a first aid kit and a bathroom!"

Someone obliges, giving him the medical supplies, then leads us to the bathroom. Vera follows at my heels, occasionally stepping on the backs of my shoes.

"Don't worry, I'll get him fixed up in no time," Avery says, closing the door behind him, and then laughs, adding, "I didn't even get a chance to leave before things blew up."

"I know," I wince as the dressings scrape against my fingertips.

"Gaddreol..." Vera whispers from behind the door. "Are you okay?"

"I'm good!" I yell, enthusiastically, hoping it sounds believable.

From the faint thumping sound against the wall, my attempt at cheering her up wasn't successful. I can't help but feel bad for her. She is still adjusting to her new body and freely moving about. While doing that, she's trying to be extra careful when it comes to her 'older brother's' blindness. And then the cataclysmic event we were both trying to prevent escalated before she could even dance with her "big brother."

"Will you still dance? Avery, will you dance with us?"

I can feel the slump in his movements, clearly not wanting to stay, but he calls through the door, "Yeah, I'll stick around and dance with you guys. Gotta look after him, right?"

He stands and crumpling sounds follow. The scorching pain in my fingers is prominent, but at least they're fully covered again. I stretch my fingers unnecessarily, before rising to my feet, reminded again of the discomfort of shoes. I fumble the doorknob until Vera opens the door for me, which causes Avery to snicker under his breath.

"Thanks! Are you ready?"

"Are you sure?" she asks, nervously, "What if I hurt you again?"

I reach my arms out to her and pull her into a hug. She lowers her chin onto my shoulder and wraps her arms around my back. For the first time I notice she's a few inches taller than me; far different from the small, frail child in Gaddreol's dream.

"I promise," I say, forcing a chuckle before adding, "Besides, if I get hurt, I have the best doctors at my disposal. Avery, too."

Vera and Avery laugh hard at my pitiful joke at his expense.

"Okay!" she excitedly exclaims. She starts to run off but stops and faces me again. "But what happened to your eyes? Are they okay?"

"He was given a test serum that gave him superpowers. We just haven't discovered which ones yet," he says, nudging my arm when he passes us.

"Hopefully, that superpower will be sight one day." She wraps her arms around me in a light squeeze before gently guiding me back to the main room.

If anyone else said something like that, I would feel annoyed. But with Vera, her childlike innocence melts my heart. All the interactions with her give me an understanding of why Avery went out of his way to protect it.

My increased sensitivity to the loud music makes the beautiful instrumentals sound grating. Paired with the swirling colors in my mind makes it hard to focus. I try to ignore both jarring sensations and follow Vera and Avery to the dance floor. From the ungraceful movements my body is channeling I may not have danced at all in my life. Maybe not even during our wedding. But it may just be the effects of the disorienting overstimulation. From the sounds of their footsteps, Vera and Avery are dancing in sync, letting the music flow through their movements.

"It must be hard to dance when you're blind," Vera says, trying to hide the disappointment in her voice.

"You have no idea."

I'm not sure if it's my blindness or the overwhelming sensations causing my inability to dance, but the reason doesn't matter when the outcome is the same.

"You look like a newborn animal learning to walk." Avery laughs.

Even when it's at my expense, I'm happy to hear his laughter again. He deserves a little reprieve from all the mayhem that's left him in a broken desolation. Plus, it's pleasant enough to soothe the nerves trying to steadily climb with every lumbering movement. A genuine smile spreads onto my face as I listen to Vera and Avery occasionally chuckling at me.

The music is less jarring now and easier to listen to as my nerves calm. Which in turn makes the colors dancing around my mind easier to watch. The purple and blue are the most vibrant with green and yellow faintly swirling through them every so often.

That doesn't mean I'm able to use the music in the same way that the two people gracefully dancing beside me can. The rhythm isn't guiding my body at all; my tedious footwear isn't doing me any favors, either. However, despite the shoes and the uncoordinated, clunky movements, I am thoroughly enjoying myself. Every time I unintentionally bump into Vera, she giggles to herself, which I can't help but join in.

"I think you're getting the hang of it!" Her excitement is genuine and encompassing.

I laugh. "It's okay, my dignity is still intact."

"Debatable," Avery says. His boisterous laughter fills the empty space between the three of us.

The instruments fade, and a staticky voice fills the room. "I want to thank everyone for coming out and dancing to your heart's content! We're wrapping up within the next ten minutes, so get the hell out! Hope to see everyone next time!"

"Thank you so much for coming with me!" Vera squeals.

"It was tons of fun," I say, which is true, but I am glad it's over.

"I'm glad I stayed. Come on, let's get you both home."

* * *

What happens when Gaddreol comes back? I wonder.

He's not going to be aware of my abysmal dance skills or the outing he supposedly attended. Those are mostly irrelevant since the details can be filled in and he will be able to approach the topic with a fluidity I don't seem to possess. It does make me wonder, though, how he will feel to know I took his place to attend an event.

What am I saying?

He won't be anything but happy that I did what I could to make his little sister happy. And Avery, too, who arguably needs it more than Vera.

"I'm glad you stayed," I say, sheepishly.

"Had to." A brief chuckle escapes him. "Looked like you needed the help."

"I was managing fairly well until running into a Vera-shaped wall," I say, causing him to laugh, again.

"Seriously, though, I'm glad I stayed, too. It was a lot of fun. More fun than I've had in forever." The joy in his voice is tangible. "You did good. Gaddreol would be proud."

Hearing that is simultaneously uplifting and dispiriting, but I'm not entirely sure why. It's an oxymoron—a melancholic satisfaction to make Gaddreol proud because he's not here to be himself.

"Thanks. I had a lot of fun, too." I say and then go up the stairs. Once I'm inside with the door closed, Avery starts the car, and drives off.

I call out to Sai, but I'm met with an empty house. Hopefully, when he gets home, I can tell him about the chaotic events. For now, I'll get ready for tomorrow. Today was already draining and I'm sure tomorrow will be no different.

A shower and some food sounds nice. Maybe a nap, too.

CHAPTER FIFTEEN

BREATHE, I THINK, reminding myself that hyperventilating would be disastrous right now. As vile as it is, the act of the kidnapping isn't the problem. It's the uncertainty of the target and the stakes that are causing the panic to build within me. It's hypocritical of me to accept this person's death, but there isn't any other choice.

All the more reason I need to stay calm; everyone is relying on me to succeed. *Don't mess this up.*

"How do you want to do this?" Avery asks, snapping me out of my thoughts.

How do I want to do this? *Honestly, I don't know.*

This is unlike any of the targets I've gone after. Sai did extensive research on each target to give me all of the resources available to efficiently execute the assassination. For this, Avery was given a picture of the man with a little information about him. He's a blend-in-the-background type of man. A nondescript thirty-four-year-old accountant. Why the director chose this man is baffling. He seems too timid to have the intimidating aura the director emits naturally.

Gregory Young.

Avery followed him to a small coffee shop that happens to be around the corner from his home. Targeting him near his house isn't ideal, but, apparently, this man appears to be a homebody. This café seems to be one of the only places he goes to besides his workplace. So I'll work with that.

"What is he doing?" I ask.

"He's got a book and a laptop with him," he replies. "Waiting for his drink, looks like."

"Is he sitting down?" I ask, but quickly add, "Tell me the layout of what you can see."

"He's sitting in the farthest corner of the place; lucky you," he says, and I roll my eyes in his direction hoping he can see. "Anyway, when you walk in the doors, the counter is on the left, attached to a bar top and the row of tables is on the right. One row of tables and it looks like five of them. He's at the last one."

"I'll go in and strike up a conversation with him." I unbuckle the seatbelt, ready to go.

"You have no shoes, no cane, and—do you even have money?" Avery sounds slightly annoyed and amused.

"Shoes distract me, and the cane is an unnecessary accessory," I state, and then pat my pockets. "I... do not have money."

The car rocks a little as he shifts himself to get his wallet from his pocket. He puts a bill in my hand and says, "Here's a twenty. I'll be across the street."

With that, I exit the car and let my feet get acquainted with the concrete. It's warm to the touch and the porous surface is smooth without many noticeable cracks or any tiny rocks scattered about. It absorbs most of the vibrational sensations, but the car pulling away tingles against the soles of my feet.

The parking lot isn't very big, so it takes no time to reach the entrance. Entering the building, I wipe my feet off on the rug and walk cautiously to the counter.

"How can I help you?" A brittle, croaky voice, presumably belonging to an elderly woman, asks cheerfully.

"May I get an iced latte, please?" I ask and put the money on the counter in front of me.

"Of course, dear. Here you are." She puts the change onto the counter, which I quickly collect.

Finding a seat is easy enough since Avery explained the layout. That and the soft echo that's likely unnoticeable by most people. I sit at the fourth table nearest to the man who is sipping a little too loud and tippy-tapping on his laptop occasionally.

"Did you mean to go barefooted?" His voice is deep and thick with an accent I can't place.

"Yes," I say, a soft smile on my lips. I keep my eyes closed in hopes of accentuating my blindness and hiding their vibrant color. "Shoes block the textures and vibrations I receive while walking, so wearing them is really difficult and awkward."

"You're blind?" he asks, sounding absolutely perplexed.

"Since birth."

"No way." His disbelief is a bit worrying. "How did you walk to the table so smoothly, then?"

"A friend dropped me off and told me the general layout before he left, so I cheated a little," I say, widening my smile a bit as he laughs at my explanation. His deep, booming laugh rumbles across my skin.

"If I tell you the bathroom is at the end of the bar to the left, you can find it without running into a single thing?" he asks with genuine curiosity.

My ability to navigate through tactile sensations and vibrations being diminished to a parlor trick is an unusual concept to me. It's been a part of my life since I could walk.

"Absolutely. Would you like a demonstration?" I ask, rising from my chair.

"I'd love one." His tone shifts to a sensual one.

The recognizable heat flushes my cheeks. *Red.*

Ignoring it, I move around the table, turning my head slightly in his direction with my eyes closed, and then make my way to the bathroom. At the end of the bar, footsteps amble in my direction, bringing my stride to an abrupt halt.

"Sorry, dear, your drink will be waiting for you at the table." The elderly woman hurries past me, narrowly avoiding bumping into me.

Gregory applauds my full stop, which feels exceptionally absurd. Once the woman passes, I continue sauntering toward the direction he mentioned. Following the bar's edge to the wall, I find the small sign next to the door, and read the braille with my pinky—the only finger that has healed enough to escape its prison.

"You were going to send me to the women's bathroom?" I shake my head; a breathy laugh comes out.

His unrestrained laugh is so powerful that I feel the vibration in my bones. He exudes amusement, saying, "Sorry, but you passed with flying colors."

I smile to myself as the colors I have seen mimic his words, flying in and out of my mind. Undoubtedly, he believes I'm smiling at him. In some small way, I suppose I am. He seems to be a charming, laid-back type of person who is easy to talk to.

"Thanks," I say, making my way back to my seat.

"I have a spot across from me, if you'd like," he offers and I can feel his eyes watching me, waiting for me to accept.

Accepting the invitation, I grab the latte and move it to his table. "I heard you typing, are you working on something?"

"Nothing important," he says, closing the laptop. "Just browsing.

How come your friend didn't come in with you?"

"While I'm pretty talented at walking, my driving skills may prove to be a bit lackluster." His laughter interrupts me, but my grin widens. "He had some other things to do but offered me a ride on his way out."

"So you don't live around here?" he asks, inquisitively.

"A few blocks away," I say, even though it's a lie. "Usually, I walk everywhere, but sometimes it's nice to get a ride."

"If you had walked, I would have missed the brilliant show. The name's Gregory, by the way." His hand meets mine, presumably to shake my hand, but he delicately traces my fingers instead. "What happened?"

"It's silly, but I bumped into an open window, causing it to fall, smashing my fingers, and then my little sister accidentally ran into me, making it so much worse." I force a chuckle to disintegrate the sudden tension between us.

My little lie isn't quite so believable when the person being told has real-world experience. I almost flinch from calling Vera 'my little sister', but I restrain the impulse. It causes me inexplicable pain to consider her as such, but I can't say for certain why that is.

I believe it has to do with my entire family, including two sisters, being gone. I hardly remember being a brother but playing that role for a day brought me a familiarity of the kinship I may never get back. Gaddreol is as close to dead as one can be and while I don't want to take his place for any reason, being able to fulfill that role was more significant to me than is even comprehensible.

"That must've been a very heavy window." He continues tracing the ins and outs of my fingers.

"Exceptionally so," I move my hand closer to his, interrupting the fluid movements, and he opens his hand to mine. "Would you like to walk me back to my house?"

"If you're leaving so soon, I'd love to go with you," he says and gathers his belongings to accompany me.

Realizing my drink is untouched, I pick it up and find it is already in a to-go cup, thankfully. I take a few sips of the overly sweet liquid until he is ready to start walking. Despite having more things in his hands, he holds the door open for me. The warmth of the concrete is far more welcoming than the cool tile.

"Thank you."

"Which way is your house?"

From the information Avery told me, left will be an easier route since it's less travelled and less monitored. Taking a sip of my drink, I raise my hand to indicate we're going left as my signal to Avery. A car starts in the distance, and while I can't say for certain it's Avery, I think it is. Gregory loops his arm through mine and escorts me to my fake house. I accept, even though it gives me less control over my own movements. Our paces are unaligned and disjointed, so he releases my arm as we cut the corner of the building.

"Are you really blind?" Gregory asks, again. His confusion baffles me, but I'm not sure what else I can do to convince him.

"Why do you ask that?" I ask, turning my head in his direction with my eyes still closed, hoping again, that it's enough evidence.

"You are walking so well without one of those sticks. I thought every blind person needed it," he says, waving a hand in my face.

"I can feel you waving your hand, you know," I say, hiding my annoyance with another soft laugh.

"Sorry, I just can't believe it."

Clearly, I think, but instead say, "Yeah, I know most blind people don't feel confident walking without their cane, but to me, it's more of an accessory than useful—unless my feet are covered."

"You're not afraid right now?" He tries to make his voice come off as intimidating. "You're in a vulnerable position."

"Am I?" Feigning obliviousness is easy.

Technically, he's right. In most cases, a person in my position is vulnerable. But right now, he can't be further from the truth. He's the one in far more danger than he can perceive. Guilt starts to infiltrate my emotions, causing my confidence to waver slightly. I focus on sipping the latte in my hand to distract me from my want to just walk away and let this man go.

"I could be a spree killer or whatever else. You never know." He laughs.

I'm fairly certain, I'm a lot closer to that qualification than you are, I think, smiling to myself about the ridiculous juxtaposition. A small, blind assassin next to a very average man.

"You're definitely not a spree killer or mass murderer. You're not unhinged for something like that. From your calculative, deliberate nature you'd likely be a serial killer," I say, thinking it would cause him to laugh, but the opposite happens. He is completely silent with a fixed gaze on me. "Sorry, that was out of line."

"No, not at all." His deep, roaring laughter returns, as he says, "I just didn't expect that."

A car speeds up and then slows to match our walking speed. "Hey, Tristan! I was looking for you at the café. You want a ride?"

"This is Avery, the friend I was telling you about," I say to the man beside me, before turning to Avery. "A ride back to the house would be great. This is Gregory."

Now, I'm two-for-two with lies potentially exposing the façade I've created. Before embarking on this endeavor, calling Avery my friend wasn't something I'd given thought to. It was improvised on the spot. Hopefully, without too much startle, he will be able to follow the lead.

"Nice to meet you, Gregory. Come on, I'll take you guys to his house. Free of charge." Avery's laugh melts away the uneasiness coming from the man standing next to me.

Gregory laughs anxiously but reluctantly climbs into the back seat. I close the door behind him and get into the front. The loud click of all the locks simultaneously going off at once makes me jump. The weight of the situation sets in with the sound, burrowing itself in the hole in my stomach.

"We're just a few blocks away," Avery says.

"Do you want to take a detour?" I ask with as much enthusiasm as possible. "Avery's a doctor and he can give us a nonpublic tour, a 'trip,' so to speak."

He leans forward and with excitement in his voice, whispers, "Are you suggesting what I think you're suggesting?"

My assumption of this man seems correct. An accountant in a likely dead-end job wants a little more out of his boring life. From the small bit of information we were given, he doesn't seem to have many friends or family in the area, so to him it may seem like a good opportunity to escape the monotonous humdrum of his mundane life. A pang of remorse punches me in the stomach.

"Anything your heart desires," Avery adds.

"Sounds great." He playfully drums the back of my seat before sitting back. "Let's go!"

I sink into my seat and listen to the sourceless sounds inside and outside of the car. The only thing to do now is let Avery take the lead. The longer this goes on, the less it feels like my test, and more of a test for him. None of this would be possible if it weren't for him.

It's weird to consider murdering people as an easier task than kidnapping them, but here we are. Murder, at least in the form I've attuned myself to, is all about timing and reaction speed. Whereas this is far more elaborate and requires acting skills which I haven't mastered. Admittedly, it's naturally easier than it should be due to my unassuming stature and perceived vulnerability.

The easy part's over.

$$* * *$$

Avery's pushing a squeaky-wheeled stretcher with Gregory's limp, unconscious body atop it. The eagerness to try everything made Avery's job comically easy. Everything that Gregory was given, I was given a placebo for. It's the first time I've truly felt a little anxious to trust someone.

If it wasn't for the last few days I've spent with Avery, I would have felt susceptible to the despicable treatment he promised me when I first encountered him. Although, if he still has those feelings about me, the director is indirectly saving my life from his potential cruelty by providing me with a life of servitude. Neither outcome is very appealing, but perhaps my anxiety was severely misplaced.

"Friend, huh?" Avery says, his voice interrupting my thoughts. "I didn't think we had crossed that bridge yet."

"Well, you didn't kill me when you had the chance, so I suppose we have unintentionally crossed that bridge," I retort.

"I was never going to kill you," he says. The remorse in his voice is sincere. "I was just being an asshole. Besides, Sai would kill me if I ever intentionally hurt you."

"Even though it doesn't unburden you of your wrongdoings, I appreciate you not taking advantage of my blindness," I say.

"I don't blame you for not trusting me. I don't deserve it, that's for sure." His voice sounds distant, pensive even.

The conversation fades as I have nothing valuable to add. I could agree with him, but it wouldn't be helpful. I could dwell on all the things he said about me during my ethereal nonexistence, but that wouldn't be good for either of us. Neither would be bringing up Gaddreol right now when his existence is a major uncertainty.

If the director is true to his word, Gaddreol will be in his body soon. Hopefully, it's still in a relatively liveable condition. Although the mutilations to his body were unnecessary by all accounts, at least the amputations are manageable.

My thoughts shift to Vera again. More specifically, how she will react to the condition of her brother's body. She already feels she's insensitive when it comes to my blindness. Hopefully, she doesn't feel the same type of accountability toward his body as she seems to unintentionally put upon herself when it comes to my blindness.

The squealing wheels stop abruptly. "We've arrived. On your right."

"Hey, Tristan!" Taz greets me as I enter the room.

"You're doing the transition?" I ask, unintentionally, raising my eyebrow.

"I'm just getting things ready. I don't perform transitions. Avery is going to do this one," she says, as he rolls the squeaky stretcher into the room.

"I am?" His confusion doesn't instill confidence in me.

"You are," Josephine answers. She grabs my arm and demands, "Sit here. Don't move."

"My task is accomplished," I remark. "I don't have to be here."

"You don't have a choice. We'll restrain you if we need to. Now behave," she scolds.

I relent and just wait, listening to the ambient sounds in the room. Taz is setting up the equipment for the transition. The machines are active and beeping as noticeably as they were upon waking up in my state of oblivion. Avery is likely moving Gregory's body onto a bed, causing the stretcher to protest ferociously.

"Leave that body be, Avery. It won't be necessary," the director declares. "Samuel, please, bring in the body."

"What was the—" Avery's voice cuts off immediately.

What is it? I ask myself pointlessly, straightening my spine as if it will help me hear things better. Not that there is anything to be heard, anyway. Everyone in the room has fallen silent, leaving the incessant beeping to fill the space. It's nearly deafening.

"Put it on the bed. Avery, help him."

My heart races, nearly bursting from its cage. Trembles course through my body and my breathing stutters. A wave of dizziness washes over me as the realization hits me.

"Sai!"

"An astute observation," the director mocks. "Are you positive you're still blind?"

"Why are you transitioning into Sai's body? We retrieved the body for you! We accomplished your menial task!" I yell.

Remorse rushes through me for reducing Gregory's life to a menial task when it's anything but. But it's quickly replaced by my rage for the director and the impuissance I feel for Sai.

"Has anyone ever told you that you tend to take things a bit too literally?" His laughter is a sickening sound.

"Sai was only supposed to be punished if I refused!" My face is scrunched from the uncontrolled rage coursing through me. Tears well into my eyes, slowly dropping when too much liquid builds up.

"Regardless of your performance, his body was always my next choice. It's only fair that Sai is properly punished for his betrayal. You are a smart man. Don't do something you're going to regret," he says, getting onto the noisy hospital bed.

"That means sit down, shut up, don't move," Josephine snaps.

Begrudgingly, I comply, folding my arms over my chest. My head tilts to the floor as the tears stream down my face. I relax my facial features to prevent the headache pounding inside my skull from getting worse. I have an aura of disorientation that makes me feel like I'm sinking inside myself, almost like I'm distancing myself from reality.

What can I do? Nothing. There's nothing that I can do now that will help anything.

If I lunge at the closest person to me, I'll likely miss and then be apprehended. Even if I don't miss, I'm outnumbered by two, possibly three people. Honestly, I'm not sure who Avery's loyalty resides with right now. Going against the director would only make his situation worse and prevent Gaddreol from being able to transition again. Siding with the director would be the most optimal choice for him, so I wouldn't blame him personally if he did, but it still puts me in a worse situation. Taz would likely be on my side, but I don't know how much good that would do.

"Alright, everything is ready. I'm administering the anesthesia to the director." Taz sounds sullen and worried.

I'm sorry, Sai... I accept defeat.

My arms are wrapped around myself in a self-soothing action, but it doesn't help. My lungs feel like they're going to collapse from my labored breathing; each breath is shorter than the last until I'm nearly gasping for air. My whole body is trembling, my legs restlessly bouncing up and down.

"Director, please count down from ten," Avery requests.

An intense tingling covers every inch of my body, electrifying all of my nerve endings. Before I can comprehend what the prickling feeling is, it's compelling my body to move, to do anything. I need to be anywhere but right here.

"Ten... nine..."

My feet move faster than I can comprehend. I bulldoze through the person hovering over me, pushing them straight into a table or counter, knocking numerous objects to the ground. The person's arms reach out, their hands trying to grab my arm, but I rip myself away from the restraining grip. My legs carry me through the door, sprinting down the hallway.

Run. Just run.

Gaddreol's countdown was met with the cessation of his life, with the tumultuous buzzing and humming that's always in the back of my mind. I refuse to listen to that atrocious death machine again. I refuse to feel the vibrations and sensations that will be the end of my husband. I refuse to let that be my pervading memory of Sai.

No amount of death I've encountered or killing I've performed could ever prepare me for this. No amount of physical training could give me the strength to listen to the director countdown to Sai's death. I'm simply not strong enough.

I'm sorry. I'm sorry. I'm so sorry. Please forgive me.

I run until I reach the elevator at the end of the hall. Hoping it will come faster, I smash the elevator button repeatedly. Doubling over from the pain in my chest, the lack of oxygen makes my body give up. My feet give out from beneath me causing my knees to slam into the tile.

I tried. I failed. I lost. You're gone.

An impenetrable, dense smog surrounds me. I'm an empty husk of pure nothingness—hollow, numb, and distant. Floating aimlessly away from my detached body. There are shrieks of agony, screams of torment, and bellows of defeat filling the empty hall. I can't feel my mouth, nor can I hear them, but I know they're happening, and I know they belong to me.

Intuitively, I know someone is trying to drag me away from the elevator that happily chimes its arrival as if all is right in the world. Maybe it is for most people, but for me, my world is crashing down around me.

Before I can drag myself forward, someone pulls me away from the platform. I know I'm thrashing around with my hands and feet flying in every direction to get them off me, but it feels like a dream where everything is weightless without any force behind it. I can't feel the strenuous effort or even who is grabbing me.

Get away. Get away from me. Please, leave me alone.

"Tristan!" Someone's yelling, I know they're yelling my name, but I can barely comprehend it. "Tristan!"

I can't go back, don't make me go back. Please.

Arms are around me, crushing me. Suddenly, the fight within me ceases. I stop thrashing, stop flailing my limbs, stop fighting the person who has their arms wrapped tightly around me. Everything stops. I feel as though I'm suspended in the air, as weightless as the day I awoke in my prison.

Am I even breathing anymore?

"Tristan. I'm here." I realize it's Taz with me as the smog lifts to a faint fogginess. "I'm here, shh."

She's not hurting me, she's comforting me. Her arms are around me in a comforting embrace, but her touch isn't warm. It's ice cold, freezing. A shiver rips through my body.

"You're okay, I'm here."

I'm not okay. It's not okay. Nothing will ever be okay.

My head shakes aggressively, expressing the thoughts I can't speak. She holds my head against her chest trying to stop the fitful movement. Her hand smooths over my hair in the same manner Sai did when he was trying to comfort me after the meeting with the director.

"Oh, Tristan, I'm so sorry." Her voice cracks and her tears fall onto my face. "I'm so sorry."

Don't apologize. I failed. I'm sorry.

Her body shakes turbulently against mine as her silent tears progress into full-body sobs. I want to reach up to wipe her face, but my body is too heavy. Gravity has beaten me down into a pulp.

Everything's derailed now. Every move we made was pulverized. Every plan we devised was obliterated. We were going to dismantle the organization together. Without Sai, that's an impossibility.

The director stole the love of my life. I don't have Sai. I don't have a family. Where do I go from here? What's the point of living if I have nothing left to live for? I can't move forward, nor can I take it back, there's no reason to remain in the present.

Transition. The poison. Take it away.

"Don't let him go home." Josephine's voice is a distant whisper, but her grating voice cuts through the fog.

Someone larger than Taz picks me up with ease. The crook of

their elbow cradles my head, while my body rests against a solid frame and my legs dangle limply over the other arm.

Avery... Why is he carrying me? Where is he taking me?

I want to push him away from me, but my body won't heed my command like it did to drag my body to the elevator. Overpowering defeat washes over me as I realize the man carrying me away from my safety gave me to incapacitate me.

What did you do to me!? I yell, uselessly, to Avery. *I should have never trusted you, you sick bastard.*

CHAPTER SIXTEEN

UNAWARE I HAD fallen asleep, I awaken with a start. I feel around myself to find I'm in the hospital bed, again. A wave of sorrow hits me before the memories of what happened flood into my mind. A hollow dread consumes me as I remember the director is in Sai's body and Sai is gone.

How could this happen? I think, trying to replay the events from the meeting up until yesterday.

I followed the request. We kidnapped a man, drugged him, and served him on a silver, squeaky gurney, and for what? Nothing. Gregory was never the target and I failed to see who was until now. I realize now that the kidnapping itself was unimportant. Also, that the test was never about Gregory; it was never about using his body for transition. The test was always about me—whether I possess the obedience to indiscriminately carry out a task I don't necessarily agree with. All the while, creating the ultimate diversion to execute his horrific scheme to obtain his ideal body.

Why did this possibility not occur to me? Avery's situation already proved the director is capable of pulling off something so depraved. So then why didn't I think he would take Sai's life away?

It never crossed my mind that the director would kill Sai when he is—was—seemingly one of the most skilled doctors at his disposal. Though, now I understand, efficacy means little when he feels slighted or disrespected in any regard.

Now, reviewing the situation with hindsight, it all falls into place. The outcome was sparked because of my assassinations. Once the director discovered my alleged proficiency in killing it was only a matter of time before he ascertained the plan we devised and then created a countermeasure for it. The perfect trap was orchestrated for our unique situation, just as it had been done to Avery and I was too witless to recognize it beforehand. I should've realized that Sai was not allowed to aid me in the task because he was meant to be the target all along.

Maybe Avery put his soul into a livable vial like Gaddreol's soul.

A hopelessly hopeful thought since Josephine and Samuel were probably stationed in that room for the sole purpose of ensuring no loopholes or potential escape plans could be enacted.

I'm so sorry, Sai. I wish I could take it all back.

Tears finally fall from my eyes, silent, but steady. Curling into a ball, I pull the blanket over my head and let the burning tears flow, unheeded.

Why couldn't it have been me? I wonder, pointlessly. The answer is clear.

If he chose my body to transition into, it would punish Sai, but it would also punish him, too. After all, to him, a sightless body is an inconvenient hindrance. I suppose I didn't think he would take Sai's body because doing so takes away one of his doctors, but control seems to be his priority above all else.

However, I think it's more than that. In choosing Sai's body, the director probably believed killing him would be extremely difficult, if not an altogether impossible task. Honestly, I'm not sure I can argue with that thought process. Even though I can't see him, I know it's Sai's face and his voice—it is him. I'm not sure it's possible for me to disconnect myself enough to conceptualize him as the director and not as the love of my life.

What if he survived like I did?!

Another despairing thought comes into my mind. Of course he didn't survive. My survival is only attributed to Sai and his deliberate tampering. As a precaution the director wouldn't allow it in any form. If it did happen, Sai would likely end up as I did, unaware of himself with constant thoughts as he tries to piece together what happened. Which would result in his imminent death anyway.

Perhaps if I can make it back to my house, the poison I use for my targets will be readily available. If it is, I can use it on myself. Unlikely, as I'm sure the director is too intelligent not to consider that a possibility. I doubt leaving will be an option any time soon. My only option is to find something around the hospital to use.

No! I have to do this. For Sai. For everyone. For myself.

Sai trusted me to carry out the assassination, so that's what I need to do. Instead of wallowing in self-pity, I need to direct any remaining strength I can manage to complete the request that Sai asked of me. Without the usual tools in my arsenal, I will need to get creative.

I can ask Avery to bring me a lethal dose of morphine to inject him with. Although, failure to execute the assassination in any way would put him in danger. Even though I was drugged by him because of the director, he doesn't deserve to be on the receiving end of the director's wrath.

If I rummage around long enough, maybe I'll stumble across something useful. Wishful thinking since I'm sure they wouldn't put me in a room with anything that could be used as a lethal weapon. Although, anything can be used as a makeshift lethal weapon.

"Knock, knock," a calm, gentle male voice says, mimicking the raps against the door.

The hazy voice I've only heard once before in a dream is now clear and direct, in the present. Hearing his voice is enough to pull me out of my stupor, abruptly stopping the unyielding tears.

I yank the blanket off and bolt upright, yelling, "Gaddreol?!"

"The one and only." He chuckles softly as he comes in, his crutch clanking with every step into the room.

"You're alive!? I can't believe it!" I yell, frantically.

A flood of emotions consumes me and I'm not sure how to feel. Relief, joy, and concern are at the forefront, but there are so many others floating just beneath the surface that I don't add weight to.

"Everyone keeps saying that, but I don't remember it at all," he says. "Avery told me you were here, so I came to finally meet you in person."

"Needed to see for yourself if I'm more than a figment of your imagination?" I try to joke, but I can't manage a smile, so I worry about it coming across as condescending instead.

"Definitely," he says, laughing softly before hobbling closer to me. "I wanted to check on you. Do you need anything?"

I shake my head. "I don't think there is anything I need right now. How are you doing?"

"This crutch is doing the heavy lifting right now, but I'm glad to be in my body." He laughs again, before adding, "Missing parts and all."

The relief I feel for Gaddreol is immeasurable. A welcome respite from my depressive state, even if it's only temporary. I'm happy the director didn't take the chance to flaunt his boundless control over Gaddreol and Avery.

"I'm glad to finally meet you," I say, "I wish it were under better circumstances, though."

"It's crazy to see you with my own eyes. Hear your voice outside of my head for once." He sounds happy, but his tone shifts to worry when he says, "You look like you could use a hug."

I nod, not trusting my voice as the mere mention of a hug brings tears to my eyes once more. Noisily, he closes the distance before sitting on the edge of the hospital bed. He leans his crutch against the bed frame before pulling me into him with his right arm. My head is nestled gently beneath his chin as he holds me tightly with his remaining arm.

My silent tears ripple through my body, causing my body to tremble against his. Absently, I grab his shoulder, pulling him closer to me, like a shield from all the sadness and suffering. I expect resistance for a split second from a limb that isn't there and then I feel the nub just below the shoulder joint. Guilt and panic course through the pain and I drop my hand in my lap, afraid of bringing attention to his dismemberment.

"It's okay, you can touch it," he assures, pulling me in tighter. "It doesn't hurt like I thought it would. Avery said they probably tested something for healing on it, so it's pretty much healed up except for some stitches."

Thank you, I whisper, in my mind. Although he isn't able to hear my thoughts anymore, I'm sure he already knows.

With his reassurance, I put my hand on his shoulder and cry until my eyes sting from drying out. All the tears I shed pooled onto his shirt, the soaked fabric rubs against my cheek, but he doesn't seem bothered by it. I'm a heaving mess, barely able to catch my breath.

Gaddreol waits for my breaths to steady before he says, "Avery gave me a little rundown of what's been happening since I've been out. Thanks for being there for him and Vera. It means a lot to me."

With a weak nod, more tears burn their way through my eyes. I'm grateful for the peace of mind I provided with the back-and-forth banter with Vera and Avery; we all needed a little silly reprieve.

In retrospect, I'm not sure it was worth it. In trying to be available for everyone else, I became unavailable for the person who ended up needing me the most. It feels selfish to even consider, but I'm not sure if it was worth it since it cost me the one person who means more to me than anything.

I am an idle participant in my own life right now and I don't know how to handle it. Everything is happening around me, just outside of my control, and I'm along for the treacherous ride.

"Are you sure you don't want me to get anything for you?" he asks, releasing me from the one-armed hug.

I shake my head and find my voice. "No. Besides, you have to get used to hopping on one foot."

"It's not all bad." He tries to sound light-hearted. "I'll be fitted for prosthetics after a while. Avery's going to get me some fancy bionic prosthetics."

"Half-robot?" I ask, feigning confusion, forcibly raising a brow.

"I believe a cyborg is the term," he mocks. "Cyborg Gaddreol!"

"Cyborg Gaddreol isn't all that appealing," I say, dramatically scrunching my face with a strained chuckle.

"I'll think of something cool one day." His genuine laugh dwarfs mine and I can't help but smile weakly.

"Doubtful, but we'll work on it." Avery's voice interjects. "Glad to see you're awake. How are you holding up?"

Not well. I shake my head again, unable to admit it openly.

"I'm sorry about tricking you the other day," he says, sounding genuinely remorseful, which is appreciative. I know rage should be my default feeling towards the betrayal, but I know he isn't in a position to go against the director. Plus, I'm not sure I have it in me to feel furious, so I fixate on "the other day."

"How long have I been asleep?"

"You've been in a coma for five days. Taz and I have been taking turns checking on you consistently. Gaddreol, too, now. The medicine I gave you, combined with acute stress, likely caused the seizure you suffered, which led to you slipping into a coma." The sincerity in his voice is undisguised by the matter-of-fact tone.

"Five days," I repeat, horrified. Five days have passed since Sai's body was taken over by the ruthless director.

"Yeah, but hey, Gaddreol got this for you," he says, walking to me.

"You didn't have to get me anything," I say, but a small paper plate is placed in my lap and a fork is handed to me.

I fumble with the fork until it finds the piece of food. It's soft and easy to pull apart. Bringing it up to my mouth, the sweet scent of chocolate and whipped cream fills my nose. Uncontrollable laughter rips out of me. "You brought me pie?"

"It's a little late, I know, so it's not the first thing you got to eat when you got your body back," he says.

"I can't believe you actually remembered that. You're the best."

The chocolate pie is rich, decadent, and far too small. It's gone in a few bites, but that's probably for good reason. I'm sure eating for the first time after being in a coma should just be a small bit of food.

Avery's voice is reserved and uncertain as he says, "I hate to be the one to ruin all this, but the director wants to see you now that you're awake."

He killed the love of my life, which caused me to suffer a seizure, and then subsequently, a coma and he still can't give me a break. *He is a despicably merciless man.*

"Okay," I whisper.

As much as I don't want to be near this wretched man, I need to face him. Compliance with his unreasonable demands may be the only way to be close enough to achieve the assassination. If I can miraculously get that close, understanding how he operates will help me formulate a plan specifically to target him in the same manner he does to everyone else.

"Are you sure?" Gaddreol asks, concerned.

"I don't have a choice," I state.

The crutch resting against the bedside falls clattering against the ground loudly enough that the echo carries through the hall. I cover my ears until the sound stops reverberating.

"You are way too clumsy for your own good," Avery says, closer now, probably picking up the crutch.

"Thanks," he says, lifting himself off the side of the bed with the retrieved aid.

After he moves, I shift my weight over the side of the bed and tentatively slide off onto the ground. A shiver runs through my spine as my feet touch the ice-cold floor. With a purposeful stretch, my body creaks and groans to life, protesting the simple action. Once the initial ache fades, I start for the direction of the door both men entered through. Gaddreol's clunking steps follow suit, and Avery passes me, leading the way.

Outside of the metallic thunk with Gaddreol's step, our walk to the elevator is relatively silent. Even the hall seems extraordinarily quiet. Not a sound to be heard in any room besides the incessant beeps of the machines. My head hangs in solidarity as we pass the rooms where so many people lost their lives.

My thoughts trail to Gregory, so I ask, "If the director didn't want him for the transition, what happened to him?"

"Unfortunately, he wasn't saved. I tried taking him down to the E.R. for recovery, but Samuel wanted to transition into his body." There's an unspoken apology in his guilt-ridden tone.

The elevator ding strikes uncontrolled, tumultuous fear into me. My throat tightens, causing shallow labored breathing. My heart is pounding rapidly, my pulse thumping painfully against my ears. My body feels like it's radiating heat through every intense tremble.

"Are you okay?" Gaddreol asks, his voice is faint and distant, I can barely hear it over my own heartbeat.

I shake my head. In absolutely no way, shape, or form can I be considered okay. In my attempt to prevent the sound of that awful machine from representing Sai's death, this ordinary mechanical ding has become synonymous with it.

My legs are restless, wanting more than anything to run away from this sound. It doesn't happen. My body is completely frozen, consumed by fear and melancholy. I can't do anything but listen to the doors close. Before this, I wasn't afraid of elevators. I was only discomforted by the nauseating instability I felt riding in it without my feet firmly on the ground.

Now, that isn't true. While the ride itself may not be frightening, I may never know. This sound is petrifying, utterly debilitating that I may never be able to set foot onto one again.

Move. Get away from the doors, I think, urging my feet, but nothing happens.

Effortlessly, Avery scoops me off my feet, carrying me away from the harrowing sound. I don't know how far he takes me from the elevator before he sets me down. I can breathe better, and the body shakes have calmed to slight, occasional twitches. My knees wobble, but I regain my balance and stabilize my breathing.

"Sorry, you weren't responding," he says, solemnly. "It's a long way up, but we can take the stairs. You can ride on my back if you want."

"No," I say, weakly. "I can walk."

"I'll meet you guys up there. Be careful," Gaddreol says, before heading back the way we came.

"You, too," Avery opens the whining door, gently guiding me inside.

I brace myself for the thunderous slam of the door, but he closes it softly so that the click is barely audible. I shuffle forward carefully to find the handrail. The old metal is coarse against my palm and the chipping paint flakes off with every slight movement.

After three flights of stairs, Avery says, "First floor down, five more to go."

✶ ✶ ✶

"Thank you," I say as Avery sets me down on a chair.

After two floors, my legs proved too weak to carry me any further. Swallowing my pride and accepting my humiliation I asked Avery to carry me the rest of the way. Without complaint, he hauled me up the rest of the stairs. His steady pace dwindled in the last few flights, and I wanted to protest, but holding myself up against his body was difficult enough, so I reluctantly stayed put.

"No problem," he says between ragged breaths.

Still trying to catch his breath, Avery pounds on the first set of double doors to the director's office. An intense feeling of dread settles in as reality finally hits me. I'm about to come face-to-face with the man who wears Sai's face.

Calm down. With a couple of deep breaths and counting a few sets of five, I manage to not break out into a fit of panic.

"It's about time you woke up." Josephine's voice sends a shiver through my body, but I stabilize myself before lifting my head in her direction. "Get up."

I obey. My knees wobble as they adjust to supporting my full weight again. My calves are screaming their protests with each step forward. Ignoring the soreness in my muscles, my head stays up high and my posture doesn't let on the discomfort I feel.

Just as always, she digs her nails deep into my arm, dragging me through the corridor into the office. Despite intrinsically knowing the path now, I allow her to feel superior and just dutifully follow. It's not like I have the strength to argue about it right now, anyway. Forcibly, she shoves me down and I sink into the chair. She scoffs but walks away from me.

Sai's scent of vanilla and sandalwood surrounds me, consuming me. A pit forms in my stomach, nausea twisting inside it.

Green. The faint color flashes through the darkness of my mind.

"You know, I'm glad that you have this body now." Her voice is overtly brazen and alluring, dragging my attention to their vulgar interaction. I bite my tongue in a futile attempt to distract myself from trembling in disgust. She adds, "It's so much prettier than the last one."

A brief kiss is shared between the two of them, but it feels like an eternity before she asks, "Do you need anything else?"

An overwhelming visceral reaction to gag at the thought of the man I've built my life with sharing intimacy with this vile woman comes over me. To prevent them from gaining satisfaction from my gross reaction, I swallow down the bile creeping up my throat. At this moment, nothing sounds better than simply curling into a ball and dying.

"That's all for now, thank you." My heart skips a beat at the sound of Sai's stoic voice. Every ounce of willpower is spent on not breaking into a million pieces.

The click-clack of Josephine's heels snapping against the tile is the only sound breaking the disconcerting silence that's filled the room. Disregarding the heavy wooden doors as she walks through them, they reverberate through the room, the abrupt echo rattling deep into my bones. Once the booming echoes subside, the only sound that remains is from our breathing. Although mine is shallower than his.

His uncharacteristic stillness causes a perilous feeling to creep over my body, uncertain of what to do or say. I can feel his eyes on me before he begins walking towards me with a cautious stride. He stops directly in front of the chair. His fingers delicately trail along my wrist. Recoiling, I rip my hand away from the grotesque touch.

Don't touch me! I think, unable to yell out physically.

Both of his hands wrap around my wrists in a gentle, but firm grip. I try to free my hands, but he tightens his grip. Without any time to react, he pulls me to my feet, wrapping his arms around my waist. He nestles his head against mine, with his face blanketed by my unkempt hair.

"My love. Nothing I can say to you will be an adequate apology for you. No words will ever be able to express to you how sorry I am for all that I put you through by asking for your assistance." The dev-astation in his voice shreds my defenses. "However, I am truly sorry."

My mouth falls open, but my breath catches in my throat. My knees buckle and my body nearly becomes dead weight, slumping against him. He catches me effortlessly, pulling me closer to him. I breathe in the calming scent I've always remembered, removing the repugnant feeling that took over moments ago.

"You're alive?!" I reiterate the same question I asked Gaddreol to the man I feared I'd lost forever. As frustrating as it is to be a blubbering mess, I accept the tears burning their way through my eyes. "You don't have to apologize. I'm just so happy you're safe."

He sweeps me off my feet, putting me onto his lap as he sits into the chair. My feet dangle over the armrest. One of his arms is tightly around my back, holding me securely against his chest. The other is loosely in front of me, trailing his fingers gently over my arms, down my palms, and over my fingertips. Calling attention to my fingers, I realize they are finally free from their gauzy confines.

"If not for the information you told me, I would not have figured out what the director was planning," He nestles his face into my hair again. "So, I have you to thank for my survival."

"I don't understand," I say, meekly.

"As difficult as it was for you, I am grateful that you told me about the details regarding the meeting. Everything you informed me of was paramount in discovering the truth. Knowing that Avery was to be your assistant in your task was cardinal. By not being able to assist you, I knew I was the target. In telling me the director is Dr. Sands, I was able to enact my own subterfuge." Despite trying to maintain a monotonous tone, he sounds exhausted and broken himself. I imagine that after surviving his inevitable death was a short-lived victory once he learned I slipped into a coma. The insurmountable fear that would create is indescribable.

Sai was able to figure out the director's motive and the means that he was susceptible to. Suffering through the complex feelings was worth it to give him the information he needed. If I had known it would lead to his safety, I wouldn't have had reservations about sharing anything.

He exhales deeply against my neck; causing goosebumps to coat my body. "Without Taz's help I would not have been able to accomplish anything, so I enlisted her to help me coordinate everything," he says. "While the director's intentions were not known, I figured he was planning to use my body to transition into. Knowing Taz was likely to be tasked with setting the transition up for Avery, I asked her if she would be willing to sabotage the equipment. She obliged happily, despite her nervousness. She severed the link attached to me. When it was time for her to detach the equipment from the director, she severed his spine. I wanted to tell you this sooner, but we didn't have much time to discuss things."

Which is true. We had no time to discuss anything at length. After the night he comforted me, I spent the next day trying to give Vera a day she would remember with Avery's help. By the time he came home from work, I was too tired to engage in conversation. Then the following day was spent performing the kidnapping with Avery.

"I'm just so happy you're safe," I say, then shift the conversation to the inevitable, "Is he still alive?"

"Yes," he says. My muscles involuntarily tense at the word. It disintegrates the hope that was starting to rise before I have the chance to feel it. "Please do not worry, he has quadriplegia now, so he's completely harmless."

Vera's wheelchair fragments into my mind, awkwardly trying to replace a small-framed child with a grown man. A nefarious man like the director being incapacitated in a wheelchair is an unthinkable possibility, but Sai and Taz made it a reality. A sickening sense of pleasure engulfs me, stopping the corrosive tears entirely. The director being in a similar paralyzed state to Vera's former self shouldn't give me satisfaction, but if anyone deserves immobility, it is him.

"What about Josephine?" I ask, gritting my teeth.

"Unfortunately, she is invaluable to gaining an understanding of the inner workings of this organization," he says, "I apologize for the physical display. It may be a charade I will have to continue until I have a solid comprehension of all the essential information we need or until the director relents."

"What are you doing with the director?" I ask, pushing away the uncomfortable situation with Josephine.

"He's in isolation." Sai's tone turns cold and distant, his posture stiffening for a moment. He relaxes again as he says, "Torturing the director is an unbecoming, daunting task."

Thinking of Sai trying to torture anyone is borderline lunacy. He is reserved, but hardly callous. The fact it is even a consideration in his mind is shocking to me. Perhaps now with Sai and Gaddreol surviving, my emotional state will become unfaltering so I can do it for him. I must admit that torturing a man with quadriplegia feels exceptionally sadistic. His heinous crimes against people are the only things preventing me from feeling monstrous.

"Have you told Avery?" I ask.

He gently shakes his head in my hair. "Not yet. Avery has dealt with so much already. I wanted him to be able to focus most of his attention on Gaddreol and himself. The only request I gave him was to look after you."

If anyone deserves a break from this grueling organization, it's Avery. Although carrying me up nine flights of stairs isn't a break, it's a little better than the emotional torment he's been put through. Hopefully, I can convey to him how grateful I am to him for carrying me up the stairs.

I nod. "Have you discovered the identities of the scientist and the engineer?"

"The trio were never too far from one another. Josephine is the scientist and Samuel is the engineer. All three of them have limited involvement with experiments in their own way." Sai's head rests on my shoulder, as he whispers solemnly. "I'm sorry. I never would have sent you to them."

"I know, Sai," I say, running my hands through his hair.

"How are your eyes?" he asks, pulling his head away from me to inspect my eyes. "They are not as luminous, but just as orange."

"Hey, look at that, I'm not a psychedelic glow stick. There isn't a consistent burning pain anymore, but my tears feel like abrasive sandpaper against my eyes," I say, wiping the tear stains from my face.

"Ask Avery for more of the eye drops," he says, before returning to the original topic. "So far I've accessed both digital and physical files, but I haven't been able to study them yet. Josephine hardly gives me a moment to myself, so studying information is not possible."

"What if I study them?" I ask before I can stop myself. "If I can get Avery or Taz to help me scan the documents and convert them, I can make braille files to review.

He shifts his body slightly so that he's facing me. He is either looking at me as though I'm crazy or a genius. "With the computer at home, everything is set up for you to use, so you shouldn't require assistance. If you do, I'm sure neither of them would have an issue with it. Are you sure you want to do that?"

"What else am I going to do with my time? At least this way, I am actually useful," I say, immediately regretting that statement. "I'm sorry."

"No, it's alright. I appreciate any help you can give. If you're sure, I can send a few files with you. Josephine likely won't notice any missing files," he says. "Actually, she may never notice. She doesn't seem to care about dealing with the paperwork. Or anything, really."

From the interactions I've had with her, it seems the only aspect of this 'job' she enjoys is being in control. Causing as much harm as possible seems to be the only thing she will willingly take part in, but mostly as an observer of the torment.

I nod and change the subject. "Did you learn anything about the kids?"

"Yes. There's a residential home nearby that's owned by Charles Sands and run by Olivia Sands, presumably related. Currently, there are thirty-three children ranging in ages from two to eleven in the facility." His matter-of-fact tone returns. "The facility is disguised as a school. Each of the children must follow a strict regimen that their purchaser decides for them."

Thirty-three kids were born and raised at the discretion of the buyer to become the perfect replacement. Whoever is teaching the kids must be involved in some form or another. I can't imagine a self-respecting person would be okay with molding tiny humans to be used as a replacement.

"They're creating their perfect bodies from actual living children," I whisper. Saying it aloud is more sickening than I expected. My stomach churns and green pops into my mind, but I push it aside. "How are we going to save them from these people?"

"We'll start with the files, discern the types of buyers and what they are looking for," he says, distantly. "Once we know who's who, we will set up meetings for them.

Lifting me to my feet, Sai brushes past me, pacing across the room. He opens a metal cabinet, presumably grabbing the files for me. Hastily, he paces the room again. He grabs my hand with a slight squeeze before the files take his place.

The folders are all roughly an inch in thickness. An abnormally large amount of paperwork on each person when the focus of the director and his cohorts only care about the immoral and financial benefits. It seems I was wrong about the precautions of this vile organization, which makes sense. Outside of the kidnapped victims, the most vulnerable position of the organization is the potential customers.

"These were filed under the section for the residential home," he says. "They're ordered chronologically, so hopefully there will be vital information."

I set the folders down on the chair and reach my arms forward, finding Sai's shoulders. Sinking my hands into his hair, I pull his face to mine. The yearning I feel for him guides my movements, pressing my mouth against his. His fervor matches mine as our lips meld together seamlessly.

The first set of heavy doors groans to life, bringing our intimate moment to an abrupt halt, the intense pining comes back with it. Sai moves away, sitting on the desk across from me. I sit back down in the chair with the files loosely under the hospital gown.

The distant metal clunk against the tile means Gaddreol is the one coming through the door. I turn my ear towards the door to listen carefully. There isn't an accompanying slam as I expect. Just another set of groaning doors open and the metal clunk hobbling through it.

"Gaddreol? Avery?" Sai asks, sounding as confused as I feel.

"Sai?" Avery asks, probably tipped off by the gentle, concerned tone he has.

"What are you doing here?" He ignores Avery's question. "What happened to Josephine?"

"Don't tell me you've taken a liking to that witch?" Presumably, Sai shakes his head since he says, "Good. Samuel called her away, so I decided to come check on Tristan. Clearly it wasn't needed. Why didn't you tell me you were alive, you dick?"

"I'm sorry."

A solid thump, followed by swishing fabric sounds tells me Avery punched Sai before pulling him into a hug. After separating, Avery says, "Good to see you, man. But, uh, what happened to Sands?"

"He's in isolation with quadriplegia," I offer, sheepishly.

"Where? I'll take a swing or two at him." Avery's excitement at the prospect of exacting his revenge is palpable.

"Avery," Gaddreol says his name cautiously as if trying to deter him from contemplating what I had considered only a little bit ago.

"Right," he says, backpedaling instantly. "Sorry."

Bizarrely, I find myself commiserating over Avery not being able to release the anger and frustration he rightfully has against the director. I'm sure he is trying to quell his malignancy to atone for his awful treatment of Gaddreol and me. However, this is a unique situation where the responsible person should be subjected to the indignation Avery has yet to unleash. In my opinion, at least.

"I have a training dummy at our house if you'd like," I offer, even though I know it will never be as good.

"Thanks," he says to me, "I'd rather spar with you when you get your bearings back, though."

Before I can answer, Sai walks over to the metal filing cabinet again. Ignoring the comment, he says, "Tristan is going to convert these files into braille to study. He already has three. If you don't mind, here are three more."

"How are you going to get them back?" Avery asks, then adds, "The witch is going to ask if you keep requesting meetings."

"I know."

"What about that supply closet on the fifth floor? It's too messy for Josephine or Samuel to ever stick their pompous noses in it."

"That's a good idea, actually," Sai agrees. "Whenever you finish with those, I will have more waiting to be taken."

"I have those sometimes." Avery laughs and gets Sai to laugh a little. Although the sound is strained, it's still melodic.

Sai walks towards me and I shift the files from my lap, standing to meet him. He pulls me into him, embracing me. He presses his lips against my ear, and whispers, "Thank you."

"Let's go before she gets back," Avery says, picking up the files I set down. "Good luck, Sai."

With that, I follow the metal clicking of Gaddreol's crutch until we leave the office. He continues down the hall towards the dread inducing metal box, while I turn to the intimidating stairway. Avery groans behind me, but he holds the door open for me.

In truth, as difficult as these stairs are, I would have chosen to go down them alone if necessary. Even though Sai is alive, the idea of going down the elevator still causes my heart to pound against my chest. Hopefully, I can logically ease my way into being okay with the daunting ping.

The long trek in silence down the stairs provides ample time to think. I can only imagine the abundant thoughts swirling around in Avery's mind. He must be lost in them as we descend the stairs. Even more so since he is pacing ahead of me in case I need help.

Just a few hours ago, Sai was assumed to be dead. Now, he's presented me with information that has the potential to change the trajectory of the organization tremendously. We just need to ensure neither Josephine nor Samuel becomes suspicious of Sai before we move the pieces into place.

CHAPTER SEVENTEEN

THE FIRST NIGHT home alone was a lot more difficult than I was mentally prepared for. I assumed that knowing Sai is alive would make the loneliness easier to manage, but if anything, it made being home away from him even more difficult.

I can't tell if the prominent stinging in my eyes is from remnants of the serum or from the fatigue nagging at my body. Ignoring the undesirable feelings, I wander through the house to find the office.

The virtual assistance in the house is attached to the computer so starting up the computer is as seamless as Sai said it would be. The voice activation and screen reading software installed in the computer make connecting the scanner and the braille embosser an intuitive experience.

It doesn't take long before a series of rapid hammering pops with a subtle hissing sound fills the house as the papers go through the braille embosser. Every pop creates a mini explosion of white polka dots in the unending black space of my mind.

The jarring sound brings up memories of Sai spending countless hours setting the machines up. And then spending even more hours diligently testing all of the components to ensure everything synced together while also being completely accessible for me.

While the machine works tirelessly through the papers, I stumble my way through the house to find the room that we prepared for my physical training. Ambling around, I find it's off the kitchen. On one side of the room is an arrangement of exercise equipment such as dip bars, and weights, and some bulky machines after that. Circling the room, I find the other side has various knives, swords, and other weaponry, alongside the training dummy Sai set up.

Cautiously grabbing a knife from one of the wall racks, I hold it with a confidence I didn't expect to have. Although it's different from the one Sai showed me, there is a vague familiarity to it. This one has a plain hilt with a short blade.

Walking forward, I softly nudge the edge of a foam mat. After taking a moment to get acclimated to the new flooring, I assume an assertive stance in the middle of the mat. My feet align with my shoulders; bending my knees, I raise my hands to my chest. With a hesitant slowness, I stab and slash into the air.

One slow strike after the next my uncertainty steadily dissolves into intrepid conviction. With the increased confidence, the blade in my hand becomes an extension of me instead of a tool, syncing fluidly with each of my movements. Every strike is more liberating and exhilarating than the last. The tentative slashes shift seamlessly into meticulous calculated slashes perfectly in time with kicks and dodges. It's a sequence that I have seemingly choreographed and practiced scrupulously time and time again.

I slash and kick to my heart's content until my body is too weak to continue. Collapsing to the ground, the blade is carefully placed at my side as I catch my breath. Through the thump of my heartbeat drumming against my ears is the sound of clapping and quiet cheering.

My head snaps to the direction the sound is coming from. Quickly grabbing the knife in my hand again, I assume a defensive position.

"Relax, it's just us." Avery says, before emitting a full belly laugh that causes me to have my own surprising laughing fit, lowering the knife. "Should I challenge you now or wait until you've rested a bit?"

"We wanted to see how you're doing. Sorry about the intrusion," Taz says. "You are really good at that, by the way."

The happiness consuming me is short-lived, quickly replaced by embarrassment that I was too enthralled to hear either of them enter. Another instance negating the idea of me being an assassin. Hopefully, the more poised and confident I become the faster I'll start to fall in line with the career path I chose.

I rise to my feet. "We can postpone the sparring for now. How long have you been standing here?"

It's strange to hear the words come out of my mouth, since a short time ago I couldn't wait to knock him out. The animosity I felt for him is gone now, but I wonder if sparring with him would provide me with the same sense of satisfaction.

"Long enough to see you get really into it," Avery says, striding through the room. "We knocked but didn't hear anything besides that loud clicking."

Despite their intrusion damaging my ego slightly, I can't find it in me to be upset about it. In place of expected anger is just endearment, knowing that they care enough to continue making sure I am doing well. Originally, I would have said something that would have only been relevant to Taz, but I've come to learn Avery isn't as heartless as he tries to seem.

"Thanks," I say. "I appreciate it. Where is Gaddreol?"

I place the knife back in its place and cross the room for the door. Crossing the threshold, I realize that the embosser is finished converting files to braille. Taking the lead, I head back to the office to gather the papers, Avery and Taz keeping pace behind me.

"Gaddreol is out with Vera." Avery sounds a little worried.

"Whatever he's doing is what he feels best for Vera right now," Taz says, reassuringly. "I'm sure things will be okay."

Gaddreol going to see his little sister as a double amputee on his own is an interesting choice. Undoubtedly, seeing him like that will shatter her perception of the organization. Before he has a chance to say anything, she's already going to understand that her body wasn't actually made for her, even if she can't fully comprehend it.

"How long does he have to wait for the prosthetics?" I ask.

"It will be another week or two," Avery says flatly, taking on Sai's defense mechanism to shield his emotions. Then he taps the plastic casing and asks, "That loud sound came from this?"

"Yeah," I answer. "The papers are on the desk, still in order, I think."

Avery shuffles the papers, before asking, "So, what are you trying to figure out from these?"

"Sai doesn't have time to analyze the files to get information on the clients, whereas I have an infinite amount of time on my hands. I'm going to read through them to determine which type of service each of the clients want," I explain, as I organize the braille papers into folders.

"Types of service?" Avery asks.

"Every person is looking for a body, but the specifics regarding each person are different. Thirty-three children are being raised for some of these people to steal their bodies. Then there are the people who are waiting for a kidnapped person of their liking."

"Do you think they have specific targets in mind to kidnap?" Taz's voice is timid, barely a whisper.

If it's too difficult, you don't have to do it. I think to her, but saying that aloud would be counterproductive, so I keep it to myself.

She's here because she wants to provide support in any way she can, which is greatly appreciated considering the sheer size of this organization alone. She'll likely continue providing any support so she can right the wrongs she committed in the name of FREE and its ridiculous theory. Not that I blame her; if I were in her place, I would do everything in my power to make up for any actions that impacted others, as well.

"Maybe, but every person who's kidnapped has to be physically healthy to be used, otherwise Sands wouldn't let them be used."

"How are kidnapped victims chosen?" I ask.

"Many of them actually come through the ER," Avery answers. "If they fit Sands' stupid health standards, they're marked. If we can convince them to stay for something more serious, it usually ends with them "succumbing to their illness." If we can't convince them to stay or miss an opportunity to incapacitate them, they get tracked outside the hospital."

"Who follows them?" I ask, but answer my own question, *We do, apparently.*

"I don't know who does that usually," Avery says, "I didn't think I'd ever be assigned to a kidnapping."

"I'm sorry you were dragged into it," I say.

Avery erupts into laughter, causing me to flinch. "You don't have a reason to be sorry. I'm sorry you were dragged into all this shit."

"On the topic of saying sorry," Taz says, "I'm sorry. You know... the director... and Sai..."

Her voice trails off with a sharp intake of air, unable to mention the horrific events that took place. Which is perfectly fine with me. I'm not sure I'm mentally strong enough to hear it again, especially not this soon.

My head drops unnecessarily, as I say, "It's okay. Sai explained it all to me. I understand."

Less than a week ago, Sai was presumed dead, I ran away like a coward, and she held me as life shattered around me. The guilt Taz feels is probably compounded by the fact she held me after she aided in the perceived devastation of my life, but if she could have just told me the truth, all the pain I felt in that moment would have evaporated.

No amount of wishing things transpired differently will make it a reality. The only thing to do now is try not to dwell on the sad aspects and maintain a pragmatic frame of mind moving forward. Easier said than done with the weight of the emotional turmoil still stirring deep within me. I imagine I'm not the only one dealing with a fragile mental state at the moment, but it's likely they are holding it together better than I am.

"Thanks," Taz says, sullenly.

I clear my throat to ease my discomfort. "Josephine and Samuel have as much to do with the situation as the director himself. Once Sai doesn't need them anymore, we'll need to deal with them just like the "customers" in these files."

"Alright. Shouldn't be too difficult if they trust Sai," Avery says. "Before I bring these files back to him, I'm going to look at them, too. I want to know what we're dealing with."

"What are we going to do with the children?" Taz's voice is little more than a soft mumble.

"If you're up for it, you should be the one to assess them," Avery says, saving me from scrambling to find an appropriate response. "You would make them the most comfortable out of all of us."

"Assess them?" Taz asks. "I can try, but I've never done a psych eval before."

"It's probably not too different from a med eval. I'm sure you could figure it out without much issue."

"Avery is right. You are the most comforting person to be around. It's something I immediately picked up on, even when I was trapped inside my ethereal state of nonexistence.

"Aw, really?" Her voice gets higher as elation shines through her worry.

"Yes," I say. "You are a beacon of hope through the dreariness."

"Thanks, guys! That really means a lot to me." I can hear the smile in her words.

"So, you'll do it?" he asks.

"Dealing with kids does sound better than the other craziness, so yeah. We'll just have to run it by Sai first."

"He'll be on board," Avery says. "These are high-profile players. How are we going to take on them?"

"Maybe if we ignore them, they'll go away," Taz offers meekly.
Would they?

The promise of immortality is not an easily forgettable concept. The people involved are not going to let the organization fade into oblivion without putting up a fight. However, what they'll be able to do about it is another story altogether. I suppose that depends on who they are and how much power they hold. If they have some influence in the hospital, it could present a problem. The other factor that is included is money. From the way the director spoke, many of the customers have already paid to fund the organization. If they've already paid, they won't give up the chance for a new body.

"I'll write a note inside the folder for Sai when he grabs these; tell him what we're thinking," Avery says. "If it comes to it, are you really going to kill these people?"

If it comes to murder, will I do it? "Yes."

"Are you okay with doing that?" Taz asks, sounding concerned.

"I am okay with murder, yes. There are people in the world that are undeserving of the air they breathe—the director being a prime example of that," I say.

"I could drink to that," Avery laughs. "I'm surprised you're okay with it. How many people can say they're okay with something like that?"

"Are you?" I ask although I'm sure I already know the answer.

"I acted like it, but no, I'm not." Avery sounds apologetic. "It was just a shitty act; a role I forced on myself to make my reality a little easier to manage."

Maybe, I don't know the answer.

Unsure of how to respond, I continue thumbing through the thick papers. The thicker papers make the files two or three times bulkier than the regular folders, so separating them is proving to be tedious. Next time, I'll be smarter and scan one file at a time, so the process is smoother.

"I chose my career to save people," Avery says, pensively.

It sounds like he wants to say more, but it's Taz who speaks up, "We will save people. First by saving these kids and future victims of FREE. Then, we'll just be the doctors we were before all this."

"Can we just resume our life like that?" Avery asks.

"Sure, why not?" Taz asks. "I know you don't think so, but you're still compassionate. It's just buried under your resentment."

"Ow. Just stab me in the heart why don't you," Avery jokes, but no one laughs.

"At least I didn't stab you in the back." From the humming sound she makes, I assume she's sticking her tongue out, before adding, "I'm serious, Avery. I know the director messed everything up, but I still think you're compassionate and caring beneath all the pain."

She's right, of course. If she wasn't, he wouldn't have gone out of his way to protect his family or Vera. I became the target of his pain and resentment, but now that he doesn't direct it at me anymore, I don't think he has anyone to point it at.

The director is incapacitated, and Josephine and Samuel are in a delicate position that makes them untouchable. When they aren't needed anymore, I'm sure he won't waste any time showing them how he truly feels.

The papers are sorted into their respective folders. I leave them in a stack on the desk and face the direction that Avery is in.

"Would it help you to take your frustration out on the dummy?" I ask, then remembering his question about sparring, I add, "Or we can spar like you want."

"Wait, really?" His tone perks up. "Yeah, if you're up for it."

"If it can give you a little reprieve, I am," I say, rising to my feet.

"Are you sure about this, Avery?" Taz asks, following me back to the training room.

"I've never trained officially, but I've gotten into a few fights here and there. Besides, he's blind, so maybe I have a chance."

Taz's abrupt laugh causes me to flinch. "I was talking about you hurting Tristan because he's blind."

"I think you underestimate him a little too much," Avery laughs. "I'm almost scared for myself."

It's strange to hear them talking about me as if I'm not here, but even stranger to hear Avery commend my supposed ability. It brings a hint of a smile to my face, though. I never thought in any capacity he would give me any form of praise.

"Okay, just be careful," Taz says, relenting.

I stride to the middle of the mat, assuming an assertive, poised stance. My stance is open with my feet aligned with my shoulders, my elbows bent rigidly at my sides a couple inches from my body, and my hands loosely balled in front of my face.

Avery's heavy footfall comes up behind me. The foam flooring noticeably indents with every micromovement as his weight shifts. Then the mat stills, which must mean Avery assumed his position, too.

"Ready?"

Before Avery can respond, Taz yells, "Don't get hurt!"

"It's fine, Taz. I'm ready." Avery says but doesn't make a move.

I make the first move, swinging my right hand towards his left side. Avery effortlessly blocks it and then retaliates with his own. Just before his arm reaches mine, a faint breeze brushes against my skin allowing me to swiftly block. The weight shift indicates his left leg comes in for a low kick. I turn my body just enough for my shin to take the impact and then counter with a loose strike that he blocks with his forearm.

With his feet firmly planted on the mat, he braces himself to deliver a quick strike that comes towards my face. Snapping both of my arms closed, my forearms take a direct hit. I stagger slightly from bracing for a harder impact but regain my composure. Then I counter with a sweeping kick, surprising him enough to knock him off his feet.

He falls to the ground with a groan and hard plop, almost heavy enough to knock me off balance. He laughs, rising to his feet, before saying, "You're way better than I expected."

"He knocked you off your feet, I'd say he's pretty great."

"Beginner's luck," he says, with an evident smile in his voice. Taz likely gives him a knowing look as he adds, "Fine, I was distracted."

"Thanks, guys," I say, chuckling.

Avery's feet clumsily sink into the mat without any rhythm as he trudges off the mat. "Another round, another time. Vera and Gaddreol are ready to be picked up."

"Tell him hello for me, please," I say, walking off the mat, in the direction of Taz.

"Sure thing," Avery calls out from another room.

"Tristan," Taz says, "the way you move is so graceful. If I didn't already know, I could never tell you are blind from watching you."

"With sight, people don't need to be aware of the nuances from other senses, but it's a skill I've taught myself and sharpened with Sai's help."

Taz squeezes my arm gently. "You're awesome, you know."

She lets go of my arm and then follows Avery, and together they make their way out the front door. With the click of the door, the loneliness pours in, freely flowing through my body.

Another night by myself.

Not that I'm incapable of being alone, but after everything that's happened over the last two months, it feels especially isolating. At least, tonight I'll be busy reading through the files Sai sent with me.

Opening the hefty files, I quickly get to work.

CHAPTER EIGHTEEN

AFTER A COUPLE weeks of monotonously brailling files, I finished working through the hundreds of clients. For the most part, many of the prospects are oblivious to the immoral structure FREE is founded upon as they're merely looking for ways to immortality. Honestly, from the obscured details, it's hard to tell if some of them are even aware of the kidnappings or if they believe it is a synthetic process.

It seems the perfect list was curated of corrupt candidates who have no issue with the kidnapping for their ultimate means. Many of the people who purchased a "hold" on the children are the mega-rich who want to pass their inheritance onto themselves disguised as distant kin. Potentially, clever if not for the disgusting reality of it. A synthetic body would have the same result.

The rich earthy aroma of coffee fills the room, followed quickly by the familiar woody scent that spreads warmth throughout my body. Sai is here instead of in the hospital.

I open my mouth, but he speaks first. "It's so nice to see you. I've missed you."

"It's nice to hear your voice," I say, a grin plastered on my face.

He sets his coffee cup on a nearby surface before wrapping his arms around my waist and briefly kisses my cheek. I wrap my arms tightly around him and stretch on my toes to meet his lips with mine.

"Josephine is requesting council with the governor, so I came to see you," he says.

The governor is the highest priority target since he is requesting the body of a political candidate who's gaining more popularity than he has. No matter how it's framed, it's a high-risk, low-reward type of situation, even when exorbitant amounts of money are involved. He'll likely not give up without causing as much havoc as possible.

The transcendence theory seems to benefit people like him more than anyone else. Most people simply want fame or fortune, but he appears to want to remain in a position of power, exactly like the director himself. While the governor is the most pressing target, the ones waiting for the children are likely to create disruptions if they're met with resistance.

Sixteen seems to be the consensus of "utilization," a grotesque term meant to dehumanize the kids. That may be in part because of the legal age of emancipation, but the true implication is probably far worse. The oldest child is eleven, which means she has five years before she just loses her life altogether.

"Does that mean—?"

He answers before I can finish asking my question. "Josephine is almost out of the way entirely, yes. She is setting up a meeting with the governor since she has established a rapport with him."

"We are finished with her after she sets up this meeting, then?"

"Yes. This is the last thing we need and then we are done with her completely," Sai states. "The outcome of this meeting is very important. If the governor doesn't secede, it may come down to killing him."

"Do you think it will come down to that?"

"I do, yes. I do not think he will approve of the alternatives we provide. He is set on obtaining his competitor's body." Sai moves away from me as he continues talking. "That is part of the reason I am here. Do you remember where your supplies are?"

He releases me, walking in the direction of the sunroom, where my supplies have resided since we moved in. Hidden inside a plain set of furniture are the tools to carry out assassinations. I'm not sure when the memories started coming, but reacquainting myself with the layout of the house helped me regain most of my memories.

"Mhm," I mumble, then ask. "With all the resources available at the hospital are those necessary?"

"The poison you use won't be tested for during an autopsy," he says, as he starts collecting things.

Sai scrounging around for things distracts my brain enough for the conversation to sink in. Josephine attending a meeting alone seems to be an unintentionally ostentatious move.

"Josephine didn't ask you to accompany her to the meeting?"

"No," he says, with a minor inflection, but continues collecting the items into a leather satchel.

"Did Samuel accompany her to this meeting?"

"I don't think I am following your thought process."

"Have you checked on the director recently?" I ask, ignoring his confusion.

"Personally? A few days ago. Why?" he asks, sounding worried.

"Obviously I can't confirm, but she may be giving the governor a warning," I say. "As far as I'm aware, she's never gone anywhere alone, so why would that be any different now?"

He stops shuffling around. "I see. You are suggesting that she is hoping to get him to side with her, for possible retaliation. I am not sure if she has discovered Dr. Sands residing in the psych ward or not. It's highly unlikely, but I will call Avery. Do you mind packing the rest?"

Sai walks out of the sunroom into the kitchen, dialing his number into the phone before I can respond. I grab the leather bag off the loveseat and run my finger along the inside to feel for what supplies he has already gathered. Most of the compartments are filled, only missing a few syringes in one part, so I add those and then close up the bag.

Walking back inside, the rich coffee smell permeates the house. While I've never been much of a coffee drinker, the aromatics make me wish I was. I grab some water from the fridge while I listen for Sai's voice. There's no sound until he stomps over to me.

"We need to get to the hospital. No one is answering," he says, keys jingling loudly with his quick stride.

I follow behind him out of the house and climb into the car, barely closing the door before he starts backing out of the driveway. The soft purring from the engine mixing with the sweeping wind against the windows catches my attention, allowing the color gray to engulf my mind. The white explosions popping through have been the only visual stimulus I've experienced as of late. It's been so long since I've had a solid color fill my mind, that I was beginning to forget what it even looked like.

"At the risk of sounding unappreciative, what are you smiling at?" Sai's voice causes the color to evaporate like a wisp of smoke.

My attention is drawn to the wide curve of my lips. I hadn't even realized I was smiling. "I was reveling in the color gray."

"A rather bleak color to find such enjoyment," Sai says, absently.

His words are distant, his attention seems to be consumed by the possibilities that could prevent everyone from answering his calls or returning them. They remind me of the first dream I shared with Gaddreol when the fluffy white clouds turned into dark gray foreboding clouds. The looming apprehension from that nightmare is present now as we close the distance to the hospital. He stepped away for a short amount of time and that seems to be enough for a catastrophe to occur.

"With my limited worldview, I don't think there is an inherently bleak color. They all have a vibrancy that is unique to them. For me, the color gray is usually accompanied by the sound of wind or the humming of machines," I respond, anyway, before fixating on the sounds again in hopes of another glimpse of the color.

"I apologize," he says. "That was an inconsiderate thought."

"Hardly. What do you think is going on?" I ask.

Admittedly, I don't know much about Josephine as a person, but she's capable of carrying out cruel actions. Taz comes to mind as a potential target. Josephine seems to regard her with more disdain than anyone else. But Gaddreol is an easy target now that he's a double amputee.

"I don't know. But we're going to find out."

As soon as the car stops, we exit concurrently, slamming doors in tandem. Listening to the swishing sounds of his fabric, I adjust my pace to match his. Maintaining pace with him, we are almost running. It seems he's trying to hurry without causing concern.

We make short work of the parking lot, reaching the sliding doors in mere seconds. Upon entering the building, a gravelly older voice calls out, "Doc! Doc, Mrs. Josephine is waiting for you in her office."

Sai stops short, half turning in the direction of the voice. "Thank you, Mildred."

We make our way through the lobby to the elevator. The initial call button for the elevator causes my breath to become short and heavy. Each breath gets shallower until I'm struggling to breathe. My pulse quickens, blood pumping hard against my ears.

Sai grabs my hand and whispers, "You're okay, I'm here."

I'm okay. He's literally right here with me.

I focus on the light pressure against my palm to not completely lose my composure when the loud ding signals the elevator's arrival. *There's a chance someone's hurt and I'm wasting time.*

While I collect myself, he holds the elevator with his free arm. Using his hand, I guide my shaky legs into the metal box. Once inside, I flatten myself against the wall with my other hand gripping my elbow. Tightly crossing my arm over my chest provides a sense of comfort and protection from the fear bubbling inside of me.

Now is not the time to have a panic attack. I force myself to take continuous deep breaths as we ascend to the highest floor.

At the top of the elevator shaft, the permeating ding counters all the progress I made throughout the ride up. Taking notice, Sai lightly rubs my palm with his fingertips. Latching onto his feathery touch, I break free from my crippling fear. I trip on the metal from, nearly launching myself from the elevator. Sai catches me from hitting the ground and then helps me stand upright.

The elevator descends with lesser dings, sending spikes of panic through my body. The cold tile beneath my feet becomes my new focal point and I use that to move one foot in front of the other until the invisible crushing weight gradually fades. By the time we reach the double doors to the office, my spine is straight and I'm able to breathe normally again. I gently squeeze his hand in an attempt at reassurance, but neither one of us knows what awaits behind these heavy doors.

The first door groans to life. It's closed gently, allowing an eerie silence to settle in before the second door groans to life. Sai's hand tenses against mine as he holds the door open for me. As I pass him, I note the strained rigidity in his posture.

The silence is broken up by muffled noises to my right, barely above knee height, and abrupt, sporadic snivels directly in front of me.

"Nice of you to finally join us." Josephine's voice is distressed.

"Let her go," Sai demands, but keeps his tone low and neutral. "She isn't part of this."

Taz? No, she's definitely a part of this. Vera.

"Shut up. Shut up. Shut up." Her tone is erratic and shaky.

Rapidly analyzing the situation around me, I gather Josephine likely has a gun held to Vera's head. Everyone else seems to be in a compromised position as a result of them trying to keep her safe. From the sound of her voice, they are roughly in the middle of the room, maybe four feet away from me.

Instinctively, I tap Sai's palm three times and he releases his grip. Unable to hear his movements, I hope he's getting out of the way. Holding up both hands, I slowly walk forward.

"Don't come any closer," she snaps. "Tell me where my husband is!"

"Let her go to her brother and we can talk about it," I say softly. Every movement I make is observed by her beady eyes as they leer at me. The weight of her gaze makes me want to fidget, but I ignore the nervous feeling, refusing to give her the satisfaction.

"Where is he?!" she asks, almost pleading.

I take a deliberate step forward. The tension in the room grows with the movement. "You don't want to hurt her."

"What the fuck do you know?!" Her voice cracks.

"She has nothing to do with this." I take another step forward. "I'm the one you want to hurt. I was brought in with the specific task of killing your husband."

"Give me back my husband!" she shrieks.

"Let her go. Then we will take you to your husband." My voice is calm and unwavering as I take a half step.

"Stop moving!" Josephine screeches. "Stop lying to me!"

I comply for a moment to listen to the subtle rustling of clothes. Josephine's fidgeting impatiently. Vera continues trying to stifle her cries, but the sporadic yelps fill the room every so often.

"I'm going to move forward, okay?" Ignoring her protests, I take another half step forward. "I'm going to reach out now. Let me trade places with Vera."

"No!" she yells, but her voice is trembling.

"You don't want to hurt her. You're angry with me. Don't take it out on Vera," I say, keeping my hands outstretched, hoping she releases the young girl.

"You ruined everything!" she screeches.

Suddenly, Vera's body crashes into my body. I quickly adjust my stance to maintain my balance, and then throw the young girl to my right and lunge forward at the unhinged woman. Hoping my spatial awareness is correct, I lean my body to the right while grabbing Josephine's forearm with my left hand and the pistol with my right, twisting it away from me and out of her grip.

The gun discharges with a loud bang resounding in my head and the room. I scream; she screams; likely the others do, too. With the gun in my hand now, I point it in front of me and squeeze the trigger. The ringing in my ears blocks out all the surrounding noise.

Someone touches my hand, causing me to flinch, but realizing it's Sai taking the gun from me, I release my grip. Once the gun is out of my hand, exhaustion takes over my limbs and my body collapses onto the ground.

A hand is on my chest applying immense pressure and I register the initial bang was me getting shot. The burning pain rushes in and

I'm struggling to take a deep breath. I raise my hand to my chest, feeling the thick liquid already coating my shirt.

I need to stop finding myself in these situations.

Everything fades into oblivion.

* * *

There's something cold and metallic pressing against the inside of my forearm. It's a light, but firm pressure that is strangely comforting. I touch it with my free hand, outlining the metal frame. Trailing up and down the long, slender shapes attached to a large object, I realize it's Gaddreol's new hand.

How long has he had his new metal limbs?

It must have been during the couple of weeks I was working tirelessly through those files, we didn't interact too much since most of his time was spent with his younger sister. And getting fitted with his new cyborg accessories. Hopefully, they are comfortable and easy to use. From the gentle pressure against my arm, they seem to be lightweight.

"Gaddreol?" I ask. "How are you adjusting to your new robotic limbs?"

He moves his metal limb away from my arm, stretching into a straighter posture from his loud yawn. "Hey, you're awake. Vera and I are here—"

"Hello," Vera interjects, her voice is sleepy.

"How long have I been asleep?" I ask, before adding, "Hello."

"A night." Gaddreol quickly picks up where he left off. "Sai asked me to stay with you when you wake up."

"Why? What's going on?" I ask.

Fumbling for the controls, I put the bed into an upright position. Although it's a small gesture, it helps me to feel more in control of the uncertain situation. This bed is surprisingly soft compared to the hard mattresses during my previous stay in the hospital.

"They're setting up a news conference in front of the building."

I failed.

While it shouldn't be my immediate thought, the assassination of the director was the main reason for being subjected to this horrific reality. If they're organizing a news conference, then they have decided to publicly disclose the corruption going on within the hospital. With his incapacitated state, I suppose it doesn't really matter. Especially since Josephine was on the receiving end of her own brandished weapon.

Without thinking, my hand goes to the bullet wound in my chest. It's taped beneath a gauze covering, so I can't feel the wound. I'm sure it's healing well. I'm also sure that my injury is one of the many reasons they've decided to take it upon themselves to expose the criminality of the organization. Second only to Vera being put in a hostage situation.

Instead of being an intimidating force facing the organization head-on, I quickly became the liability that requires constant care. The entire operation we devised appears to be little more than a misguided, ill-advised deflection. It seems my initial assessment of my shortcomings is accurate.

Keeping my tone flat, to not reveal my feelings of self-doubt, I ask, "Why are they setting up a conference? I thought they wanted anonymity in the organization."

"After what happened they felt this was the safest route."

After what happened, I repeat.

After severely miscalculating Josephine's motivations, allowing her erratic thoughts to become reality, taking Vera as a hostage. After I was shot in the chest while disarming the crazed woman.

It's the correct decision, and logically, I'm aware of that fact, but emotionally, I can't distance myself from feeling like it's happening because I let everyone down. Trying to dismantle this disgusting organization without rousing suspicions was the goal, but in trying to achieve that, a young girl was taken hostage. If I had been able to accomplish what was asked of me, then none of this would have happened.

Focusing on whether I'm to blame is counterproductive, so I ask, "What happened to Josephine?"

"She died from her injuries," he says without any inflection.

Josephine wasn't my initial target, but she is the one I killed. Guns aren't my specialty, nor my preferred method, but it did get the job done, albeit a lot messier than I would have liked. Mostly, I'm just glad the only casualty in the event was me.

"Thanks for saving me," Vera says.

Her voice is soft like she's trying to be small and invisible, possibly feeling guilty because of me getting shot. Each of their tones and demeanors feel cautious, like they're both tiptoeing around the horrors that just unfolded to protect my apparent fragility. A shift from

Vera being the one requiring protection. Perhaps I'm reading too much into it because of my diffidence.

"I'm glad you're okay," I say, attempting to diffuse any negative feelings she's harboring.

"Me, too," she squeaks, sounding uncomfortable.

"We can't thank you enough," Gaddreol adds.

A light set of footsteps close the distance to me. It's likely Vera as I don't think her older brother has mastered the art of stepping lightly with his new metal limb. She stops when she reaches the left side of the bed.

"Can you shake my hand? I'm holding it above your left side."

Her question catches me off guard, but I oblige, twisting my body to reach for her outstretched hand. The small motion causes the pain to radiate throughout my chest. I force my face to remain expressionless, to not contort from the spike in pain.

She grabs my hand and squeezes it with firm pressure, shaking it slightly. "Thanks for dancing with me. And being my big brother for a day."

Big brother, I repeat. The words are simple, but the vigor in her words stabs me right in the heart. She isn't like my younger sister, but being recognized as a big brother again is more overwhelming than I was prepared for.

"Um, what?" I ask. It's the only thing I can manage to say before I can process her words. "You're welcome. I didn't think you'd know about that."

"Yeah," she giggles, but it sounds forced and dreary. "Gaddreol is a real bad liar, so he told me the truth. He told me how you were stuck in your own head."

The tone in her voice is harrowing but powerful. As she says it, she loosens her grip on my hand and then presses her head lightly on my shoulder. It brings tears to my eyes knowing she is relating our experiences.

"I hope this is okay."

"Yes, of course," I say, blinking the tears away. Gently, I rest my hand on the back of her head.

"I'm glad you're okay," she repeats.

Vera's voice is small and feeble now, but it doesn't seem like she's talking about the situation that just occurred with Josephine. Rather, she's saying she's glad I didn't end up with her former existence. But I think it's also weighing heavily on her now since she understands that her situation isn't the innocent change she originally believed it to be. I can only hope that she isn't taking it personally. I don't want her to feel she needs to return to an immobile state, nor do I want the guilt to consume her.

"I'm glad you're okay," I repeat, barely a whisper, trying to keep the sadness from consuming my voice.

"Is it okay if I call you Bat?" she asks. The sudden shift catches me off guard and I can't stop my bellowing laughter at her words.

"I'd be honored if you called me that." Which is true. It's a delight to be called that after my self-proclaimed mole analogy.

The TV comes on with Avery's voice uttering thanks, interrupting our exchange. Vera releases my hand and I lift my hand from the back of her head as she moves away from the bed.

Avery clears his throat before saying, "Hello, my name is Avery Johnson. I am a general surgeon here at Sampson Hospital. My colleagues standing up here with me are Sai Reid, a trauma surgeon, and Tessa Garcia, an anesthesiologist, respectively. We've gathered everyone here to share with you all the private organization that Director Charles Sands has been operating inside the walls of this hospital.

"Without the fear of retaliation from the director or his late wife, Josephine White, I am here to share my story. The organization is named Forced and Rapid Evolution. Hundreds of lives have been taken; justified by what they called the Transcendence Theory, the purpose of which is to transcend our morbidity and mortality alike.

"I am one of the numerous victims that have been subjected to his ideals. The body that I'm in belongs to Adrian Johnson, a nurse who was fresh out of college. By taking my soul from my body and implanting it into his, Charles effectively killed Adrian Johnson."

Vera's soft sobs break through Avery's monologue. She probably chose to be here, but I can understand why it is difficult for her to hear. Her reality is shattering and listening to Avery speak his truth is as harrowing as her own.

"My real body—the body of Avery Johnson—is being preserved within the walls of the hospital. It has been preserved to be used in the form of blackmail. If I came forward to expose the director I was going to be framed for the murder of Avery Johnson, as Adrian Johnson.

"Through coercion, I participated in the illegal activities within this organization, and I am fully prepared to take accountability for my role." Avery's voice falters and he stops talking.

"My name is Sai Reid. My role in the organization is to transition a person from one body to another. I have personally performed over three hundred transitions with Tessa Garcia's assistance. I participated in taking the lives of hundreds of people and I, too, am fully prepared to take accountability in my role.

"Now that the three at the head of the organization no longer prove to be a threat, we decided that the best course of action is to share our knowledge. After we removed Charles Sands from his position, we discovered a children's residential home that his daughter, Olivia Sands, oversees. These children were born for the sole purpose of being transitioned into, but we are going to have the children moved to another facility with full evaluations.

"All of the files we found have been reviewed and analyzed, so we are aware of who the clients are. The victims of the organization are not documented, but we are creating a comprehensive list so that we can provide closure to the families.

"The director is inhabiting the body of his son, Matthew Sands. As a result of a failed attempt to take my body for himself, Sands is incapacitated and being held in the psychiatric ward."

Taz interjects, "We would like to continue pursuing the goal of the organization through ethical means, such as synthetic bodies. It is a readily available technology, but the director felt the results took too long for his clients, so he chose illegal means to achieve the desired result.

"Josephine White was transitioned into a synthetic body, so it has proven to be an effective tool. Through biotechnology and robotics we have a variety of options available to give people a better life.

"My name is Tessa Garcia, better known at the hospital as Taz. I am a trained anesthesiologist. My role in the organization is like my role in normal operations. I ensure the patients' safety. I have not taken part directly in the illegal aspect of the organization, but I'm prepared to accept any accountability for the wrongdoings within the organization."

"We will answer any questions you have," Sai says, ending their statements.

The TV is shut off and Gaddreol asks, "Are you alright, Vera?"

"No," she says, her voice trembling. "Are they going to get into trouble for this? Are the kids going to be okay?"

"Honestly, I don't know what will happen," Gaddreol says. "I wish

I had a better answer, but this is a delicate situation."

Now that Vera is faced with the emotionally taxing truth, it must be so overwhelming for her, but she still directs her focus on being concerned with everyone around her. The strength she displays is reminiscent of Gaddreol's. It seems like she is trying to dismiss her personal feelings, so she doesn't worry anyone. Sometimes, we need permission to be vulnerable, a gentle push to release the things we're trying to keep hidden.

I shift my legs to the side of the bed toward the direction they're sitting. Finding my strength, I stand up. Once the dizziness passes my feet glide towards the siblings. Stopping in front of them, I sit on my knees and offer my hand, outstretched in the air. Her hand meets mine, allowing me to grasp it in mine.

"Vera, it's okay to feel sad. It's okay to feel anger and gratitude clashing against one another about your newfound freedom and the reason it's available to you. My situation with Gaddreol was in some ways reminiscent of your own lived experience and it's okay if you have conflicting feelings regarding that, too.

Your concern for the kids and doctors involved is admirable. But none of that should cause you to feel obligated to push your feelings away. You have all of these complex emotions that want to take their course, and you're allowed to let that happen."

Her hand trembles in mine as her body starts to shake. Heavy droplets fall onto my hand as she pulls our clasped hands up to the bridge of her nose, squeezing tightly. Her tears flow, and her quiet sobs gain force until she's nearly choking.

Her body shifts forward, which from the swishing fabric, it sounds like Gaddreol has adjusted himself to comfort her. She leans away from me, presumably into her older brother's embrace. The sadness she's been feeling radiates in her voice as she sobs and wails to her heart's content. The pure exhaustion and dread in her tiny voice is more difficult to listen to than when Avery broke down.

It sounds like all the pain and frustration she's been harboring throughout her life is coming out alongside the horrors of everything she's faced recently. Having a new body at the cost of someone's life, her brother losing his limbs, and becoming a victim of a hostage attempt. None of those things by themselves are easy to deal with and yet they're all compounded into a mass of anguish for Vera.

"Thanks, Bat. Thanks Gaddreol."

CHAPTER NINETEEN

INVESTIGATING THE STATEMENTS made during the conference are federal agents. They are interviewing everyone that could be directly or indirectly involved. Including Vera, who is in the office with them now. Gaddreol is accompanying her since she is a minor. Once they are finished interviewing her, I'll be next.

I'm not particularly excited to be questioned about my story, but I can't wait to be out of these stiff chairs and into the comfortable leather chairs inside the office. The cane loosely in my hand reminds me of Gaddreol's nervous fidgeting just before we were separated. I clench my fist to resist giving in to the same compulsion.

The heavy doors open and a woman with a slight nasal ring to her voice says, "Thank you, Miss Adair. Mr. Tristan Reid, please, follow me."

Rising to my feet with the cane outstretched before me, I can feel the sharp energy shift once she realizes I'm blind. Vera touches my arm as she walks by me, causing me to stop for a brief moment. The agent doesn't say anything, but she holds the door open for me and quickly passes me to hold the second door. Once inside, she directs me to the set of chairs that are now facing each other instead of the desk. I take a seat and she sits across from me.

"For the record, state your name," she says, her tone stern, but soft.

"Tristan Reid," I say.

"Are you in the body you were born with?"

"Yes."

"At the end of the interview, we will get a DNA swab from you. Are you okay with this?"

"Yes."

"Do you know why we're here today?"

"I am going to share my personal experience."

"Correct. So why don't you begin with how you became involved in the first place."

"Alright. Well, I'm sure you know, Sai Reid is my husband. He is an integral part of the hospital and the organization. The director decided Sai knew too much and was more of a liability than an asset, so he was going to use me as blackmail. To save me from the cruelties the director is capable of, we decided to transition Gaddreol into my body."

A disgruntled sound comes from the woman before she says, "Why was that the solution you decided on?"

I expected to be questioned on how we knew blackmail was the primary goal, but I suppose after hearing Avery's and Gaddreol's stories, mine is relatively tame by comparison.

"In placing Gaddreol in my body, we circumvented the danger to both of us. We felt this was the safest option while putting me in a compromised position that would appease the director."

"Were you afraid of death?" she asks.

"Of course, but it seemed to be a prominent factor if I didn't take the risk anyway," I say.

"So what happened once you made the decision?" she asks.

"Gaddreol took over my body and I was trapped in isolation, but alive, kind of. Once we were separated, the director assigned a job to me. The job turned out to be a diversion to target Sai."

"What was the job assigned to you?"

"Kidnapping Gregory Young for the director to take over, but that turned out to be a decoy. Samuel is using the body of Gregory now."

She clears her throat loudly, then asks, "You're blind, correct?"

"Yes. Since birth."

"If you've been blind since birth, why would Charles Sands think you are capable of committing such an act?"

Occasionally, I hear grunts from people as they shift and fidget. Likely tired of standing around waiting for these interviews to be finished.

"I don't think he did, which is why the task was assigned to me."

"Please explain."

"I think he was giving me a task he believed I was incapable of accomplishing. In passing, I was to work for him, and failing meant there were to be consequences for both Sai and me. As a master of manipulation, he didn't appreciate Sai undermining his authority, so I believe it was supposed to be a lose-lose situation causing the most emotional damage possible."

"I see. Will you share what transpired with the kidnapping of Gregory Young?"

"Avery and I learned Gregory's intimate schedule and followed him to a cafe that he frequents occasionally. I was dropped off while Avery parked the car in a nearby parking lot to keep an eye on my movements. I struck up a conversation with Gregory and asked him to walk me home, which he happily obliged. Avery pulled up next to us on our walk through the alleyway and asked if we wanted a ride. While Gregory was hesitant, he didn't object and came with us. With the mention of drugs, we gained his trust fairly easily."

My head wants to drop from recounting the horrific act. Luring an innocent man to his death is not something I ever wanted to do, but it's something I accomplished with Avery at my side. I straighten my posture, keeping my head facing the direction of the woman in front of me.

"So, you lured him in with your blindness and gained his trust with drugs?" she asks, trying to maintain a stern tone to hide her disgust.

"Yes."

"Then what?" she asks, her ankle smacking the chair leg when she shifts her position.

"Once Gregory was unconscious, Avery pushed him on a gurney to one of the rooms used for transitioning. I walked with him to the room, where Tessa was already setting everything up. The director, Josephine, and Samuel showed up together and I was made to sit in a chair and wait. While I sat there, Samuel brought in Sai's unconscious body for the director to transition into. I didn't know it at the time, but a paralytic drug was given to me to force my compliance. It didn't act fast enough so I ran out of the room and down the hall until my body gave out at the elevator."

"From your perspective, what happened next?"

"I slipped into a coma for a week. Gaddreol was the one who first came to see me upon waking up. He and Avery accompanied me to meet with the director, which is when I learned Sai was still alive. I offered to help him study the files since he didn't have the time to do it for himself with Josephine at his side. It took a couple of weeks to braille all the files, but in doing so I learned fifty-six clients are still actively waiting on a body to transition into. Twenty-five of them are highly prominent clients such as the governor, the secretary of state, and the chief of police among other high-ranking positions."

"Thank you. Next, would you mind sharing the incident involving Josephine?"

"I'm not sure how she discovered his identity; I presume it is something he said or did that tipped her off. While he believed she was having a meeting with the governor, she took Vera hostage at gunpoint. I assume she used her to put Avery, Gaddreol, and Tessa in compromised positions. Sai figured it out and drove us to the hospital. At the time we didn't know what the situation was, just that no one answered Sai's calls.

"Once we made it inside the office, Josephine yelled at us to stay put and Vera was making strained noises, so piecing the situation together was fairly intuitive. Without really thinking about it, I took over and talked Josephine down. When she released Vera, I lunged at her to get the gun. I succeeded but ended up getting shot in the process. I turned the gun on her and fired the weapon. I learned the next day that she died from her injuries."

"You're blind, but you were able to disarm a sighted woman with a gun and then aim it at her to kill her? Am I understanding that correctly?" she asks, disbelief clear in her voice. Some of the other people in the room mimic her disbelief with displays of snickering or fake coughs.

"Yes."

"How did a blind man accomplish something that two sighted men couldn't accomplish?"

Being blind doesn't equal incompetence. She seems to believe that blindness is an inherent weakness. If things were different, I wonder if she would agree with the director and his assessment.

"I nearly lost my life in a knife attack years ago. I survived, of course, but I didn't want to be defenseless, so I studied martial arts and trained with a variety of different weapons, including firearms. While I never expected to use a gun against someone, I'm glad I had the knowledge to save Vera. As to why the others present in the room couldn't accomplish that, I don't think anyone in the room that day was proficient with weapons of any kind."

It's far more nuanced than that. No one has the same response to stressful situations. Avery, Gaddreol, and Taz likely had frozen or fawned responses to not agitate Josephine further. Sai reacted similarly, allowing me to take the lead since I had a fight response.

"I see. Is there anything else you feel is important to tell me?"

"I don't think there is anything that you aren't aware of, so no."

"Alright. Well, thank you for sharing your side of things. We will get a DNA swab and then we're finished for now."

Footsteps close the distance, and then a man simply demands, "Open."

I comply and the Q-tip is swirled throughout, covering nearly every inch of my mouth before he takes it away. "Thank you."

The interviewer stands, so I do the same and listen for her to step away before following her. She holds both doors open for me, again. Sai is waiting for me outside the office, coming to stand at my side immediately.

"Thank you, Dr. Reid, for your cooperation. We'll be in touch soon."

"Of course, anything you need, please do not hesitate to ask."

His hand finds mine and we walk away as the door shuts behind us. His fingers gently stroke mine in a soothing gesture as a comfort to both of us. It's a habit he developed after the knife attack that he does during particularly stressful times.

* * *

Avery invited us all to a fine dining restaurant. Much to my dismay, I'm wearing a pair of dress shoes with a linen suit. Cane in hand to help me feel stabilized, since it isn't necessary to guide me with a large group of people near me.

Sai must look nice. A smile widens on my face as I think about how gorgeous he must've been on our wedding day.

Seeing him without a frankensteined picture would be the only reason I would consider transitioning into a body with sight. Perhaps if the trials continue, I can keep doing them with a lesser amount of the serum. I highly doubt any results will come of it, but it would be worth a try, if it doesn't hurt too much.

Although, hearing his smoky voice and melodic laugh is enough. That and smelling the scent that has become synonymous with him. Also, feeling the soft touch of his skin.

Speaking of, his sweet scent surrounds me as he wraps his arm around my waist. "Are you ready to go?"

"I'm ready. Do you know why he invited us out to dinner?"

"No," Sai says, plainly. "We'll have to find out once we get there."

His arms drop from my waist, and he heads for the door. I follow him, carefully placing one foot in front of the other. Gripping the banister, I descend the stairs with more difficulty than expected. Despite my delicate steps, each one sends a sharp pain from the bullet wound into the rest of my chest, causing a burst of grunts to escape me.

Once I reach the last step, I stop to catch my ragged breath. Sai is beside the car with the door open, but I can feel his gaze fixated on me, watching, waiting to make sure I'm able to continue without assistance. I straighten myself and walk unimpeded to the car.

"Are you alright?" Sai asks after I close the door.

"Yes, I'm okay," I say. "Just a little pain, but I'm fine."

"Do you mind if I play some music?" he asks.

Outside of dancing with Vera that day I haven't listened to music since Gaddreol took over my body.

"No, why do you ask?"

"If we listen to music, the chance for you to see the color gray goes with it." He states in his matter-of-fact tone.

A smile curls my lips. "Music has colors, too. A lot more than just gray."

Classical music starts playing on the radio and a light show that weaves intricately with the instruments. It reinvigorates colors that were starting to dissipate. The violin resembles a rich purple, the cello a deep blue, the drums are vibrant green, and the keyboard a striking red. There are other instruments playing harmoniously with duller colors, but those four are the most prominent. My head sways rhythmically with the music as the colors swirl pleasantly around my head.

"This is beautiful."

"I'm glad you can see the music," he says, the smile on his face is clear in his voice. "But I am sorry to say we have arrived."

The car stops and he shuts the engine off.

"That's alright. The colors are magnificent, but I'm excited to be in everyone's company," I say, shuffling out of the car.

"You made it! And you've got shoes on!" Avery's boisterous laugh floats through the open air.

His voice is deeper and huskier than it was. *Did he transition back into his body?*

"Avery, you look great. As do you, Gaddreol."

"Thanks. As do the both of you. I'm glad you are here," Gaddreol says, "Now we're just waiting on Taz and Vera to get here. They're on their way."

"Where did they go?" I ask.

"They went dress shopping," Avery says.

I'm glad that Vera has Taz as a companion. Her relationship with Gaddreol is fantastic, but having someone like an older sister could be invaluable to the young girl. Taz has quickly taken a liking to her, too, it seems. I'm sure they will both look lovely.

"Sorry we're late. We found so many beautiful dresses, Vera had a hard time choosing. But look at how fabulous she looks!" Taz says, as the pair walks up to us.

"You both look fabulous!" Gaddreol beams.

"Thanks," Vera says. "Bat! Taz took me to get my hair done. It's braided, do you wanna feel it?"

Normally, I wouldn't, but her enthusiasm is too great to ignore. "Of course! They did a fantastic job. Do you like it?"

"I love it. Come on, I'll lead the way," she says, grabbing hold of my hand, half-dragging me through the restaurant with her.

The host directs us to our table with Vera dragging me along. As sweet as it is, it's more disorienting than she realizes. I focus on every movement she makes to make micro adjustments, so I don't trip over my own feet. She even pulls my chair out for me before taking her own seat between Gaddreol and Taz. Once everyone sits, the waitress takes the drink orders.

Taz says, "The appetizers we'll have are Smoked Gouda Stuffed Jalapeños, Caviar Tartlets, Brie Stuffed Mushrooms, Bacon Jam Crostini, Swordfish Skewers, and Dates Stuffed with Goat Cheese and Salami. I'm sorry, I took over and ordered different things for everyone to try. Is that okay?"

"That's fine. I'm sure it's all going to be great," Gaddreol says.

"There's a lot of stuffed appetizers," Vera says, giggling softly.

Sai leans closer to me, asking, "They have seared scallops or filet mignon, would you like either of those?"

"Seared scallops are fine, thank you," I whisper.

"I really appreciate you guys coming tonight," Avery says, "I'm just going to get it out of the way. I'd like to ask you all to attend my brother's funeral. It'd mean a lot to me and my family. That same night, the hospital is hosting a candlelight vigil for all of the victims and families."

By doing the news conference, a weight was lifted from Avery. He sounds like himself again and now he's finally able to give his family the closure they need. The organization took more from him than most and if going to his brother's funeral provides him with solace, I doubt anyone would deny the request. Hopefully, the upcoming candlelight vigil will give the families of the victims the same chance.

I'd love to come to your brother's funeral, I think, but that's rude and borderline inappropriate.

"We will come to support you and your family," Sai says, saving me from potentially embarrassing myself.

My palms start to sweat and I'm not sure why. A bizarre reaction to offering support to someone in their time of need. Trying my best to ignore it, I wipe my hands against my pants.

"I'll be there for you, too," Taz says, and I hear fabric rustling, which I assume is her reaching out to touch Avery in a comforting gesture.

"Me, too," Vera chimes in. "I think I might cry though."

"If you cry, it's okay," Gaddreol says.

"You and me, both," Avery says, trying to remove her worry.

The waitress comes back with the appetizers, and everyone gives their entree orders. Taz distributes the appetizers evenly and passes the plates around the table, earning everyone's gratitude.

After grabbing one of the items from the plate, I turn to Sai and he says, "It is the date stuffed with goat cheese and salami."

As soon as I pop it into my mouth, an explosion of sweet, savory, and tangy flavors blends together, complimenting the consistency. "This is delicious."

"I really don't like the goat cheese-salami-date thing," Vera says, and I imagine her nose is wrinkled in disgust.

For some reason, thinking of the possible expression on her face reminds me that I have some semblance of what everyone sitting at the table looks like except for Taz. Even when I asked her what Sai looks like, it never occurred to me to ask what she looks like. I grab the appetizer with a toothpick in it next.

"Are you alright?" Sai asks. "That is the swordfish skewer."

"Yes, but I realized how rude I was before," I say, before turning my head in Taz's direction. "Taz, may I ask you what you look like?"

The swordfish is tender and flavorful, but one bite isn't sufficient to be satiating. At this point, I'm pretty sure Sai is a mind reader as he puts a toothpick in my hand so I can have another bite of the delicious fish.

"What?" She says around a mouthful of food. After an audible gulp, she adds, "Totally! Think Marilyn Monroe—a gorgeous, drop-dead blonde bombshell supermodel."

Stunned silence falls on the table before everyone erupts into muffled laughter trying to contain their noise level. Avery speaks between his chuckles, "You're ridiculous, you know."

I grab another appetizer and Sai whispers, "Mushroom stuffed with brie." This one is enjoyable, but it lacks the dynamic flavors like the first. It's an appetizer that you can get from many different restaurants.

"Just a tiny bit. I'm around five-nine and a little chubby. My eyes are plain brown, and my hair is brown with bouncy curls. Oh, and my skin tone is a little lighter than Avery's."

I force the images together as best as I can to see the little bit she described. It's probably the least accurate image I've tried to piece together so far since I can only see either a small child or a big man, and changing those physiques is nearly impossible. But I can see the brown curls and the brown eyes atop Avery's skin tone. Though I'm sure they're not the same color, they are in my forged picture.

"From what I can make out in my mind, you are beautiful."

I try the jalapeño stuffed with smoked gouda next. It has cream cheese that compliments the smoky and earthy flavors quite well.

"Aw, thanks! You've got to try the caviar tartlet. They're so cute! I've never tasted anything like it!" Taz exclaims, so I feel around my plate to find that next.

A small bite-size tart with caviar and a small mixture of sour cream, mayo, and shredded cheese. She's right in that it's unlike anything else, unique in every sense, but it may be one of the better appetizers of the bunch.

"I don't like that," Vera says. "Sorry I'm wasting your money."

"Hey, don't worry about it," Avery says.

"We're just glad you tried it," Gaddreol adds.

"I liked the bacon jam thing a lot," Vera says, humming a sound of contentment.

"Would you like mine?" I ask.

"No way. You won't get to try it then," she says, dismissively.

Since she declines, I shove the crispy mini baguette into my mouth. Vera's right. It's by far the best appetizer of the night. The savory flavor from the bacon jam pairs well with the creaminess of the cheeses and the sweetness of the honey. Possibly the most immaculate blend of flavors put into a bite-sized piece of food I've had the pleasure of tasting.

"I'll get you some more," Avery says.

"Thanks!" The young girl exclaims.

When the waitress returns with the entrées, Avery gets another order of the bacon jam crostini appetizer for her. Everyone quietly enjoys their food, with only occasional sounds of silverware hitting plates and sounds of enjoyment. Although the entree tastes good, it is overshadowed by the star of the show. The more extravagant appetizers that were brought to the table were the best part. Vera had the right idea when she wanted more.

"Here you are, sweetheart," the waitress says.

"Thank you, so much!" Vera whisper-squeals her words.

There's a muddled clink sound that's very close to me, and then Sai says, "You have a surprise on your plate."

Reaching out, I fumble around my plate until finding another crostini on my plate. For a moment, my eyebrows crease, but the tension releases as a small smile forms. "Thanks, Vera."

"You're welcome. You seemed to really enjoy it, too."

My facial expressions must betray my feelings more than I thought, especially when food is involved. The small bite of food is as flavorful as it was the first time I ate it and I'm glad it's now the lasting impression of the fancy meal. Once everyone finishes their meals the three doctors debate whether or not Avery should pay for the whole meal. In the end, the other two relent, letting him pay for the entirety.

Thankfully, Vera doesn't drag me around the restaurant again, so I dawdle in the back of our large group. The slow pace is greatly appreciated when I feel this unstable. It seems our group is walking in silent pairs from the table to the outside. The cane bumps into someone. I open my mouth to apologize, but the person runs into me, taking my breath away, enveloping me in a tight hug.

"I'm sorry, Tristan," Vera says. "Before I knew you were, uh, you, I was really mean. It was weird to see my brother as you, but you are perfect as you."

"Don't worry about it, okay? No hard feelings," I say, wrapping my free arm around her shoulder.

"Promise?" She asks.

Questions like this remind me that even though she is a teenager in age, her life experience is reminiscent of a child. I doubt whatever she said that could be misconstrued as mean was anything more than playful banter. She's far too caring for intentional malice.

"Promise."

"Thanks, Tristan," Gaddreol says, touching my arm for a second.

"My pleasure," I say, dropping my arm, and then Vera releases her death grip, stepping backwards, seemingly satisfied with my response.

"Thanks again," Avery says. "I appreciate you guys more than you know. I'll send the details for the funeral."

Everyone exchanges goodbyes before setting off to their own cars. Each step is followed by the looming presence of what's to come. The only certainty is the funeral that will undoubtedly weigh heavily on everyone in attendance. Beyond that is the uncertainty regarding the outcome of all the unwilling participants involved in FREE.

CHAPTER TWENTY

A BROKEN, BLURRED image of Avery dissipates upon waking up. The picture isn't clear, it's barely recognized as one at all. If I had eyesight, it likely would have been missed altogether. Today is the funeral and it seems to be weighing heavily on my mind to the point it's latching onto the only image I have that resembles the young man who lost his life.

The funeral is occurring at noon and most of my stuff has already been picked out prior, so I should have plenty of time to prepare myself. The shoes issue is sorted out already since Avery confirmed it's okay if I don't wear any.

A delightful aroma of coffee and maple syrup fills the room before I hear Sai's soft footfall coming towards the bed.

"Good morning, Tristan."

"Good morning. Breakfast in bed? What's this for?"

Quickly, sitting up, an uncontrolled stretch takes over my body and for a brief second, I worry I'm going to knock the tray out of his hand. He waits patiently until I settle into a sitting position before placing the tray across my lap.

"With today's events, I thought you may be feeling anxious, so I wanted to do something to ease those feelings," he says. "I brought you orange juice with the waffles."

"You are amazing," I say. "You didn't have to do all of this."

Tears threaten to fall even as the smile touches my lips, but I'm not sure I understand why. The funeral is for someone I've never met, but it is affecting me more emotionally than I expected it to, which Sai seems to intuitively pick up on. Perhaps I was sleeping fitfully, so he wanted to give me something to look forward to when I woke up.

He plants a brief kiss on my cheek before grabbing his coffee off the tray and climbing onto the bed next to me. There's a soft hissing sound from him grabbing a book from the bedside table. He doesn't get to read often, so I eat my breakfast in silence.

It doesn't take long before it's completely gone. Sai notices, asking, "Would you like me to take that back?"

"No, it's alright, I've got it," I shift the tray and he grabs it while I get up. He hands it back to me and I take it to the kitchen.

Small tasks are easy to overlook, easy to take for granted until you lose your ability to perform them at all. Less than a month ago, taking this tray would have been an arduous, impossible task. Now holding things, unbalanced or not, is nearly effortless again. Walking through the house is instinctual, again. The different textures aren't necessary anymore, but they're like a physical map for my feet to follow, which is a strange comfort.

The matte tile in the kitchen smoothly shifts into solid hardwood in the hallways, which then abruptly shifts to plush carpet in the bedroom. Once I get back into the room, the rustling fabric tells me Sai is getting ready for the funeral. I grab my clothes and begin doing the same.

"We have ten minutes." He says in his usual matter-of-fact tone.

Getting ready is a lot easier now that my fingertips have mostly healed. The daunting buttons on the vest and the tie are a little challenging but doable. Sai comes out of the bathroom over to me. He smooths my hair to the side.

"Thanks. How do I look?" I ask.

"You look amazing."

Putting my hands on his chest, I say, "Not as good as you."

"You cannot say that with certainty," he says, and I can hear the wide smile on his face.

"I'm pretty sure I can," I tiptoe, and he bends down with a tender kiss. "Are you ready to go?"

"I am, yes."

His hand is on the small of my back and he walks with me through the house. Once outside, he locks up the house and I walk down the steps, feeling the tiny grooves in the wood, noticing how unique each plank is. The warmth from the morning sun on the concrete radiates through my feet—a comfort I didn't know I needed. The car is unlocked as I approach, so I climb in, Sai right behind me.

The car starts and beautiful instrumental music plays. Instantly, the colors come to life in my mind, dancing to the rhythm of the music. My eyes close automatically, as if that will give me a better view of the swirling lights.

"Hey, Sai," I say, "Would it be alright if I walk up with Gaddreol? If he and Avery are okay with it, too, I mean."

"Yes, of course," he says, concern steady in his voice. He seems to want to ask if I'm okay, or something similar, but he doesn't.

I don't offer anything more because I don't know what to say to that. Why do I want to walk with him instead of Sai? I suppose it's because the funeral feels intimate and personal to me in a way that Gaddreol can empathize with better than anyone else. It doesn't matter much, since if they reject the request nothing will change, but it feels important to ask.

The longer the ride is, the harder my heart pounds in my chest. The colors feel more anxiety inducing assault than a peaceful light show at this point. I rest my head against the window, allowing the vibrations to rattle against my skull. Surprisingly it's a much-needed distraction to help ground me, keeping me from being overwhelmed. Sai rests his hand on mine, and I squeeze it, probably a little harder than necessary.

"Are you ready?" he asks.

No. I think, but say, "I think so."

With that, we make our way to where the funeral service is being held. It's outside, which makes sense why Avery said it's okay if I don't have shoes. The grass is dewy from last night's rain, causing my feet to sink into the softened dirt. To most, I'm sure the sensation of the ground turning to mush underfoot is off-putting, but it isn't bothersome to me in the least. Although it does dampen the usual vibrations, I still prefer it to shoes.

"Hello, Sai, you look lovely. How are you doing, sweetie?" an older woman says, her voice shattered. She must be Avery's—and Adrian's—mother. "And you must be Tristan. If only we'd met under better circumstances, but it's nice to meet you."

"I am sorry for your loss. If there is anything we can do for you and your family, please do not hesitate to ask," Sai says.

"I'm so sorry for your loss, Mrs. Johnson."

"Thank you, lovelies. The service is starting soon. Avery is by the sitting area." Her voice cracks when she says his name. The pain she must be feeling is inconceivable—vast and torturous. To finally have closure about her missing son, only to reveal the death of her younger son. My stomach ties itself into knots just thinking of the sheer devastation she must feel.

Sai leads me to the area where everyone is gathered, chatting idly. Avery excuses himself from someone and then gives a quick hug to Sai and me. Gaddreol gives a brief hug, too, before handing each of us a long-stemmed rose to toss into the grave for Adrian.

"Thank you for coming," Avery says, sounding just as broken as his mother.

"Of course," Sai says, plainly.

"If this request is too much, please say so, but I was wondering if it would be okay to walk up with Gaddreol," I say, sheepishly. A nervousness courses through my body, a prickling sensation running over my skin.

"Yeah, sure," Gaddreol says. "Are you alright?"

Am I alright? I should be, but I don't think I am. It's not my family that's affected by this tragedy, but there's a sadness that plagues me, looming over my thoughts.

"I think so. But is it okay if we go last?" I ask.

"Yes," he says. "I think it's time, let's take a seat. I'm going to sit up front with Avery and Vera."

I hope Vera isn't too upset by all of this either.

"Good afternoon, everyone. I'd like to thank you all for being here. I am Quinn Johnson, eldest brother to Adrian Johnson. We're gathered here today to celebrate the life of Adrian. He was young and full of life, always throwing caution to the wind to follow his heart and passions. We express our gratitude for the time we spent together and the memories we shared. Adrian, your time with us was short but will never be forgotten. We grieve the farewell we give as we accept your departure from this world. You will remain in the hearts and minds of all who love you. Thank you for being the best son, brother, and friend you could be."

"That was beautiful, baby," their mother says in between her wails.

"Please now place a rose on Adrian's grave. Take as much time as you need," he says, stepping away from the podium.

"Since you want to wait until the end, I'm going to take Vera up now," Gaddreol whispers. I simply nod.

I close my eyes, listening to the sounds around me from the quiet, indistinct mumbles of those saying their farewells, to the soft and loud cries of distress and anguish dispersed here and there over the grim serenity of the graveyard. Beyond this gathering are distant sounds of birds chirping and cars driving through the city; a melancholic reminder that even when we pass, life around us continues.

The long stem twirls absently between my fingers when metal gingerly touches my hand. "You ready?"

No, but that doesn't matter.

I nod, following him to the grave. My knees come into contact with a loose rope around the hole. The small interaction makes my legs want to crumble as if the light touch gave my body permission to give out. To prevent myself from collapsing, I sit on my knees. Gaddreol's hands gently rest on my chest and back, ensuring I don't fall, releasing his loose grip when he realizes I'm not falling. Sitting isn't the most appropriate, but it's marginally better than accidentally losing my balance.

Hello, Adrian. We've never met, but it feels like there is a strong kinship between us. Perhaps it's because I met your brother trying his best to emulate your tenacity. I don't think that's it, but rather because I may be the only person who understands what happened to you on a spiritual level.

It feels selfish to even think that, though. Sitting here with you now reminds me of the moments I begged for my death, while you never even received the choice to decide for yourself. Your death wasn't a choice you made, you were a victim of your circumstance, through and through. For that, I sincerely apologize.

My heart grieves for you, grieves for the countless victims yet to be known, and grieves for the disembodiment I experienced.

Your funeral marks the beginning of the end. The end of the horrors created by that man, the end of the pain this organization caused, the end of the treacherous organization itself. With you, the devastation will bring regrowth and through that, beauty will flourish. What happened to you, and so many others, is inexcusable, but your death will bring about truth and unity.

Thank you for being who you were meant to be. I wish I could have met you in life.

In your name, I promise to live my life to the fullest. Thank you.

The rose in my hand feels heavy like it's bearing the weight of my words within it. I toss it into the grave as the tears stream down my face.

I didn't realize Gaddreol wrapped his arm around my back, but his hand is gently rubbing my shoulder. Accepting his embrace, I lean onto his shoulder, resting my head as the tears flow freely.

I didn't expect attending a funeral for someone I've never met to be this emotional. We've never met, but I feel a closeness with him that I'm not sure any possible explanation would be adequate.

Vera sits on my other side, grabbing my hand. "It's okay, Bat."

My tear-stained face is puffy, and I know my eyes are red. Now that I've thoroughly ruined Gaddreol's clothes as well as my own, I should probably get to my feet. I start to stand, but both people on either side of me stand first and drag me to my feet. Vera pulls me into a hug, ripping the remaining breath from my lungs.

"I understand," she whispers, her voice is coarse.

If anyone understands, it's her. Her experience is the closest thing to what I'm dealing with right now. I feel ashamed, but it didn't cross my mind how much this funeral must be affecting her poorly, too. To be on the opposite side of the transition, to be in the same position that Avery was in to lead to this moment in the first place. She must be hurting, yearning for forgiveness, just as Avery is.

She lets go, and then someone's broad chest slams into me, their arms wrapping around my shoulders.

"Thank you. I'm glad my baby brother means a lot to you, too."

"You don't have to thank me." I manage to push the words out of my breathless body.

He releases me abruptly. "Sorry, I didn't mean to crush you."

Truthfully, Vera did. I just couldn't catch my breath between the two. No point in saying that, though. I'm just glad to be able to expand my lungs again.

"Are you alright?" Taz asks.

"I think so, yes," I say. "Sorry about my emotional display. I—"

Sai cuts me off. "Tristan, we will never understand what you went through during the transition, but we are understanding of your emotions and how you need to process them."

"No one here judges you for any of that," Taz adds.

"Yeah, my mom's just waiting to give you a bear hug because she said you look like you could use it." Avery's soft chuckle is a peaceful noise through the sorrow, bringing a smile to my face.

Avery's—Adrian's—mom just lost her son but wants to comfort me, someone she doesn't know. She is an amazing woman with a commendable amount of strength.

"I'd like that, actually," I say, mentally preparing myself for another round of tears to pour uncontrollably from my eyes.

It feels like the sea of people around me move away at once for this woman to come through. She pulls me into a motherly embrace, the type that makes you feel safe and loved. The kind I haven't felt since being a kid myself. Sinking into her arms, I accept the warm embrace. She's barely five feet, but the strong energy she carries with her makes her feel taller, larger than life.

"My baby will always be in our hearts," she says, but quickly adds. "Avery told me a little about you, what happened to you. Just like my sweet baby, you didn't deserve that."

"Thank you, Mrs. Johnson," I say, sobbing into her shoulder.

I miss my mom, I think as she rubs my back.

Her comforting embrace reminds me of my mom who I haven't been able to hug in years. In fact, everyone around me right now reminds me of my family—of a new family. All these people around me have love and care for me, that I mutually have for them. I'm glad to have everyone here with me.

"Thanks, everyone," I say, pulling away. "Attending this funeral for Adrian has given me consolation I didn't even know I needed."

"I'm glad you can find healing in this. Even in his death, my baby gives back to this world. Now, I'm sorry, but I need to excuse myself. I'll be just over there if you need me."

"What happens now?" Vera asks.

"Now that we've said goodbye to Adrian, people usually hang out and talk for a little bit, taking the chance to get together with people they haven't seen in a while," Gaddreol answers.

"If you're ready to go, Gaddreol can take my car and I'll get a ride with Quinn," Avery says. "I don't want you guys to hang out any longer than you want, especially since tonight will be the vigil."

"Are you sure?" Gaddreol asks.

"Yeah, no worries," he says. "I'll see you tonight."

With that, everyone gives Avery a hug and their condolences before taking their leave.

* * *

Hundreds of people have shown up in support of those who suffered because of the director. Bundles of overwhelming idle chats come from every direction. Because of Sai, I'm at the front of the hospital, so thankfully I'm not overwhelmed by the conversations. On either side of me are Vera and Gaddreol.

"What are we supposed to do now?" Vera asks, leaning down to whisper in my ear.

"It's kind of like Adrian's funeral. We're just using candles instead of roses to pay our respects to all of the victims."

"Thanks, Bat."

"Of course."

The crowd grows quiet, and Sai speaks. "Thank you for coming out tonight as we honor the victims and their families. Through the memories we share, their beautiful souls live on. Taz would like to share a poem with everyone as we light the candles." His voice is sorrowful and heartfelt, emotions he doesn't usually display.

I want to reach out to comfort him, but I don't move. Gaddreol lights the candle in my hand and Vera's. The open air gets heavier with the burning wax smell from each lit candle.

I can imagine every doctor who participated in the transitions must have an immense amount of guilt. Being faced with grieving families weeping for their loved ones as well as everyone else here offering their consolation must be difficult to process. It's one thing to know you've hurt many people with your actions, it's an entirely different thing to witness it for yourself.

"Thank you, Sai. Hello, everyone. I'm going to get right into it.

"Wherever you need me, I'll be there,
My memory, lives on in your heart,
My voice, you'll hear in the wind,
My smile, you'll see in the sunshine,
My laughter, you'll hear in the birds chirping,
My embrace, you'll feel in your favorite blanket,
My beauty, you'll see in the stars,
Whenever you need me, I'll be there."

"I'm not a poet, but I feel that the people we love live in our hearts and in the things we surround ourselves with. They're never truly gone, nor forgotten," Taz says.

A beautifully somber instrumental song plays through the open space. Rich and vibrant strings of blue, purple, and green move fluidly in my mind like gentle waves. The strings dance and move in synchronization with the music. For a moment, I wonder if anyone standing here listening to this music experiences it in the same way that I do now, but I doubt it.

"Cyn... Cynthia!" A woman exclaims, her trembling voice grows louder as she presumably rushes over to us.

As the song ends, I feel Vera's body jerk away from me, and she produces a quiet yell. "What are you doing?"

"You're not Cynthia, are you?"

"I'm sorry, ma'am. This is my little sister, Vera." Gaddreol says, positioning himself in front of me and Vera.

"Cynthia is my daughter. You... you have her—" she says, her voice cutting off abruptly by her sobs.

"Am I your daughter, miss?" Vera asks, unintentionally making the woman cry harder.

I assume the woman pulls Vera away from me since her body is away from mine now. That and Gaddreol moves slightly closer to where the woman's voice is.

"I'm so sorry, ma'am. My little sister was transitioned into your daughter's body before we knew what was happening."

"Can I ask why? Why my sweet girl?"

"Unfortunately, I don't know why she was chosen," Gaddreol says. "Vera was paralyzed as a small child, unable to walk or talk, so I signed up without knowing that living people were involved. I can't express how sorry I am that this happened to your daughter."

"Oh, sweetheart. You poor baby. I'm so sorry, too. Why do bad things happen to innocent kids?"

"I'm sorry for taking Cynthia's body, miss," Vera says, her voice a soft whisper. "I'll give it back."

"How old are you, sweetheart?" The woman asks between sobs.

"Fourteen."

"My beautiful girl was fifteen. She had a brain aneurysm, and I was told she died during surgery, they asked me if her body could be studied since aneurysms are rare in kids. Cynthia always wanted her body to be used to make people's lives better when she died..." Her voice fades as her cries increase.

I wonder if she died during surgery from an aneurysm or if she died when Vera was placed in her body. In the end, it doesn't really matter when the result is the same. A young girl lost her life, and a caring mother lost her daughter.

"Cynthia sounds like an amazing kid," I say. Saying the young girl's name aloud is a closure I didn't know I needed.

"She is—was the best child a mother could ever hope for. Vera, can you promise me you'll take care of my beautiful daughter's body?"

"Wait, what?" Vera asks.

"My daughter's dead and I'd do anything to bring her back, but it's not possible. You're alive and well and two beautiful young girls shouldn't lose their lives," the woman says. "If my beautiful daughter could see that her death gave life to someone else, she'd be so happy. Please just take care of yourself, and Cynthia."

"I will. Thank you, miss," Vera says, her voice a mix of sadness and relief. She stumbles backwards into me, probably released from a hug. I can't see it, but somehow, I know she is crying because of the woman's blessing.

"My name is Deborah and if it's okay with you two, I'd like to give you my number. And if you ever need anything, please call me," she says, presumably handing him a piece of paper with her name and number on it.

"Yes ma'am. I'd like that a lot," Vera says.

I find myself wanting to say something else, but there's nothing for me to say as this isn't my situation to offer input, so I remain silent, and they continue their exchange without my interruption. I put my hand on Vera's shoulder, and she squeezes it. Gaddreol exchanges information with the woman so that she can know what's going on with her daughter's body at any given time.

"I'm going to the memorial. Don't hesitate to call me if you need or want anything." Deborah says, giving Vera one last hug before going to the temporary memorial erected in front of the hospital.

A permanent memorial is being made, but the temporary one is a placeholder for people to commemorate the deceased. Whether they choose to leave items or just have their moment of silence for the victims. If someone suspects their family member is a victim, but their name isn't on it, they can add their contact information to a list Sai has. With over six hundred victims I imagine there are a lot of unnamed people who have been lost in time. Hopefully they all find their own peace.

"What was that about?" Avery asks, sounding concerned.

"The girl whose body Vera has is named Cynthia. That woman is her mother, Deborah," Gaddreol answers.

"What'd she say?"

"She gave me her blessing," Vera spits the words out through her tears. "And her number so we can call her. She wants me to keep living for her daughter."

"I'm sorry, Vera," Avery says. "Are you okay?"

"No, but yes." Her snivels turn into muffled sobs, and I assume he pulled her into a hug as she did to me earlier.

The innocence Vera has is unrivaled by everyone involved in this wretched experiment. Hopefully, the blessing from Cynthia's mom will give her the closure she needs to begin healing, allowing her to find the closure she deserves.

"She was super nice. I don't want to disappoint her," Vera says.

"Disappoint who?" Taz asks. "No one'll be disappointed in you, ever. No matter what."

"What if I can't live up to her daughter?"

"Vera, that's not what she meant by that," Gaddreol says. "No one wants you to be anyone but you. The only thing anyone wants, including her mother, is for you to be happy and healthy."

"Yeah, what he said," Avery joins in.

"Just remember, we're all here to help you adjust to your new life however we can," Taz adds. "Whatever you need, we got you."

"And if we don't, we will figure it out," Sai says.

"Between the five of us, I think we can find a brain cell to use," Avery laughs, causing Vera to giggle, which infects everyone else in our small circle with laughter, including me.

"You guys are the best," Vera says, her laugh fading away.

"Things are winding down; do you want to head home now?" Gaddreol asks to which Vera agrees.

The pair take their leave, but Taz, Sai, and Avery stay behind to make sure the vigil ends without any issues. The conversations are dwindling so I'm fairly sure most people have left or are leaving now.

"How are you feeling?" Sai asks, wrapping his arm around my shoulders.

"After everything, I think I can finally say I'm okay. Really okay."

It's the first statement since transitioning that I've been able to say with complete confidence and conviction. I finally feel a sense of peace despite all that's happened and the unknown of what's to come. The past won't haunt me, and the future won't frighten me.

It's strange to think that going into this I was borderline solitary with only Sai at my side and now I've come out of this with friends willing to do anything for me and I would do the same for them. Although it was pure hell during the transition, I am grateful for the new companionship in my life that arose from it.

"Can we go home?" I ask, resting my head against his shoulder.

"Of course."

EPILOGUE

THE SHADOW OF what happened in FREE looms over the hospital even a year later. The shadows may never go away, but we strive to displace them by replacing them with hope. Through a little bit of ingenuity and innovation, of course.

Hope for a better quality of life. Hope for acceptance. Hope for unity.

FREE is demolished now. In its ashes, rises a new organization known as A.J.'s Foundation, in honor of Adrian Johnson.

The putrid stains on the hospital aren't going away any time soon, but at least the founders of FREE are rotting in prison until they die. Charles is still in his son's body serving thirty consecutive life sentences. The judge wanted to put him in his own body, but it was destroyed by experimentation, so he remains in the same body until he dies when Matthew can finally be put to rest. Samuel on the other hand, was placed back into his body and likely won't live to serve more than ten to twenty years of his consecutive life sentences.

As for Gregory, well, he died as he lived. Although he was one of the many victims who were named, no one came to claim his body. Avery and I paid for him a burial site and a gravestone. I visit his grave occasionally to pay my respects and just talk to him, since more than anything, he needed a friend as much as I did.

Many of the victims who lost their lives have been named and returned to their families. Their names have all been added to the permanent memorial in front of the hospital. Unfortunately, there may be more that we will never know about since Charles won't talk to anyone regarding the past.

The transitioned patients have all either returned to their original bodies or received a synthetic body. A few of them have decided to stay in the organization to help improve the synthetics and robotics.

The children have been placed into new homes, with the proper care and teaching they deserve. They seem to be thriving in their new environments. Olivia Sands wasn't charged with anything, but I'm unsure of what happened to her.

I, along with every doctor involved, have been acquitted of any charges due to duress. Many have moved on from the hospital, but many more have taken their place. Doctors, scientists, engineers, roboticists, and researchers alike have joined A.J.'s Foundation, expanding it further so that more research and faster development can be done on synthetics and robotics. With this research, people will be able to have their new lease on life without damaging side effects.

The unethical experiments have been completely eradicated, but redeveloped trials are being done for drugs and ailments. I've been a part of a different set of blind studies, but there hasn't been any improvement. My vision will likely never improve, but at least it can provide valuable data that will hopefully help others.

For the moment, assassinations have taken a back seat in my life. I've been compiling the names of customers who are complicit in the kidnappings and murders but were acquitted due to a lack of evidence or not tried in the first place due to their high-ranking positions. I have amassed a catalogue, but acting right now would be foolish since the incident is still fresh in everyone's minds.

In the meantime, I've been directing my energy into the new foundation. My role within A.J.'s Foundation isn't defined, but I help anywhere it's needed. Whether that be aiding in experiments as a participant or an assistant, or simply filing paperwork, I'm content with what I can offer.

Vera and Gaddreol help with the organization, too. Just as I do, Gaddreol assists where he's needed. But Vera is learning from the engineers and roboticists while attending school full-time. Once she graduates, she'll be working with teams to create synthetic bodies and cyborg components for those who want them. Vera still keeps in contact with Deborah, sharing with her all of the accomplishments she's made.

Sai, Taz, and Avery are highly regarded by many people for their courage to go against Charles and his abhorrent organization. They have primarily returned to their usual work in the hospital but assist the organization when they're able to. Their priority always remains giving people the best chance at life that they can.

Every week, the six of us meet up to do something. Whether that be going out to eat, doing a random activity, or just spending time together talking about things. The seven of us now, since I got a new addition in my life. Mole, my new service dog, a labrador retriever, accompanies us at every gathering.

I never physically transitioned, but this experience transformed me in so many ways. It tore me down, piece by piece, allowing me to rebuild myself. It took losing almost everything and having my world literally stripped away from me for me to realize that things I once perceived as weaknesses were never such things. Requesting assistance or needing help to achieve something doesn't mean I'm incapable or useless. Being reliant on someone or something doesn't mean my independence is gone. As grievous as this experience was, I'm grateful for who I've become.

Thank you for sticking around with me to the end!

Transcendence Theory is the first book I've written.

I appreciate everyone for taking the time to read it. I sincerely hope you enjoyed reading it as much as I enjoyed writing it.

Whether you loved it or not, I would greatly appreciate a short review.

Made in the USA
Columbia, SC
19 August 2024

40748981R00130